PON

10/05

D0467136

Seasons

Seasons
Bonnie Hopkins

West Bloomfield, Michigan

WARNER BOOKS

NEW YORK   BOSTON

Copyright © 2005 by Bonnie S. Hopkins
All rights reserved.

Published by Warner Books with Walk Worthy Press™

Warner Books

Time Warner Book Group
1271 Avenue of the Americas, New York, NY 10020

Walk Worthy Press
33290 West Fourteen Mile Road, #482, West Bloomfield, MI 48322

Visit our Web sites at www.twbookmark.com and www.walkworthypress.net.

Printed in the United States of America

First Edition: October 2005
10 9 8 7 6 5 4 3 2 1

Library of Congress Control Number: 2005924165
ISBN: 0-446-57846-0

Book design by Giorgetta Bell McRee

To my gracious Heavenly Father, who began and completed this work. Each time I tried to make it my story, You faithfully redirected it back to the right path. All praise, honor, and glory to Your name.

To Kym Fisher, who believed from the very beginning and never doubted her mother could accomplish this God-given assignment (thanks, Squirt), and Rev. Harold Fisher, whose wisdom in the Word was so helpful.

To my little inspirations: Nicholas and Sydnee Fisher, whose unceasing joy and enthusiasm for life encourage me and give me hope for the future.

And

In memory of
Timothy Fisher and Taylor Hopkins,
who fought a good fight and brought a brief, but strong,
light into the world.

Acknowledgments

To my WONDERFUL supporters:

Kym and Rev. Harold Fisher, Cynthia Johnson Biggers, Reba Ball, Margaree and Kevin Mitchell, Jewel Mitchell Walker, Andrew Johnson, Sandra Hopkins, Arnetta Johnson, Lula Nelson, Tanja and Reg Murray, John and Virgie (fabulous) Montgomery, Janine Moore, Carroll Roesler, Yvette Chargois, Joyce Walker, Erika Larkin, Lydia Cannon, Sylvia Teague, DeDe Greene, Rhenae and Clem Abrams, and Alice Burnam.

You have fervently prayed and made yourself a resource by asking (or telling) me what you could do to help. And when I did ask for help, you graciously responded and got it done. You have regularly encouraged me through cards, e-mails, and phone calls, or perhaps spoke a kind or encouraging word when it was most needed. You listened patiently when I whined and complained (even when I knew you were thoroughly sick of me). You harassed and pushed when I was in one of *those* places. You constantly sent or called with all kinds of helpful information. Some of you have just been there . . . a quiet but strong leaning post of support and wisdom.

Whatever the case, I simply say a heartfelt THANKS to all of you, and may God richly Bless you!

To those of you not listed, but who have supported me through prayers and positive thoughts for the success of *Seasons*, please know that I am grateful.

To Denise Stinson and the Walk Worthy Press staff! Only a new author can understand what it means to get "the call." I will never forget the day I received that call that ushered me through the door and brought us to this point. Thank You! Thank You! Thank You! And God Bless you! I am eternally grateful for the wonderful opportunity you so graciously provided for me to tell this story.

To Time Warner Book Group and editor Frances Jalet-Miller and copy editor Susan Higgins, I am abundantly appreciative of your conscientious hard work and expertise. (You guys are great!)

To the readers! I enjoyed writing *Seasons* for you. And as I wrote, I prayed that this book would bless you, and encourage and inspire you to walk through your seasons in victory. I am supremely thankful for your support, and I hope this story will help you remember to trust God through every season, because as the characters so aptly demonstrate, SEASONS DO CHANGE!

Seasons

To every thing there is a season, and a time to every purpose under the heaven:

A time to be born, and a time to die; a time to plant, and a time to pluck up that which is planted;

A time to kill, and a time to heal; a time to break down, and a time to build up;

A time to weep, and a time to laugh; a time to mourn, and a time to dance;

A time to cast away stones, and a time to gather stones together; a time to embrace, and a time to refrain from embracing;

A time to get, and a time to lose; a time to keep, and a time to cast away;

A time to rend, and a time to sew; a time to keep silence, and a time to speak;

A time to love, and a time to hate; a time of war, and a time for peace.

Ecclesiastes 3:1–8

Prologue

Ooooh! This is not good! Jaci had come face to face with the unsettling fact that there was no more time for thinking, analyzing, or prevaricating. She was just minutes from walking down the aisle.

Questions and doubts continued to torment her. *What am I doing? Have I lost my doggone mind? How did I get myself into this? I'm so set in my way of thinking and living, do I even want a husband?*

She nervously paced and fought the sensation that the walls were closing in and vital air was thinning. *Why these questions now? This should be a settled issue. Definitely not a good thing!*

She talked out loud to herself, verbalizing her thoughts—her doubts. "My life may be deficient in certain areas, but I've managed to obtain a modicum of peace and contentment. I'm self-sufficient, free to go and do as I please, and too old to be changing things at this stage of the game. Love aside, do I need to be giving up life as I know it for the unknown . . . marriage?"

She swallowed repeatedly in an effort to quiet the butterflies that churned in her stomach. They had to number in the hundreds! *What is wrong with me? Why am I stressing like this?* She yearned for the comfort and peace of her family room— pictured herself in blissful solitude, reading a book or watching a good movie—far removed from this wedding scenario. But wait . . . she loved this man!

Old demons who had made a home in her mind years before wouldn't be quieted. *But can you . . . do you dare trust him?* Frustration filled her as she recalled that her family room, cluttered with the belongings of out-of-town relatives, was anything but serene right now. She shook her head, trying to clear it. *I don't need to be in here alone with all these crazy thoughts!*

She stuck her head through the door and called out for her daughter. "Randi!" Hearing the stress in her mother's voice, Randi rushed into the room followed closely by Sister Sadie. Jaci looked at them, distress evident on her face. "I'm having second thoughts about this ya'll. I just don't know if I should be getting married. Is Jason here? Oh God, what if he's changed his mind? What if something goes wrong? Is all the wedding party here? Do I look okay?" She nervously fired off question after question.

Randi admired how beautiful her mother looked in the exquisite custom-made gown. "Mama, everything is fine, you look beautiful, and I know you're not questioning God's blessings."

"I just don't want to make a mistake," Jaci whispered. "You know I had lost all hope of this ever happening. I thought I was destined to remain single. What if I was right?"

"Mama," Randi said with impatience. They'd had this conversation many times before. "You may have had a long wait, but don't you think God has come through in a great way? I mean, look at Jason—handsome, rich, and crazy about you. You can't get any better than that."

Jaci smiled waveringly. "He is something, isn't he? I guess that's why I'm having such a hard time believing this is happening. I keep thinking it's too good to be true. What if I'm just grasping after long dead dreams?" Her voice grew faint, weighed down by doubt. "What if this is a mistake I'll end up regretting?" Her eyes filled with tears. "I couldn't stand that."

Before Randi could attempt to calm her mother's frazzled nerves, someone called for her and she turned to tell them she would be there in a second. She grabbed her mother's hands and spoke hurriedly. "Mama, you're just having some prewedding jitters. Relax! Everything's going to be fine." She tossed a worried look at Sister Sadie before walking away.

Sadie Brooks listened to the troubling conversation between Jaci and Randi and shook her head as sadness dimmed her happiness. *I've got to talk to this girl!* she decided.

Sadie was like a mother to Jaci. Sadie remembered when the young mother had joined the church many years ago. After it became apparent there was no husband in the picture, Jaci had been judged as "unacceptable" by many of the members. Oddly, her child was warmly accepted and embraced, while Jaci was deliberately ignored. Jaci had been hurt and puzzled by their rejection but finally stopped seeking their acceptance and concentrated on serving the Lord. But something about Jaci had touched Sadie's heart. She had shunned the masses, taken Jaci under her wing, and now enjoyed a mother-daughter relationship with her that others envied. *Help, Lord,* Sadie prayed. *The devil is trying to use Jaci's past hurts to destroy her future. Please give me the right words to say to her.*

Jaci took deep breaths, but calm eluded her. She couldn't stop the disturbing memories of the last few months. *I've been stalked, attacked, had my life threatened, and almost lost my job* over this man. *Randi's father even showed up making demands. Was the Lord trying to tell me something?*

Her legs trembled and she badly needed to sit down before she fell. A chair across the room beckoned, but the need to run from the room and out of the church as fast as she could became paramount. *Should I? If this marriage is a mistake, wouldn't it be better to stop it now?* The temptation to run was strong, and the demons in her mind pressed their case. *Think! Remember all you've been through during the last few months! What about these questions, doubts, and fears plaguing you? What if they are trying to tell you something? Remember the difficult years—years that are now behind you. And most important, think about the peaceful existence you've obtained. Do you want to give it up for the unknown? Girl, you better think!*

In the midst of her confusion, one lucid thought finally broke through. *Pray! Oooh, thank You, Holy Spirit.* She began praying out loud frantically. "Lord, I've talked to You about this marriage for months and I believed it was in Your will and purpose. But why am I stressing like this? Father, I need You to quiet these doubts and fears and show me what to do. Now! Please! Before I do something I'll regret!"

But the dark memories and tormenting doubts refused to be quelled. Was she about to make a serious mistake?

"Lord, are You going to answer? Please guide me, Father." The churning in her stomach turned to nausea.

"What's wrong with me?" she asked in self-disgust while clutching her stomach. "I'm too old, been through too much, know better than to let myself be stressed out like this. Surely my long, difficult journey has taught me something! Father, what are you telling me?"

A few seconds later, she turned and walked across the room as swiftly as her shaky legs would carry her.

"Jaci!" Sister Sadie frantically called. "Wait a minute!"

Memories

$\mathcal{G}$raduation day from college was a scary, exhilarating, wonderful occasion!

Twenty-one-year-old Jacetta Winters clutched her college diploma tightly and thanked God that four years of year-round classes had finally paid off. Exuberant and optimistic, she overflowed with hopes and dreams. She was ready for challenges to be overcome and adventures to be explored. Look out world; she was ready for anything! Or was she? Years later, she would remember that day and recoil in embarrassment at her extreme naïvete.

The next week, back home in their small Riverwood, Arkansas, community, Jacetta and her six cousins rejoiced in their victory. From birth the cousins had been inseparable and their notorious shenanigans had gained them reputations of being both villains and heroes. Now, with the exception of one who had dropped out to get married, they all celebrated becoming college graduates.

Identical green eyes, a Winslow family trait passed down from Jacetta's maternal grandparents, stared out from the face of each cousin. "Ya'll, the only thing I regret is that for the first time in our lives, we're all going our separate ways," Jacetta told them tearfully.

"I know," C.J. answered in a shaky voice. "Can you believe it? Dusty going into the Marines. Buddy headed to Michigan to take a job, and Big Ben moving to Little Rock to be a high school coach. Now who would have figured that!" They all looked at Big Ben and laughed.

"I'm really going to miss ya'll." Jacetta's eyes traveled around the circle. "I'm already wondering when we'll see each other again." She found them solemnly staring back at her, probably wondering the same thing.

Seeking to lighten the mood, Gina asked, "Is everybody else all set to leave? I know I'm not." The cousins had been excitedly talking about their plans for months, but as some of them had already discovered, and others would soon learn, the best of plans could fall apart in the blink of an eye.

"Buddy and I are driving to Little Rock with Big Ben to catch our flights," Dusty explained. "It wouldn't do to hang around too long. We might change our minds about leaving."

"It'll probably be next weekend before I leave," Jacetta answered, then looked at C.J. "What about you, Cij? When are you leaving?"

C.J. looked down and answered, "I don't know exactly. But it'll be soon."

Dusty decided to mess with Nita again. They had been teasing her all weekend about her pregnancy. "Nita, you sure this guy you married is okay?"

"Yes, Dusty. How many times do I have to say it?" An uncomfortable grin covered Nita's face. "And I'm so glad Jace and I will be living in the same city. At least we'll be able to see each other often."

"Well, you certainly didn't waste any time getting knocked up, if that's an indication of anything," Buddy said, causing Nita's face to flush in embarrassment.

Big Ben, who had always been a softie, looked as if tears weren't far off. He finally spoke up to cover his emotions. "It sounds like everybody but Gina and C.J. are set to go. Gina, you planning to hang around 'the Wood' for a while?" Gina dropped her head to hide the brief look of pain that crossed her face. "I don't think so," she answered quietly.

He looked at C.J. "What about you, 'Red'? You still planning to follow that basketball player?"

C.J. gave a nod of confirmation. "Yeah! And call me 'Red' again and get punched out," she threatened.

"Okay, okay!" Buddy said, interrupting the old argument and falling into his usual role of leader. He looked around the circle and said in a serious tone, "We have to stay in touch, everybody. If I don't hear from you, I'm coming to look for you. Take care of yourselves and don't do anything I wouldn't do."

Everybody else let out loud groans. "If we did, we'd really be in trouble," Gina said. They laughed and hugged again before going separate ways.

The next week, as they traveled to Dallas, Jacetta sat in the backseat of her parents' car looking out at the passing scenery and fighting tears. She was leaving her small, close-knit community filled with big plans to work a full-time job and take night and weekend courses toward her master's degree.

Riverwood, lovingly referred to as "the Wood" by the younger generation, represented her place of security and nurturing, so she wasn't surprised by the mixed emotions swirling through her. Although ambitious dreams and well-thought-out goals were firmly in place, fears of the unknown clogged her throat while feelings of homesickness were already settling in her heart.

Jacetta was a private person, so she hated the thought of moving in with her uncle's family. Uncle George recently retired from the military and his family relocated to Dallas a few months ago. Their small stopgap apartment was already cramped, but Jacetta's parents insisted, arguing that her uncle and aunt could look out for her, which would also give her a chance to save a little money before getting her own place. True. But she still didn't like it.

Thankfully, she already had a job lined up! Her aunt helped her secure a position in municipal government. The entry-level pay wasn't great, but the job as interviewer and planner for the city's neighborhood improvement program was right in line with her career aspirations in public administration. *Thank you, God!* At least her independence was in sight.

The last thing her dad said to her before heading back to Riverwood squelched a little of Jacetta's excitement. "Now, don't you go getting in no trouble out here, girl. You do, don't come running back to my house. Just remember how you were raised." His harsh words brought tears to Jacetta's eyes until she reminded herself that her dad had always felt it was his duty to put a damper on anything that resembled joy. Little did she know then how close her father came to prophesying her future.

Things were going well! Jacetta was enjoying her job, learning her way around, and taking courses toward her graduate degree. She excitedly checked her growing bank account regularly, anxiously looking forward to the time she would be able to move into her own place.

Never in her wildest imagination could she have dreamed up Maxie Jackson!

Her uncle had car trouble one day and coworker Maxie gave him a ride home from work. Of course, Uncle George invited him in for a beer. And naturally, he introduced Maxie to his little niece who had recently moved to town. And yes, the little country girl straight from the woods felt the foundation of her goals crack a little when she looked into Maxie's handsome face and dreamy eyes. How was she to know that the glow in Maxie's eyes was one of anticipation as he eyed his next conquest?

Jacetta went out with Maxie several times before she had finally enjoyed some solitary moments to share the exciting news with her cousins. One Friday evening, everyone else decided to go out to dinner, leaving her alone in the apartment. Ordinarily she would have been out with Maxie, but he had been called in to work. As soon as the family left, she immediately began to dial numbers, looking for her cousins to tell them about Maxie. She couldn't reach Nita and Gina, but did eventually track down C.J. "I've met him, Cij!" she cried excitedly. "I have met the man of my dreams. And he is so . . . ooo . . . fine. Whoo!"

"Oh my ears!" C.J. groaned at Jaci's loud, excited screaming. "Now calm down and tell me who 'he' is."

"His name is Maxie Jackson. He's older, about thirty, and soooo handsome and sophisticated! He's just slightly taller than I am, and you know I like tall men. But other than that, this man is perfect."

She was disappointed when C.J. didn't share her excitement.

"I don't know, Jace," C.J. said after listening quietly. "You're telling me that this older, good-looking man is unattached and interested in you?" She paused, reluctant to tell Jaci that life in the real world had already torn away her rose-colored glasses. She hated to sound cynical but felt she had to warn her cousin to be cautious. "Jace, are you absolutely certain this guy is not already married or hooked up with somebody? I mean, he sounds almost too good to be true. And remember what Grampa used to say? If something looks too good to be true, it probably is. Just be careful, okay? It might just be your innocence and the challenge of adding a fresh notch to his belt that he's after."

Her feelings were a little hurt by C.J.'s pessimism, so Jacetta changed the subject; they talked a while longer, getting updates on each other and their cousins. "So how are you and Randy doing? You guys planning to tie the knot anytime soon?"

"Well he's asked, and I've said 'yes,' but we haven't set a date. He's anxious to see how things go his first season. He's looking good so far though." Randy was beginning what he hoped would be a long career in professional basketball.

"That's great, Cij. Be sure to keep me posted. You know, I was so glad that with Nita and me living in the same city we would be able to see each other regularly, but I've only talked to her once since I got here, and then she hurried me off the phone and never called me back. And I haven't talked to Gina at all. Can't even get a number for her. I heard she decided on the spur of the moment to move to Oakland with her old roommate, Clariece. I didn't even know they were that close."

"Me neither," C.J. replied thoughtfully. "I haven't talked to them either. I can understand Nita's reasons a little. At least she has an excuse—getting married and pregnant, all within a year. That's a lot of adjusting to do. But Gina hasn't been in touch with anyone. I don't know what her problem is."

After Jacetta hung up, she still felt a little miffed at C.J. She stood in front of the mirror, looking at herself critically. She was five-foot-five and admittedly overweight, but thankfully the extra pounds were evenly distributed in all the right places. Her thick hair was a reddish-brown color, but she kept it dyed black and wore it in a short Afro. She hated the soft, naturally wavy texture of her hair and was often teased by her uncle when she applied harsh solutions to it, trying to get the hard nappy look she wanted. "Girl, do you know how many women would kill for the kind of hair you have?" he asked.

She groaned as she took in the honey-toned skin, which was marred with numerous dark blotches and spots caused by the acne she constantly fought. Thank God for makeup.

She reluctantly agreed with C.J. that there was nothing special about her. In all honesty, her almond-shaped eyes and large shapely legs were her best features.

"Oh well," Jacetta finally said to her reflection in the mirror. "So there's nothing spectacular about the way I look. At least Maxie is mature enough to look beyond just outward appearances."

Whatever his reasons, Maxie Jackson aggressively pursued Jacetta and monopolized the little free time she had. To keep her from having to ride the bus, he dropped her off and picked her up from work and school whenever his schedule permitted. If they were not together, he called her at regular intervals to let her know he was thinking of her. Jacetta was on cloud nine.

A few weeks after they started dating, one of the women— a regular in Maxie's crowd—pulled Jacetta aside. "Look, honey, I figure nobody's taken the time to tell you, but Maxie's married, honey."

Jacetta's jaw dropped in shock and she fell off of her cloud with a thud. "Why in the world would you tell me that?" she asked the woman, anger apparent in her tone. "Maxie is not married."

The woman made an indifferent gesture. "I'm just telling you because you're young and dumb and don't have a clue. You can do whatever you want to with the information. I just felt like you needed to know the truth."

"I don't date married men, Maxie," Jacetta blurted out as soon as they were alone. "If you're married you should have told me."

Maxie's head shot around in surprise. "Who told you I was married?" he demanded.

"One of the women who hangs out with us. I think her name is Geneva. Anyway, what does it matter who told me? The only thing in question is whether it's true or not."

"Ha! It figures. Geneva's just jealous. She's been after me for years, and I'm a little hurt and disappointed in you," he said, reaching over to open the glove compartment. "I thought we had more trust than this between us, but let me show you something just to set your mind at ease." He pulled out a thick envelope and handed it to her. She opened it and saw that it was a divorce decree. As she read it she was so relieved, and it never crossed her mind to question why he kept the papers in his car.

After he saw her relief, Maxie quickly pressed his advantage. "I've been divorced for a while now, although not too many people know it. But even if I were still married, don't you know I love you so much I would willingly leave her?"

His words filled her with joy, but she shook her head sadly. "I'm not a home wrecker, Maxie. But since it's a moot point there's no need to discuss it."

Maxie's confession of love was followed immediately by his plea that they fully express their love for each other. Jacetta had refused to let things go beyond a certain point.

"We're both adults, with adult needs," Maxie pressured. "I know you're reluctant to take our relationship to another level, but I believe you love me just as much as I love you. Baby, we're going to spend the rest of our lives together, so there's no reason for us to wait. Please, sweetheart, I need you so much."

She actually fell for that old line! Years later, Jacetta would still be wondering why. Maybe she was flattered that this much older man had placed them on the same "adult" level. Maybe it was because she was actually overwhelmed by his profession of love. Maybe it was simply because she really loved him. Whatever her rationale, she agreed to go to his apartment with him. She convinced herself that since Maxie was the man she would soon marry, she was actually giving him the gift of her love and commitment.

A couple of months later, she was out with Maxie and his friends on their regular Friday night club-hopping circuit. But fun was the last thing on her mind. *How could I have been so stupid to let this happen?* This question had taken up residence in her mind, consuming her thoughts. Throughout the evening she was quieter than usual. She should have been feeling excitement about going apartment hunting the next day. But instead, Lord, she was miserable!

She always felt uncomfortable around Maxie's older, worldly wise friends who got a kick out of teasing her and making fun of her greenness. *Why do I let them make me feel like this?* she wondered. But she knew for sure that the news she had for Maxie would only confirm their opinion of her. As the evening wore on, she was torn between extending her time in their presence to delay the inevitable, or ending the evening so she could finally talk to Maxie.

After what seemed like interminable hours, they were finally in the car heading toward her apartment complex. A slightly tipsy Maxie tried to coerce her into going home with him. "Come on, honey, it's Friday night and you don't have class tomorrow. Let's spend some time together."

Jacetta's nerves were stretched to the limit, and curiously, for the first time, she wondered if this man and his partying lifestyle were what she truly wanted. "No, Maxie, I can't. I told you I plan to go apartment hunting tomorrow."

"You can spend the night and I'll go with you and help you find a place. Or better yet, why don't you just move in with me? That's what you should be doing anyway. It'll cut down on your expenses and give us more time together."

"I don't think so," she mumbled, almost overcome by anxiety. She had already gone against enough of her long-held values, and look where it had gotten her. She noticed they were turning into the parking lot. As soon as he parked the car, Maxie began to kiss and caress her.

"Come on, babe, loosen up! You've been uptight all night."

Knowing she couldn't put it off any longer, she swallowed nervously and hoped her vocal cords would cooperate because somehow, she had to get the words out. She condemned herself for being such a coward—heck! She'd always had the courage to confront any situation. Until now. She took a deep breath and began speaking. The words came out in a tight, squeaking voice. "I'm pregnant, Maxie. I . . ."

"You're what?" he yelled, interrupting her and quickly moving away from her.

She continued in words that were rushed, choppy, and unsure. "I know this wasn't planned, but now that it's happened, we need to decide what we're going to do." She stole a look at him and noticed his response was anything but enthusiastic. His body stiffened and his ardor mysteriously disappeared. His unexpected reaction cut into her emotions, bringing tears to her eyes. This was not the way it was supposed to play out. He should have been taking her in his arms and assuring her that everything would be okay.

Instead, he was quiet for long moments before asking angrily, "How did you let that happen? And just what do you expect me to do about it?"

O . . . *kaaay!* Not exactly a positive response. She was hurt and disappointed, but she *had* just hit him with some unexpected news. "Well, I guess we need to decide if we're going to get married or . . . exactly what we're going to do." Her tear-filled voice and body language pleaded for reassurance, which didn't come.

If possible, his voice was colder, harder. "That's easy. There's not much I *can* do since I'm already married."

"What?" Shock and confusion coursed through her. *Why was he lying?* "Maxie, you're not married. You showed me your divorce papers, remember? And I know you live alone." A nervous giggle escaped as she tried to hide her hurt.

Maxie shrugged nonchalantly. "We . . . eeell, let me put it this way. Those divorce papers I showed you? They were from my first marriage. I'm still married to my second wife. Off and on anyway. We're kind of on the outs right now."

His words delivered such a devastating blow to Jacetta's heart that it felt almost physical, and a distressing question exploded in her head. *Oh Lord, what have I done?*

"S-s-second w-wife!" Jacetta was so upset she started stammering. "You n-n-never said anything about being m-m-married twice."

Her youth and inexperience made her easy prey for Maxie's deliberate attack. "It's not my fault if you took it for granted that I had only been married once." *Which was what I intended you to do,* he thought. "And when Geneva opened her big mouth and told you I was married, I had to do something to prove her wrong and pacify you." He spoke in a tone of self-righteous indignation. "I should have known better than to get involved with a stupid little hick."

Hurt and anger caused tears to slide down her face. The words *used, fool, stupid* entered her mind and made her cringe as she realized how easily and eagerly she had been taken in by him. It didn't lessen her despair to know she wasn't the first and wouldn't be the last to find herself in such a predicament.

Her cousin C.J's words came back to haunt her. "*Jace, are you absolutely certain this guy is not already married or hooked up with somebody? He sounds almost too good to be true. And remember what Grampa used to say? If something looks too good to be true, it probably is. Just be careful, okay?*"

Why hadn't she listened? Maybe if she had . . .

Shame engulfed her, winning the battle over all other emotions. She knew this shame would be with her for the rest of her life. Not only had she dishonored herself, but also she had dishonored God, her family, and all the people back home in

Riverwood who with so much pride and expectation had sent her off.

Her daddy's words, *"You get in trouble, don't coming running back to my house,"* popped into her mind, bringing other harsh realities: She couldn't go home and she couldn't stay in her uncle's already crowded apartment. Also, she was in a precarious position on her job because she had been there only a few weeks. Basically, she was homeless—and pregnant. Suddenly, another emotion took center stage in her mind—fear. *What am I going to do?*

She looked at Maxie with anguish etched into her face. "But why? Why would you lie and deliberately mislead me? What could I have possibly done to deserve this kind of treatment from you? I love you, Maxie, and I thought you loved me."

She kept staring at him in stunned disbelief, remembering how flattered and over-the-moon happy she had been when he started pursuing her. Now, she was struggling to understand the rationale behind his calm announcement that he was married, that love wasn't a part of the game he was playing, and that if she was too stupid to know that, it wasn't his fault.

"So, Geneva was telling me the truth after all," Jacetta said while sobbing heartbrokenly. How had she gotten to this place? Pregnant. Alone. Ashamed. Terrified.

Maxie looked at her and said impatiently, "Don't start with the childish hysterics. Even if you are pregnant, it's not the end of the world. We'll deal with it later, but I need to go ahead and leave now."

"But . . . what am I supposed to do, Maxie? You have to help me! It's your child too!"

Maxie shrugged his shoulders and looked out the car window. *Well the fun is over with this one. It's time to move on*, he thought to himself.

He remained silent for so long that Jacetta brokenly asked again, "Please, Maxie, what am I going to do?"

"Look!" he yelled at her. Her whining was getting on his nerves. "I thought you knew what to do to keep this from happening, but evidently, you didn't have sense enough to do that, so you have yourself to blame." He turned the ignition to start the car. "If I were you . . ." he paused briefly, effectively letting her know it was her problem, and hers alone. "I'd start thinking about how to get rid of this baby."

Jacetta gasped, trying to comprehend what she was hearing. "You mean an abortion? I can't do that! Not as long as there are other alternatives." She was furious and wanted to slap him for even making that kind of suggestion. "You want to kill this baby, Maxie? Your own child?" She was yelling at the top of her voice but couldn't seem to help herself. "You can forget it!"

Really wanting to get away at this point, Maxie looked at her, thinking, *Am I going to have to throw this woman out of my car?* He had no intention of dealing with this, now or ever.

"Look, you do whatever you want to," he said with indifference. "I told you I have to go. If you don't want to follow my suggestion, that's up to you."

Jacetta's shoulders slumped. Her pride wouldn't let her beg him anymore. She opened the car door and stepped out. Before closing the door, she leaned down and said, "Maxie, I hope to hear from you soon, but if I don't, just remember one thing: God is merciful, but He's also just. It might take years, but you *will* regret the day you rejected me and your child. This baby and I will make it, Maxie. God will see to that."

Maxie wasted no time in speeding out of the parking lot without looking back.

Jacetta had never felt so alone as she watched the taillights of his car disappear. Distraught, she looked around the dark parking lot, knowing she couldn't face going into the apartment where there would be no privacy. But she had nowhere else to go. She found a dark corner behind the trash container, where she sat down on the cold ground and cried bitterly as she released her dreams into the night.

While tears streamed silently down her face, she spoke to the only One she knew Who would never leave or forsake her. She didn't care who might come along and hear her. "Father, forgive me. I've sinned and done what I knew was wrong. And my actions have resulted in a child. Lord, I need You like I've never needed You before. Please have mercy on me and help me."

As the days passed, her fervent hope of hearing from Maxie gradually faded. He had seemingly dropped off the face of the earth, leaving Jacetta alone to face the cold winds of winter. She knew that if she and her child were to survive from this point on, she could only depend on herself and the Lord.

The innocent, carefree, enthusiastic Jacetta was gone! Maxie had given her a crash course in life and in just a few moments she had changed from a breezy spring idealist to a stormy winter realist. She resolved that from now on, her trust would be hard won and that she'd always be suspicious that people—especially men—were out to fulfill their own selfish desires at her expense.

More than two decades would pass before God, in His own triumphant way, would show her that it is He Who controls the seasons.

Moments

Jaci

*J*aci Winters worked in municipal government as a supervisor in the Housing Compliance Department. She was assigned to oversee the Hearing Coordination responsibilities of the Demolition and Abatement Division. As part of the legal process, the city held public hearings to give property owners one last chance to plead their case before their dangerous building or inoperable vehicle was demolished or hauled away. Jaci and her staff coordinated the hearings and made sure the information provided by the regular inspectors was accurate before it was presented.

Although Jaci had several people assigned to her, she was heavily involved in the day-to-day operations, which included making quality assurance on-site inspections before each hearing. Jaci was a dangerous-building investigator before her promotion to supervisor, and she had always hated going into dangerous buildings to take pictures of the violations. She took the job because it paid so much more than other positions and she had desperately needed the higher salary. She still hated doing the on-site inspections, but she did it to keep her staff on their toes. There was no way they could be lax in doing their job because Jaci made sure she was familiar with the fine points of every file. She learned the hard way she had to cover herself.

Today, she was working with senior inspector Bill Whitmore, doing final inspections on buildings scheduled for the next hearing. While on the way to the next address, Jaci studied the file and mentally geared herself up for whatever they would find. Dread filled her when they arrived. The building, completely obscured by trees, overgrown vines, and weeds, wasn't visible from the street. Jaci and Bill approached the abandoned building, carefully searching for the best path to reach it. Wielding a machete, Bill beat down tree limbs and underbrush to create a narrow path, and Jaci closely followed, uttering her usual prayer: "Please, Lord, let the snakes and any other culprits lurking around be more afraid of me than I am of them."

"You know, Bill," Jaci said loudly, hoping to scare away anything or anyone creeping in or around the building, "I'm really starting to wonder if this job is worth it. There's no telling what we're going to find when we reach that house. How long have we been trying to get it demolished? About eight years? And the owner is still fighting to keep it up. What could he possibly want to save it for?"

Still vigorously beating at the underbrush, Bill answered, "Probably using it for some kind of tax write-off. People have all kinds of ways to get around the system." When they finally reached the structure, he observed, "I don't believe the regular inspector has been here in quite a while. It'll be interesting to see what's in the file. Some of those guys make it so hard for the rest of us. Who is the inspector assigned to this area anyway?"

Jaci flipped through the file log trying to find the last date an inspector had visited the building. "Hmmm, from what I can determine, Daniels is the inspector, and he was here last month," she said. "But look at the last date marked on the building—that says six months ago. Uh, uh, uh! Daniels would be mad as heck if we reported this."

The front door of the building was missing. They tread carefully over the rotten wood of the porch and stepped cautiously over the threshold, only to find another decaying floor inside. Jaci lifted her camera and snapped shots of first one violation and then another. As they moved about inside the dark structure, Bill lifted his high-powered flashlight to provide as much light as possible.

"I don't think we need to go any farther," he told Jaci. "Did you get a shot of the collapsed roof and caved-in floor over there? That should be enough to prove this one needs to come down in a hurry. There ain't nothing anyone can do with this except bulldoze it."

"You're right about that! Let's get out of here," Jaci said with relief.

They retraced their steps and stood on the dilapidated porch to mark the date of their visit on the front of the structure. "Get a shot of this, Jaci," Bill said, busily writing with a permanent marker. "I want to show Daniels that some of us actually do our jobs."

Jaci focused to get a close-up photo. "I like the way you think, Bill. I'm thinking seriously about showing these pictures to his supervisor. What Daniels and others fail to realize is that they actually put people in danger when they don't do their job."

As they stood there, they heard a low, threatening growl a second before a large dog with a chain secured around his neck rounded the corner of the building. His growling quickly became loud, aggressive barking and the dog's sharp teeth were bared, ready for attack.

"Oh no!" Jaci yelled as she jumped off the porch and landed in a dead run. From behind, she heard a splintering noise, then a string of curse words, as Bill, hitting a spot on the rotten porch that wouldn't support his weight, watched his foot disappear into a new hole.

The dog stopped momentarily, as though trying to decide which one to go after. Since Bill was closer, the dog headed for him. Bill quickly removed his foot and leaped from the porch. He kept looking back, expecting the chain around the dog's neck to tighten up and restrain him. He cursed again when he saw that a large piece of wood, apparently once a part of the structure, was attached to the other end of the chain and being dragged by the dog. Jaci, who was hurriedly fighting her way back through the path they had made, looked back and saw both Bill and the dog gaining on her. She tried to speed up.

When she saw the street, she mumbled a breathless "Thank God," but kept running. Bill overtook her, struggling to get the car keys out of his pocket and hoping the dog's progress would be hindered by the undergrowth, giving them time to jump into the car. When he looked back, to his amazement, the dog was still in pursuit, dragging the piece of wood as if it were weightless.

Jaci reached the car as Bill nervously tried to get the key in the lock, but the keys fell to the ground and Bill yelled, "Run, Jaci!" The dog had cleared the underbrush and bore down full speed on them, with the chain and wood trailing behind him.

They both took off again, fearing the dog was going to take a chunk from their backsides any second. When they reached the end of the block and dared to look back, they noticed that the dog had stopped midway down the street and stayed there, as though in obedience to some remembered command.

Jaci dropped her clipboard and camera, threw off her hard

hat, and bent over, hands on her knees, trying to catch her breath. She thought, *doggone it, I'm getting too old for this!* As soon as she was able to talk, she said, "Now we know why Daniels didn't mark the house with the dates of his inspections. He hasn't been near that house since God only knows when. He's in big trouble! That file should have indicated that there's a vicious dog on the premises."

"True," Bill reluctantly agreed while struggling to regain his breath. As a senior inspector, Bill walked a fine line between the inspectors and management and was often forced to defend one or the other. "He deserves to be reported for this one. Or better yet, I'm more inclined to think a good butt whipping would serve the purpose."

As they drove back to the office, Jaci's thoughts reflected her frustration. *Is this all I have to look forward to?* Shaking her head, she silently talked to the Lord. *Father, You know I appreciate all of Your blessings. But, Lord, is this all it's ever going to be? Is there nothing in Your plan for me but more loneliness, more dangerous buildings, and more vicious dogs? Father, this is Your world and You own everything in it. Lord, surely, You have something else for me.* She sighed. *Nevertheless, Father, thank You for what I do have.*

Jaci had no way of knowing that her season was about to change; that even then she was at the heart of conversations taking place hundreds of miles away in Dallas; that the person who had swept her dreams away like a tornado over twenty-two years before was about to bring more stormy weather into her life. Neither could she know that her future held another man who would help her weather the storms and would also bring refreshing breezes and new beginnings of springtime. Yep! Torrential winds were about to blow, sending Jaci through a season that would leave dramatic and irreversible changes.

J.P.

J.P. Gilmore and Herbert Williams sat in the reception area of the Housing Compliance Department, waiting to see Wynola Dickson. J.P. was ticked off. Their appointment had been for three o'clock, thirty minutes ago, and he didn't have this kind of time to waste. He realized he probably had made a mistake in calling the woman, but he hoped she might help him to get regular listings of buildings the city planned to demolish.

As he sat there steaming and considering walking out, J.P. idly looked through the glass wall to the elevator in the hallway as its doors opened. Two men, obviously in the midst of an amusing conversation, stepped out. As one spoke, the second one laughed so hard he fell against the wall. "Aw man, you're lying on her, I know you're lying!" he cried.

"I swear, man, I ain't lying. That lady flew by me so fast I saw dust flying from her feet. That woman can run! That dog was never going to catch her."

Another man walking down the corridor noticed the commotion and strolled over to them. "Man, you gotta hear this!" the second man said, and began to repeat the story. Before long, the third man was bent over with laughter. "I wish I had been there," he said between fits of laughter. "I would give anything to have been there. Where is she? Probably had to go home, didn't she?"

The elevator doors swung open again and J.P.'s heartbeat went into overdrive when a beautiful woman stepped off. She wore black jeans, a blue long-sleeved oxford shirt, and heavy, mud-encrusted boots. Her long hair was pulled back in a ponytail and showed the imprint of where the hard hat she now carried had been sitting on her head. A camera and a

small purse were slung over her shoulder and she was juggling
the hard hat, a clipboard, and a cold drink in her hands. Her
mouth thinned when the three men broke out in laughter, and
she shook her head disgustedly.

"You just couldn't wait to tell them, could you? You low-
life jerk! Well did you tell them about yourself?" The men
broke up again, doubling over and falling against the wall.

Shaking her head again, the woman entered the reception
area and walked toward the receptionist's desk, as a beautiful
smile replaced her frown. "Hey, Mrs. Hinson, how're you
doing? Any messages?" An answering smile spread over the
elderly lady's face behind the desk, who handed the woman a
stack of messages. "Hi, Miss 'J,' I can't complain. I won't ask
how you are. I can see you're tired. How did it go out there
today?"

"Don't worry, you'll hear all about it from those characters
out there when they finish laughing."

She turned to leave and noticed the two men sitting across
the room watching her. "Oh hi," she said, directing her gorgeous smile toward them. "Have you all been helped?"

J.P. felt the breath leave his chest. The smile lit up her whole
face and revealed beautiful teeth behind well-shaped lips,
which he instinctively knew would be a joy to kiss. And those
eyes! Green and sparkling like emeralds, they pierced him to
the core and caused his body to go into overdrive.

He responded with a large smile of his own, forgetting all
about being ticked off at Wynola. "Yes, we have, thank you.
We're waiting to see someone."

"Okay." She turned to the receptionist again. "See ya later."
She retraced her path through the double-glass doors leading
into the corridor. Nearing the men, who were still standing
there with amused expressions, she pointedly turned her head
away from them as she walked by.

"Ran into any dogs lately?" one of them asked. She kept

walking without acknowledging his question. The men busted out in loud laughter again.

J.P. watched her as far as he could see her down the long hallway. "Wonder who that is?" he mumbled to Herbert, who was just as engrossed.

"I don't know, but sure would like to," Herbert replied.

Never in his life had a woman he didn't even know affected him so strongly, and J.P. decided that he would make it a priority to find out who she was.

Maxie

Maxie Jackson was tired of the hospital room at Parkland Hospital in Dallas. He shifted around in the lumpy visitor's chair, trying to find a comfortable spot while he impatiently waited for his wife. Although he was awaiting his release, he still didn't feel well after having triple bypass heart surgery. He had been in the hospital almost two weeks after suffering a massive heart attack and was anxious to feel like his old self again. His doctor told him it would take a while, but he couldn't help wondering just how long. He didn't like sitting idle all day because it left too much time to think. He was usually on the go, enjoying life and pursuing whatever entertainment had his attention at the moment. This sitting around was for the birds.

He was mulling these thoughts over when a woman stuck her head in the open door of his room. It was Viola Wright, a woman he had known for years.

"Hello. Aren't you Maxie? Maxie Jackson? Yes, that is you. I was just walking by and saw you sitting here. You remember me, don't you? I worked with Jacetta Winters way back, years ago."

Maxie looked at her suspiciously. "Yeah, I remember you. I haven't seen you in years. What are you doing here?" he asked.

"Oh, I'm just visiting my aunt, who's right down the hall." A curious look swept over her face. "You know, I've stayed in touch with Jacetta over the years. She's done well in Houston. And that beautiful daughter!" Viola couldn't stop herself from going there. She didn't know all the particulars, but knew enough to guess that Maxie had treated Jacetta very badly. "Her daughter got married a few years ago, and it was really a lovely wedding."

Maxie remembered Jacetta Winters well. She was the little hick who had tried to trap him into marriage by getting pregnant. Huh! Someone should have told her he wasn't falling for that. Better women than she had tried that trick.

But now, for whatever reason—maybe boredom—even though he tried to act nonchalant, his interest was triggered. He didn't know for sure, but had to assume the woman knew he was the father of Jacetta's child; otherwise, she wouldn't be telling him all this—would she?

"So, what brought you here?" Viola asked nosily.

"My old ticker blew up on me and I had to have heart surgery. I'm getting ready to go home now though. Just waiting for my wife to get here."

"Uh huh." Viola looked at him with thinly veiled dislike. *You're probably just getting started with your troubles, sucker. You reap what you sow in this world,* she thought. She turned to leave, saying, "Well take care." She left hoping that Maxie would suffer as much as he had caused Jacetta to suffer. "I know Your Word is true, Father. May his moments of reaping be upon him," she prayed softly as she walked down the corridor.

Strange! The word popped into Maxie's mind after the

woman left. Strange that someone would mention Jacetta Winters and her child to him, especially at a time when he couldn't do anything to divert unwelcome thoughts. Over the years, if a thought about Jacetta or her child happened to enter his mind, he quickly pushed it aside as he went about his pursuit of self-gratification. He hadn't even been interested enough to try to find out the child's sex. Now in his dreary hospital room—twenty-something years later—he chuckled, congratulating himself. So . . . he had another daughter.

Two weeks later, Maxie ran into Jacetta's uncle, George Winters, as he entered the drugstore. George was brimming over with news of how well Jacetta and her daughter were doing.

"Man, let me tell you about that niece of mine. I was a little worried when she left here and moved down to Houston, but she's done real well. You know she always was real smart. She went down there and got a good job with the city. Been there over twenty years, and her daddy was telling me the last time I talked to him that she's thinking about retiring in a little while. Wants to do something different. We drove down there for her daughter's wedding, and I tell you, Jacetta's got a really nice house with a swimming pool in the backyard. I'm really proud of that girl."

"What kind of dude did she marry?" Maxie asked, filled with curiosity.

"You know," George answered slowly, "she never did get married. I guess she was too busy working and raising that child all by herself. My brother acted a big fool when she came up pregnant. Told her not to even think about coming back to his house, so I guess she was focused on what she had to do. My brother done regretted his words many times over the years. Especially after he saw how hard she was working. She wouldn't even take any help from him when he did try to give it. Anyway, now he can't help but feel guilty about everything.

Sometimes it's not the things you do, but those you don't that cause the deepest regrets."

Now this is too weird, Maxie thought. He hadn't seen George in years. They had parted on bad terms, since George hadn't been too happy with the way things had gone between him and Jacetta. To solve that problem, Maxie transferred to another branch of the company they both worked for, then made sure he stayed out of George's way.

A bevy of strange and unfamiliar emotions stirred within Maxie as George continued singing Jacetta's praises and talking about how well her child had turned out. Emotions he couldn't identify or understand assaulted him. And when he finally pinpointed them, he discovered to his amazement that he was actually feeling disappointment. In his mind, it looked as though the game had been won, and accolades were being given to the winner, but he was unable to share in the victory because he hadn't even shown up to play in the game. Ironically, he also identified envy and even loneliness creeping in as he thought about his run-down rented house and pillar-to-post lifestyle. He'd literally had to beg for help when he'd gotten sick. *Wait a minute!* He scolded himself. *Why am I questioning my lifestyle? I love it! Must be these health problems messing with my mind*, he consoled himself.

George's words grabbed his attention again. "Jacetta's daughter, Randi, already has one child and another one is on the way. She ain't wasting no time is she?" he said laughingly.

Unexplained anger flared in Maxie's mind. *Why did these people keep referring to her as Jacetta's daughter? They knew she was his daughter too.* Before he realized he was going to ask, he said, "You wouldn't happen to have Jacetta's phone number, would you?" He didn't know if George would give him the information even if he had it, but surprisingly, George searched through his wallet and found the number.

"You know, I just happen to have it on me 'cause I've been

planning to call Jace. I've been thinking about going to see her. Now that I'm retired again I can do that," he said, chuckling.

Maxie understood why the guy so willingly gave him the number when George continued in a serious tone, "You need to call her, man. You didn't do right by Jacetta and that child . . . we both know that. And I have always felt some responsibility since I brought ya'll together. But the most important thing now is to get to know your child. Randi is a nice young woman. If I were you, I wouldn't leave this world knowing I had a child I had never seen. And it's not fair for Randi to go through life not knowing her father. And I gotta tell you, you have truly ripped yourself off by not being a part of her life." He began to walk away. "Well, I guess I'll be moving on. Take care of yourself, man." George hoped what he had said would cause Maxie to regret his callous treatment of Jacetta and their child. But he had a disturbing thought. *Maxie still might not be man enough to fully understand what I was trying to say to him.*

As Maxie waited for his prescriptions, his mind raced all over the place. After all these years, two conversations had come up about Jacetta within a couple of weeks. It made him nervous. He normally didn't believe in coincidence, but this one could really bug him if he let it.

Not wanting to return to his lonely little house after getting his prescriptions, Maxie decided to drive over to his brother Joe's house for a while. He hadn't been there long before he found himself telling Joe about the two conversations he'd recently had about Jacetta.

Joe immediately jumped him. "Man, I told you when that was going down that you were going to regret how you treated that girl one of these days. You didn't even tell Mother she had another grandchild did you?"

"Naw man! Why would I do that? That girl didn't mean nothing to me."

"Well, all I got to say is, where are your other children? How often do you see them? And how well do they know their grandmother? Or vice versa? They don't even go see her. Not to mention you."

Maxie had two other children—a boy and a girl—both older than Jacetta's child.

His son, James, was the product of his first disastrous marriage. He had neither loved nor cared for James's mother, but the woman had been shrewd. Vicious threats from her family, and her having him thrown in jail for not supporting the child, had forced him to take the course of least resistance and marry her. The marriage only lasted until she realized he had no intention of adhering to the marriage vows. But he'd been stuck with paying child support after the marriage ended or she would have happily sent him to jail.

A few years later he was shacking with a woman who got pregnant with his daughter Andrea. Again, he was forced into marriage out of self-preservation when another woman on his job started causing all sorts of problems and disruptions for him. Despite his practiced techniques in shaking unwanted women, the low-life woman wouldn't leave him alone, insisting he was going to marry her. His supervisor made it clear that he had to get his personal business straight or he would be out of a job. So, Maxie had done what he had to and married his daughter's mother. Not that the marriage meant anything to him. It was a means to an end that he quickly found a way to use to his benefit.

He smiled at his slyness, remembering how many women he had fooled by showing them his divorce papers from his first marriage, conveniently leaving out the fact that he had remarried.

Now, feeling the heat of his brother's words, he exclaimed, "Man, I see my kids all the time. Especially Andrea whenever I'm over at her mother's house. She's doing all right."

"But, Maxie, when have you spent any quality time with her?" Joe harassed. "How many children she got now? What about James? How many children he got? Do you even know? Man, you're pitiful! Here you are, old, sick, broken down, and needing someone. And because of the raggedy life you've lived, your own children and grandchildren don't know or give a darn about you. Pitiful!"

When Maxie's children were young, he loved playing the part of the doting father whenever it suited his purposes. He picked them up and paraded them all over town, showing them off and taking credit for their well-dressed appearances and sharp intelligence. After they got old enough to understand what was going on, they refused to go anywhere with him. So, he had merely left them alone except for seeing them occasionally, out of curiosity.

"Man, those women kept me broke taking care of those kids. Every time I turned around it was something." Maxie defended himself. "I'm just glad they're grown and finally out of my pocket. When Jacetta came up pregnant, I knew I wasn't dealing with any more child support hassles."

Joe shook his head. "Then why did you get her pregnant? Man, you were old enough to be more responsible. Just didn't have a thought for anyone but yourself."

"Well, Jacetta should have taken responsibility for herself. I didn't make her do anything. And anyway, I'm not even certain that baby was mine."

"Aw, please! You know there was never any doubt that baby was yours. You even bragged about Jacetta being a virgin. And you monopolized all her time to make sure no other dude could get to her. So, you can save that old "how do I know it's mine" line. But I remember from talking to her a few times that Jacetta was pretty close to God. And I have a strange feeling about these out-of-the-blue conversations you're having about her. God may be getting ready to show you that turn-about is fair play."

Maxie felt an unfamiliar shiver run down his spine at hearing his brother's words. Jacetta's last words to him—something along those same lines—suddenly popped into his mind. *Now why did I remember that after all these years?* he thought, then shook it off by attacking his brother. "Man, here you come with that old God mess again. I ain't interested in hearing it. Anyway, if you're so self-righteous, why didn't you do anything to help her?"

"You don't know how much I have regretted not doing any-thing to help that girl," Joe said sadly. "My only excuse is that I was tied up in my own issues around that time. But I still feel bad about it. And if I feel bad, you ought to be feeling really rotten."

There was no way Maxie would ever admit it to his brother, but the unexplainable emotions of loneliness and disappoint-ment struck him again. Andrea and James hadn't even come to see him since he'd been sick. They treated him with the same indifference that he showed toward them. Suddenly, his life looked very bleak and empty.

Two weeks later, Jacetta remained at the forefront of his mind. Maxie didn't consciously make the decision, but some-how he knew he would call her. He didn't really remember much about how she looked, but he did remember her love and adoration for him. Her feelings for him had made it very easy for him to exploit and take advantage of her. *I've got too much time to think!* He scolded himself for his empty life. But inevitably his mind would return to Jacetta and *his* daughter. The descriptions painted about their lives stirred a deep yearning within him, filling him with the desire to see for him-self. Why? He didn't know. Was it about the daughter he had never even seen? Maybe. Could it be curiosity about Jacetta, whom he had dumped without a second thought? Not hardly!

It was more than likely the effects of his health problems, and the undeniable fact that he was growing old. Whatever the reason, he wanted to see Jacetta and his daughter and grandchild. He made a sudden decision . . . he would do just that!

Jaci

*J*aci always felt mentally depleted after a hearing. Thankfully, all had gone well, and as usual, her staff wasted no time heading for home. She sat idly at her desk, knowing she too needed to leave, but dreading the long drive and the horrific traffic she would have to deal with. She decided to kill a little time by checking on her cousin C.J., who she knew could probably use an encouraging word. After suffering through years of her husband's infidelity, C.J. had made the difficult decision to end her marriage.

"Hey, Cij! What's going on, girl? You're not sitting over there feeling sorry for yourself, are you?"

C.J. laughed. "That's what I like about you, Jace. Shoot from the hip and aim right between the eyes. And no, that's the last thing on my mind. I'm over here packing and throwing stuff away. Lord, what junk we accumulate! Why do we do that?" She paused before continuing. "Jace, I really appreciate all the moral support you're giving me. I'm so glad we live near each other while I'm going through this."

Jaci smiled at her cousin's words. "C.J., how many times do I have to tell you? I wouldn't have it any other way. By the way, do you want me to go apartment hunting with you Saturday? My invitation stands—you're welcome to stay with me until you find a house."

Just talking to her cousin lifted C.J.'s spirit and had her feeling better. "Yeah, girl. And I really appreciate your offer, but I need my own space. I'm not the best company for anyone right now. I've gotten a list of apartments from Apartment Locators I think I might like. I guess it doesn't matter a whole lot, since I'm not planning to stay there long. But I do want to be comfortable for however long I'm there. Are you still coming to help me pack tomorrow?"

"Yep. I'll be there as early as I can in the morning," Jaci answered, thankful that her four-day workweek made it possible for her to help.

"Good. I can sure use your help, and it's not going to be nothing nice. Randy still hasn't come to clean out his things and I have my hands full just dealing with mine, plus the furniture and household stuff. I really didn't think the house was going to sell this quickly. I mean, we just put it on the market a couple of weeks ago, and we've already got a contract on it. It wouldn't be an issue if the buyers didn't want to begin redecorating right away. They want to be able to move in as soon as the sale is complete. But I'm not mad at them. They're paying some big bucks for which I am very grateful. It's just putting me under pressure to get all our stuff out as soon as possible. Of course, a lot of it will have to go into storage, but that can't be helped."

C.J. seemed to be taking everything in stride but Jaci knew she had to be in a lot of pain over her dissolving twenty plus years of marriage. She searched in her mind for a way to bring a little sunshine into her life. "Hey, Cij! Why don't we meet somewhere for breakfast in the morning? Then we can start packing on a full stomach and work through until we're done."

C.J. hesitated. She really didn't feel up to going out for breakfast, but Jaci was doing too much to help her get through this mess for her to be disagreeable. "Okay, breakfast. Where?"

Hearing in her cousin's voice that breakfast wasn't appealing, Jaci decided to do something different. "You know what, Cij? Forget breakfast. It's going to be hard enough getting myself up and across town early in the morning. We don't need to be wasting time going out to breakfast. We can do that anytime. You just have yourself up and ready to tackle that monstrous house when I get there." C.J. had always felt that the house was too big for just the two of them, but her husband, Randy, a former pro-basketball player, had insisted on buying it.

Jaci hesitated a minute. "Cij? Have you talked to Randy lately?"

"Girl, yes! He's still pissed about the divorce settlement. He really thought he was going to walk away with everything just because he's a popular sports personality. He was too stupid to realize that would work against him after all the scandals he's been involved in. He didn't want me to get anything, and I could have lived with that. But you know me, tell me I can't have something and I dig in for a fight. And after all, I have a dead child and years of pain and humiliation invested in this marriage. But neither one of us thought I would end up with the house and half of his bank account. Whew! How sweet it is! Anyway, now he's hinting around about trying to patch things up. He realizes that he's not going to be able to maintain the lifestyle he's grown accustomed to. But he's crazy if he thinks I'm going *there* again! No way!"

Jaci laughed. "Good for you! Randy ought to know by now not to mess with the Winslows. He's seen us in action. Anyway, I'm going to get off and head on home. I'll see you in the morning."

Early the following morning, Jaci stood in line at the local New Orleans Poboy, a place popular for big, fluffy pancakes.

She decided to surprise C.J. with a big breakfast and studied the menu intently, unaware that she herself was being studied.

In fact, J.P. Gilmore, in line behind her, stared at her so hard he had to be reminded to move up as the line moved. He was sure this was the woman he had seen at the Housing Compliance Department a few days earlier. If she turned around enough for him to see her eyes he would be certain. Dressed in khaki shorts, which hugged her shapely hips and revealed big beautiful legs, and a green short-sleeved shirt, she looked delectable, and J.P. was looking so hard he almost forgot where he was again. Dang, she was beautiful!

Jaci spoke to the lady behind the counter for a long time, making sure her order was correct. Her wavy hair was pulled back and held in place with a clip, and J.P. watched as she thoughtlessly pushed an errant curl out of her face. He had to forcefully control the impulse to reach around the people between them to run his hands through the soft curls.

She turned to respond to something the person behind her said, and J.P. got a better look at her face. It was her! Her green eyes danced in merriment as she joked about the big pancakes she loved. As she moved over to the checkout counter, he knew her large carryout bag had to contain more than one order. He swallowed his fear that she might have been buying breakfast for herself and a man.

Jaci paid for her order and worked her way back through the crowd toward the door. Her eyes met the bold stare of a handsome guy who looked vaguely familiar, but she quickly looked away. A woman couldn't be too careful. The man's eyes followed her progress, causing Jaci to feel very uncomfortable and to hurry out the door to her Jeep as fast as she could.

J.P. almost followed her to the parking lot but managed to stop himself. He didn't want to scare her off, and he did know where to find her. He cheered himself with a promise that he would get to know this woman as soon as possible.

J.P.

*T*he Gilmore family gathered for their regular after-church Sunday dinner, and, as usual, the conversation centered around the family business. The family owned a real estate agency that serviced Houston and surrounding counties.

J.P.'s parents, Cecelia and J.P. Gilmore Sr. (known as "Big Pat"), along with Big Pat's twin brother, Stanley, had run the flourishing business for several decades. Illness had forced Stanley into partial retirement a few years before, and now J.P.'s parents wanted to gradually hand the running of the company off to their children. J.P. bore most of the burden since his siblings refused to accept much responsibility. Typically, Big Pat was browbeating Ronald, J.P.'s younger brother by two years, about taking a more active role in the business.

"Ron, when are you going to step up to the plate and start helping out with the business? We're just about killing Junior—he's trying to run both his company and the family business. Your sister is off doing her own thing, so you know we can't expect any help from her. And it's time for me and your mother to start taking it easy, do some things we been wanting to do."

Ron was feeling the heat. He had little interest in the real estate business, preferring to concentrate on his architectural firm.

"Pop, I got my hands full with my own business. I've told you, I don't plan to ever step up to that plate. I'll help out now and then if I have time, but I'm not going to commit to any-thing else. If I let ya'll, I'll be roped in like you've done with J.P., and next thing I know, I won't have time for my own busi-ness."

His mother jumped in. "Well, at least J.P.'s not neglecting his family like you are. He's managing to run his software com-pany *and* the family business and doing both real well."

"That's him, Mama," Ron said agitatedly. "I can't do that—or rather, I'm not going to do that. If he wants to spread himself thin like that, then all power to him." He gave J.P. a dirty look that said, "look what you've done now."

"Well, like I said, he's doing well in both. And I don't hear him complaining."

"But his heart is in developing computer software, and if he had the time to fully pursue that without family ties obligat-ing him, he would probably be doing even better."

J.P. had opted out of the conversation and just sat back lis-tening. He was tired of the same old argument, and beyond that, he found he liked the challenge of running both busi-nesses.

He finally said, "Current business trends indicate that di-versity in business is a wise thing. Having all your eggs in one basket is not a good thing in this fickle economy. If one goes into a slump, I have the other one to fall back on. But a little help would give Mom and Pop a chance to relax a little."

"Nope. I'm not committing to nothing." Then, totally changing the subject, Ron said, "J.P., if you want to walk the construction site, we'd better go. I have plans for later on."

"Now, I like this housing development project," Big Pat said, following them as they headed out the door, Ron with a frown and J.P. with a resigned smile. "See, if ya'll would join up on more things like this, you could really be raking it in," he yelled to them from the doorway.

They got into their vehicles and drove the short distance to the cul-de-sac where J.P. lived and where eleven other custom-designed houses sat in various stages of construction. As they inspected the progress of the homes they were building in a joint venture, J.P. brought up the subject again.

"I think architecture and real estate are more compatible than real estate and computer software. I'm not complaining . . . don't get me wrong. I'm doing real well since I decided to handle more commercial properties. And I'm finding some good deals by watching the properties being condemned by the city. It ain't bad, man. You ought to come on and try it."

"Nope."

"Listen, man," J.P. continued, "I've found a way to gain quick access to information on newly condemned commercial properties. Quite often, I can pick up some good deals by making an offer to owners who just want to dump the property fast. Remember Wynola Dickson? She's one of the managers in the Housing Compliance Department."

"That old hag that's been after you for years?" said Ron. "Man, how can you even think about it? You gon' get yourself killed. You know she's open for some play with you. And that crazy husband of hers knows it too. I wouldn't even mess around with that. Find another way. Do it the way you been doing it. But leave that alone."

"Who are you to be giving advice on being careful? If I recall, you're the one always having to leave with your pants under your arm."

"That's me," Ron answered smugly. "I can handle that. You can't."

"And how you figure I can't?" he asked, then chuckled. "You're right, I've gotten too old for that kind of stuff. And you have too. My mind won't even flow that way anymore." He waved his hand in dismissal. "Anyway, as I was saying, I had an appointment last week to talk to Wynola about hooking me up with some leads. Man, she had me and Herbert sitting there cooling our heels for almost an hour waiting for her." He shook his head disgustedly. "I didn't appreciate wasting our time like that, but I'm glad I went, because two good things came out of it."

"What?"

"I met an interesting woman while I was there—sort of. That's one. And the other is that I found out I can't deal with Wynola. When we finally got in to see her, she didn't have any interest in discussing business. All she wanted to talk about was what's happening on the social scene, and of course she was in her element, flirting with both of us. I tried to steer the conversation back to why we were there by telling her that I didn't want to take up her time. That all I needed was for her to direct us to the right source to get a list of condemned commercial buildings that are scheduled to be demolished. She just waved her hand, and said, 'oh honey, I can help you with *anything* you need.' I knew then I would have to find another way. Heck, I was so frustrated when I left her office, I was ready to wring her neck. It was a big waste of valuable time."

"What do you mean you sort of met an interesting woman?" Ron asked. "Either you did or you didn't."

"See! I knew you were going to pick up on that! You didn't hear anything else I said."

"That's me, man—what can I say?" Ron answered, smiling broadly and spreading his hands.

"Anyway!" J.P. continued, ignoring him. "I'm going to avoid Wynola from now on. I've already found out from talking to some of the inspectors on the street that I need to talk to a guy by the name of J.C. Winters. They say he can give me whatever information I need. So I'm going to start going to those abatement hearings they have whenever I can. This Winters fellow is the person who handles those hearings for the city. That's where I could use your help. You could attend those hearings for me."

"Nope!"

"Well, man, just go with me to the one next week and meet this guy. That way, if I ever need you to attend one, you'll know what the deal is. We don't have to go to all of them, just often enough to keep up with what's newly condemned. Come on, man! You owe me that much. And if you don't, I'ma tell Mama. Pop just full of talk, but Mama gon' get a stick after your behind sooner or later. You know that don't you?"

"Now, you know you wrong for that," Ron said with a chuckle.

"Whatever it takes," J.P. replied with a non-apologetic grin. "The next hearing is Thursday at ten. Come by the office around nine Thursday morning and we can ride together. Sometimes parking is a hassle." Shaking his head, Ron got in his car and drove away.

Thursday, J.P.'s reaction was almost comical when he walked into the room where the hearing was held. The beautiful, professionally dressed woman presenting the city's case was none other than the lady he had seen and had such an unusual reaction to in the reception area that day, and again in the restaurant the previous Friday. But the most shocking surprise was that this woman and *Jaci* Winters were one and the same.

Ron didn't have to be told that this was the woman who had captured his brother's attention. He watched with amusement as J.P.'s eyes seldom left the woman, taking in everything about her. He acknowledged his brother's good taste in women and wished he had seen her first.

J.P. was so captivated that he gave up any pretense of following the progress of the hearing and gave his full attention to her. She looked to be in her mid-thirties, was about five-foot-five, and the navy blue business suit she wore did little to hide her well-proportioned, curvy body. Her flawless honey-toned skin looked smooth enough to eat and her hair was a tantalizing enticement. The thick, reddish-brown tresses hung in soft curls that begged to be touched. Her eyes captured his attention again. Could those mesmerizing green eyes really be natural, not tinted contact lenses? And those legs! Big, shapely, and slightly bowed at the knees—he almost salivated. J.P. was definitely a leg man.

"Hey, man," Ronald said, giving him an elbow jab in the side. "You better catch your eyes before they fall out of their sockets. And while you're at it, grab your tongue, too, cause it's almost dragging the floor."

"*That's* Jaci Winters! That's the person I need to talk to."

"I thought you were turning this thing over to me? You said you didn't have time," Ron teasingly reminded him.

"Well . . . I might be able to find a little time here and there," J.P. said. "We'll see how it goes." He turned his eyes back to the woman.

"Those inspectors were right about her," he whispered to Ron. "She obviously knows her job well. These owners don't have a chance." They watched as Jaci calmly but firmly responded when the disgruntled property owners tried to dispute the evidence presented against their properties.

"She has excellent PR skills doesn't she?" J.P. continued to praise her. He admired the way she stood her ground, refusing to back off on the incriminating evidence she had gathered. She presented the information in an organized and straightforward manner, giving the number of times the buildings were found in violation, producing pictures of the violations, and in many cases, showing signed statements from neighbors concerned about the unsafe buildings in their neighborhoods. The owners were well aware of the violations, but they still resented being brought to court about them.

"She is good!" he said as he watched owner after owner lose, but leave appeased, as she expertly offered recommendations and solutions that provided a win-win outcome for both the city and the owners.

"That woman's got you sprung, brother," Ron said, a gleeful smile on his face, as they left the building. "Man, I never thought I'd see the day. But I just saw it. The big tree in the forest has toppled." Ron laughed at his own statement. "What are you going to do if she's not interested? Or what if she's married?"

"She's not wearing a wedding ring," J.P. answered as fear filled him. "If she were married, she'd be wearing a ring. No man in his right mind would let a woman like that walk around without a ring. Naw. I'd be willing to bet, she's not married." He sounded like he was trying to convince himself.

"Well, what kind of angle are you gonna use to get to her?"

"I don't know, man," J.P. answered irritably. "But I'll figure something out."

As soon as he had a chance, Ron told Big Pat about the woman that had J.P. in a spin. "You need to go check her out, Pop. This woman has Junior's nose open wide enough for an eighteen-wheeler to pass through it. And he don't even know if she's married or not."

"How does she look? J.P. ain't worked up over no ugly woman is he?"

"Oh no!" Ron answered. "She's all right. In fact, I may have to give him a little competition."

Big Pat gave Ron a hard look. "I know you don't mean that. There's plenty women out there. Go find your own."

"Just joking, Pop, just joking."

J.P. had attended several hearings before Big Pat decided to tag along and see what the situation was for himself. He knew J.P. hadn't missed a hearing yet and hadn't uttered one complaint.

"Uh huh!" Big Pat said when they entered the room, and J.P. headed straight for Jaci to say hello.

"What was that 'uh huh' supposed to mean?" J.P. asked suspiciously, when they found seats and sat down.

"Oh. Nothing. I'm just here observing, you know."

All during the hearing, his dad watched him, while J.P. watched Jaci. He noticed everything. Her interactions with the hearing board and the property owners were guided by an unquestionable knowledge of city ordinances. She orchestrated the smooth flow of the hearing from beginning to end. The more he saw, the more he liked. The more he liked, the more he cautiously searched for flaws and chinks in her armor. Common sense told him that nobody was perfect.

He had introduced himself to her and her coworkers after attending a couple of hearings and explained his purpose for attending. She had proven to be a great source of information by providing him with an updated listing of condemned buildings on a regular basis. She was friendly, but not overly so, remaining professional at all times.

At first this was a little unsettling because J.P. was accustomed to women falling all over themselves to get to him. He was encouraged, however, after he saw her firmly rebuffing the attentions of other men who blatantly came on to her. He observed her covertly throwing business cards and slips of paper with hastily scribbled phone numbers into the trash and concluded that she was definitely not on a manhunt. For some reason that fact impressed him. He was tired of empty-headed women whose only goal was catching a man. Somehow he didn't think she fit that mold, but he really wanted to know what made her tick.

"Okay," Big Pat said as they walked to the garage after leaving the hearing. "Want to tell me about this woman who has you all hot and bothered?"

"What are you talking about, Pop? What woman?"

They reached J.P.'s SUV, got in, and headed back to the office. Big Pat gave him a scathing look. "Now you know, I wish you wouldn't try to snow an old man. Son, I been over that road before."

J.P. couldn't do anything but smile. "So that's why you decided to tag along today. Ron opened his big mouth, and you just wanted to spy on me."

"You know anything about her? Is she married?"

"Nope, don't think so. I've been watching her for a while, and yes, I'm definitely interested in her. I just haven't figured out how to get through that professional armor she wears. I've watched a whole lot of other guys try to talk to her and get shot down."

"Ump! You must be slipping. The J.P. I know, with the reputation he has for being a connoisseur of women, wouldn't even have a problem. Unless . . ." Big Pat hesitated as a thought crossed his mind. "You know, she may be a switch hitter—not necessarily interested in men."

J.P.'s mouth fell open and his blood ran cold. He hadn't even considered that. "Don't even go there, Pop! I've watched her dealing with both men and women. If that were the case, I would have noticed a difference. She relates to everybody the same way."

"These days you have to be watchful for everything, son, and that's not always easy to spot. Just keep your eyes and ears open and be careful. You'll find out what you need to know. I'm anxious to see how the great lady's man is going to handle this myself!" Big Pat chuckled, thinking he couldn't wait to tell his wife about the woman. "Just your hesitancy in approaching this woman tells me how important she could be to you."

J.P. grunted. "The reports of my great success with women have been greatly exaggerated. I'm not nearly as notorious as people think. Being a single, well-to-do businessman in this city makes me a target for women of every description. And frankly, I wouldn't be a man if I hadn't indulged a little, but honestly, Pop, I've been tired of that lifestyle a long time."

"Well, I'm glad to hear that," Big Pat answered thoughtfully. "Every man eventually reaches that point. If he's the right kind of man, that is. Some, like me, get there at an early age, while others are old men before it happens. The important thing is to get there at some point, and sadly, some never get there. It's a tragic thing for a man to live his whole life and not know how good it is to love and be loved by a good woman."

J.P. nodded his head affirmatively. "I want what you and Mom have. A life of commitment to each other. Sharing, loving, and working together, serving God together, going on vacations and just experiencing life together. You raised us up to be reasonably productive adults, and Lord knows I don't know what I would have done if ya'll hadn't been around to help me with Patrick. It's taken me some time, but I now appreciate what you have together and it's definitely what I want for myself."

"Well, what are you waiting on? You're not still licking your wounds over Vivian?"

He gave his dad a dirty look. Vivian, J.P.'s ex-wife, had left him for an older, wealthier man when his son, Patrick, had been a toddler. "Heck naw! That's way behind me. But like I said, I want the right woman. One who wants the same things I want. I'm nearly forty-four years old, and I've already wasted too many years. I don't relish the thought of one fruitless relationship after the other, or spending the rest of my life alone. It's finding that elusive woman that's proving to be a challenge. Most of the women I meet these days turn me off. If they're not fickle, fake, and immature, they're hard, calculating gold diggers. Some of 'em are just plain old, low down, and dirty. But whatever group they fall into, they seem to lack the desire or the ability to build a meaningful relationship, and they all leave a bad taste in my mouth."

"So what makes you think this woman is any different?"

"I guess it's the way she carries herself, and some quality or trait in her that reaches me on a level that no woman has touched before. Every time I see her I want to touch her, kiss her—something! Beyond that, I can't pinpoint what it is, and it's driving me crazy! Usually by this time, most women are throwing themselves at me. But beyond being helpful, she hasn't. That intrigues me. And there's nothing funny about her either. The man in me wouldn't react to her this way if she weren't all woman."

Big Pat laughed, enjoying his son's distress. He had waited a long time to witness it. "Yep. That's how I felt about your mother when I first met her. She had me crazy, too." He laughed again, remembering, before saying, "Well, I'm sure the woman realizes you're interested. Maybe she's just smart, biding her time just to string you along a little."

"No," J.P. answered thoughtfully. "Frankly, I don't think it's even occurred to her that I may be interested. And anyway, I don't think that's her style. Since she's not an easy woman to approach, I'm a little stumped, but believe me, I'm just waiting for the right opportunity."

"Well, son, whatever you do, pray about it. Let the Lord guide you. That way you'll know you're moving in the right direction and won't be making a mistake."

"Yeah, I'm doing that, Pop."

Jaci

wo weeks later, Jaci hurriedly gathered files and placed them into a portable filing cabinet, while she laughed and talked with her coworkers. Relieved that another hearing was behind her, she noticed frowningly that a few people were still mingling around the large room.

"These stragglers must really be pleased with the decisions they got on their properties," she whispered to her assistant, Gloria. "They act like they don't even want to leave."

The hearing had been reasonably uneventful, and that always made Jaci breathe a sigh of relief. The worst-case scenario would be to present incorrect information at the hearing and cause the city to lose the case. Some owners would stoop to any level to discredit the city's case in hopes of holding off the demolition of their condemned buildings. Her years of experience had taught her that some inspectors couldn't be trusted to provide correct information. So, she and her staff worked extremely hard, checking and double-checking facts, to assure that their information was as accurate and up to date as possible.

It was Thursday and the end of her four-day, ten-hour-per-day workweek. She sighed tiredly as she mentally went over all that she needed to do on her days off.

"Hey, Jaci," Bill called from across the room where he was stacking chairs. "You're in a hurry to get out of here today. You must have big plans for the weekend." He knew Jaci usually stayed at work while everyone else rushed out.

"As a matter of fact I do," she said. At their surprised expressions, she continued, "I have yard work and house work to do. I promised my cousin I would help her move, and I still have to get somebody out to look at my roof. It's at the point where it's got to be replaced, which I'm definitely not ready for. There's no telling how much it's going to cost, so I gotta look for a way to earn some extra money. Yeah, I need to be outta here real quick today."

"No date?" Gloria asked slyly. "I can't believe you don't ever have a date, Jaci. Frankly, I don't think you're telling us everything."

"Ha! When do I have time for dates? Or better yet, *who* do I have *to* date? Girl, you know there are no men out there."

"Uh! Uh! There are men all around," Bill threw in. "You just refuse to notice them."

Jaci again said, "Ha!"

Their lighthearted bantering continued as they worked to put the room back in order and prepared to leave, all the while cutting their eyes at the two remaining men still in deep conversation and evidently in no hurry to leave.

They noticed one of them was real estate developer J.P. Gilmore, who attended the hearings in search of potential properties he could purchase.

"What's that drop-dead gorgeous J.P. Gilmore still doing here?" Gloria whispered. Jaci glanced across the room to where the good-looking man stood. Well above six feet, his muscular body was always immaculately dressed, whether it was casual or business attire; the clothes molded his body as though custom-made for him. They probably were.

"I don't know. But are you complaining? Just enjoy the view," Jaci replied, still sneaking looks. His wavy black hair, sprinkled with a few gray strands around the sides, complimented his pecan colored skin. And his classically handsome face included piercing dark eyes and a wide sensual mouth topped by a well trimmed sexy mustache. *Yep! Definitely a hunk!*

"Don't you think he looks a little like Judge Joe Brown?

Even his mannerisms and the way his deep voice resonates when he talks—it gives me goose bumps!" Gloria stated.

"Well, any way you size him up, Mr. Gilmore is a hunk," Jaci agreed. "Not that it excites me. It's just a fact. I found out a long time ago that good looks on the outside often hide a rotten inside. He is something special to look at though. *Just looking* being the operative words."

"Um, Um, Um! I sure could be tempted to find out what's on the inside if I had the chance," Gloria added, staring unashamedly at J.P.

"Jaci," Bill said, walking over to where she stood, "why don't you talk to that contractor over there with Gilmore? He might be able to give you some leads on good roofers."

The men turned and moved toward them. J.P., who had purposely waited for the right moment, walked up to Jaci. "Good hearing, Ms. Winters, and thanks for the information on the commercial properties. I really appreciate your help."

"No problem," Jaci said. "It's all about getting rid of those dangerous buildings."

"I see you guys are trying to get out of here," J.P. continued. "I hope I didn't detain you, but I was hoping to get a chance to speak to you." When Jaci gave him a questioning look, he continued. "It's not about the hearings, it's on a totally different matter. Is it okay if I call you tomorrow?"

"Sorry, I'm off tomorrow. But I'll be here Monday. You can call any time after eight." Although Jaci arrived at seven, she used the first hour each morning to organize and focus on whatever she had to accomplish over the course of the day.

J.P. pulled a business card out of his pocket, scribbled some numbers on the back, and handed it to her. "Well, if you get some time over the weekend, give me a call. If you don't get me at the office, try the home number or the cell anytime. Just leave a message; if I don't answer, I'll get right back to you."

"Okay," she answered slowly, with a puzzled look.

J.P. waved good-bye to them, and as he walked away, he turned and pointed to the card, saying, "Please don't throw that away."

Jaci blushed, realizing he must have observed her doing just that with others. Turning away in embarrassment, she rushed to catch the contractor to talk to him about her roof.

"Girl, what is wrong with you?" Gloria asked minutes later as they walked down the hall to their offices. "That hunk wants to talk to you and here you are acting crazy. You'd better call that man tonight!"

"Pul . . . lease!" Jaci said, rolling her eyes. "You know that guy probably has a wife and hundreds of women after him. No thanks! I can do without that kind of drama."

Gloria shook her head. She couldn't figure Jaci out. She was not only beautiful, she was a kind, caring person as well. She tried to get along with everyone, but refused to let people get too close. She had problems with both the men and the women in the department. Gloria knew it was because of the reserved way she carried herself. People who liked gossip and mess couldn't handle that.

In the years they had worked together, Gloria knew of only one man who had gotten to first base with her. Evidently it hadn't worked out well, and since then, Gloria watched as several other men around the department tried, but failed. Jaci would often comment about a man being fine or a hunk, but she rejected the many flirtatious advances she received, so she had earned the reputation of being a cold fish and was often the target of unkind words and jokes.

After quickly putting things away, Bill and Gloria called out, "Good night" to let Jaci know they were leaving. Jaci kept working to clear her desk and pondered J.P. Gilmore's request that she call him. She had no intention of calling him over the weekend, but was admittedly very curious. What could he possibly want to talk to her about? He was probably just living up to his reputation as a playboy, she concluded. Maybe she should throw that card in the trash, she admonished herself.

Jaci was the topic of her coworkers' conversation on their walk to the parking lot. "What do you think makes Jaci tick? As far as men are concerned, that is," Bill asked Gloria.

"I don't believe she thinks much of them. I think maybe she's been badly hurt at some point."

"Yeah. She's had some bad experiences," Bill said thoughtfully. "How long have you known her?"

"About ten years, since she became supervisor of hearing coordination and hired me as her assistant. Why?"

"Well, I've known her ever since she came to the Housing Compliance Department—more than twenty years. She's worked all over the department, from clerical to administrative positions. Did you know she made history by becoming the first woman investigator in the Dangerous Buildings Section? I give her a hard time sometimes, but I have a lot of respect for that lady. That's a dangerous and uncomfortable job, even for a man, but for a woman, doubly so."

"Yeah," Gloria said. "She told me about some of her experiences when she first became an investigator. She said the biggest problem wasn't the actual work, but the people here in the department. I don't know why people are so hard on a woman trying to make it up the ladder the right way. But Jaci said there was no way she was giving up. She's a tough lady, that's for sure."

"You ain't telling me nothing I don't know. The only reason she got the investigator position was because of management's fears of gender discrimination lawsuits. The threats weren't coming from Jaci, but she's the one who ended up with the job because of her qualifications and experience. After getting the position, she received very little support from management. And she had to deal with some pretty rough treatment from the men in the department who either wanted the position or felt it should have been given to a man."

"Was it really that bad?" Gloria asked.

"Oh man! That lady was programmed for failure in so many ways, it's a wonder she made it. That's how she gained my respect. I admit, at first I was kind of grudging, too, because I just didn't think a woman could handle the job. But when I saw her hanging tough and refusing to give up, I knew she had to be motivated by something other than just wanting to be the first woman to hold the position. I started helping her. I took some heat, but I just couldn't stand by and watch her struggling like that. And when I started helping her, some of the other guys jumped in and helped her, too. It was only later that I found out she was a single parent and needed the higher salary."

"Oh, Bill, I'm so glad you did that for her. She's a very caring person and will do anything to help you. Remember when I had surgery a few years ago? She would come up here on weekends and bring her daughter to help me keep up with my work so Wynola wouldn't try to replace me. I'll always be grateful for that. You know, I think that Gilmore guy is interested in her, but Jaci won't cooperate."

As they were talking, J.P., who had gotten detained by someone on his way out of the building, was slowly driving out of the garage. When he saw them standing there in deep discussion, he pulled over and stopped. The thought occurred to him that these two people worked closely with Jaci and perhaps he could pump them for information about her. He got out of the car and walked over to them.

"Hi. I just thought I'd let you all know how much I appreciate all the help you guys give me. It saves me from having to go through a lot of hassle for the information."

"No problem, glad to be of service," Bill said.

Seeing an opportunity for them to play matchmakers, Gloria jumped in with both feet. Giving Bill an eye that said, "follow my lead," she said, "You know, we were just talking about our boss, Ms. Winters. If it weren't for her we probably wouldn't be able to offer you much help. She's the one who's worked and fought hard to get our division to where it is."

"Right," Bill kicked in. "I was just telling Gloria how much I respect and admire Jaci. She's been our supervisor for several years now, and I haven't regretted a minute of it. Jaci has the division so organized that a punch of a button will give you anything you need to know about any building on file. And I gotta tell you, it hasn't always been that way. Man, I remember when it would take us days to locate a file. And then, nine times out of ten, no current information would be in it. But now, it had better be in there or somebody's butt is in serious trouble."

"Is that right?" J.P. asked, eagerly taking in everything they were saying. "So, Ms. Winters is something else, huh?" He felt like he had hit the jackpot.

Bill started chuckling. "You better believe it. Needless to say, she's become an expert at anything to do with the demolition process."

"How did she end up coordinating these hearings?" J.P. asked.

"They practically forced it on her," Bill answered. "Jaci already knew the administrative paper flow and the kind of documentation needed to get a structure demolished. After she became an investigator, and she was the first woman to hold that position, it didn't take long before she was finding ways to improve how information was collected and expeditiously transferred to the file. And like I said, she's a stickler for detail and hard work. Her production was soon way over everyone else's and her files never got kicked back. The powers that be soon realized it was in their best interest to utilize her abilities to increase overall production. So they created the

Hearing Coordination Section and put Jaci in charge of it. I agreed to come over and work with her. Best move I ever made."

J.P. had heard enough. They had given him an idea for a plan. "It's been good talking to ya'll. I gotta go but just wanted to let ya'll know how much I appreciate your help. I'll talk to you guys later. Thanks again." He waved to them as he got into his car, feeling good about what he had just heard and about the plan forming in his mind.

Maxie

Maxie sat in his worn recliner, TV remote in hand, idly flipping through channels, but his mind was on Jacetta—again. He tried to recall how she looked, but he couldn't put a face with that sexy voice he had heard on her answering machine. He knew she couldn't be bad looking since he didn't deal with unattractive women. But he did remember her being a little chubby. That was all right too since he didn't like skinny women either. "I bet she's really fat now," he said to himself, deciding to ask George about it.

"Hey, George, how's it going, man?" Maxie asked when he heard George's voice on the phone. "I hate to bother you, but I've tried to follow your suggestion and call Jacetta. I've dialed the number you gave me several times, but I always get an answering machine. Under the circumstances, I'm reluctant to leave a message, you know?"

"Oh, so you decided to call, huh?"

"Yep. She sure sounds different, but you know I'm relying on an old memory. She still look about the same?"

The first time Maxie called Jacetta's number and heard the husky, sensual voice instructing the caller to leave a message, he had been so intrigued he hung up, then called right back, just to hear that voice again. Her voice didn't sound like that when he knew her.

"Well, Jacetta is a hard person to catch," George answered. "Probably still working two jobs—always has. But the last news I heard, her daughter was having problems with that baby she's carrying. Serious problems. You just gon' have a hard time catching her. And you messed up big time when you cut out on her, man. And I'm not just saying this because she's my niece either. Jace is a beautiful woman. I never have figured out why she's not married. The men in Houston must be blind or crazy."

"Oh really?" Maxie asked, a sliver of unexplained excitement running through him. "Well, I guess I'll just have to be patient and keep trying until I can catch her."

After his conversation with George, he decided that it might be better to just take a trip down to Houston. It was only a thirty-minute flight and he could easily get Jaci's address. Yes. That was a more interesting course of action he decided, and he began to plan a trip to Houston.

Jaci

Jaci tried to push J.P. Gilmore to the back of her mind as she went about her weekend activities, but thoughts of him intruded at regular intervals. What could he possibly want to discuss with her other than Housing Compliance business? She knew of his reputation with women and didn't believe he had that kind of interest in her, because from what she had heard, he went for the young and beautiful, and she certainly didn't fit either description. Curiosity nearly got the best of her, and she almost dialed his number a couple of times, but she managed to fight off the temptation. No, she decided, she would wait for his call on Monday.

Monday was hectic! An unscheduled staff meeting interrupted her plans to begin writing the disposition reports from Thursday's hearing. And her daughter called and begged Jaci to accompany her to a doctor's appointment. Randi's second pregnancy was turning out to be difficult.

Jaci knew she probably wouldn't be returning to work, so she was trying to get as much as possible done before leaving. It was almost lunchtime when she remembered J.P. Gilmore's promised call. Oh well, it must not have been too important, she decided.

As if her thoughts had somehow been communicated to J.P., Jaci's phone rang, and when she heard his voice, she couldn't help but wonder: *Wow! what's up with this?*

"Ms. Winters, how are you today?" She felt a shiver travel down her spine. His deep voice caused all kinds of reactions in Jaci. "I hope I caught you before you had lunch. I was wondering . . . if you're free, I'd like to take you to lunch. I apologize for the short notice, but it's been one of those mornings."

The invitation was the last thing Jaci expected, so she was caught off guard and left floundering for a response. She finally pulled her haywire thoughts together enough to recall her plans. "I . . . uh . . . I can't today. I'll be leaving here shortly for a doctor's appointment with my daughter."

"Well, how about dinner then? That would be better anyway, since we won't have to watch the clock."

Again, Jaci hesitated. She really didn't know the man and had no idea what he wanted to talk to her about. Under these circumstances she didn't feel comfortable going to dinner with him. "I don't think so, Mr. Gilmore. I'd better not make any plans. You never know how these doctor visits will go."

"Okay. But before we go any further, I have a request. Would you please call me J.P. or Jason. Every time you call me Mr. Gilmore, I look around for my father."

Jaci laughed. "Only if you'll call me Jaci, or Jacetta."

"Whew! I'm glad we got past that! Now, how about dinner tomorrow night? Think you can make that?"

"Sorry, I have choir rehearsal tomorrow night. Let's make it lunch and you've got a deal." She could tell J.P. was disappointed, but he covered it well. They arranged the time and location, and just as she was about to hang up, he said, "Tell me if I'm too presumptuous, but is anything serious going on with your daughter?"

"No, but it's very nice of you to ask. Hopefully, it's nothing a little time won't cure. She's just having some complications with her pregnancy."

"Pregnancy!" he yelled in an amazed voice. "You have a daughter old enough to be pregnant?"

Jaci laughed. "Yes, and if that's a shock, you'd better sit down for this one. I'm already the grandmother of an eighteen-month-old."

After a stunned silence he said, "I see I have a lot to learn about you, Ms. . . . uh, Jaci. I never would have thought you were a grandmother."

"Well, thank God it's not the case with me, but you know these days you can find grandmothers in their twenties."

"Yeah, I guess you're right."

Jaci had another restless night as she raked her mind for some fathomable reason for J.P.'s request to talk to her. She really hoped he wasn't seeking a casual affair. For some reason, she knew she would be very disappointed if that was the case.

The next day, she was nervous all the way to the restaurant.

What if he doesn't show up? What if all he wanted was to make some kind of pass. Jaci made a lifestyle of rebuffing passes and had finally gotten to a point where her body language and the way she carried herself sent the message that she was not interested. Men still made passes, but she could tell they were doing so only to see if they could get a different reaction from her.

Her fears about his not showing up proved to be groundless. As soon as she turned into the parking lot, she saw him waiting for her in a prominent place where he couldn't be missed. Pappadeaux's was one of Houston's most popular seafood restaurants and also one of her favorites. They made small talk until they were shown to a table, where J.P. solicitously seated her before taking his own seat. She knew what she wanted to order because she always ate the same thing here.

When she told him this, he looked astonished. "Why don't you try something different today? This is our first meal together, so start a new tradition."

Jaci didn't know how to respond to that suggestion, so she adamantly stuck to her usual, then began worrying about what was coming next.

She didn't have long to wait. "I know you're curious about why I wanted to talk to you," he stated. "First, let me say how much I admire the way you do your job. You're very good at what you do. Do you like your job?"

Really curious about where this was headed, she answered slowly. "I guess it's like most jobs, you love some aspects and hate others."

"Oh? That's surprising. What part of your job do you hate?"

"Well, there's another part of my job that you probably know nothing about. What you see at the hearings is just the culmination of a long process. By the time we get to that point, we have to be certain we've dotted every 'i' and crossed every 't.'" That's where my staff and I take over. We're kind of like the quality assurance arm of the department, making sure every detail is accurate before any kind of housing violation goes to a hearing."

"Yes. Being in real estate, I have a general idea of the process. And I've already noticed how good you and your staff are at what you do. But what part of it would you like to do away with?"

"Having to go into those dangerous and sometimes collapsing buildings is extremely difficult, even though I've been doing it for years now. I don't ever know what I'm going to encounter in a building. And believe it or not, finding a dead body is not my greatest fear. It's the live ones, and those of the animal kingdom that I fear the most."

"You mean you go into those buildings?" At her nod of confirmation, he continued. "Alone!?" He sounded upset. "Why? Why would you put yourself in danger like that? That's no job for a woman!"

Jaci tensed up. She caught enough flack from her coworkers, she didn't need it from him. She cautiously answered his question. "Well, I seldom go in alone anymore. I always take one of my staff with me, which doesn't reduce the dangers, just makes them a little more bearable. But when I became an investigator ten years ago, I had to go alone."

"Why? You still haven't answered my question. Bill told me you were the first woman to hold the position. Was it so important to become the first woman investigator that you put your life at risk?"

"No. Of course not!" She was getting a little miffed at his attitude. "That was never my motive. And if you must know, I needed the investigator's salary. I couldn't care less about being the first woman to hold the position. Is this why you invited me to lunch? So you could hassle me about my job?" she asked a little testily.

"No," he answered slowly, still trying to process what she had told him. "Actually, I wanted to offer you a job."

"A job?" she asked, feeling both relief and surprise. Then she listened in wide-eyed astonishment as he told her he was the owner and CEO of Information Tech, a software development company, and explained what the job entailed.

"Am I correct in my understanding that you work only four days a week?" he asked. After her affirmative nod, he continued. "I would like for you to come and work for me part-time. You would be researching and collecting detailed information from potential customers. Information that will assist in the development of comprehensive and effective software programs to meet the customers' needs."

"But . . . I don't understand. Don't you have to do that up front? Before developing the software?"

"In cases where we're customizing it for the customer's specific business, yes. And we often have to go through months of trial and error before getting the software working to the customer's satisfaction," he explained. "I've found that if we obtain more of the small, seemingly insignificant pieces of information often overlooked initially, we can ultimately save time and money, and maintain better customer relations."

With cautious but growing excitement bubbling through her, she felt she needed to confess. "J.P., my knowledge of computers is very limited. I know how to produce documents in several programs, and, in fact, I manage to make a little extra money from time to time doing word processing and graphic design jobs, but that's the extent of my computer literacy."

J.P. continued in his deep, sexy voice that did unexplainable things to her insides. "This job doesn't require a lot of technical knowledge. I need someone who is conscientious, dependable, and who has the ability to pay attention to small details. I've watched you in those hearings and I know you're that kind of person. It's all about customer service and getting to the root of what my customers want and need. Jaci, I believe you're perfect for this."

Although relieved that he hadn't made some ridiculous proposition, she was reluctant to commit herself before thinking long and hard about it.

"It sounds like something I'd like to do and I could certainly use the extra money," she said, thinking about the cost of replacing her roof. "But I don't know . . . it sounds almost too good to be true. I learned the hard way to never leap before taking a good long look."

"I can understand that. And if I'm making this sound like it's that good—take my word for it, it's hard, demanding work. That's why finding the right person is critical. It's very hard to find a conscientious individual with integrity and an eye for detail. I really need someone full-time, but at this point, I'll take what I can get. Most of the work is local, but some travel is required. Would that be a problem?" He badly wanted to ask the question uppermost in his mind, but her wall of reserve made it difficult to find a way to approach it. He had to resort to fishing around for the information he needed.

"The travel would be okay as long as I can plan it around my regular work schedule." In all honesty, it sounded both intriguing and like an answer to her prayers.

J.P. noticed her struggling and could guess some of her concerns. "I wouldn't ask you to do anything that conflicts with your regular job, or that would interfere with your life in a negative way. You will always have the privilege to accept or reject assignments. I need someone to relieve me of some of these quality assurance responsibilities, and like I said, it's vital that I have the right person. As you know, I'm heavily involved in my family's real estate business and wish to expand our commercial holdings. But I can't afford to neglect my other business interests either. My V.P. takes up a lot of the slack, but he's beginning to get pretty stretched too."

"How much . . . I mean uh . . . what does the . . . uh . . . what's the salary?" Jaci finally managed to ask. He quickly named a figure that caused her mouth to fall open. "You're kidding!" she exclaimed loudly, causing heads to turn in their direction.

He looked at her calmly and said, "No, I'm very serious. I know to get quality, you have to pay for it." J.P. felt her hesitancy and suggested, "Why don't you think about it. You don't have to give me an answer right now. Just call me when you make your decision. You still have my card, right?"

Jaci observed the amused look on his face and knew she had been right in her conclusion that he had watched her throw men's unwanted phone numbers into the trash. "Yes, I still have it."

Her lunch was untouched as Jaci excused herself on the pretext of needing to get back to work. Her stomach was in too much turmoil to eat anyway. She prayed silently as she drove back to her office. *Father, please give me the wisdom and guidance I need to make the right decision. I know I need the money and the job really sounds fascinating, but I know that everything that shines isn't necessarily gold. And most importantly, Lord I want to be in Your will and purpose.*

J.P.

J.P. had been troubled since his lunch with Jaci. The thought of her going into those dangerous buildings weighed heavily on his mind. He couldn't understand why a woman would put herself in danger like that. But he didn't know the whole story, he reminded himself.

It took more than a week, but she finally called and accepted his job offer. He had literally given a joyful whoop! "Jaci, I promise, you won't ever regret this. The timing is perfect. I'm bidding on a job for a hotel in D.C. on Friday. Can you go with me so I can start showing you the ropes? We'll leave Thursday evening, do the assessment on Friday, and return Friday night or Saturday morning."

"It'll be a push to get ready, but sure, I'll be able to go." After a brief pause, she continued. "But is one day enough to get the kind of information you need to develop an effective program?"

J.P. laughed. "See there, that's what I mean. That detailed mind is already working. And to answer your question, yes, I believe so. They've already completed a preliminary survey and supplied enough data to get us started. We'll go over it on the plane and plan the best way to proceed. We'll primarily be looking for the small things they may have overlooked, details that will help us tailor the right program for their needs. We'll do that by talking to employees from the top all the way down to the lowest level. We'll review their current procedures, look at their records, and just observe how they conduct business."

"Okay. Sounds clear-cut enough. But I confess, I'm more than a little nervous about this."

"Don't be. You can relax since you're in training. But you will have to observe closely. I'm a pretty hard taskmaster and you should know, I expect a lot from my employees. And by the way, since I value my life, I have to ask, will your husband or significant other mind you traveling out of town with another man?" He boldly fished for information.

"No. That's nothing for you to worry about. But you're scaring me with all this hard taskmaster talk. Now I'm wondering what I'm getting into. I don't want to find myself trying to do a full-time job on a part-time basis. I want to make it clear that I'll only be held accountable for part-time responsibilities. Otherwise, I'd better bow out right now."

"I'm not unreasonable, Jaci. You'll be okay. You want to ride to the airport together? We'll be flying out of Hobby."

"No, I'll get myself there. I promise to be on time."

He knew that was her way of trying to keep things on a professional level, so he didn't push the issue and provided the flight information.

Their arrangements worked out smoothly. They met at the airport with no problem, and though Jaci was obviously nervous, she tried to cover it. He searched for a way to put her at ease, wishing he could tell her that her accompanying him meant more than the prospect of getting the luxury hotel account.

As they studied the information on the plane, he was even more certain he had made a sound decision in hiring her, even beyond his ulterior motive of getting to know her better. Her limited knowledge of computers didn't hinder her logical mind, and she brought up questions and pointed out customer relations details that the hotel and his staff had overlooked in their preliminary data.

After checking in, and as they walked to their rooms, he asked about dinner. "How long will it take you to get ready for dinner? I don't think it's any dressier than what you have on. In fact, we'll probably be fine with what we're wearing."

Jaci tried to beg off. "I think I'll bypass dinner. I'm kind of tired and I want to be well rested for tomorrow."

But J.P. wouldn't let her. "You have to eat and we still need to go over a few things. I won't keep you up too late. Anyway, the hotel manager may join us and give us a jump start on our work."

Jaci looked a little uncomfortable. "You're the boss."

"Think you can be ready in say . . . forty-five minutes?"

"Yeah sure," she answered before entering the room next door to his.

The remainder of the trip went as he had predicted. They worked all day Friday and well into the night, going through the hotel's records and talking to employees. The process took longer than expected but Jaci was in her element. She dug right in, enthusiastically typing information on the laptop computer he brought along, often with comments or suggestions of her own. He loved it.

It was after ten when they wrapped up things in the hotel office and headed to their rooms. "I'd like to go over everything again, compare notes, and see if we've overlooked anything before we leave. Are you up to doing that tonight?"

"Well, I'm tired, hungry, and sleepy, so I don't know how much help I'll be, but I'll try."

"Okay, okay! I know I'm acting like a slave driver—it's just that when I'm on a roll, I hate to stop. Why don't you take a thirty-minute break and get your second wind, then come on over and I'll feed you. We'll get down to work after we eat. It shouldn't take long."

"All right, sounds good." She realized when she got to her room that she was surprised at herself. She hadn't hesitated at all about going to his room to work. She was amazed at how relaxed she now felt in his presence. *What a difference a day makes,* she thought with a smile. She showered and slipped into slacks and a casual blouse, ran a comb through her hair, put on lip gloss, grabbed her purse, and knocked at his door in just under thirty minutes.

"A timely woman! I don't believe it!" J.P. said with a smile as he opened the door.

"I don't play when it comes to my stomach," Jaci joked.

J.P. looked at her and knew he would have a hard time concentrating on work. Dressed casually in slacks and a short-sleeved blouse, Jaci looked beautiful. Her beauty packed more of a punch because she was totally unaware of it. She hadn't dressed to impress or seduce, as he had come to expect from women. It was clear that comfort had been her only objective. But he *was* impressed. And he was seduced by her lack of pretentiousness.

"I went ahead and ordered dinner. I didn't think you'd want anything too heavy, so I ordered a chef salad with a fruit and cheese tray. Is that okay?"

"Perfect."

"Let's just relax while we wait for the food. Have you been to D.C. before?"

"Yes, I was here years ago for a wedding. That was a short trip too. Someday I want to come when I have the time to tour the Smithsonian, the memorials, you know, the whole tourist scene."

"We could stay over if you want and do a little sightseeing. Sometimes you just have to seize the moment. Come here, let me show you something."

He opened the French doors leading to the balcony and led the way from the room. "If I'm not mistaken, you can see the White House from here."

"Oh wow!" She followed him onto the balcony. "I wish I could say yes to staying over, but I need to get back tomorrow. Now where is the White House?"

He pointed it out to her, along with some other points of interest. "I spent a lot of time here years ago. But I haven't done the tourist thing either. I've heard it takes more than a day just to get through the Smithsonian. I'd like to do that one of these days too."

They stood close together on the balcony and looked out over the dark streets. J.P. caught a whiff of her fresh, clean scent. He liked perfume on a woman, but the mere smell of soap on Jaci was wreaking havoc on his senses.

"Jaci, I . . ." A loud knock on the door interrupted him. Sighing frustratedly, he went to let room service in.

"You call this light?!" Jaci's mouth dropped as she took in the large bowl of salad, a tureen filled with some kind of soup that produced a wonderful aroma, a tray of fruit and cheese, assorted crackers and rolls, and a dish filled with melon balls. A bottle of sparkling cider sat in an ice bucket. "This is wonderful, J.P."

They ate leisurely while they went over the hotel assessment. The meal was almost finished when J.P., taking note of everything she ate, observed that Jaci hadn't touched the rolls. "You don't like bread I see? Or are you on some kind of diet?"

"Oh no. I love bread, but I don't particularly care for rolls that are so hard you almost pull your teeth out trying to bite into them. These things could be used as baseballs." She grabbed one and began tossing it into the air like a baseball. "I bet if one of these hit somebody in the head, it would knock them out cold."

J.P. walked across the room to the corner and grabbed a long stem silk flower from a tall vase and positioned himself, holding the flower like a baseball bat. "Okay, pitcher! Let's see what you got."

Jaci stood, wound up, and threw the roll, as hard as she could. He swung with the flower, hit the roll and sent it flying across the room, where it hit a framed picture on the wall. J.P.'s deep laughter filled the room, while Jaci stood with her hands over her mouth, mortified at what she had done.

"Oh my God! I can't believe we just did that! I'm so tired, I must be out of my mind. Here I am throwing bread around in the middle of the night." She picked up the roll and held it up, showing him it was still intact. "See what I mean. Hard as a rock."

He walked over and looked down at her with an expression on his face she hadn't seen before. "I've really enjoyed this time with you, Jaci. You're a lot of fun." He moved closer and cupped her face in his hand. "You're also one of the most beautiful women it has been my privilege to know. With the most beautiful eyes." He leaned down and kissed both of her eyes. "And the most kissable lips," his lips lightly brushed hers, "that I have ever seen." His lips returned and rested longer on hers. "In fact, everything about you is beautiful."

With eyes closed and on tiptoes straining to reach his lips, Jaci knew she was going to scream if he didn't kiss her the way she yearned for him to. Her arms went around him and pulled him closer.

J.P. groaned, then said, "Oh honey, I don't know if we should be doing this," before his lips covered hers in a deep passionate kiss. She was the one who groaned then, and tried to get closer to him. "God, Jaci!" he said, then kissed her softly on the forehead. "I'm throwing you out of here right now. Come on, out you go." He propelled her across the room, opened the door, and pushed her through it and into the hallway, slamming the door behind her.

Jaci stood on the other side of the door, drawing deep breaths to gain control of herself. Oh Lord! Talk about coming undone! She had really lost it! She turned to walk the few steps to her room, then realized she didn't have her purse and room key. She knocked on his door and waited. The door opened just enough and he handed her the purse before slamming it again.

Jaci dazedly opened her door, walked into her room, and sat

down heavily on the bed. What in the world had gotten into her? She had just acted in a way that was totally out of character. Never had she imagined herself in that kind of scene with J.P. Gilmore. She was sitting there puzzling over her behavior when the phone rang, startling her.

"Hello?" she answered softly.

"I don't know what the heck just happened, but I wanted to say good night. See you at seven in the morning, okay?" He paused a few seconds. "Jaci? Are you all right?"

"Yes."

"I apologize. I didn't plan on that happening, believe me. I wouldn't do anything to harm you or our friendship. You know that, don't you?"

"It's okay, J.P. No harm done. Good night." She hung up the phone and shook her head in amazement. *What was I thinking? I should be very grateful to him. If he hadn't stopped, I might have done something I would really regret in the morning.* Deciding it was just a fluke, she convinced herself not to waste any time analyzing it, but instead to just forget it and get some much needed sleep. In her prayer before getting into bed she added, "Lord, I don't understand what happened tonight, but strengthen me in my weakness and help me to be very careful around Mr. Jason Gilmore."

"I'm very pleased!" J.P. told her the following morning on their way to the airport. While they waited to board the plane for home, he continued talking about the intricacies of the software he was developing for the hotel. Neither gave any indication that something out of the ordinary had happened between them. "I have no doubt we can produce a software program to fit the hotel's needs, but I'm not certain we'll make the cut because they're concerned that we're too small to handle the level of technical support they're going to require. I am very satisfied with what we accomplished, though, and I know after talking with the manager that he'll keep us in mind. You never know what might come up at a later time. They were certainly impressed with you." He said smilingly, "How do you feel about things so far? Think you're going to like it?"

"I think so," she answered. "It's like putting a puzzle together, and I love jigsaw puzzles. So, I think I'm really going to enjoy it."

Since they both liked the window seat, they had agreed that Jaci would have it on the trip from Houston and he would have it on the trip back. He followed her onto the plane to their assigned seats in first class, admiring her from behind. When she stopped beside their row, the man sitting in the seat across the aisle jumped up to grab her carry-on bag. Smiling down at Jaci, he asked, "Is this your seat? Here, let me put this up for you."

"No. That's okay. I'm going to keep it with me. Thanks though."

Jaci stepped back to let J.P. slide into the window seat.

J.P. noticed the man smiling at Jaci and looking at her like he could eat her in one bite. "Go on honey, you can have it," he told Jaci.

"No, it's okay. We agreed, remember?"

"Jaci, we're holding up the line. Will you go on and sit down!"

She shrugged and scooted into the window seat. He followed her and took the aisle seat, then reached over to buckle her seat belt.

"I think I can handle that," she told him in a soft voice, before digging in her carry-on bag for a book.

"What're you reading?" he asked, trying to gauge her feelings.

She held up the book for him to read the cover. *Trying to Sleep in the Bed You Made.* "Interesting title. Was there any particular reason for selecting that book?"

Ohhhh yeah! she thought, but said, "Not really. My book

club is reading it for our next meeting. One of the members read it and said it was pretty good."

"So you like to read, huh? I wonder what else I don't know about you?"

"I would guess there's a whole lot about me you don't know," she answered with a smile.

He grinned. "Yeah. But not for long if I have anything to do with it."

She pretended she didn't hear his last comment, and after the plane took off, she read for a mere ten minutes before she felt her eyes getting heavy. She closed the book and twisted around in the seat until she found a somewhat comfortable position.

"Would you like a pillow and a blanket ma'am?" the flight attendant asked.

"Yes, thank you, I certainly would," Jaci answered appreciatively.

She went through the process of getting into a comfortable position again, and before she knew it she had drifted off.

"Jaci? You want some lunch?" J.P.'s voice invaded her sleep-dazed mind.

"No thanks," she whispered before slipping back into sleep.

J.P. woke her when the plane was about to land.

After landing they walked with the man who had been seated across the aisle to the baggage claim area. Jaci found out he was from Arkansas and was traveling to several states on a business trip.

"Oh! I'm from Arkansas, too," she told him excitedly. "Where do you live?"

"Little Rock," he answered. "But I grew up in Camden."

"Oh really! I'm from Texarkana—or what might be called the suburbs," she said laughing. "I know a lot of people from Camden. How long are you going to be in town? Do you know where you'll be staying?"

The man quickly pulled out a card and wrote the name of the hotel on the back of it. J.P. took the card and put it in his pocket, giving Jaci an irritated look.

They retrieved their bags and walked out of the airport. As soon as Jaci stepped through the door, a man called her name. She turned and waved, then walked toward him. J.P. followed her and watched as she and a tall bald-headed guy hugged each other. She finally turned back to him.

"J.P., this is my friend, Leon. Leon, my boss, J.P. Gilmore." The two men shook hands before Leon grabbed her bags and put them in the car, then opened the passenger door for Jaci.

Jaci waved to him as they pulled away from the curb, leaving J.P. standing there feeling like someone had punched him in the gut. No wonder Jaci hadn't wanted a ride to the airport with him, he thought angrily. She had a ride.

He and Jaci spent a lot of time on the phone the following week, discussing the information they had collected and how it would be applied to the software program. He used it as part of her training and was pleased with her progress so far. She was going to be an asset to his company in a significant way. He asked her point-blank who was the man who had picked her up from the airport. He had to know, but her answer didn't bring him the relief he'd hoped for.

"Leon? Leon is the choir director at my church."

"You guys seemed to know each other pretty well," J.P. commented.

"We do. I've known him for years. He's a pretty good friend."

J.P. berated himself. Why was he so reluctant to push for information? He had never been intimidated by a woman—with the exception of his mother, who could intimidate the president.

The time he had spent with Jaci convinced him that he wanted a deeper relationship with her and he was even more determined to make it happen. He spent hours strategizing about that when he should have been concentrating on other things. He hadn't spoken to his family since his trip to D.C., but he knew the questions were coming sooner or later. He had hoped for later.

"How are things progressing with your lady?" his brother Ron asked as they sat in J.P.'s family room watching the Tennessee Titans lose yet another game.

He groaned. He was discouraged by Jaci's actions since their trip. She had reverted to her old, reserved persona—her outer armor securely back in place.

"You would have to ask! I don't know, man. I thought I had made some progress when we went to D.C., where I saw a whole new side to her. In fact, we actually had a lot of fun together." He remembered their easy camaraderie and the heated scene in his hotel room. He still couldn't believe the powerful chemistry between them. But that balloon had quickly popped with the appearance of the man at the airport. "Since then, it's like we're back to square one. The only thing I'm sure of is that I want a relationship with her, but no matter how hard I try, Jaci won't let me get close. She won't go out with me. I have to go to a hearing or call her for a job just to see her, and every time I try to slip in questions and comments that would shed light on her personal life, she adeptly sidesteps them and returns to business. When I ask about her daughter—I told you she has a grown daughter, who's expecting a baby?—all she'll say is that things are still not going well. I'm really struggling with this one. I think she might be a little afraid. We've already discovered there's a strong physical attraction between us."

Ron's head popped up. "How did ya'll find that out? What exactly happened in D.C.?"

J.P. looked at him pointedly. "Now brother, you know that's none of your business. Back off."

Ron, suitably reprimanded, tried another line of questioning. "Did you offer to help with her problems? Every woman has some kind of problem she needs help with, and sometimes offering help will soften her up. Maybe there's something I can do, you know, to help fan the flames a little." He grinned at his own suggestion.

J.P. gave Ron a "give me a break" look. "She just tells me it's not my problem. And that there's nothing I can do."

Ron laughed, enjoying his brother's frustration. "This lady sounds like she's a hard nut to crack. I'm just trying to help."

"Nope. I can handle my own affairs."

"Speaking of affairs, exactly what kind do you want with this woman? I mean, do you want something short- or long-term?"

"Right now, I'm just trying to get to know her. There's plenty of time to decide where it's going after we get past that point."

"Well just remember to enjoy the game and then run if things start getting too serious."

"How do you know I don't want them to get serious? Man, I'm tired of the games. I want a good woman to settle down with."

"Aw naw!" Ron's reaction was one of shock. He was happy in his confirmed bachelorhood and thought his brother was too. "I know that's not J.P. Gilmore, legendary ladies' man, I hear talking about settling down. Man, you're working too hard. You need to take a break and have some fun."

"I know what I need. And right now it's to get to know Jaci Winters. I told you I'm ready for a change. Have been for a long time."

Ron gave him a look that said "traitor" before turning away.

J.P. hadn't talked to Jaci in almost two weeks and was starting to get a little anxious. He didn't have an assignment for her at the time and was working on an excuse to call her when it seemed a higher power intervened, providing him the perfect opportunity to spend some quality time with her. A call came in from a customer about a software problem and instead of assigning someone else to work it, J.P. decided to go himself and take Jaci along. He said a brief prayer before calling her.

"Jaci? J.P. here. How about driving down to Galveston with me Friday on a troubleshooting job? This is an existing customer who is not happy with the software we developed. They claim it's not performing as promised. We have to determine if it's actually the software or incorrect application of it," he explained. "This will give you another perspective on the overall process we go through in the development of efficient programs and will show how important it is to work with the customer both before and after the software has been installed."

"Sure. I guess so. What time?"

"Galveston's only an hour's drive away, so why don't I pick you up about nine? That'll get us there in plenty of time for our ten-thirty appointment."

"I can meet you at your office. That way you won't have to drive across town to pick me up."

"Nope. I'll pick you up. And please don't argue this, Jaci." He had decided to stop allowing her to put up barriers between them.

His plan was to use the trip to break down some of Jaci's reserve. After picking her up Friday morning, he executed his strategy by telling her about his son and the ups and downs of getting him through high school and into college.

"I didn't know you had a son," Jaci exclaimed, turning toward him in her seat as much as the seat belt permitted. "How old is he?"

"Nineteen. He's lived with me since he was ten. After a short, rocky marriage, his mother and I split up and she remarried right away and had a couple of other children. It was rough on Patrick. The new husband tolerated him until he got older. Then his tolerance ended when Patrick, who had always felt like an outsider, began acting out."

"Oh my. That kind of situation is never easy for a child. That's one of the reasons I remained single. I didn't want to put my child in a situation where she was vulnerable and merely tolerated."

Bingo! J.P. thought. That answered his question about her marital status.

"That was probably a good decision. Patrick was shipped back and forth between us until we all got tired of it. I tried to stay out of it as much as possible, but he's my son and I didn't want him to feel like I was abandoning him. Patrick was angry and hurt that his mother didn't take his side in the conflicts, but she was still his mother and he loved her. So, when I suggested that he move in with me, mainly just to show my support, I expected a negative response. Nobody was more surprised than I was when he asked if he could come right away. It was the middle of a school term and although it was a big adjustment for both of us, we worked it out and handled it pretty well."

"So, does his mother and her family live here? Or did he have to move from another city?"

"Yes, they live in Chicago. Patrick went through a lot of changes when he first got here—new city, new school, new home environment, the whole works. And he was at a pretty susceptible age, so I really had to be there for him, you know, give him a lot of attention, spend lots of quality time with him, the whole parenting scene. Thank God my family—especially my parents—were able to pitch in and help. I don't know what I would have done without them."

"I'm impressed. I never would have considered you a single parent. Do you ever regret your decision to have him live with you?"

"Heck no! I wouldn't do anything differently, even if I could. Many times when people assumed I was out partying or chasing women, I was actually at home with my son. It's very gratifying for me to see the well-adjusted young man he's grown into and know I helped to influence that process. I wouldn't trade that for all the tea in China."

"I do understand," Jaci said. "I missed out on quite a lot as far as dating and pursuing a lot of dreams are concerned. But when I look at the woman my daughter, Randi, has become, I almost burst with pride and joy. Sometimes I feel like she was a little girl one day and then without my realizing how or when it happened, she was all grown up and telling me she wanted to get married. I often tease her when she walks into a room by asking her who she is and what has she done with my baby. I don't have to wonder how she turned out so well. All her life, my constant prayer to God was that He would make up the difference between my shortcomings as a parent and what she needed. He did that. Although I would have preferred for her to do some things differently, like waiting a while before marrying and getting her college degree before having a family, all in all, she hasn't done badly."

J.P. was overjoyed with the way the conversation was going. Jaci was relaxed and open and seemed to be enjoying the conversation as much as he was. "It sounds like you two are still pretty close, even though she's married and left home. Is her husband an okay guy?"

"Oh yeah. He treats her well, works hard, faithfully serves the Lord. What more can I ask for in a son-in-law? And of course my grandson is just the icing on the cake. He's the sunshine of my life."

This is good, J.P. thought. It was going much better than he had hoped. "What about Randi's father. Does she see him often?" J.P. knew he was treading on thin ice, but he needed to know. He could have kicked himself when he felt her imme-diate withdrawal.

"No, she doesn't," she answered in a quiet, cool voice, and turned away from him to stare out the window at the passing scenery.

He hurriedly sought to mend the breach. "Obviously, I've touched a sensitive issue with you. I'm sorry, I didn't mean to pry. It's just that I'm enjoying sharing information about our lives, and I guess I got carried away and went too far, huh?"

Jaci was quiet for a few minutes, then she turned to look at him, her large eyes, now more gray than green, reflecting her turbulent emotions. "No, I'm sorry. I'm the one who should apologize. I'm pretty touchy on the subject of Randi's father. You see, we haven't seen hide nor hair of him since the night I told him I was pregnant."

J.P. almost ran off the road as he stared at her in amazement. "What!"

Again, Jaci was quiet for several minutes. Then, drawing a long breath, she said, "I admit I don't like to talk about him. He treated me badly and hurt me very deeply. In fact, it took years of struggling—with the shame of having a baby out of wedlock, against the joy of receiving such a special gift from God—before I could move on. Add to that struggle the com-mon survival issues of barely making ends meet while raising a child alone and you get a very difficult existence. If it hadn't been for my child, I probably would have given up. But with the help of God, we made it."

J.P. was still trying to deal with the matter of the man who had abandoned her. "But what about her father? Why did he do that? Did he think the child wasn't his? Any fool can tell you're not the type of woman who sleeps around. Do you mind sharing what happened with me?"

She hesitated. "To be honest, not many know the full story, but no, I don't mind sharing it with you. Frankly, I don't know what his problem was, other than being just plain rotten and no good. That's one reason it was so hard for me to deal with it. I still can't comprehend, even after all this time, why I was foolish enough to fall for someone like that. Yes, I was young, straight out of college, and straight from the woods, not the country—the backwoods—but I wasn't dumb or ignorant. I knew right from wrong. I was still a virgin at that point and planned to remain one until I was married. But I let that man with his sophisticated ways and smooth talk convince me to ignore good judgment, disregard my carefully laid out goals, and act in a careless, stupid way.

"So, whatever his problem, I've had to accept my own responsibility in everything. I could have said no, and gone on with my plans, or I could have at least acted more responsibly and insisted on some kind of protection. But I was so . . . overjoyed that this man was interested in me that I didn't do one sensible thing, and the consequences I've had to live with have made me very cautious and careful in my dealings with men."

This explains a lot, J.P. thought. "I think you've been too hard on yourself. I know you believe in God's forgiveness, don't you? If He's willing to forgive you, don't you think you should be willing to forgive yourself? And I bet there were some other variables at work in the scheme of things, too. For instance, you said you were a little in awe that a man like him would notice you. Right? I'd bet he was a lot older and able to exploit your youth and inexperience. Right?" Jaci nodded yes to both of his conclusions. "By the way, does he live here or is he in another city?"

"I have no idea where he is. The last I knew, he was still in Dallas. I left there and moved here when Randi was only a few months old. And yes, you're right, I did have a hard time forgiving myself, even after I asked for God's forgiveness. Not just for having a baby out of wedlock, and not being able to provide for her as I would have liked, but also for so carelessly tossing away God's plan for my life. I can't blame him for that. I was young—he's more than ten years older than I am, but like I said, I knew right from wrong."

"So, tell me, what happened when you told him you were expecting?"

Jaci looked out the window at the cloudless blue sky and in a quiet voice related to him the events of the night she told Maxie about her pregnancy. She didn't question why she chose to tell him the story, other than an unexplained connection she felt to him—maybe because of the time they had spent together, or maybe because she was finding it so easy to talk to him. Whatever the reason, she wanted to share the sordid details with him. She left nothing out . . . telling him everything, the defunct divorce papers Maxie had shown her to convince her he was not married, his admission to having a second wife when she announced her pregnancy, his blaming her and insisting she "take care of it," his lies that he would be in touch. The whole sad story spilled out, as the scenery outside the car slid past them.

J.P. felt his gut tightening as anger consumed him.

"If I could get my hands on that poor excuse of a man, I would choke him for the disgraceful way he treated you. I sincerely hope our paths never cross." *No wonder she is so cautious,* he thought. She had been callously used, then tossed aside like an unwanted rag doll. She hadn't deserved that.

He realized they had reached Galveston and wondered where the time had gone. They spent the next few hours with the client, and J.P. managed to straighten everything out, despite being distracted and in a hurry to finish. Jaci was also less energetic than usual. Her traumatic revelations had deeply affected them both.

"Are you in a hurry to get back home? If not, let's take the ferry across the bay," he suggested when they left the small building where the company's offices were housed. He nearly lost his footing when Jaci swiftly agreed. He had expected a right-out NO, or at least an argument.

"I love this island," she explained. "It would be sacrilege to come down here and not take a ferry ride and eat seafood."

J.P. was overjoyed. She had just answered his next question. "Well, why don't we make an afternoon of it? Let's browse the Strand and then go down on the beach. How about it?"

"I'd love it," she replied.

Jaci

They spent the afternoon exploring every store on the Strand. Jaci willfully pushed the memories from the past aside, reminding herself of the promise she had made to never let that episode steal another moment of her life. Poking around in antique and novelty stores was always a fun and relaxing activity for her. And she remembered from their D.C. trip that, surprisingly, J.P. could be a lot of fun. He didn't disappoint her. He got into the spirit of things and wanted to buy everything she picked up to look at. She couldn't get him to understand that half the fun was in just looking.

"Let's go over to the strip. That's where I usually do all my shopping," she smilingly confided. They did, and after going in and out of every shop along the strip, they both had bags filled with all sorts of junk, like T-shirts, sea shells, and little bottles of sand.

"You want to eat now or head for the ferry?" J.P. asked.

"Let's eat first, then take the ferry ride," she said. "That way, we can head home when we get off the boat."

"Okay. Sounds like a plan and I know the perfect place to eat."

They enjoyed a delicious seafood meal and talked about all kinds of things, but their liveliest discussion centered around spiritual beliefs, especially as they related to the single and dating scene. It was amazing how alike they were on basic values, and how the way they had been raised influenced the kind of parents they had become. Jaci laughingly asked, "Did you ever find yourself doing or saying something to your child that you swore you would never do when your parents did it to you?"

They laughed harder as each one acknowledged guilt. "Yep. The famous 'I brought you into this world and I'll take you out' flew out a few times. And the one that my son vividly remembers is 'as long as you're living under this roof and sticking your big rusty feet under this table, you'll do as I say.' He loves to remind me of that."

Jaci nodded. "Yeah, I still cringe over that one myself." After eating, they drove around the small island, admiring the wide assortment of beautiful cottages dotting the beach. Jaci confessed that she had always wanted to own one of those waterfront homes.

It was almost twilight when they got behind a long line of cars waiting to board the ferry. There was a relaxed, comfortable atmosphere in the car that made Jaci gratefully acknowledge what she called one of her "moments": a rare occurrence in which she knew there was not another place she would rather be than where she was at that very moment.

They boarded the ferry, then got out of the car, quietly watching the vast waters and enjoying the antics of the seagulls that hovered low to capture the breadcrumbs passengers threw.

"Oh wow, look at those stars," Jaci said. "Somehow they always look bigger and brighter when you're out in the open."

They stood quietly and watched the stars beginning to twinkle against the darkening sky and the gorgeous full moon striving to show itself from behind passing clouds, which cast a beautiful reflection upon the sea.

"Yeah. It's great to see nature at its best and be able to appreciate the beauty of it," J.P. answered.

Everything was working together to weave a feeling of contentment and peace within her. She had never enjoyed the company of a man as much as she was enjoying this day with J.P. *I'm having a great time,* she thought, *but considering the fact that I'm probably not the most exciting woman he's spent time with, hopefully he's not bored.* She tried to sneak a look at him. Busted! Her eyes collided with his, as he stood there unashamedly looking down at her with an expression she couldn't comprehend.

She shivered in reaction to their shared look. Immediately, J.P. stepped behind her, enfolding her in strong arms. "Are you cold? Do you want to get back in the car?" he asked huskily, running his hands up and down her arms in an attempt to warm them.

"No, I'm fine, I was just thinking about how much I'm enjoying today."

"I'm enjoying it too. In fact, I'm finding that I always enjoy myself when I'm in your presence."

Jaci didn't know how to respond. Although she liked the feel of his strong arms embracing her and decided to be quiet and just enjoy the moment, she cautioned herself—*careful, remember this man has a potent effect.*

After a while, J.P. whispered in her ear, "You're a hard woman to get to know. But I refuse to give up because I believe you're worth the effort, no matter how hard I have to work." When she didn't respond, he continued. "Jaci, I don't think I've ever been as entranced by a woman as I am with you. Are you involved with anyone right now?"

"No. Why?" Jaci's heart beat wildly. She knew where his question was leading and felt uncomfortable because she feared her answer would spoil the moment.

"Because you're a beautiful, intelligent woman whom I enjoy spending time with. And I think you know I would like us to spend more time together to get to know each other on a more personal level." When she didn't speak, he continued. "Do you think that's possible?" She was definitely not making it easy for him.

"Well, I have some very strong opinions about the dating scene, and after you hear them, you may not want to get to know me better," she answered. "And since we're on the subject, are you involved with anyone? That road goes both ways you know."

He laughed, realizing he should have expected that question. "No. I'm not going to lie and say I don't go out occasionally, but there's no serious involvement with anyone. So tell me about your strong feelings regarding the dating scene. I want to hear it."

She pulled away and stepped to his side so she could look at him as they talked. "I don't have to tell you after our conversation on the way down here that I'm very leery of any kind of relationship with men. But there are several other reasons I don't get involved easily. First and foremost, I don't believe in casual affairs. But that's the norm in today's dating world, and you're thought of as obsolete if you don't do it. It amazes me that although we're constantly hearing about how AIDS and other STDs are rampant, people are still sleeping around, thinking it can't happen to them. Many of them are not even using protection and not getting tested to find out if they've been exposed.

"You have to understand," she continued. "I deal in reality. I'm too old and wise at this point in my life to act stupid or coy. I've dealt with the consequences of that kind of foolishness too long. Although I've always wanted a husband and a family, I'm not going to violate my principles again in an effort to make it happen. Experience was a very good teacher." She grimaced, recalling all she had suffered because of poor judgment. "I believe honesty and commitment should be the foundation of a relationship. A lot of men run from that and have no intentions of maintaining a monogamous lifestyle—married or not."

She paused to get his reaction. When he remained silent, she continued. "You won't hurt my feelings if you don't agree with me, but you did ask, and I'm merely telling you how I feel. In any case, honesty at this point makes more sense than lying. At least we'll know where we stand. So . . . Would you like to gracefully withdraw and say forget it? I gotta tell you, a man who lies just to get things to go his way is likely to get a whipping," she said with a smile.

He saw that behind the smile, she was serious. "No, go on," he said slowly, wondering if he really wanted to hear the rest of what she had to say.

Not missing a beat, Jaci continued. "Like I've said, I have some serious trust issues where men are concerned. And the men I've had the misfortune to deal with have done nothing to change that. In fact, they've more or less proved it's not even worth the trouble. Any man I date would have to understand that and be able to deal with it," she chuckled. "Usually when I get to this point, the man has concluded that he's dealing with a crazy woman and runs so fast it's hard to tell he was ever here. Do you want to continue this conversation or stop here and cut your losses? Speak freely—I can handle it."

J.P. hesitated. This was some heavy stuff coming from this woman. *Do I want to take this any further?* he asked himself.

"No! . . . I understand where you're coming from," he finally answered, searching himself at the same time. He wanted to be honest. Frankly, he was often tempted to revert to his old ways. But he knew he was tired of the same kind of women and the same meaningless relationships. Knew it wasn't taking him where he wanted to go. Knew it was time to stop half-stepping and try another way.

"I appreciate your honesty and everything you've said, but I'm not other men. I was, I admit, indulging in that dating scene like some of them, but I'm not anymore. And regarding the trust issues, as long as I know what I'm dealing with, I can handle it. Now, do you think it's possible for us to spend some time getting to know each other? Let's just see where it takes us."

"Before I answer that question, tell me exactly what you're looking for. I mean, why do you want to get to know me? You have a reputation for being a ladies' man. I just told you how I feel about that. It occurs to me that maybe I'm just a challenge to you. If so, I'm not interested in seeing where it can go, I already know it's not going to be a good trip for me."

"Wellll. Uh! Let's see." Again, he took a long time answering. "You really don't beat around the bush do you?" He laughed nervously. "I'm thinking about this because you've been very candid with me, and I want to answer you honestly. I guess the best way to explain is to tell you about my parents. After forty something years of marriage, they still love and care for each other. They are at their happiest when they're together, and they're together a lot. They have a level of trust and commitment between them that's uncommon in the world today, but it brings them a lot of peace and contentment. One day it dawned on me that because of my lifestyle, I was missing out on something great.

"I'm sure you've heard that it's insanity to keep doing the same thing in the same way and expect a different outcome. I want what my parents have, and to get it, I knew I needed to make some serious changes. I admit I was out there—and I'm still tempted some times—part of that scene you described—

going from woman to woman in pointless encounters. But I'm not crazy, so common sense prevailed. I still date, but it's for a different purpose now. I've committed my life to Christ and now want to commit myself to one woman. And I want to be healthy and able in every way to fully enjoy life with that special woman. I would at least like to explore the possibility of your being that woman.

"You're not the only one who has been betrayed. My son's mother left me for another man before I was able to make enough money to keep her happy. So I know what it's like to be hurt. And for years I've been running from commitment in fear of a repeat of that. But at some point you have to decide to stop looking back toward the past and move forward into the future." He gave a silent thanks for Sunday's sermon. "Now that we know where we stand, can we move forward?"

His description of his parents' life together filled her with yearnings that had been pushed into forgotten corners of her mind. *Oh to have a hope for that kind of life.* Could she take a chance? Should she? "Okay," she heard herself agree. "As long as you understand where I am on certain issues and continue to be honest and up-front with me. If at any point, you decide you want to move on, tell me. I can deal with it. I'm definitely not into sharing," Jaci said, looking at him, without a hint of a smile.

"I've heard everything you've said, and just for the record, I'm not into sharing either. I'm very happy we had this conversation." He smiled and drew a deep sigh of relief as unexplained happiness bubbled up in him. He pulled her back to their original position.

They were quiet for several minutes as he held her close to him, enjoying the feel of her soft body against his. "What are you thinking about?" he asked softly.

Jaci sighed before answering. "I was daydreaming a little. Don't laugh now, but one of my fantasies has always been to

come to this or some other island with my husband and to experience the romantic ambiance, go to sleep, listening to the
waves crashing against the seashore, and watch the moon's
magic reflecting on the water. And then to wake up early
enough to share the joy of the sunrise. It would be like coming into harmony with God, nature, and each other, you
know?"

J.P. groaned softly and tightened his embrace. Her words
caused a deep longing within him. *Oh please, God, let it be me,*
he prayed. "That's a beautiful fantasy, honey, and not difficult
to make a reality. I'll be one very unhappy brother if I'm not
the one sharing it with you." Despite her admitted hang-ups,
her honesty and openness intrigued him. Nobody could accuse her of being fickle or shallow. She knew who she was and
what she wanted. It would take a man of character to hold her.
He sincerely hoped he had it in him to be that man. "Do you
hear what I'm saying, Jaci? I could very easily stake my claim
on you right now and I wouldn't be going anywhere."

"Yeah, I hear you. I think we're caught up in some kind of
romantic spell right now. It'll pass."

Her unusual peace and contentment with less than favor-
able circumstances blew his mind. She knew what she wanted
but was prepared to live without it if she had to. It made him
want her more. "What if it doesn't pass? What if we don't
want it to pass?" he pushed.

"Shhh . . . hh! Don't break the spell, Jason. Let's just enjoy
it."

He grinned, relishing the way she had said his name. He
started planting kisses from her temple to the side of her face
and neck. "Come here, sweetheart." He said as he turned her
in his arms and hugged her tightly. "Awwww, honey, you feel
so good in my arms," he said before kissing her. Jaci's last co-
herent thought was that the darn spell had gone too far.

They were so lost in the kiss that it took a moment for the

noise to register. A man and a woman standing near them loudly cleared their throats in an effort to get their attention. "Excuse me!" the man said. "I just thought you folk might like to know we'll soon be reaching land."

J.P. grinned broadly. "Thanks. I was just trying to keep my lady warm."

"Looks like you were doing a pretty good job of it," the man stated as he and the woman headed to their car, laughing all the way.

Jaci covered her face with her hands. "I'm so embarrassed. Two old people out here in public acting like kids . . . Can we just get in the car?"

"Honey, don't break the spell now, okay? We still have the trip back across the bay, and I don't want to spend it without you . . . and the spell. I don't see anything wrong with what we were doing. It's a romantic night. Most of the people on the ferry were probably doing the same thing." He led her to the car and opened the door, then closed it after she slid in. He went around to the other side, got in behind the wheel, and turned to her, reaching to cup her face in his hand. "In fact, I'd like to pick up from where we were before we were so rudely interrupted."

He leaned over and kissed her forehead, her eyes, nose, and then her lips. Jaci backed away, praying, *Lord, deliver me from temptation.* "Jason, I think we should just enjoy the ride, okay."

"Okay, sweetheart." He didn't back away from her though. "Can I at least keep my arm around you?"

"I guess that's okay," she answered in a soft voice.

Before they knew it, the drivers in cars behind them were blowing horns and yelling at them to move so they could disembark. Jason groaned, "Not again!" and hurriedly drove off the boat and down the road to find a place to turn around, then pulled in behind the line of cars waiting to catch the ferry back to the other side. They didn't even think about getting out of the car this time.

"Some spell, huh?" Jaci said after a while. "I don't know what's gotten into me tonight."

"Whatever it is, it's gotten to both of us. I say let's just go with the flow? I'm enjoying it."

"Yeah, I am too," Jaci answered. "You know, it's been a really good day. Ever experienced one of those rare moments in life when you just know there's no place else in the whole world you'd rather be than right where you are?" At his nod, she continued. "Those moments are supreme blessings and I've learned to savor them. Today has been one of those moments in my life. It's been fun."

He too was filled with a rare contentment. "It has been fun. And like I said before, I ain't going nowhere. Hopefully, there'll be many more of these moments for us."

Suddenly remembering the couple laughing at them earlier, she cringed and asked, "Can you imagine what was going through those people's minds? Probably something like, 'Some people just don't know how to behave in public.'" She laughed and he soon joined in, and before long, they were cracking up.

"Uh uh! I think they were enjoying the show and wishing it were them. They've probably forgotten how to do it."

"Or they're asking themselves if they really want to," she said, giggling.

A few minutes later, she went into a deep, thinking mode. The atmosphere between them was no longer comfortable. In fact, Jaci admitted to herself, it was charged with electricity. She was aware of J.P. in a way she had been fighting against and feared feeling about any man again. Briefly Maxie came to mind. *Stop!*—she told herself sternly, *don't even go there. There's no comparison between the two.*

As if picking up on her thoughts, J.P. spoke. "You can tell

me if you don't think it's my business, but have you been seriously involved with anyone since Maxie?"

"No. But like I said earlier, I've tried. I've always wanted to share my life with a special man. I've dated off and on, but nothing worked out. Then after one of them went after Randi, it scared me so bad, I decided to give up on dating."

"What! Some guy you were dating went after your daughter?" J.P. asked.

"Yes. As Randi got older, I really tried to be extra careful about who I brought around her. I was always watchful, and if I saw the man looking at her in a less than acceptable way, he was quickly sent on his way. But, I hadn't picked up on anything with this one guy. I suppose I trusted him because he worked in the department and he seemed to be a Christian and an okay sort of guy. But he was really a wolf in sheep's clothing. That was brought home to me in a disturbing and traumatic way when Randi was fourteen or fifteen. I thought everything was going all right with this guy, then I went home one day, and Randi was waiting with the news that the dirt bag had been calling her and coming to the house when he knew I wasn't home. She had been trying to handle it on her own, reluctant to tell me because she knew I really liked the guy."

"Oh God!" J.P. exclaimed. "What did you do?"

"I confronted him. And he boldly admitted that Randi was a pretty little girl, and he was attracted to her." She shuddered with remembered anger and disappointment.

"Darn it! I don't know what's wrong with some of these dudes. They have to be messed up in the head to do something like that," J.P. said in frustration.

"Killing that sucker would have been too good," Jaci said, her hands clenched in rage as she recalled the incident. "I really wanted to choke him with my bare hands, and of course I couldn't since he's much bigger than me. I finally settled for calling him and telling him how disgusting and pitiful he is, and that if he came anywhere near either of us again I would call the police. I also had an attorney friend call to tell him I was considering filing charges against him, and to inform him that pedophiles are dealt with in an extremely harsh manner by the criminal justice system. We knew I didn't have a case since he hadn't touched her, but we hoped to fill him with such terror that he wouldn't ever look at another child in that way. I told one of the men on staff about it, you know Bill— and he also had a long talk with him. I don't know the extent of what Bill said to him, but the guy almost runs in the other direction whenever he sees me."

"So have you dated anyone since then? That's been seven or eight years ago."

"Oh yes. After Randi left for her brief stay at college, I thought, okay, coast clear. Now I don't have to worry about her anymore, so I can try it again. However, that backfired in my face too. It seemed that the brothers assumed I was so man-hungry and lonely that I'd fall for anything. They'd wait until they thought the timing was right, then insist on moving the relationship to the next level. Some of them went for the gold right off the bat. Bam! Let's live together. One had the audacity to show up one night with his suitcase. Oh man did he get a mouthful—and I got an earful from him—something about being an uptight, frigid old maid. After that, I gave it up. Why subject myself to that kind of scene?"

J.P. shook his head in disgust. "You've just had the misfortune of running into the lowest life forms out there. There are some decent men who are looking for decent women."

"Can't prove it by me. Anyway, I've made myself content being alone and I have peace about it. The Lord will give you peace about any situation if you ask Him."

"That sounds like you've given up on God's ability to send the right person into your life."

"No. But I've stopped trying to find him myself. If God has

someone for me, He's fully capable of bringing him into my life and giving me the wisdom to recognize him. I'm just not putting my life on hold, or putting myself through a lot of bad experiences trying to do it myself."

"I understand that, but you've got to keep an open mind about it. If your mind is closed, God could send him and you could very well miss him. Remember you promised to give us a chance to get to know each other. If your mind is closed to the possibilities, it's not going to happen. You know that don't you?"

She did know that. And during the drive home, Jaci retreated into deep thought as she contemplated the past and her warranted mistrust of men. She looked toward the future with more than a little uneasiness.

When they arrived at Jaci's house, J.P. spoke to her in an excited voice. "Jaci, it has been a great day! I think we've started laying a good foundation to build a relationship on. I promise you I'm not like those jerks you described today. It may be hard for you to believe at this point, but I'm willing to do whatever I have to do to prove myself different. I know you're apprehensive—have every right to be—but keep an open mind about this. Okay? Let's go to dinner one night. Will you call me and let me know when you want to do that? I can adjust my schedule to fit yours."

"Okay. I'll call you." But she was experiencing so many mixed emotions that she had no intention of going out with him again until she had everything sorted out. She acknowledged there was something budding between them, but her past dictated that she tread very carefully. For the second time in her life, she knew a man had the power to hurt her very badly.

Despite her unsettled personal issues with J.P., things continued to go well on the jobs she did for him. Most were in town, but occasionally, he asked her to travel to another city.

In that case, she would leave on Thursday evening and fly if the assignment was in a distant city, or drive if it was a short commute. Fridays were spent interviewing company employees and researching records for the information she needed to make her recommendations. She returned on Friday evening or Saturday morning, depending on how early she completed the job, and arranged to drop by J.P.'s office on Saturday, or they met somewhere for lunch the following week so she could submit her report.

J.P. became creative in finding ways to spend time with her. Since she had still not agreed to a formal date with him, he tried to extend their meetings into dates, and because of some weakness in her that she couldn't control, he was successful a few times, and she had enjoyed these times in spite of herself.

She was determined to keep her distance until she could sort out her feelings and deal with the powerful physical attraction between them. Just the memory of their kisses curled her toes and scared her shoes off. He was astute enough to recognize her volatile response to him and pushed his advantage every time they were together by thoroughly kissing her. She realized he was gradually breaking down her defenses and tried to strengthen her resolve to take things slowly with him.

Jaci recalled the day she had prayed for change. She was thankful for the delightful moments she had experienced recently, as well as the new exciting happenings. But before she could savor, and put them in perspective, other issues began to explode from every direction, bringing stormy weather and causing movements in her life that would alter it and usher in a new season.

Manipulations

J.P.

J.P. was frustrated. While Jaci sought ways to keep them apart, he prayed and searched for ways to dispel her fears and convince her to give them a chance. Although he understood her cautiousness, he was certain about the growing feelings between them. He had manipulated her into going to the movies with him a few times, and had even coerced her into accompanying him to one of the black plays that had come to town. Each time he went out with this woman whom he secretly thought of as *his Jaci*, they would have a great time, leading him to hope things were finally moving to another level. However, much to his disappointment, the wall of reserve she expertly erected around herself would be back in place the next time he talked to her. A war of wills was definitely under way, but Jaci didn't know the extent of his resolve and persistence. He wasn't a successful businessman by accident. The same determination that was applied to his business affairs was also applied to Jaci. He sent flowers, left "thinking of you" messages at both her home and office, and coaxed her into spending time with him every time he had a chance.

His breakthrough came in an unexpected way. He had

dropped by the Housing Compliance Department primarily to see Jaci, but on the pretext of obtaining the list of condemned properties. Fully expecting to be intercepted by Wynola, who he believed had instructed the receptionist to advise her whenever he was in the building, he was elated when informed that Wynola was in a meeting. "Is Jaci available?" he asked the receptionist.

"She's in her office, just go on back," the receptionist told him. Although he felt that the woman was unprofessional in not announcing him, he was grateful for the small bit of luck, thinking that Jaci might have refused to see him if she had warning. He hurried down the corridor toward the wing where Jaci's office was located, turned the corner, then walked slowly so he could read the name plate on each door.

He heard her husky voice, speaking in a tone that suggested she was upset. When he found her office, he saw that she was on the phone and was indeed very upset, but was attempting to comfort whoever was on the other end. "Try not to worry, honey; I'll be there as soon as I can. I'm leaving now to pick up Sean."

He watched as she hung up and dropped her face in her hands, drawing deep breaths in an effort to calm herself. Without thinking, he stepped inside and closed the door. "Jaci?" he said softly. "What's wrong? Is there anything I can do?" She straightened quickly, shock and surprise evident in her face.

"What are you doing here?" she asked in a voice so full of emotion he felt his own heart constrict.

"What is it, Jaci?" he asked again. "Will you tell me or am I going to have to shake it out of you?"

She gave him a look that said "just try it buster," before stating, "It's Randi. She's having serious problems with her pregnancy. Her blood pressure is at a dangerous level. It's so bad the doctor wants her to go right to the hospital." As she talked, she was collecting her purse and briefcase.

"I'll drive you," he insisted as they started toward the closed door.

"No, that's okay. I have to pick up my grandson from the day care center first. I don't want to put you through all that trouble."

J.P. caught her arm in a firm grip. "I'm driving you, no arguments, Jaci." Seeing his determination, she merely pulled away from him and walked out.

They picked up Sean, then drove to the hospital. When they arrived, Randi was already installed in a room, so they went directly in to see her. Introductions were made and J.P. observed that Randi, who looked just like her mother, also exhibited Jaci's same strength. She was hooked up to several intravenous tubes, yet she maintained a positive attitude and was even joking around.

As family members and close friends arrived, he was introduced simply as a friend—a role he happily assumed. He was delighted and intrigued to observe *his* Jaci discard her professional persona and happily interact with everyone in a warm and loving way. This was the real Jaci, and he looked forward to the time when she would be like that with him.

He couldn't believe he wasn't bored as hours slipped by, and he was actually content to sit there and watch the caring support among Jaci's family and friends. He spent much of his time in the waiting room, keeping Sean occupied and talking with an older woman who was introduced to him as Sister Sadie, a church member who told him she had "adopted" Jaci and Randi years before. He occasionally walked Sean to his mother's room or carried him when he went outside to make calls on his cell phone. He joined in when Jaci, Sister Sadie, and others gathered in a circle several times and asked God to keep Randi and the unborn baby in His care. He felt himself yearning to be a part of this loving circle. His own family was pretty tight knit, but he felt an overwhelming desire to be an intricate part of hers.

After the staff gently but firmly threw them out of the hospital, J.P. drove Jaci back to her building to pick up her truck. Then, despite the fact that they lived on opposite sides of the city, he insisted on following her home.

When they arrived, he gently lifted the car seat off the backseat of his SUV and carried the sleeping baby into the comfortable and beautifully decorated house, where he instantly felt at home.

"You have a beautiful home, Jaci," he said, taking in the black art that covered the walls. "It's not hard to see that you love baptism scenes." He walked around the house and examined what had to be every conceivable baptism scene in existence. The colors in each framed print coordinated with other decor and furnishings in her home. "Did you do the decorating yourself?"

"Are you kidding me? What you see is a hodge-podge of stuff collected over the years. The secret is to keep the same central color and style. That way things look like they belong together even if they don't. Anyway, it's comfortable and homey. Yes, I do have a weakness for baptism scenes. It's hard for me to resist one when I see it. Why don't you find yourself something to drink while I put Sean to bed. This little guy has had it."

She left the room carrying the sleeping child, and J.P. went into the kitchen, found some coffee, and started a pot. He didn't necessarily want coffee, but would use anything to extend his time in her presence. Her home felt different from his. It took a minute to realize what it was. It felt like home. While he busied himself with the coffee, J.P. analyzed his feelings for this woman. He knew she was different from every other woman he had known. He recalled his ex-wife of many years ago—the only woman he had come close to committing to.

They had gotten married when she became pregnant, but there had been constant conflict throughout the short-lived marriage, and she eventually left him for a man she felt could take better care of her than he. Although he didn't regret the marriage's ending, he had been hurt and angry at the way she had done it. The only good to come out of it had been their son. Since then, all the women who had gone through his life meant nothing. When things ended, he said good riddance and moved on to the next one. He already knew this would not be the case with Jaci.

When Jaci returned to the family room, he was on the sofa watching the late news and drinking coffee. She sat down beside him, and they began talking about the happenings in the news.

He was comfortable, content, and without a thought of leaving until he noticed her weariness; he guiltily jumped up.

"Oh honey, I apologize. Here I am talking your head off and you're too sweet to tell me to get out so you can get to bed. Come on, walk me to the door."

Jaci walked him to the door and stood looking up at him with eyes that reflected the light of her foyer.

"Thank you for being there for me today," she said softly. "I would have made it, but it would have been so much more difficult. You've already been so good to me that I hate to ask, but there's one more thing I really need from you." His inquisitive gaze searched her face. Knowing Jaci wouldn't ask for anything unless she absolutely had to, he braced himself, preparing to provide whatever she needed.

"Can I please have a hug?" she asked softly.

J.P. threw his head back in a hearty laugh. Seeing her perplexed look, he sobered. "I haven't lost my mind. You just surprised me, and believe it or not, I wanted to ask you the same thing, but I didn't want you to think I was trying to . . .

you know . . . take advantage of you at a vulnerable time. But I sure do want to hold you in my arms."

As he spoke he pulled her into his arms and held her tightly against him. "Oooh, honey, I'm always amazed at how good you feel in my arms." He groaned with the intensity of his feelings, before finally looking down into her eyes.

"Sweetheart, do you have any idea how I feel about you?" He saw uncertainty enter her eyes and immediately cautioned himself to exercise patience. He didn't want to destroy the fragile bond they had created between them tonight. "Forget I asked—I know you don't."

He kissed her gently and continued to hold her. He spoke to her in a shaky voice. "From now on, you won't have to ask me for a hug. That's one thing you can count on from me, okay? And another thing, we're supposed to be getting to know each other, remember? This thing between us is not going to go away honey. We're too old to play games and waste time. I'm still waiting for that call to go to dinner. I don't want to push you, I know you have some issues, but promise you'll call me soon, okay?" Not waiting for an answer, he gave her another tight squeeze, then opened the door and left.

Jaci stood immobilized with her back against the closed door for a long time after she heard his truck back out of her driveway. *Lord, what am I going to do about that man?* she asked as all of her insecurities rushed in to haunt her. *What could a handsome, wealthy man like J.P. possibly want with me?*

She had no idea that at that same moment, another man— a man from her past—was plotting his re-entrance into her life, which would bring further confusion and excavate the root cause of her insecurities.

Maxie

*M*axie stopped the car in front of the spacious house with the beautifully landscaped yard and looked again at the address scribbled on the piece of paper. It was the right address. The one-story brick house with white trim and large white columns looked inviting from the street. At the double windows on both sides of the entryway were flower boxes with an array of colorful flowers flowing out of them. Large potted plants placed along the porch gave the attractive house a welcoming and appealing look. What kind of job did this woman have? he wondered. It must be a darn good one, or else she had help from someone—most likely a man, he decided.

He got out of the rental car and walked to the front door, continuing to take in everything about the house. He pushed the doorbell and heard it ringing from within the house. No answer. He repeated the process, still no answer.

"Yoo-hoo! Excuse me, sir, but can I help you?"

Maxie turned around to see a little old lady standing in front of the house across the street shielding her eyes from the sun to get a better look at him.

"Yes ma'am. I'm an old friend of Jacetta Winters. I'm from out of town and thought I would look her up while I'm here. Do you know when she'll be home?"

"I'm afraid not, young man. She doesn't have one of those nine-to-five jobs. She has to stay there until the job is done. I keep an eye on the place for her. Nobody comes around that I don't see." She made sure he understood the message she was trying to convey by making a gesture with her hands when she said "nobody."

Undaunted, Maxie confidently continued. "Do you happen to have her work number? I sure would appreciate it if you could give it to me. You see I really want to see her, but I'm in town just for a short time."

"Of course I have the number, but you know I can't give it to you. That kind of thing is just not done these days—I mean, you could be one of those stalkers or something—no sir, can't do that. The best I can do is let her know you came by. Who are you?"

Choosing not to answer her question, Maxie turned on his famous charm. "Aw, ma'am," he said with a big smile, coaxing her. "I know you can look at me and tell I'm a good guy. And like I said I just happen to be in town and decided to drop in to see her."

She noticed his refusal to tell her who he was, so the old lady looked at him with shrewd eyes. *A slickster if I ever saw one*, she thought. "Nope. The best I can do is what I already offered. Maybe you shoulda let her know you were coming."

He realized he was getting nowhere with the old lady, so Maxie got back into the car and drove slowly down the street. He checked out the neighborhood. Nice. He would definitely be back.

Jaci

Jaci's life got hectic. She felt as if she were meeting herself as she ran from work, to the day care center to pick up Sean, to the hospital to see Randi, then home to collapse, only to start all over the next day. Randi's husband, John, had literally set up residence in the hospital, leaving little Sean in the shared care of his grandparents. Sean spent most nights with John's parents, but Jaci picked him up from day care every day and dropped him off at their house after taking him to see his parents at the hospital. He spent the weekends with Jaci so the other grandparents could get a break.

Taking on projects for J.P. was out of the question, and she was grateful that although J.P. called frequently, he never mentioned anything about an assignment.

Randi had been on total bed rest in the hospital for several weeks where both her and the baby's conditions were kept under close observation. It was the first Sunday in June, and Jaci awoke feeling almost as tired as when she had gone to bed. She decided she and Sean would attend early morning church services and dragged herself out of bed with a groan. After church, they stopped on their way home to do some much needed grocery shopping. As she strolled up and down the store aisles tossing items into her cart and trying to keep Sean from grabbing things off the shelves, her pager went off.

"Oh, oh, Sean, wonder who's beeping us?" she said to the squirming little boy. She pulled the pager out of her purse and saw it was the hospital's number, followed by "9 1 1." She grabbed Sean out of the grocery basket, leaving it sitting in the middle of the aisle, and ran to her Jeep where she dug her antiquated cell phone out and called the number showing on the pager.

"Hello, I'm Jaci Winters. Someone just paged me." Jaci spoke breathlessly into the phone, anxious over what she was about to hear.

"Oh yes, Ms. Winters, your daughter asked us to contact you. The doctor has decided to go ahead and deliver the baby. Do you know how to reach her husband? He hasn't responded to our pages."

"He's probably at church," Jaci said, her mind racing with this new development. "I'll see what I can do."

She set about tracking John down as she drove to the hospital. When they all arrived, Randi was already in prep for surgery. A nurse told her that Randi had gone into premature labor, and the doctor, concerned that both the underdeveloped baby and Randi's high blood pressure wouldn't be able to withstand a normal delivery, had decided to do a cesarean.

Jaci called others to let them know, and it wasn't long before family and friends filled the waiting room. They prayed and settled down to wait.

Word finally came that the little girl, weighing barely three pounds, had been delivered and that both mother and baby were doing well.

Jaci's life grew even more frenzied. The baby, who Randi and John named Jasmine, was transferred to Children's Hospital where pediatric specialists had the expertise needed to give premature babies the best possible chance. Randi remained down the street in Hermann Hospital, where she recuperated from the emergency surgery while the doctors continued to treat her blood pressure.

Jaci's mind and body were on automatic as she went to work and ran between the two hospitals every day. She didn't stop to think, she just did it.

Randi's condition eventually improved enough for her to go home. Naturally, she insisted instead on proceeding directly to Children's Hospital, where she stayed beside little Jasmine for as long as her own body and the hospital personnel permitted.

It had been so long since Jaci had taken an assignment from J.P. that she seriously considered letting the job go. When she tried to talk to J.P. about her concerns, he refused to discuss it.

"I don't know how many times and ways I have to say no, Jaci. There is no need for you to quit. In fact, it might do you some good to get away from this situation every now and then. This has been going on a long time, and you've been running yourself ragged. I know you're concerned about the baby and Randi, but you've got to take care of yourself, too. That job is the last thing I want you to worry about."

"J.P., I really appreciate all the kindness you've shown me and my family. I want you to know you are a blessing. I don't have to tell you how much I like the job because you see how excited I get about every assignment. And not only that, it's flexible, and pays more than I think it should—not that I'm complaining. But . . . well, it's not fair to you and your other employees for me to continue to hold on to the job when I'm not able to fulfill the requirements."

"Why don't you let me worry about that, Jaci? I know what the situation is, and I don't have a problem waiting it out. You're very good at the job, so it's in my best interest not to let you quit."

"J.P., I don't think . . ."

"No, Jaci, don't think about this. That's what's wrong now, you're doing too much thinking."

Jaci backed off, but was still uncomfortable with the way things stood with the job.

J.P.

J.P. increased his efforts to show Jaci how much he cared. He sent flowers to both Jaci and Randi every week and couldn't describe how happy it made him when he regularly received their thank-you notes.

He kept close tabs and knew the baby was steadily improving, so he was able to talk Jaci into taking a job in Corpus Christi.

"Jaci, you need a break from this situation. Corpus is close enough that you can get back here in a hurry if you need to," he pressured. "You've got to be exhausted, and getting away will do you good." She reluctantly agreed that she did need some time away and they made plans for her trip. J.P. prayed that everything would be okay.

Jaci

*J*aci decided to use a vacation day from her regular job on Thursday and leave a day early. She took a flight out Wednesday evening and was on the job early Thursday morning. She actually enjoyed herself, although worry over Randi and the baby was constantly in the back of her mind.

When she boarded the plane Friday afternoon, she felt good about what she had accomplished but was glad to be heading home. Although she had checked in with Randi regularly, she couldn't help feeling a little uneasy about leaving town because she was accustomed to being there for her daughter's every need.

Jaci was on pins and needles when the plane landed in Houston. Maneuvering as swiftly as she could around the slower moving crowd, she headed to the bank of telephones as soon as she entered the terminal. She punched in the number to Children's Hospital because she knew Randi would be there.

When she finally heard her daughter's voice on the phone she said, "Well, it's about time. It's frustrating having to go through all those people to get to you. How's my granddaughter?"

Randi immediately cried, "Mama, when are you coming home? The baby's having problems. Mama, can you please hurry home now?"

Alarmed, Jaci's heartbeat escalated. "I am home, or in Houston anyway. I just got off the plane. What's going on?"

"Jasmine started having trouble breathing this morning and they need to remove some kind of blockage."

Jaci felt fear consume her. "Oh Lord! I'll be on my way as soon as I can get to my truck. I had planned to go by home first, but I'll come straight there." She hung up the phone and resumed her trek through the busy airport to catch the shuttle bus to long-term parking.

She was rattled. The baby had been progressing nicely when she left. What in the world could have happened? She retrieved her Jeep and forced herself to concentrate on the horrendous traffic heading south on Interstate 45. After settling into the flow of traffic, she talked to the Lord:

"Lord, I don't know what I'm going to find when I reach the hospital. Whatever the situation is, please keep little Jasmine in Your care. And Lord, strengthen Randi and John and enable them to keep their trust and focus on You and Your power to bring little Jasmine through this. You've brought them through so much, Lord. Please don't leave them now.

"Father, You've been so good to our girl. You've kept her strong and helped her to be a witness and inspiration to the parents of other babies in the intensive care unit and the doctors and nurses as well. They draw strength from her, Lord, and I'm grateful to You for making her the strong person she is. And Lord, when I see her unwavering faith, I can't help but be filled with joy and thanksgiving. Because I know it's only through Your grace and mercy. When I think about how she was conceived and the life of lack and hardship we went through, I realize what a special gift she is and I thank You for her. Lord, whatever happens, I praise You for all You have already done."

Jaci's prayer and praise continued all the way to the hospital.

When Jaci stepped off the elevator at the hospital, Randi stood waiting for her. This struck Jaci as unusual, since Randi was seldom away from little Jasmine's crib. Jaci's heart plummeted. *Uh oh!* she thought. *Something is drastically wrong.*

They walked to the waiting room where John was already sitting, and Jaci quietly began praying again.

An hour later they still restlessly awaited word on the baby. Jaci decided to make a few calls. J.P. was one of the people she needed to call. She punched in his home number, knowing he would not be there, but she needed to let him know she was back. Everything else could wait. When she heard his voice on the answering machine, she was relieved, but couldn't help thinking, *Wow! The man's voice sounds so good!*

"J.P., this is Jaci," she said quickly. "Just wanted to let you know I'm back. I'm at the hospital. I'll call you later and set up a time to come by with my report."

Later that night Jaci yawned continuously as she battled to stay alert in the fast-moving freeway traffic. The baby had come through the surgery, was stabilized, but was still critical. There was nothing they could do but continue to pray.

"Lord! I'm tired," she said to the interior of the truck. Her eyes were gritty, making it difficult for her to see clearly, and she was hungry but refused to stop for something to eat.

As she entered her driveway, she felt the familiar wave of satisfaction wash over her. How she loved this house. It wasn't her dream home, but it was certainly a step in that direction. She gave her usual praise to God for the house and for the college professor she had met on one of her many part-time jobs, who sold it to her. After he accepted a position in another city, he had drastically reduced the price of the house so she could afford it. What a moment that was when she and Randi moved from an apartment into their own home. She used the event to teach Randi that if she served the Lord and obeyed His Word, He would always supply her needs.

Jaci drove into the garage, pushed the remote to lower the door, and debated whether or not to grab the bags that she had hastily tossed into the Jeep at the airport. When she heard the phone ringing, her mind went immediately to the baby. She nervously jiggled the key to unlock the door leading from the garage into the kitchen but it took too long, and by the time she reached the phone, the answering machine had clicked on. She stood anxiously by, waiting for the beep to find out who was calling.

J.P.'s deep voice entered the room. "Jaci, I know you're not still at the hospital, I just called there and talked to Randi. She told me you were on your way home. Call me as soon as you get there."

I don't feel like talking to you right now. She pushed the button to retrieve her other messages. *Nothing I have to deal with tonight,* she decided as she headed into her bedroom and shed her clothes. She berated herself as she got undressed. "I should never have let J.P. talk me into taking that assignment." She knew that it was irrational, that what was happening with Jasmine would have happened regardless of whether she was in town or not. But still, she would have felt better if she had been there.

The phone rang again just as she finished undressing. "Oh noooo!" She wailed tiredly and contemplated letting the machine answer but changed her mind. *It could be Randi, I'd better get it. I've got to invest in one of those caller ID things.* Jaci was always years behind in new technology. It changed so rapidly, she figured, why bother?

She rushed to pick up the phone. "Hello," she said in a cautious voice.

"Hey! What's happening?" The casual greeting suggested

they had just spoken yesterday, when in fact, it had been well over twenty years since she'd last heard that voice. But she recognized it immediately. Stunned, with all kinds of emotions running rampant, she was unable to answer the man's cavalier greeting.

"Jacetta? What's happening? You're a hard lady to catch. I've been calling you for weeks now—even made a trip down there, but you were nowhere to be found."

Jaci's mind went into turmoil. *Oh Lord! How should I respond? Do I hang up? Go stone crazy on his behind? Act like the good Christian woman I'm always claiming to be?* The hardship and struggle; the fears and rejection; the social, emotional, and financial toll that single parenting had taken on her—all cried out for her to curse his behind out, then hang up. But because she had called on the Lord, she knew she had to at least try to handle it His way.

"Maxie," she said calmly, but in a shaking voice. "What in the world do you want?"

Maxie casually explained that he had run into her uncle who had given him her number. Under her breath, Jaci berated her uncle's thoughtlessness. Aloud she said, "Now why would he do that? And better still, why would you want my number?" Her chaotic thoughts vigorously sought a reasonable explanation for his calling after all this time. Why now, when the years of struggling to eke out survival for herself and her child were over? Why now, when she was burdened with other issues?

Jaci recalled all the years she had hoped and prayed for this call . . . to hear this voice . . . to not be so utterly alone in raising their child . . . when just a little support from him would have made a gigantic difference in her child's life. But that child was a woman now, married with children of her own. Now, all this voice represented was an unneeded problem. She dug into her reservoir of inner strength to deal with this added stress. "What do you want?" she asked him again, valiantly holding on to her anger.

Maxie arrogantly said, "What do you mean, what do I want? I believe I have a right to check on my daughter if I want to. By the way, how is Randi doing? Your uncle was telling me something about her baby being in the hospital. I should have been informed about all of this before now."

Jaci quickly and totally lost it! "What! . . . Who! . . . do you think you are, mister? You don't have any rights where my daughter is concerned. You have some kind of nerve calling here trying to act like . . ." She sputtered. "You do not! And I repeat, do not! have a daughter. I took your advice. Remember your advice about what to do with our child? Well, as far as you're concerned, I did that. And in case you didn't know, that's irreversible. You can't change your mind about that."

Maxie, as cool and collected as he could be, came back with a ready retort. "I do have a daughter. Her name is Randi and if you had let me know where you were, I could have been a part of her life down through the years. In fact, you're the one who deprived me of a relationship with my daughter. You are the one who sneaked off to Houston with my child. You are the one responsible for her not knowing me, and you're the one wrong in this situation, not me."

Jaci dropped the phone and grabbed the top of her head, which felt as if it were about to blow off. She tried to think of some curse words strong enough to fling at him—words that would adequately express her rage. But the few she knew were much too mild, and even they were hiding somewhere in her shell-shocked mind. She was quiet for so long that Maxie must have thought she had hung up. She could hear him yelling, "Jacetta! Jacetta! You there?"

She picked up the phone. "This is ludicrous," she quietly stated. "I'm not going to argue with you. The time for that is long past and I'm not going there. But for the record, let me tell you something, you low-life bastard. I won't go into how you deceived me by pretending you were not married. I realized long ago that was actually a blessing in disguise. But I want you to know, I worked right up to the hour I went into labor. And I was back on the job after only two weeks because I couldn't afford to lose anymore time off. Otherwise, we would have starved to death. I didn't leave Dallas until *my* daughter was several months old. In all that time you couldn't—or wouldn't—be found. I'm still waiting for the call from you to let me know how you were going to help me. But I guess all of that was my fault too!" By this time Jaci was screaming into the phone. "Now, how YOU have the audacity to tell ME I'm responsible for your not knowing your child is beyond me."

Her head was pounding, her hands were shaking, and her heart was beating so hard it felt like it was about to burst through her chest. She definitely didn't need this!

Maxie, not to be outdone, went on to say how hard he had tried to keep track of her and the baby. "I always knew where you were until you left town. You were doing all right. So don't try to put that guilt trip on me. You shouldn't have left town with my baby."

Jaci's head almost exploded. She tried to calm herself, thinking it was stupid to let this man give her a stroke. "You are crazy, but like I said, it's over and done with. It's not even worth discussing. Now why are you calling me?" Jaci muttered through clenched teeth.

"I want to see my daughter and grandchildren. Your uncle said she has two children, and that one is in the hospital. What's wrong with the baby? How old is it? How old is the other one?"

Jaci fought to regain a modicum of control. She spoke quietly but forcefully into the phone. "I don't have any information to give you about *my* daughter and grandchildren. I will tell her that you inquired. Of course, I'll have to explain who you are (*God forgive me for lying—Randi was well aware of who he was*) and why you want this information. As far as she knows, you're dead. If she chooses to talk to you, I'll let you know. You may call me back in a few days. I really have to go now. I can't say it's been nice talking to you."

"You told my daughter I was dead?! Wh—"

She hung up on him.

Jaci fell across the king-size bed. *I can't believe this! Oh God, what is going on?* Tears of frustration slid down her face. *Every time I get on top of one problem, another one pops up! Lord, I'm so weary.* As if on cue, the telephone rang again.

There was no question as to whether she would answer it—NO! After the beep sounded on the answering machine, she heard her uncle's voice. "Hey, Jace, this is Uncle George calling from Dallas. Just wanted to let you know that I ran into Maxie a while back, and we've been talking every now and then. I gave him your phone number. He uh . . . he's been real sick—some sort of heart trouble. When he asked for your number, I gave it to him thinking he needs to get to know his child and grandchildren. I hope I'm not too late calling. I doubt he'll call anyway. I hope everything's okay. Bye."

"Doggone it uncle!" Jaci yelled to the empty house, "You are way too late!" Her tears continued. Maxie's calling and demanding to see Randi added to her already overloaded mind and physically tired body. It was like the proverbial last straw.

The phone rang, and again, she let the machine answer. She heard J.P's voice.

"Hello? Jaci, it's J.P. again. Please pick up the phone or call me back as soon as you can."

In agitation, Jaci yelled back at the phone. "No!" She was not up to talking to him. But before she could get back to her contemplation, she heard her pager go off. "Darn it!" She knew he would keep calling and paging her until she answered. She picked up the phone on the nightstand, called his home number, and hoped he wouldn't be there. When the answering machine picked up, she gave a sigh of relief and left her number. Her relief was short-lived. A few minutes later, her phone rang. Accepting the inevitable, she picked up the receiver and said, trying to sound as normal as possible, "Hello." There was a pause on the other end.

"Jaci? What's wrong? Have you gotten some bad news on the baby? Is Randi okay? What is it?"

Jaci racked her tired brain for a response. She really didn't want to tell J.P. about Maxie's call, but she couldn't lead him to believe something was wrong with the baby. He was almost as concerned about the tiny infant as she was, and had been through too much with her to mislead him. She tried to play it off as stress getting the best of her.

"I don't know, I guess I've just let everything get on top of me. The baby had to undergo a really serious operation today and she's in ICU. I'm worried about Randi trying to be a superwoman when she hasn't had time for her own body to heal properly. The hearing I'm working on is troublesome. There's a new problem every day. And now I have this person on the phone bugging me about his job. I'm totally stressed out."

"Jaci!" J.P.'s voice indicated his aggravation. "I don't believe you're stressed over the hearing, you've been doing them long enough to know they always come off just fine. Randi is okay and hanging in there. The baby came through the surgery and is doing okay, isn't she?" At her softly spoken "yes," he continued. "And you know doggone well I'm not calling you about my job. You're crying aren't you? I know you well enough to know you don't cry easily over your own problems. Everybody else's maybe but not yours. Now what's going on? What has you so rattled?"

Silence. She dithered—trying to come up with a plausible

explanation—one that would satisfy him. *Why was she reluctant to tell him about Maxie's call? She questioned herself.* But not long on patience, J.P. spoke before she had formed an answer.

"Jaci, I'm coming over. I'll be there as soon as I can fight my way through traffic. Do you need anything? Have you had anything to eat?" When she responded with a choked up "No," he made a disapproving sound. "That's part of the blasted problem right there. You need to eat. I'll stop and pick something up."

J.P's kindness pushed her over the edge. Sobbing quietly as she hung up the phone, she prayed, "Lord, help me get myself together before he gets here." She was angry with herself for letting Maxie's call affect her like this. She had promised herself long ago that she would shed no more tears over that episode and for the most part had kept that promise.

She went into the bathroom and was horrified when she looked in the mirror and saw how she looked. A shower was definitely in order. After her shower, she threw on jeans and a T-shirt and tried to prepare herself to deal with J.P. Just how much should she tell him? There was no reason not to tell him about Maxie's call, other than her reluctance to break down further barriers between them.

J.P.

As he traveled across the freeway on his way to Jaci, J.P. wondered what kind of food he could pick up that would be somewhat nutritious. *Lord, I have a bad case for this woman and I need to hurry up and do something about it.* Why this particular woman? He didn't have an answer. He just knew that he cared very deeply for her, that he would have absorbed all her hurt and pain if he could, and that he wanted to spend the rest of his life with her. It scared the heck out of him.

When he arrived at her house with a bag filled with chicken burgers and fries, he noticed her red eyes, but she was calm and in control of her emotions.

They sat in the family room and ate on TV trays. When they finished, he looked at her, waiting. He wanted her to open up and talk to him about what was wrong, but knew that would probably not happen.

"Why didn't you call me on my cell phone this morning? If I had known what was going on, I would have come by the hospital and sat with you."

"I just didn't want to bother you with any more of my personal problems. Lord knows, you're doing enough already. And I . . ."

"Jaci!" he interrupted. "How many times do I have to tell you, it's no bother. You bother me when you don't give me the chance to help you. You're always complaining about Randi trying too hard to be superstrong, but who do you think she got it from? Everybody, including you, needs a shoulder to lean on sometimes. Jaci, every man is not like Randi's father. It's time you understood that."

Jaci sighed tiredly. "J.P., I'm not going to apologize for who I am, nor for standing on my own two feet and handling my own problems. If you came over here to yell at me for doing that, then you'd better leave. I'll come by your office around ten in the morning and give you my briefing on the Corpus job."

His patience wore thin. "That's not why I came over here and you know it *Jacetta.*" He made a point of stressing her full name. "I came because I care about you, and I know something has really upset you."

Jaci

*J*aci felt shame burn through her for being so ungrateful. She dropped her head into her hands and spoke in a quivering voice. "I'm sorry. I . . . do know better. Strange you should call me that—Jacetta, I mean." She took a deep breath to quiet her emotions. "Because the thing that really got to me and threw me over the edge tonight was a call from Maxie. And that's what he calls me."

"What!" Incredulity was written all over his face. "Randi's father called here tonight? Why?"

"He was demanding information about Randi and the baby and . . . everything. He sounded so cavalier, as if it doesn't matter that he's been missing all these years and has every right to be calling now. Anyway, we had a terrible argument. I . . . I . . . think if I could have gotten to him, I would have tried to kill him. I was just that angry. Anyway, he uh . . . he wants to see them." She felt tears slide down her face. "Oh God, help me not to hate him!" she prayed.

J.P. listened quietly, wanting to comfort her but knowing she needed to give vent to her anger.

"The fact that he's done nothing to help us get to this point doesn't faze him in the least. And I find that insulting. We went without so much—never had enough of anything. And where was he? Somewhere hiding from us and having a good time. And now he has the nerve to waltz back into our lives making demands and acting like a concerned father. That's extremely hard for me to deal with. And I don't want him anywhere near my child and grandchildren. I had just hung up on him when you called."

"And why couldn't you tell me that over the phone, Jaci?" he asked softly. "Why were you so determined to handle this by yourself? Honey, when are you going to realize I want to share things with you? And don't worry, Maxie will find out that he's lost his opportunity to be nothing but a good-for-nothing jerk in Randi's eyes. Now . . . tell me how I can help. Believe me, I'll gladly punch that sucker out for you," he said, smiling that gorgeous smile of his.

His words lifted her spirits. "Good. I would greatly appreciate it. My uncle George called and left a message right after I talked to Maxie and said that he's having some health problems. It might not take much to kill him."

"My pleasure, baby. I can't think of a thing that would make me happier," J.P. said, chuckling, but meaning every word. The guy had a butt whipping coming and J.P. wanted to be the one to do it.

"Anyway, I told him I would talk to Randi to see if she wants to see him. He's supposed to call back in a few days. You know . . . , Randi really doesn't need this right now," Jaci said in frustration. "But he doesn't care. He even had the nerve to accuse me of leaving Dallas without letting him know. Never mind that I couldn't find him. He's conveniently forgotten that he told me to get an abortion and then hid from me. He's turned it all around in his mind and basically, he's convinced himself that I'm responsible for everything he failed to do."

"If I ever see that jerk . . . !" J.P. said angrily. "Baby, he almost destroyed you, do you know that? And after all these years, as hard as you've worked to build a good life for you and your daughter, you still don't realize what a rare and beautiful lady you are. Yeah, I would like to do some real damage to that lowlife." While he was talking, he moved closer and pulled her into his arms.

Jaci cried again. Not over Maxie, but because this strong and kind man was her friend. She wrapped her arms around him and held him tight.

J.P.

*T*hey sat like that for a long time. Not saying anything, just holding each other. J.P. again thought about the powerful feelings he had for her. And as they held each other, he wondered if he could be the kind of man he knew she deserved. He had been around and experienced all kinds of women, but Jaci was the one who touched a place deep within himself that he hadn't even known existed. She made all other women insignificant to him. She was special and, he conceded, had captured his heart.

When he felt her relax against him and realized she was asleep, he knew he should go home, but he hated to leave her.

She stirred in his arms and whispered, "Please stay with me tonight." J.P. couldn't say no. "Okay, but just for a while. Come on, you need to go to bed."

When they got to the bedroom, Jaci slipped out of her jeans but left her oversized T-shirt on and got into bed. He slipped off his shoes and followed her. "Have I lost my doggone mind?" he asked himself as he got into the bed. She slid over to him and laid her head on his chest with one arm draped across him. He held her until she fell asleep. When he attempted to slip out of the bed, she mumbled "no" and began to kiss his neck and chest.

"Jaci, stop baby. This is not a good idea. You're not yourself tonight and I can't take advantage of that. I think I should leave now."

Again, she mumbled, "No, stay with me please. I don't want to be by myself tonight."

He leaned over and kissed her lightly. "You are a beautiful and desirable woman, and as much as I would love to stay here with you, I can't, honey. You're very vulnerable, and I'm not the strongest right now. If I stayed, there's no telling what would happen, and if it did, I wouldn't be much better than Maxie. Come on, walk me to the door."

Maxie

axie's thoughts were anywhere but on the pictures flashing on the tube. *Jacetta.* The forceful woman he had spoken to was definitely not the same timid, soft-spoken one he remembered. For some reason this intrigued him and made him want to know more about this present-day Jacetta. At any rate, if she thought she was going to keep him away from his daughter and grandchildren, she had another think coming. He picked up the phone.

"Hey, George! How you doing man?"

"Great!" George answered. "What's up with you, Maxie? You still coming along okay?"

"Oh yeah, man. I'm doing okay. I was wondering if you had talked to Jacetta lately?"

"No. Not really. I've talked to that answering machine of hers, but not her directly. Why? What's up?"

"Well, I finally talked to her and told her I wanted to see my daughter and grandchildren. She's kind of bitter—wouldn't tell me anything. Yelled at me and told me that I don't have a daughter as far as she's concerned. She sounded nothing like the Jacetta I remember."

George grunted. "What in the world did you expect? For her to roll out the red carpet and say come on in? You got to be crazy if you thought that. Fact is, you mistreated her, Maxie. And she's had a rough time surviving. She's had to work two or three jobs most of her life. And from what I understand, she been doing a man's job for years just to make a little more money. So frankly, I understand where she's coming from. You would, too, if you put yourself in her place. I ain't got no sympathy for you, Maxie. All said and done, this is my niece we talking about."

"Yeah, I know that," Maxie replied, giving little regard to what George had said. "I even took a trip down there to talk to her, but she wasn't home. What kind of job did you say she has? It must pay okay, judging from that house."

"She works for the city. Something to do with condemned buildings—I don't really know what. Why? Why are you so interested in the kind of work she doin'?"

"Didn't you tell me she never got married?" Maxie asked.

"Yeah, that's right," George answered suspiciously. He didn't like the direction of this conversation. "Maxie, like I told you: You need to be trying to make peace with your daughter. Why are you asking all these questions about Jacetta's personal life?"

"Well, I'm just curious, man. That's a pretty nice house she's living in, and I'm just wondering if she's hooked up with somebody."

"If she is, it ain't none of your business." George felt his temper rising.

"I just don't want any trouble from some dude while I'm trying to work things out with Jacetta and my daughter. You know what I'm saying? Jacetta said she was going to talk to my daughter and for me to call back in a few days. I don't want anybody trying to interfere."

"You ain't got nothin' to work out with Jacetta," George replied testily. The guy's arrogance was causing him to flex his hands into fists. "It's too late for that. She's moved on with her life and is doing real good." George felt contempt for his own foolishness. "You know, my wife told me I didn't have no business giving you that girl's phone number and now I'm starting to think she was right. Maxie, you go starting some trouble with my niece, you'll have more trouble than you can handle, and not just from me either. A lot of people are still itching to kick your tail over the way you treated her. Don't make me sorry for trying to help you get things right with your kid. It was never my intention to cause anymore problems for Jacetta."

Maxie realized he had pushed too hard in his quest for information and tried to direct the conversation back toward cordiality. "And I appreciate everything you've done, George. I know you're just trying to help. All I was saying is that I need to know what I'm up against. That's all."

"You just need to concentrate on your daughter at this point. Jace is going to do what she said she would, but like I said, she's out of the picture as far as you're concerned."

That's what you think, Maxie mused to himself, but said, "Thanks, George, I owe ya, man. I'll check back with you next week sometime."

J.P.

J.P. watched as Jaci stepped out of her Jeep and walked around to open the rear door to dig inside for her briefcase. He was standing in his fourteenth-floor office looking out of his corner window. He noticed how her jeans clung to her curvy butt and shapely legs as she strode toward the building. There was something about Jaci that brought out all of his male instincts. *What was it about this woman?* he wondered, watching her stepping with a poise and assurance that he knew had been hard-won and long in coming.

The woman had no idea of the power she packed. She was both velvet and steel. And when her protective shell fell away, it revealed pure woman—in all of her softness and strength. He still questioned his sanity in leaving her last night. Was he going soft in the head or something? No doubt about it, her enticing femininity awakened a masculine monster inside him. She actually didn't know why other women envied her and men lusted for her—including him. "Okay, okay!" he said out loud. "I admit it."

"Excuse me?" a voice said from the door of his spacious office. Herbert Williams, his second-in-command, stood there with a thick stack of files in his hands and an amused look on his face. "Just what are you confessing to, my fearless leader?"

Embarrassed at being caught talking to himself, J.P. chuckled and said, "You don't want to know. And if I told you, I'd have to kill you."

"Uh oh!" Herbert said. "This is heavy stuff I'm hearing. Do I need to be concerned?"

"Maybe," J.P. answered. "Just between you and me, I may be headed into a midlife crisis thing and going soft in the head."

Herbert came in and sat down as J.P. took the chair behind the large masculine desk. "Are you okay, man? I mean, really, there's nothing serious going on is there?" J.P. simply smiled and reached for the folders in Herbert's hand. They started talking about the status of various jobs as J.P. flipped through the folders. Herbert was explaining the problems they had encountered on one of their software programs when J.P. suddenly remembered Jaci. She should have been announced long ago.

"Let's wrap it up for now, Herb. Jaci is here and should have been announced and in here by now."

"Okay." Herbert quickly got to his feet. "Jaci's bumping me

huh? Interesting!" he said jokingly. J.P. might have a reputation for being a playboy, but when it came to work he was conscientious and a hard taskmaster. Herbert walked to the door and turned to ask when they could finish up, but J.P. was on the phone asking Linda, the receptionist, if Jaci Winters was in the reception area. Her reply did not please him and he asked her to come to his office.

"Stay here a minute, Herb, I want you to hear this." A few minutes later, Linda appeared in his doorway. She was forty-something—tall, light skinned, well built, somewhat attractive. She had been with the company a little over a year and made no secret of her interest in more than an employer/employee relationship with J.P. But beyond the fact that he made it a policy not to date employees—Jaci being the exception, of course—he'd discovered she was one of those calculating women he despised. She had been so obvious in her pursuit of him that he had gone into a self-protection mode, making it a point to keep things strictly business with her, and interacting with her as little as possible. Too often, she showed up at social affairs when she knew he would be there and attached herself to his side until he found a way to shake her.

Now he was thankful for the wisdom and insight that had directed him to steer clear of her. He probably should have fired her when he realized her intent, but she had turned out to be a pretty good employee, and it was easier to keep her than to go through the trouble of looking for a replacement.

She entered his office smiling. "What can I do for you boss?"

J.P. waited expectantly to see if she was going to mention Jaci. She knew his instructions regarding visitors. They were not to be kept waiting either on the phone or in person. The staff person they were seeking should be notified immediately of their phone call or arrival, and was to acknowledge them and indicate how long they could expect to wait.

He now recalled Jaci jokingly saying on more than one occasion that to conduct business with him at his office, she had to plan plenty of time on her schedule. Now his suspicions were growing as to why.

Without waiting for an invitation, Linda walked to a chair in front of his desk and sat down, while J.P. continued to wait. She must have thought he was finally noticing her interest in him. Her smile got wider, and she casually crossed her legs.

When he saw her smile, J.P.'s anger began to simmer. He reined in his temper and quietly asked, "How long has Ms. Winters been waiting in reception?" Linda's smile slipped a little, then she waved her hand dismissively. "Oh, that Jaci Winters woman? She can wait."

His anger increased. "How do *you* know she can wait? Who does she usually see when she comes to this office? Did you notify me that she was here? How do you know I'm not in a hurry to complete my business with her? Who gave you the authority to make this kind of judgment on our visitors' importance? Have you ever kept Ms. Winters or anybody else waiting like this before?"

By this time, Linda's mouth was hanging open and a big "oh! oh!" clearly showed on her face. She opened her mouth to speak, but nothing came out. She tried again, sputtering, "I . . . I . . . I knew you were with Herb and I didn't want to disturb you. I knew you all were going over those important status reports."

J.P.'s temper shot up further at her explanation. A vein in his forehead visibly throbbed and his jaws had clenched. Herbert realized Linda was in big trouble and tried to come to her defense. "Uh, J.P., I'm sure Linda was just trying to be conscientious. She didn't mean to overlook or overstep the rules in any way." The look J.P. leveled at him caused Herbert to quickly cease his efforts.

"Let me be real clear, Linda. You listen closely, Herb, be-

cause I expect you to assure follow-through. When I give instructions, I intend for them to be carried out completely and
without any interpretive nuances. If you didn't understand
these instructions, you should have asked questions. Now,
Linda, if you would like to continue working here, please express your complete comprehension of all instructions." At
her hesitation, he literally spit out, "Now, please!"

Linda was totally caught off guard. This was definitely not
going as she had hoped. She finally managed to mumble, "Yes,
sir, I understand."

"Then I suggest you follow them or look for another job.
Please show Ms. Winters in now. She's waited long enough.
And don't ever keep her—or anyone else for that matter—
waiting like this again."

When Linda left, Herbert remained and set a steady gaze on
J.P. "What going on, man? Linda slips every now and then, but
all in all, she does a pretty good job."

J.P. looked at him angrily. "She didn't follow instructions,
Herb, and this is not the first time. The receptionist is the first
point of contact for this office. We can't afford any laxity
there. That's why I pay that person a good salary. She can
make or break this company by the way she treats people. I
built this firm on the foundation of consistent, first-class customer service. That's why we've gained the level of success we
have. I'm not going to let a silly employee destroy that by
treating people badly."

"Yeah, you're right," Herb said as he opened the door to
leave. He shook his head in consternation. He was usually so
engulfed with work that he became oblivious to what was
going on around him. He liked Linda and had even considered
asking her out until he realized she had her eyes on J.P. Beyond
office matters, she generally ignored him, lighting up only
when J.P. was around. He was astute enough to know when
someone wasn't interested. Obviously, Linda wasn't as astute.

Linda

Linda Adams stomped back to her desk, furious over what had just happened. She was desperate to the point of dementia. She was forty-five and unmarried, with nothing resembling a prospective husband. She had come to work for J.P. with one goal: to make him her husband. She came from a wealthy Louisiana family (her father was a doctor, her mother a college professor). She needed a husband who fit certain social criteria—and J.P. definitely did. All her siblings either had high-profile careers or acceptable mates. She was the only one who had not yet "arrived," and she was tired of being the butt of their cruel jokes and put-downs. Linda had never been interested in a career but had concentrated on finding a wealthy husband to give her the social prominence she craved. She depended on her looks, light skin, and family connections to give her the advantage. But those attributes hadn't been enough to off-set her grasping desperation and pushiness with men, which had caused them to run as fast as they could when they discovered what she was like. She had even resorted to stalking a few men after they lost interest and tried to end things with her. A couple of them had even filed charges against her.

This pitiful receptionist job was just a means to an end—her road to becoming Mrs. J.P. Gilmore. After setting her sights on J.P., Linda decided that a change in tactics was called for. Her new strategy was to demonstrate what an asset she could be to him socially—every prominent businessman needed a socially astute wife. She also did whatever was necessary to eliminate any other woman in the picture. Although her plan was taking longer than she liked, the payoff would be worth it. J.P. was handsome, wealthy, and highly respected.

She recalled the party he had given for the employees last year, when she had walked through his beautiful, spacious home and pictured herself there as his wife.

While she sat at the receptionist desk every day answering the phone and greeting visitors, she dreamed of the time when she would walk through the office as the boss's wife, commanding the highest respect. She had noticed how J.P. looked at Jaci Winters. How he often left the office with her. There was no way she would allow a little nobody civil service worker like Jaci Winters disrupt her plan. No! Jaci Winters had to go. Linda didn't plan to lose this one. She only worked a few hours on Saturdays and she still had work to finish, but she picked up the phone and dialed a number.

"It's time to get someone out of the picture and I'm going to need a little help," she said into the phone, then she listened for a moment. "Yeah. Her. I have a feeling things have gone further than we realized."

Jaci

While Jaci sat in the reception area of J.P.'s office waiting to see him, her mind mulled over the events of the previous night. She couldn't believe Maxie! Calling her after all these years and making demands. Even more unbelievable was her actions with J.P. She shook her head in amazement. *Had that really been her?* Now, she would have to try to reestablish some distance between them.

After her usual long wait, Linda had finally told Jaci to go on back to J.P.'s office. "Hey, baby, how are things this morning?" J.P. asked, embracing her tightly. Jaci stiffened and tried to back away, but he ignored it and held her a little longer, waiting for her body to soften against his. But to his disappointment, she pulled away.

"I'm really sorry you had to wait so long in reception. I just ripped Linda up one side and down the other for that. Tell me the truth, does she do that to you often?"

Jaci hesitated. *So that's why I got such an ugly look from Linda.* "Look, I know you're a busy man, and Linda is just doing her job. I don't mind waiting. I told you before, I plan for a long wait whenever we meet here."

He was shaking his head. "No, no, no. You are to let me know if it ever happens again. It will never be acceptable, but you're dealing with too much right now to put up with that kind of treatment, so I want to know, okay?"

Jaci nodded yes and then got down to briefing him on the assessment she had just completed. Neither one mentioned the previous night's events. When they finished talking about her trip, J.P. immediately changed the subject. "Will you go out to dinner with me tonight?" Jaci shook her head before saying, "No." J.P. moved closer to where she was standing. "Why not? Jaci, you can't keep running away from this. Sooner or later you'll have to accept that there's something between us. After last night, you have to know that the feelings are not going away."

She looked at him angrily. "That was a cheap shot. You know what kind of frame of mind I was in last night."

He pulled her into his arms. "I'm sorry, sweetheart. I don't know why I said that. You're right; it was a cheap shot. You have me so messed up I don't know whether I'm coming or going. I need to have things settled between us. I can't stand being in limbo like this." He kissed her gently.

There was a brief knock and an older man with silver hair entered without waiting for an invitation. His striking resemblance to J.P. assured her this was his father. He walked into the office and took in the couple standing there embracing.

J.P.

J.P. turned toward his father, but kept an arm around Jaci. "Jaci Winters, please meet my dad, J.P. Gilmore Sr., better known as 'Big Pat.' Pop, this is Jaci Winters, the lady I've been telling you about."

"Well hello, Jaci, I'm glad to meet you," Big Pat said, crossing the room as he inspected her from head to toe.

Jaci extended her hand to shake his. "Hello, Mr. Gilmore. It's very nice to meet you too." She pulled the straps of her purse and briefcase onto her shoulder, preparing to leave.

"I've heard a lot about you, young lady." Big Pat continued his scrutiny of her. "I understand you're doing a good job for my son. I appreciate that, but when are you going to put him out of his misery?"

"Put him out of his misery? I didn't know he was in any misery." Jaci looked at J.P. with puzzlement. "What kind of misery are you in? And what do I have to do with it?"

An embarrassed smile covered J.P.'s face. "Nothing, honey. Don't pay any attention to him."

Big Pat went on, undaunted. "Girl, you've got this man so tied up in knots he can hardly do his job. Can't have that, since he's running two businesses and already has too much on his plate. He needs a woman, a wife. And he thinks you're the one for him. So when are you going to marry him?"

"Pop! Cut it out," J.P. yelled.

"Marry him?!" Jaci tried to pull away from J.P. to head toward the door. He didn't let go, but guided her across the room to the door where he looked down at her. "Sure you won't change your mind about dinner tonight?" He knew the answer but had to ask.

She shook her head. "I'm sure."

"Well, can I call you later? Maybe I can come by for a while." He hated that his dad was witness to his desperation but couldn't seem to help himself.

"You can call, but I probably won't be home."

He looked at her hard. "Where will you be? At the hospital? Maybe I can come by there."

"No, I won't be at the hospital. Look, I have to go. Nice meeting you, Mr. Gilmore." She was so rattled she didn't notice that the older J.P. didn't respond but was studying them intently.

J.P. leaned down and kissed her lips softly. "I'll call you anyway."

Jaci left the office almost running, not wanting to even contemplate what the senior J.P. had said about marrying his son. "He's crazy," she said to herself, walking rapidly down the corridor.

"Boy, you're in big trouble," Big Pat said, laughing as he watched his son running his hands over his head in a continuous gesture of frustration. "That woman's all up under your skin." He laughed harder at J.P.'s frustrated response.

"She runs hot, then cold. I never know what to expect. But dang! I'm so crazy about her I can't see straight." He paced around the office in agitation.

Big Pat continued to laugh. "That's obvious. But if you have to go down, it may as well be for a woman like her. She's beautiful and seems very nice too. I like her. You got your hands full though, because I think she's got a mind of her own. We still have a tee-off date? Somehow I don't think you'll be much good on the course today. What's this about Jaci going to the hospital?"

J.P. explained a little about the baby and all that Jaci had been through over the past few months. "I'm trying to be patient since she's dealing with so much right now. I almost fired Linda this morning for making her wait in reception for no reason. If I hadn't seen Jaci on her way in, there's no telling how long Linda would have had her waiting. I don't know what's wrong with that crazy woman."

Big Pat rubbed his chin thoughtfully. "I do. She's set her cap for you, and she's trying to run the competition off. I heard her on the phone when I came through reception. She was talking about how she was going to get rid of somebody. I'll bet anything she was talking about Jaci. She bears watching, son. Something about her I ain't never liked. Better yet, get rid of her!"

Jaci

As Jaci passed through the reception area, her mind spinning over what had just happened, she almost didn't realize that Linda's quiet but viciously spoken words were directed toward her. "You think you're smart, don't you. Playing up to J.P. like you are. Well, let me just tell you in case you are suffering any misconceptions. J.P. is spoken for—he's mine, and you don't have a snowball's chance in hell with him. So move on, honey, and stay away from him, or I will move you myself. I mean every word I'm saying. And don't tempt me because I'll be glad to show you."

Jaci stared at her for a moment before shaking her head and

escaping through the door. She really didn't need anymore drama in her life.

After reaching her truck, she got in and sat there for a minute, trying to process what she had just experienced. She shook her head again. *Lord, it's amazing how much trouble I get into just minding my own business.* As she drove out of the parking lot, she pushed her troubling thoughts to the back of her mind and decided to stop by her office.

She called the hospital to check on Jasmine as soon as she arrived at her office, and, after being told that the baby was stable, Jaci decided to go through her in-box to clear it before checking her messages. She wasn't anxious to retrieve the troublesome messages that were inevitably waiting on her voice mail. Since this was Saturday, hopefully she would get through a lot of work without interruption and take some pressure off of next week.

Of its own accord, her mind went back to J.P., and she cringed in embarrassment when she remembered what had transpired between them last night. What in the world had gotten into her? Thank God, once again J.P. had acted with some restraint because she certainly hadn't. It seemed she had none where he was concerned. And this morning, his father's ridiculous remarks about her marrying him made her realize she had to get things under control between J.P. and herself. No way was she going to put her emotions in the hands of a man until she was ready to deal with the repercussions.

Her desk phone rang, causing her to jump in surprise. *Now who would be calling here on a Saturday?* she wondered. Curiosity made her pick up the phone. "Hello," she said in a cautious voice.

"Girl, what are you doing at that darn office today?" her friend Lena yelled into the phone. "You still haven't gotten it have you? Newsflash—you ain't a superwoman! Everybody needs to rest sometimes, Jaci. Now what could have been so important that you had to go to that pit today?"

Jaci began to laugh. "Girl, how you doing? And I know I ain't a superwoman. I just decided to come by here and clear my desk a little because next week is going to be hectic. But guess what I'm doing? I'm sitting here thinking about stuff best forgotten. Figure that."

It was good to talk to Lena, one of the few true friends she had made over the years. Lena was an attorney with the city, and they occasionally collaborated on cases where owners filed suits against the city for demolishing their dilapidated houses. They got together often to lament over the lack of men in their lives and supported each other through the ups and downs of failed relationships and the ongoing survival struggle.

Jaci told her about the trip to Corpus Christi, gave her an update on the baby's condition, and then told her about the call from Maxie. Lena couldn't believe it.

"Just how did that bastard fix his mouth to even speak to you after all these years? And did you curse his tail out and hang up?"

Jaci told her about the conversation with Maxie, and J.P.'s subsequent kindness, without going into too much detail.

"And you won't believe this! I went by J.P.'s office this morning to give him my report, and guess what? His father came in while I was there, and, girl, he had the nerve to ask me when I was going to put J.P. out of his misery and marry him. Can you believe that? I was so embarrassed."

Lena was quiet for long minutes. Jaci was about to ask if she was still there when Lena finally took a deep breath and said, "Wellllll, I think Pops has the right idea. I mean . . . J.P. has been leaning over backwards to show you he's interested in more than a roll in the sack. You need to open up and give him a chance. You never know, Jace, he could be the one."

It was Jaci's turn to be quiet as she remembered just how close she had actually come to rolling in the sack with him, and at her invitation. "You may be right," she said finally. "We are very attracted to each other. But the thing is, I don't know where I want it to go. I have some serious fears about getting hurt again. I don't know if I could handle that. Oh, and let me tell you about Linda, J.P.'s receptionist." Jaci felt it was a good time to change the subject.

"Oh yeah, the old witch who always makes you wait so long to see J.P.?"

"Yep. That's her. And you nailed it when you called her a witch. This morning J.P. caught on somehow to what she was doing and called her in. Whatever he told her, it must not have been good, because when she came out, she gave me a real dirty look before telling me I could go on in. Then, when I passed her desk on the way out, she threatened me."

"She what!? Jaci, exactly what did she say?"

Jaci repeated what Linda said, ending with, "You know I need that kind of drama like I need a hole in my head."

"You need to tell J.P. what she said. Let him deal with her. And then you need to give this thing with J.P. a chance, girl. Nothing ventured, nothing gained. Listen, I'm not going to keep you. But don't stay there too long, Jaci. I cooked up a lot of food, so come by and eat before you go *home!*" She stressed the word "home" because she knew Jaci was most likely not going home before stopping by the hospital to check on the baby. She was right.

Arriving home later that evening, Jaci felt more hopeful about the baby than she had ever dared. Jasmine was showing definite signs of improvement since the surgery, and the doctors were guardedly optimistic. Her good feelings didn't last long.

There were two disturbing messages on her answering machine. One from Maxie demanding to know whether she had talked to Randi yet. And the other from her mother, advising that her paternal grandmother was not doing well and wanting to know when Jaci could come to Riverwood to see her. Jaci had deliberately kept the seriousness of the baby's condition from her parents, so they had no idea what was currently going on. They were under a heavy burden themselves, taking care of her grandmother and dealing with their own old-age troubles.

"Oh, Lord!" Jaci said to the empty house. "This couldn't have come at a worse time."

She had still not talked to Randi who was already dealing with so much that Jaci was reluctant to dump the sudden appearance of her long-lost daddy on her. She had hoped, somewhere in the back of her mind, that Maxie would just go away. But apparently he was not going to do that. She was going to have to do something real soon.

She called her mother and got the full scope of her grandmother's condition. She conceded that, yes, from the sound of things, she did need to go right away. She hung up and began making travel plans.

Monday, as she prepared for Thursday's hearing, something else happened to put even more pressure on Jaci. She was summoned to Wynola Dickson's office and reprimanded for being discourteous to a citizen. Jaci searched her mind, but for the life of her couldn't recall doing anything even remotely like that. She always put herself in the other person's shoes and tried to treat them as she would like to be treated. She knew she hadn't deliberately done or said anything objectionable to anyone, but with so much going on, maybe she had done so unconsciously.

"If I did something like that, it wasn't done deliberately, and I'll gladly apologize," Jaci said. But when she asked for the name of the citizen she needed to make the apology to, Wynola refused to supply it.

"I have the right to confront my accuser," Jaci insisted, "It could be that someone has either lied on me, or at the least misunderstood something I said."

"You don't have the right to anything," Wynola stated coldly. "And there's never any excuse for that kind of conduct. I've received many complaints about you over the years, but since you've done a reasonably fair job, I've chosen to overlook them. But this time you've gone too far. If it happens again, I'll start disciplinary actions toward removing you from your position."

Jaci was dumbfounded. Never had she received less than an acceptable performance review in all the years she had worked for the city.

"I've never heard about any complaints before," she told Wynola. "And I don't recall my performance reviews ever showing that my work was below par in any way." Jaci got angry. "I don't know what's going on, but something's not adding up. I've worked too long and hard in this department to be dealing with something like this. And I certainly don't like the idea of walking around with this kind of cloud hanging over me." Jaci made a mental note to request prayer from her church.

Wynola felt a little sliver of concern run through her. She knew Jaci's past performance reviews would show the truth of Jaci's statement, but she refused to back off.

She smiled nervously. "As long as you understand that I won't put up with any further misconduct, you'll be all right. I don't have anymore time to waste on you today, I'm late for a meeting."

Jaci left Wynola's office with an unsettled feeling. For some reason she felt an overwhelming desire to talk to J.P., but she quickly quashed it. He was already much too involved in her affairs.

She told her staff what had happened, asking if anyone

knew anything about it. They were all shocked and angered by the accusation.

Bill Whitmore had the most volatile reaction. He had been around long enough to know everything about everyone in the department. It was a well-known fact that Wynola had gotten her position because of political connections and that she was basically an airhead without basic knowledge of what the job entailed, with no interest in learning. He also knew what Jaci had gone through to get where she was and despite what was going on in her life currently, she was still one of the most valuable employees in the department.

"What in the world is wrong with that crazy woman?" Bill shouted. "After all these years, she should know that's not your style. She'd better realize what side her bread is buttered on. Without your hard work, she probably would have been out of here a long time ago. Naw. Something else is going on, and I'ma find out what."

Bill decided he would call the department director. The two men had been hired around the same time, and although it was not widely known, they had maintained a close friendship over the years. Bill had cheered and helped his friend on his way to the administrator job, while he happily chose to stick to inspection work. He had never infringed on their friendship with personal requests, but he was going to do so now.

Jaci tried to concentrate on preparations for the hearing and for the trip out of town. She dreaded the six-hour drive to Riverwood, but knew she had to go. She put in her request for time off and was shocked when it came back from Wynola unsigned with the word DENIED written across the top in red.

Normally she didn't take a lot of time off work. She had grown into that habit when her child had been young and prone to childhood sicknesses. Jaci had gone to work many times so sick she could barely stand, reluctant to use her sick or vacation leave on herself. Even during her daughter's illness with the baby, she had seldom missed any whole days. She would use only as many hours as necessary, and spend the rest of the day on the job.

She took the form and headed to Wynola's office, praying for help from the Lord as she went. "I need to see Wynola," she said walking pass the secretary without stopping.

"Wait! She's busy right now," the secretary called as Jaci walked through the open door to Wynola's office.

"Tough," Jaci replied.

She walked across the large office to Wynola's desk and asked, "What is the reason for this, Wynola?" She threw the form on the desk and stood, waiting for the woman to get off the phone.

Wynola looked at her with distaste and took her time ending what was obviously a personal call. She then turned to Jaci. "What do you mean barging into my office like this? You really are tired of working here, aren't you? It means just what it says, 'denied,' or can't you read?"

Jaci couldn't believe the viciousness of the woman. "Lord help me," Jaci whispered before responding. "Yes, I can read. I asked you for the reason it was denied. I have the time and there's nothing that my staff can't handle if I'm out of the office a few days. So why?"

Wynola looked at Jaci with a smirk. "Because I felt like it. Now get out of my office."

Jaci picked up the form and walked slowly toward the door. It occurred to her that she had been wrong in her approach. She turned around and found the woman staring at her with open dislike. "Wynola, the reason I need this time off is because my grandmother is very ill, and I have to travel out of town to see her. I'm asking again. May I have this time off?"

"I'm sick of you with all your personal problems. You've been working below par for the last several months now, with one problem after the other. I'm not putting up with it anymore. If you can't handle the job, get out! I know somebody who can." She stood up behind her desk and literally screamed the last sentence.

It was clear the woman was not going to change her mind, so Jaci turned and left the office. She vaguely registered the presence of other people on her way out, but her eyes were so full of tears of anger that she couldn't see who they were. She went back to her office, still not believing what had happened. That she should have to be dealing with something like this, after so many years on the job and what she had thought was an excellent record, was beyond her comprehension. She started talking to the Lord.

"Father, I don't know what's going on here, but I know You do. Whatever it is I know You're able to handle it. I ask that You will do that right now. I thank You, Lord, for the victory in this situation. And Father, I pray for Wynola. I know You're able to minister to her in whatever way she needs You. Have mercy on her, Lord, and bless her. And above all else, save her and let her experience Your love and peace."

In her spirit she heard the Word of God whisper, "*Stand still and see the salvation of the Lord.*"

Again, she told the staff what was going on. They had worked together too long for her to be anything but honest with them. If Wynola was gunning for her, she would probably go after them next. "It seems I can't do anything right around here all of a sudden. First, I'm reprimanded for being rude to a citizen. And now, my vacation request is being denied. Wynola told me she's tired of my personal problems and my working below par. I do know I'm going to see my grandmother. If that means I'll lose my job, then so be it, but I have to go."

Her staff was unusually quiet this time. And before long, Bill had disappeared out of the office.

Jaci may have been reluctant to go over Wynola's head, but

others were not. The next day when someone knocked at her open door to get her attention, she was surprised to see Ed Shannon, the department director standing in her door.

"Oh Lord, what now?" she asked, not bothering to hide her agitation.

Ed Shannon rarely interfered with day-to-day personnel matters in the department, leaving that to the divisional managers. He encouraged employees and managers to work together to solve personnel problems without his involvement. But he was too troubled by what was happening to take that approach this time.

He looked at the woman sitting behind the desk, observing her frustration and the tiredness in her eyes and spirit. He had never known her to act in any way other than with cordial professionalism and graciousness. That was missing today and he knew she was definitely a woman at the end of her rope. He was aware of what had been going on in her family and knew that in spite of everything, she had still managed to do her job in an exemplary manner. He thought about all the commendations that the department had received because of her hard work and creativity. He had never heard anything of a negative nature about her from a citizen. Even when citizens complained about their properties being condemned, they were always complimentary of Jaci's sensitive assistance.

Ed had already heard about Wynola's mistreatment of Jaci from Bill Whitmore and two other division managers who happened to be in Wynola's office when it happened. He also knew that when the Gilmore family, who were personal friends of his, as well as the mayor, heard about it, he would also be hearing from them. J.P. had already jokingly told him Jaci's days in the department were almost over.

"Jaci, I understand you've been denied some vacation time," Ed said, while his thoughts ran ahead of him. "Is that true?"

"Yes, sir, it is."

"Do you know why?"

"No, sir, I don't. But that's not surprising since I just learned from Wynola that there have been other complaints made against me by property owners. Evidently, I'm close to losing my job and didn't even know it." Her anger erupted despite her trying to control it. "That really blows my mind. I've busted my butt in this department all these years and I'm just now learning that my work is below par." She leveled a hard look at him. "So, why do I have the honor of your presence? Are you here to tell me to clear out my desk?"

When he heard the anger in her voice, Ed realized the department hadn't done well by her. Even though management had not supported her, she carried out her responsibilities well. He had convinced Bill Whitmore to transfer into the division when Jaci took over as hearing coordinator, hoping Bill's support would help turn the tide of resentment caused by Jaci getting the position. And it had to a certain extent. But there continued to be widespread petty jealousy and dislike of her. He had left it alone, hoping it would work itself out. It hadn't, yet Jaci seemed to handle it okay.

Now he realized he should have taken the lead in support of Jaci because for some reason, Wynola had turned against her. It was evident that Wynola was out of control, and if he didn't take action, this situation could escalate and cause repercussions he didn't want. Why the devil Wynola had suddenly decided to wage this malicious attack against Jaci was beyond him!

"Absolutely not!" Ed answered Jaci. "I'm just as much in the dark about this as you are. I've already heard about what happened in Wynola's office, and believe me, I'm going to get to the bottom of it. In the meantime, I came to personally let you know that your request for time off is approved. I know you don't abuse your leave benefits and I see no problem with your taking the time. I heard it's a family emergency. Is that right?"

"Yes. My grandmother is gravely ill in Arkansas."

"I'm sorry to hear that. Where's your leave form? I'll go ahead and sign it." Jaci handed him the form, which he looked at for a long time before signing his name. "Will you make me a couple of copies of this when you get a chance? Just give them to my secretary," he said as he handed the form back to her.

"Yes, sir, I will."

"Everything is cleared with Wynola. Go on and see about your grandmother. And don't worry about your job. You'll be okay."

He heard her softly spoken "Thank you very much, sir."

As he walked away, he heard her say, "Thank you, Heavenly Father, for Your delivering, conquering power on my behalf." He wondered if he was numbered among the ones she had asked Him to conquer. The thought didn't sit real easy in his mind.

Ed decided that the mayor was going to hear about this from him first before Big Pat Gilmore got to him. He and the mayor needed to have some serious conversation about employee job performance or the lack thereof. Wynola Dickson held her high-ranking position because of her husband's political connections. But she had done very little to actually carry out the responsibilities. Ed had inherited the problem and hadn't rocked the boat because Jaci and other employees in the division made sure the work was done. But now, in his opinion, it was time for Wynola to go because apparently, she had lost the ability for rational behavior.

Jaci was shocked at her grandmother's condition. Although very old, her grandmother had been in reasonably good health until recently. Now she was seriously ill and the prognosis for recovery was not good. A nursing facility was recommended to the family; however, her dad and his siblings were reluctant to place their mother in a nursing home, but Jaci and her brothers supported their mother in accepting the doctors' recommendation. Her grandmother required more care than her parents, up in years themselves, would be able to provide.

Jaci returned to Houston with a heavy heart. Her grandmother's condition, the baby, Maxie's demands, and her job situation made it seem as though trouble was on every side. She struggled not to become perplexed but instead to just jump in with both feet and deal with everything so she could move on.

"My daddy!" Randi said, amazement and other emotions spreading across her face. "Where has he been all this time? Why does he want to see us now? What's his game? He has to have one."

"Honey, I can't answer any of your questions. He called me out of the blue a few weeks ago and demanded to see you and the kids. I don't feel comfortable about it, but he is your daddy and I don't think he's going away. The last thing I want to do is stand in the way of your meeting him. You know that I've always been honest with you about how things happened with me and your daddy. It was his decision not to be involved in your life. You know I've made several efforts to locate him over the years, to give you the opportunity to meet him, but he couldn't be found. Why all of a sudden he surfaces now—making ridiculous demands—I don't know. It's your decision. I can't make it for you. If you don't want to see him, it's fine with me. But I have a feeling he's going to have to hear it from you. You'll eventually have to face him yourself. That's where you'll get all your answers."

"He's been sick, you said? You think maybe that's why?"

Jaci laughed. "Yeah, he could be a sick old man trying to

clean up his act while there's still time. I don't know. Whether that's the case or not, you have to do the right thing—the thing that you can live with."

"So, you're telling me to see him, huh? How could you do that after the way he treated you . . . and me? As far as I'm concerned neither one of us owes him anything."

"Honey, I'm not telling you to do anything. You are going to have to communicate your desire to him one way or the other. Like I said, he'll never believe me if I tell him you don't want to see him. Of course, I'd be happy if you told him to go jump in the deep blue sea. But again, it's not my decision. Basically, I'm out of it at this point."

"Mom, you're never going to be out of it. It took both of ya'll to get me here. He ducked out on me, but you ain't going nowhere. If I do talk to him, I'll let him know real quick that as far as I'm concerned he's just a stranger. He'd better not try to disrespect you in any way either. He'll be laid out on the floor! He won't get a chance to die from sickness, I'll kill him."

A little choked up, Jaci said, "Okay. I'll give him your telephone number and tell him to never, ever, call my house again."

J.P.

J.P. left messages for Jaci at every number he had for her. By the time she returned his calls he was fit to be tied. Anger didn't define what he felt when he learned Jaci had left town without letting him know.

"Don't ever do that again!" he spoke softly, but forcefully. "I'm serious, Jaci. I know you realize how much I care for you, and that I would be worried about you. You were wrong not to at least tell me you were going out of town. All I'm going to say is, don't ever do something like that again. I think you owe me that courtesy."

"Wait a minute! I don't owe you anything, Mr. Gilmore. And working for you doesn't make you responsible for me. I'm an independent woman and don't have to answer to you or anyone for my actions."

"Believe me. I know you're an independent woman. And even though I probably don't have the right to feel responsible for you, I do, because I care about you. What if something had happened? I wouldn't have even known you were out of the city." When she didn't respond, he continued in a soft voice.

"Jaci? Are you running scared because of what my dad said to you about marrying me?"

"No!" she yelled. "I just . . . he just . . . kind of caught me off guard. But no, I'm not running scared." He knew by her reaction he had come close to the truth.

"I think you are. I think that's what prompted you to leave town without letting me know you were going. Honey, I'm not trying to take control of your life or anything, I'm just in lo—" Where had that come from? He had almost told her he loved her. "It's just time you learned to let someone take some of the pressure off of you. And Jaci, I don't plan on that being anyone but me."

"I don't want or need you or anyone else for that matter to take pressure off of me. I've come this far by myself. And I haven't gotten to this point letting someone else run my life, J.P."

"I'm not trying to run your life, sweetheart. I'm just trying to show you how much I care. And I'm not arguing with you about it anymore. I don't know what I'm going to do about you. I believe we have something special between us. Something I'm not willing to throw away. You know it, too, but you're not ready to accept it."

He paused, waiting for Jaci to say something. When she remained quiet, he continued. "Anyway. That's all I have to say on that issue. How about coming to my house for lunch Saturday? You can meet my son. He's been bugging me about it ever since he talked to my dad. So will you come?"

"I don't know. I mean . . . Not that I don't want to meet your son, it's just that I don't want him to get the wrong idea about us."

"Well, I've met your family and friends. What ideas have they gotten about us?"

"None. Because the circumstances were different, and you know it."

"Well, I had already told him all about you. And then his granddad really laid it on about how beautiful and nice you are, and how he's already asked when you're going to marry me. So Patrick is really chomping at the bit, wanting to meet you, check you out, and see what has his old man all shook up."

"Well, I don't think it's a good idea. He may draw the wrong conclusions."

"I do. And whatever conclusions he draws will be his own. Besides, you *do* owe me, lady, for almost giving me a nervous breakdown. Now here are the directions. Be here around two."

Jaci

The following Saturday, Jaci found herself nervously trying to decipher her hastily written directions to his house, filled with an overwhelming temptation to turn around at any time. She didn't particularly like social functions, and she had no idea who besides J.P. and his son would be there. *Why hadn't she been firm in her refusal?* she asked herself for the hundredth time. He couldn't force her to come. The worst he could do was fire her, and she could live with that. In fact, that might have been her simplest solution—to just quit. But she had never been a coward. And now wasn't the time to start. Whatever happened, she would survive it.

When she pulled into the circular drive of the large two-story home and double-checked the address to make sure she was at the right house, she wasn't surprised. She knew he would have a beautiful home. She was also extremely relieved that there were no other cars in the driveway. She hoped that meant there would be no other guests.

Nor was she surprised when she entered the beautiful, professionally decorated house. "Jason, it's lovely!" she exclaimed when she stepped into the wide foyer.

"Come on, let me give you the ten-cent tour. It's just a place to come to for sleep and other necessities, as far as I'm concerned."

As they walked from one room to another, Jaci had to keep herself from gasping in admiration. The layout of the rooms and their size led her to ask, "Is this a custom-built home? I mean normally you don't find houses like this in this area."

"Yes, it is custom built. I had an idea of what I wanted, and my brother designed it. I looked all over the area, once I decided this was where I wanted to live, and didn't find anything I could settle for. So . . . I decided to do my own thing. This is the result. As it was being built, and especially after it was finished, we had so many inquiries about buying it that my brother and I decided to buy and redevelop this entire cul-de-sac. Most of the houses were old and run down and being used as rental property anyway, and the owners were happy to sell them. You know, there's a big wave of people wanting to move back into this area. It's close enough to the center of things—downtown, the sports arenas, freeways—that it's suddenly an attractive area for those tired of the long commutes."

"So have you had any problems selling the other houses?"

"We can't get them up fast enough. We've already sold most of them and have pending contracts on the rest. It was a good decision."

"Are you happy with yours?"

"Like I said, it's really just a place to crash. It doesn't have that homey feeling I thought it would have, you know. Goes to show you, a house does not necessarily make a home. But maybe one day that will all change." He gave her an unexplained long look.

As they emerged from the second floor and headed into the large family room, a tall, good-looking young man entered from the backyard. He looked so much like J.P. that Jaci didn't have to guess who he was. When Patrick saw Jaci, he smiled and walked toward them with his hand outstretched.

"Hi, I'm Patrick," he said, shaking her hand.

"Hi, Patrick, how are you? I'm Jaci," she stated, with an answering smile covering her face.

"Will you two give me the honor of introducing you?" J.P. asked, a frown marring his handsome face.

"Jaci, I'd like you to meet my son, Patrick. Patrick, please say hello to my friend, Jaci Winters."

Jaci and Patrick looked at each other and burst out laughing, causing a look of dismay to cross J.P.'s face. "Are you guys laughing at me? What's so funny?" Although he was a little put off at being the butt of their amusement, he was relieved that they seemed to like one another.

"You are, Pop. Would you please lighten up. Hey, Jaci. I'm happy to finally meet you. I been trying to get Pop to invite you over for a long time. Glad you finally made it."

Jaci threw a puzzled look at J.P., but she followed Patrick's friendly conversation as he told them he had the fire going in the pit and the coals were almost ready. "So, what else are we having?" he asked. "Do we have to eat that sorry potato salad from the deli? Jaci, can you make good potato salad?"

"Pat!" J.P. yelled. "Watch your manners. I didn't invite Jaci over here to cook."

Jaci was just about to sit on the large sectional couch, but instead walked toward the spacious, well-appointed kitchen.

"Let's see what you have. I may be able to throw something together. Ummm." She said after a cursory look in the refrigerator. "You don't have the makings for potato salad—not even the potatoes!"

"That's because he hasn't gone to pick up everything else. I do the meat, but everything else comes from the deli," said J.P.

"Well, let's make a list of what you need to buy at the store, and we'll be in business in a little while."

"Why don't you go to the store with me?" Patrick asked. "I'm a terrible shopper. I'll probably forget half the stuff I'm going after."

"No!" J.P. said irritably. "She's not going to the store with you, Pat. Now go ahead and make a list of what we need and get going."

Jaci looked around for her purse. "I may as well go with him. Otherwise I'll just be watching you doing your thing with the meat."

"That's the general idea," J.P. said, frowning.

Jaci found out quickly that Patrick was a consummate con artist. When they left the grocery store, they had the makings for potato salad, baked beans, green salad, and cheesecake. "Now I'm beginning to understand. I think you had an ulterior motive for wanting me to come over. Namely, a home-cooked meal. That's all right because you're going to help. Just get your fingers ready to do some potato peeling and onion chopping."

As they worked together preparing the food, Jaci realized she had forgotten all about being nervous and was having a good time. Patrick was a love and fun to be around. And J.P. was enjoying his role as head chef.

They managed to put together a decent meal, with Jaci doing most of the cooking. Patrick was proud of the fact that it had been his idea. "Just think, we could have been dying of food poisoning from that deli food."

"And now those dishes are just screaming for your attention," J.P. reminded him.

"Aw, Pop. Don't mess up a good thing. Those dishes are not going nowhere!"

"Yes they are, son. They're going into the sink, dishwasher, whatever—and then into the cabinets. Now get to it."

"Aw, man!" Patrick grumbled, but headed into the kitchen. Pretty soon, running water and the noise of banging pots and clinking china were accompanied by blasting music as Pat busily attacked the dirty dishes.

"I like your son," Jaci told J.P. as they sat close together on the sofa. "He's a bit of a con artist, but he's a lovable one."

J.P. gave a loud laugh. "Wow, you are sharp. It usually takes a little longer to discover that fact. Yeah. He learned at a young age how to get his way. And he does it in such a way that it's hard to say no or get angry. If I didn't know him so well, he would run all over me."

"And who did he learn these particular skills from?" Jaci asked with a smile. "I mean, you don't just pick up those skills, you have to be taught."

He looked at her and said with smiling sarcasm, "And just what are you inferring? That he learned them from me?"

"You know the saying: If the shoe fits . . ."

He tackled her—tumbling them to the floor where he proceeded to tickle her, demanding that she take it back. The tickling eventually evolved into kisses. Soon, they both realized it was time to stop. J.P. asked if she wanted to go out to a movie or watch one there at home.

"I'm too full. Let's just stay here. I should be heading home before long anyway."

"Uh, uh! Don't even think about it," he told her, pulling her over to the entertainment center that housed a big screen television, a sophisticated sound system, and a wide array of videos and DVDs.

They were arguing over which movie to watch when Patrick came bounding down the stairs, looking like a different person in dress slacks and a sports coat.

"Wow!" Jaci said. "I almost didn't recognize you. Where are you going all spruced up?"

"I'm heading back to the yard. Got a hot date tonight. Jaci, I'm really glad I got a chance to meet you, and it was great spending the day with you. And thank you for fixing that great food. I might have to come back tomorrow to finish off the leftovers. Hope we can do it again real soon." He leaned down to hug her and pecked her on the cheek.

"Pop, if I don't get by tomorrow, I'll call you sometime next week, okay?"

"All right son, be careful. And don't forget to get some hot studying in along with the hot dates."

"Yeah, yeah, yeah!" Patrick answered before the door slammed behind him.

"What? He doesn't live here with you?" Jaci asked.

"No. He's a student at UH and lives on campus. He had scholarships offered at some other really good schools, but preferred to stay close to home."

"That's great! It says a lot about your relationship. A lot of kids can't wait to get as far away from home as possible."

"I've noticed the same thing with you and Randi. I'd say we've both done well where our kids are concerned."

"My answer to that is that the Lord made up the difference."

"Well, you did your part too, okay?"

He pulled her close and began planting kisses on her neck, face, and finally her lips. All thoughts of the movie were gone. Before long, Jaci knew it was time to flee temptation.

J.P.

J.P. was fighting a losing battle. He tried to force himself to concentrate on other things—things he needed to focus on—but inevitably, his mind returned to Jaci. It drove him crazy remembering her softness, her kisses, her passionate response to him. How wonderful it had been to have her presence in his home, and how he wished she would never leave. The physical attraction between them was explosive. When they got close to each other it was like one of them was the match and the other gasoline.

It scared him! Even though he knew he cared deeply for her, and probably loved her, it made him think seriously about giving up life as he had known it. And although he convinced himself that this new life was what he wanted, the reality of its happening was more than a little disconcerting.

His brother Ron was getting a real kick out of it. "Okay, let me get this straight. You bent outta shape over this woman and she don't even want your sorry tail? That's classic. Man, I don't believe this! I mean, I could see it happening with a hottie like Sheila or Brenda. Even that witch Vivian. But this chick looks like she'd freeze an ice cube from ten feet away. Dang, brother, you gone soft in the head or something?"

J.P. didn't care to explain that the cool façade Jaci presented to the world went up in smoke when they were together. "You don't understand because the only way you relate to women is sexually. When you meet a woman who can reach you on other levels, you'll understand what's going on. Until then, back off."

"Naw, I ain't backing off, man, naw!" Ron said forcefully. "You're the legend, man. I gotta save you from yourself." He picked up the phone and dialed a number. "Hey, Walt, what's happening? I need you to round up Charlie and T.C. and come on over to J.P.'s house. We got some serious de-programming to do. Yeah, man, dude thinks he's in lo . . . ve."

J.P. could hear his friend Walt on the other end, laughing his head off along with Ron. Oh well, he had known this was coming as soon as Ron discovered his deepening feelings for Jaci. He loved his brother, but he often wanted to knock his block off.

Ron was a confirmed bachelor and ultimate player. The only thing he got serious about was his work. When it came to designing structures, Ron was dead serious, and on it. The demand for his architectural designs was big, and growing every day. J.P.'s house and the others they were constructing had boosted Ron's career dramatically.

As J.P. glanced around his house, he appreciatively took note of the intricate details. After describing what he wanted, J.P. had basically given his brother carte blanche. The results were the ultimate in design, beauty, and practicality. It was a showplace that had made the list of "houses to see" in the city. The outside was eye catching. Built in a circular configuration, it was unique in appearance. White brick covered the entire exterior, offset with the unusual placement of windows and angles. Semi-circular steps led up to the double etched-glass front doors, and a step inside revealed a very special place. Skylights and dormer windows were strategically placed to give a light and airy overall effect.

The downstairs rooms flowed in an open layout and included formal living and dining rooms, a large family room, a state-of-the-art kitchen, a home office, a library, and an exercise room. The upstairs rooms were built around the outside perimeter of the lower floor, providing an open balcony that overlooked the downstairs rooms. Spacious bedrooms encircled three sides of the house's upper level. The remaining side showcased an open game room. The game room then opened on to an enclosed sunroom, which overlooked the backyard and swimming pool. A curving stairway circled up from the foyer to the upper level. Another stairway led down from the game room into the family room. The whole effect was breathtaking. Yes, his brother had built him a great house. And a well-known interior designer had done her thing in decorating it.

He reined in his thoughts and prepared himself for attack. The guys would tear him to pieces with every negative thing they had ever heard of, or experienced, in relationships. And most of them had horror tales. They would extol the virtues of the bachelor life, then they would demand to meet Jaci, the woman who had somehow caused him to step into insanity.

He could take it, but knew he was reluctant to expose Jaci to them. He was having a hard enough time trying to talk her into merely accepting their feelings for each other. She would run from him as fast as she could if these guys ever got hold of her.

By the time his brother and friends left that night, J.P. wasn't even sure of his own name, and was actually questioning his desire for a possible future between him and Jaci. What could he have been thinking about to want to give up his life of freedom for a ball and chain? And he was the one pursuing it! *Oh God, I'm so confused,* he cried to himself.

He had a long talk with his mother the next day, and told her everything. He could count on her to help him put things in the right perspective.

"J.P., you've always known your own mind. Why are you letting Ron and that bunch of heathen friends of yours change it? Maybe you need to reconsider if your feelings are that easily swayed about this woman. You probably need to back off and give this some more thought."

"I thought I had it settled, Mom. This woman is the epitome of everything I've always wanted in a woman. She's beautiful inside and out. We're good together. We enjoy the time we spend together. It's like I'm better, happier, when I'm with her. And I guess the main thing is, she's not chasing after me. The fact that I have money hasn't even fazed her. And she doesn't just go to church; she loves the Lord and is actively serving Him. She's caring, considerate, loving. Patrick just loves her. And she's got as many hang-ups about us deepening our relationship as I do—probably more. But she makes me feel like we could have what you and Pop have together, if we could ever get to that point."

"I've heard all about her from your father and Patrick," said his mother. "They think she's the bomb, as the kids say. I wouldn't know, since it seems like I'm the only one who hasn't met her. But honey, you have to follow your own heart and mind. If this is the woman you want, then don't question it, go for it. But if you still have doubts, don't jump into anything. Pray about it, and seek your answers from the Lord. Just take your time. You've waited this long. A little more time won't hurt, I don't care what Dad and Patrick say. Just remember, Dad and I didn't start out where we are now. Naw, honey. We went through some real sticky places to get here. And that's the way it's going to be with you all. Relationships and marriage are hard work, as you should already know from past experience."

"Now, Mom, don't even bring up that fiasco with Vivian. You know that was a mistake from the beginning. This is totally different."

Cecelia's curiosity about the woman increased. She knew her son well, and any woman who had him in this kind of torment had to be special. "All I know is, if you plan to live, you better bring this girl around here to meet me. I mean that!"

"Okay, Mom," he answered, chuckling. He always felt better when he talked to his mother.

He knew he had some serious thinking to do about where he wanted to go with Jaci. He figured the best thing to do was to follow his mother's suggestions to pray and take his time.

He backed off. As hard as it was, he stopped calling and pursuing Jaci.

Jaci

Jaci hadn't seen or heard from J.P. in almost two months. She was devastated, but told herself it was best that it happened now. She reached deep within her spirit to draw on the Lord's strength and peace that had seen her through so many difficult places, and once again, moved on with her life.

"Girl, I don't have to tell you how much I hate to go to that thing Saturday night," Jaci said to Gloria as they prepared files for the next hearing. "The only good thing about it is that we're going together. I couldn't tolerate going alone. Did you get something to wear yet?"

Gloria flashed a big smile. "Yeah, girl! I found just the right outfit, and, honey, I'm going to be catching, cause it's really bad! I hope you got something to pop some eyes out too. If not, I'm taking you shopping myself. If we have to go, and you know we do if we want our jobs, we might as well make the most of it."

Jaci was amused. "I have something I think will make you real happy. I went shopping with Lena, and you know her. She practically forced me into buying this little black dress. It's short—has a halter top and a hem made of fringe. In fact, I'm going to have a whole new look Saturday night. I think it'll surprise even you."

The annual Thanksgiving Benefit Dance was something Jaci dreaded every year. This year would be worse because of the tense atmosphere between her and Wynola. She'd prepared herself for a fight after returning from Arkansas, but although Wynola had nitpicked and found something wrong with everything Jaci did, there had been no mention of the days she had taken off.

Since it was mandatory for all employees to attend the benefit, she had to go, but she made her usual plans to make an appearance and then sneak out at the first chance. The event was sponsored by the Housing Commission of Houston and was a party as well as a Thanksgiving fund-raiser for needy families. The entire housing industry participated and competed by bringing canned goods and other donations. Those who enjoyed parties looked forward to it every year since there was an abundance of food, drinks, and entertainment.

Gloria and Bill Whitmore met at her house so they could all ride together. They both gasped when they saw Jaci. She had swept up her long hair on top of her head in a sophisticated style and wore a sexy black dress that did little to hide her voluptuous curves. "You look great!" they told her.

Being among the first to arrive, they had their pick of tables. As more of their coworkers arrived, their table became crowded and more chairs were pulled up. It amazed Jaci how a different environment changed her colleagues' attitudes toward her, especially considering the way things stood between her and Wynola. Usually in conflicts, her fickle and unprincipled coworkers flocked to the one they perceived as having the most power. And in this case, that was Wynola. But some of the same ones who gave her a hard time in the office couldn't seem to get close enough to her tonight. How was Jaci to know, since she didn't participate in office gossip, that the word around the department was that Wynola's tenure in the department was about to end?

Surprisingly, Jaci was having a good time. Bob Johnson, who had been trying for years to get a date with her, tried to hog all her dances. And for once, Jaci was enjoying the attention she usually rebuffed.

"Just so you know, Bob, tonight is all about having a good time, nothing more," Jaci told him.

"Aw, baby, don't burst my bubble. You know how long I've been waiting for a chance with you," Bob answered.

"Yeah, me and every other woman in the department—young, old, married, single, black, white—you name it. You don't discriminate, you go for them all."

"Baby, you're looking so good tonight, you just say the word, you got me all to yourself for as long as you want me."

"Right. Until some little young chick comes along and shakes herself at you. Then you'll be gone before I can blink my eyes." They laughed as they talked and danced around the floor.

Jaci didn't know that J.P. had entered the room and was angrily watching them. A casual observer would be amused at the shocked expression covering J.P.'s face when he found Jaci on the crowded dance floor. At one point between dances, he started across the room toward her table, but before he could get there, Bob grabbed her hand and pulled her back onto the dance floor. J.P. went back to his seat. But his eyes remained glued to Jaci.

When Jaci returned to the table, Gloria motioned her to the empty chair next to her. She leaned over and whispered, "Girl, there's a certain man here who hasn't taken his eyes off you, and he doesn't look too happy either. Did you know J.P. was going to be here tonight?"

Jaci sent a hurried look around the room to see if she could spot him. "No, but so what?" Although she appeared to be unconcerned, her heart started beating double time.

"Well, like I said, he's not looking too happy. In fact, he started over here once, but when you got up to dance with Bob, he went back to his table. He's been watching you all night. I think the man is totally pissed. Wynola's sitting at his table and you know she's up to no good, so be prepared for anything."

"He has no reason to be pissed at me," Jaci said in a low voice. "I mean, after all, we're not . . . there's nothing between us."

"You couldn't tell that by the way he's watching you tonight," Gloria responded. "And he has been really nice to you. You have to admit that."

"Yes, I do know that. But then he stopped communicating with me. And I absolutely refuse to chase after him." She hoped her hurt and bewilderment over J.P.'s apparent change of heart didn't come through in her words. Her high spirits suddenly disappeared. "Let's just have a good time until we can leave, okay?"

Bob claimed her again for a slow dance. Jaci loved to dance and it had been quite a while since she'd had the opportunity, so she really enjoyed the rare treat of dancing to some of her favorite oldies classics. When the song ended, Bob offered to get her something to drink and she returned to the table alone. Just as she sat down, J.P. appeared beside her.

"Can I speak with you a minute, Jaci?" he spoke quietly over her shoulder. Heart pounding, and forced enthusiasm in her voice, she said, "Well hi, J.P., what's up? I didn't know you were coming to the dance. How have you been?" She was puzzled by his silence, and when she noticed his stiff, unsmiling countenance, she decided Gloria was right. The man was pissed!

"Let's walk outside," he said as his hand closed around her arm and pulled her up from the chair. He kept her close to him as they left the room. When someone attempted to halt their progress to say something, J.P. ignored them and tightened his grip on her arm. Surprised stares followed them as they exited the room. Jaci was embarrassed and becoming angry. What was his problem anyway?

It had been he who had broken contact with her. She had to conduct all her dealings with his company through Herbert Williams. She assumed he had grown tired of her with all her family problems and decided she wasn't worth the trouble. His behavior was irrational and unacceptable.

When they got outside the room and down the corridor a ways, he stopped and looked down at her angrily. "What in the world has gotten into you? Why are you letting that guy put his hands all over you like that?"

"What are you talking about, J.P.? I'm just having a good time. And what I do is my business. What's wrong with you? Why are you acting this way? I haven't seen or talked to you in weeks, now here you are acting like someone who's lost his mind. Well hear this, Mr. J.P. Gilmore. You have nothing to say about what I do! Now, I'm going back inside, so let go of my arm."

"What you're going to do is go back in there and get your stuff, then tell that crowd you're with that you're leaving."

"No, I'm not! Just who do you think you are, mister? I didn't come with you and I'm not leaving with you."

"I'm up to here, Jaci," he said, pointing above his head. "I've watched all I'm going to watch tonight, and you are leaving. I don't have anything to lose; these are not my coworkers. And I will make a scene that none of them will ever forget if you don't leave with me now. Don't think I won't. So, go and get your coat. Did you drive or are you riding with someone?" When she barely nodded yes, he said, "Well tell whoever you're riding with that I'm taking you home."

She stood there looking at him for a long time. In turn, he looked at her with angry eyes that communicated to her that he meant what he said.

"Will you tell me why you're doing this, J.P.?" she asked softly. "I'm at a loss. I don't know what's going on here, and I don't appreciate how you're acting. I'm trying to remain rational and I wish you would too."

J.P.

J.P. knew Jaci was right to demand an explanation, but he was so intent on getting her out of there that he couldn't think beyond that point. He came to the dance on the off chance that he would see her. He knew her attendance was required, so in spite of not communicating with her for so long, he figured he would come, dance with her, and help her through the night. Jaci had mentioned how she disliked having to attend the event, so he expected her to look and act like she didn't want to be there. Man, was he shocked!

He began searching the room intently for her as soon as he arrived. When he spotted the sexy woman with the short revealing dress, showing off a pair of gorgeous legs on the dance floor, he had looked appreciatively, but continued to look for Jaci in the crowd. When the lady whirled around to face him and he realized she was Jaci, he almost fainted. Why was she dressed like that? And what was she doing dancing with that guy like that? Then he became angry. Very angry.

He felt like a fool. He had backed off, true enough. But never had she been far from his thoughts. When he remembered what he had expected—to be her rescuer, and maybe get the chance to dance with her, to hold her in his arms, he felt very foolish in the face of reality.

He immediately began plotting ways to get her out of there, finally concluding that he would have to strong-arm her; otherwise, he knew she would refuse to go. And indeed, there she stood, demanding an answer to why he was acting this way. He had no answer, at least none he could share with her in the middle of a crowd. He just knew that he wanted her out of there—with him.

"Jaci, just get your things and let's go. Or do you want me to do it? Where's the check stub for your coat? Where's your purse? How did you get here?" He looked at her with a scowl. "And don't tell me you came with that clown you've been dancing with!" He let her arm go and walked determinedly back toward the ballroom.

"Wait! Okay. I'll go with you. Just let me get my things. I'm really angry at you for doing this, J.P.," she said before walking away. He watched as she went back into the ballroom and wondered what the heck had gotten into him. He knew he was all the way wrong, but couldn't seem to control his actions. He just hoped he could come up with an explanation that would help Jaci find it in her heart to go easy on him and maybe someday, to forgive him for his high-handed, uncalled-for actions tonight.

Jaci

*J*aci tried to appear as if all were well as she told Gloria and Bill she was leaving. They were surprised. "What's going on, Jaci? Is everything okay?" Gloria asked, looking at her closely. Jaci gave them a brief explanation about J.P. wanting to drive her home so they could talk, but they knew her well enough to know she wasn't real happy.

"Jaci, you sure you're ready to go?" Bill asked, a worried expression on his face. "Want us to drive you home? It won't be a problem." Bob also looked concerned. "I can drive you home, Jaci. We're having such a good time, I sure hate for you to leave now."

"No, you guys, everything is fine. I . . . uh . . . J.P. and I need to talk. Ya'll stay and have a good time. I'll see ya'll later." She grabbed her purse and went to get her coat while J.P. waited for her at the door. Bob watched as Jaci and J.P. walked out the door together and shook his head sadly. Playing the field was getting old.

Linda

*L*inda Adams sat at the table where J.P. and several of his staff had gathered. She had followed J.P. and Jaci into the corridor, where she covertly watched the heated encounter between them. She came to the dance tonight hopeful that this would be the night she caught J.P.'s eye. Dressed in red from head to toe, she knew she looked good. She refused invitations from other men to dance, while smiling invitingly at J.P. to let him know she would welcome his invitation. He ignored her and kept his eyes focused somewhere across the room. It took her a while to see who he was watching so intently, and when she saw Jaci Winters on the dance floor, looking beautiful in a short black dress, Linda knew she would have to act quickly. She took the bull by the horns and asked J.P. to dance with her. She felt about two inches tall when he absently said, "No thanks" and left the table to walk across the room to where Jaci was sitting.

"I'm sick of that hussy!" Linda said when she sat back down at the table. "And you haven't done anything to help," she hissed at the woman sitting next to her.

"Are you crazy? Linda, I've put my job in jeopardy manufacturing stuff to harass her. What else do you expect me to do?"

"Huh! Well it hasn't been enough," Linda said with total disregard for the other woman's concern about her job. "I'm going to get rid of that little witch, with or without your help."

J.P.

J.P. opened the door and Jaci slid into the car. She watched as he walked around to the driver's side. When he got in and started the car, he asked, "How are Randi and her family doing?"

She was tempted to tell him to go to hell. "I should tell you it's none of your business, but they're all doing well." She noticed a smile playing around his mouth as he worked his way out of the parking lot and into heavy traffic. Jaci fumed. How dare he laugh at her? She didn't see anything amusing.

"J.P., you haven't answered my questions. What is going on? Why are you coming off with this caveman act tonight?"

He merely glanced over and said, "We'll talk when we get home." He noticed that when they were alone and amiable, she called him "Jason" in a way that heated his blood. However, when they were around others, or she was upset with him, he was J.P. He was feeling a deep need for her to call him Jason again.

Jaci was so distracted she'd hadn't noticed the direction J.P. had taken. "This is not the way to my house. Where are we going?"

"We're going to my house so we can talk. Your friends will probably call your house to find out what's going on. At my house, we won't be disturbed."

"This is ludicrous. I want to go home. What in the world has gotten into you?"

"You're not going home right now."

Jaci turned her face away from him, silently fuming.

Thirty minutes later, he pushed the garage door control and pulled the Jaguar in beside the large SUV already parked there. They entered the house and continued to the large family room. Jaci again admired the beautifully decorated house. Too large for one person, she thought, but that was his business.

"Okay. Let's talk, so you can take me home," she told him as she sat down on the leather sofa placed strategically in front of the big screen television.

Now that he had her here with him, J.P. didn't know what to say or where to begin. She wouldn't understand his need to get her away from the dance. She was such an innocent about the way she looked and the impact she had on men. Maxie and the other jerks she had encountered over the years had really done a job of crushing her self-esteem, and in spite of the way she had picked herself up and moved on, somehow a positive self-image hadn't made the journey. She thought of herself as unattractive and unappealing, convinced she lacked whatever it takes to attract a man or to maintain a relationship with him if she did.

But he saw her differently and wanted to be her friend, lover, and protector, shielding her from the wolves seeking to devour her. But how would he express that to her?

"Jaci, I honestly don't know where to begin," he said as he sat down beside her on the couch. "I can understand your puzzlement over my actions tonight, and truthfully, I'm puzzled myself because this is all out of character for me. You asked a little while ago if I had lost my mind. Maybe I have, I don't know." J.P. cringed; feeling out of control like this was simply not him. He looked at Jaci with frustration, figuring he may as well be honest—what did he have to lose? "I love you, sweetheart," he admitted. "I've never felt this way about a woman. Something in me yearns for you, wants to protect you, to be with you. Frankly, it scares the heck out of me, especially when I consider that you might not feel the same way about me."

Jaci looked at him incredulously. "Right! What an interesting way you have of showing that love," she said sarcastically. "Considering the way you disappeared from my life without a word. You must think I'm Winnie foo foo."

"I don't blame you for feeling like that, but please, just hear me out, okay?" He paused to collect his thoughts, knowing his next words would alter his life one way or another. "Because of my fear, I ... uh ... convinced myself that I needed to back off and sort out my feelings and decide exactly what I wanted. Now I know—that wasn't the way to handle it. And sweetheart, I apologize for not communicating to you what was going on with me, and especially about the way I've acted tonight." He reached out and took her hand, timidly, as if he expected her to snatch it away. He was relieved when she didn't, but the expression on her face didn't offer much encouragement.

"When I saw you tonight and you seemed to be having such a good time dancing with that guy, well . . . I was petrified that I may have lost you! Here I am an old man dealing with these feelings for the first time in my life. Sooooo! To put it bluntly, I'm vulnerable when it comes to you, and I can't tell you how much it scares me."

He waited for her reaction to his confession, but she sat there quietly, with her head down, saying nothing. He continued. "And yes, I'm mad. I saw red and lost all rational thought." He jumped up from the sofa, walked a few paces, and turned to stare down at her with a frown on his face. "Why were you carrying on like that with that dude? You acted as though you enjoyed him being all over you. Well I didn't like it at all! And my only thought was to get you out of there before I did something stupid like punching him out."

"You know, you're making me really nervous," Jaci finally said, still looking down at the floor. "You sound like a jealous lunatic. It would be different if we had a settled understanding between us. But you just admitted that you backed off, without even bothering to let me know what was going on. So what was I supposed to do?" Her green eyes flashed angrily when she finally looked up at him. "Huh? Did you expect me to sit around all sad and miserable? I don't think so, J.P. You gave me flashbacks to what I went through with Maxie. And you already know, I'm never going there again."

He sat back down beside her groaning loudly and covering his face with his hands. "Oh God, honey. I am so sorry. I didn't think. It was never my intention to put you through that. All right, I know I didn't handle things the way I should have, and there's no excuse for it other than confusion and fear. But as far as tonight goes, I admit I'm jealous! And even though I might be acting like it, I'm not a lunatic. I knew how much you dreaded going to that dance and the only reason I showed up was to help you get through it. It was like a bucket of cold water had been thrown in my face when I realized I might have lost you to that dude.

"I know I've handled things badly. I guess we should have had this talk a long time ago, but to be honest, I don't think either one of us was ready."

"No, maybe we weren't," said Jaci, her brilliant eyes looking directly into his. "But the way you decided to handle it really hurt me. What makes you think we're ready now? Has anything changed?"

"Absolutely!" He grabbed her hand again, caressing the soft skin on the back of it. "I know beyond a shadow of doubt that I love you and want to build a life with you. I can only hope you feel the same about me. I'm so sorry for the deplorable way I've acted, but I can tell you now that it's a settled issue with me. And if this hadn't happened tonight, I would have been on your doorstep very soon. I was coming to you with my heart in my hand and believe me, I wasn't leaving until everything was cleared up between us."

Tears flooded Jaci's eyes and ran down her face. It took her a minute to answer him. "You keep saying you're not going anywhere. But your actions prove differently. You did leave without a word or explanation to me, J.P. That makes me afraid to trust you."

"Jaci." Agony filled his voice and tears filled his eyes. *How could he have been so stupid? So callous in his treatment of her?* "Sweetheart, I realize I hurt you, but I love you with all my heart. Please forgive me. We have something good. Don't throw it away because I gave in to my doubts and fears. And if you must know, I was in hell the whole time I was away from you. I know you might have a hard time believing me, but I promise I'll spend the rest of my life showing you how much you mean to me. I'm not like Maxie, sweetheart. Nothing like him. Please, honey, give me—give us—another chance."

Jaci

*J*aci was stunned. Anger, attack, argument were what she'd expected. Not this heartrending confession. She didn't know how to respond since she had planned to let her own anger sustain her in the confrontation. But he had destroyed that with his softly spoken plea. She looked at him, trying to gauge his sincerity, and found him looking at her in that special way he had. It was a look that said she was the most precious thing he had ever seen.

For reasons she couldn't explain, more tears filled her eyes and flowed down her cheeks. When J.P. asked her why she was crying, she couldn't answer him, just shook her head and let the tears flow. She had given much thought to their powerful physical attraction and to the possibility of a serious relationship between them, and she had prayed for God's wisdom and guidance.

J.P. moved closer to her and pulled her into his arms. "You're making me cry, too, and you know men aren't supposed to cry!" he joked nervously. "I know we've got a lot of issues but I would really like for us to settle some things between us tonight."

Jaci cried harder. Because even if she had wanted to, she couldn't have said no. "All right," she said brokenly.

Relief filled him and caused more tears to fall. He tightened his embrace and kissed her.

"As much as I enjoy it, I didn't bring you over here for this," J.P. said as he pulled back.

His heart broke into pieces when she moved away from him and said in a quiet voice, "I think I love you too, Jason, and that's not an easy thing for me to say." Looking deeply into his eyes, she continued. "I have to tell you, admitting it makes me feel like I'm sitting in a canoe without oars in the middle of the ocean."

He chuckled. "Wow! Sweetheart, I can definitely relate to your illustration. Just remember I'm there too. At least if we drown, we'll do it together." He pulled her back into his arms and kissed her deeply.

Between kisses he said, "Jaci, you've torn down all my defenses. Everything I am is yours. I will never intentionally hurt you again. Now, I'm realistic enough to know we're going to fuss and fight like all get out. But as long as we keep loving each other and talking through our differences, we'll make it. That's what I want with you, Jaci. Life with all its ups and downs. What do you say? Do we begin building a life together?"

Jaci's eyes filled with tears again and it took a minute to get herself together to speak. She drew a deep breath. "Okay, but just know this. You pull something like this again—leaving me hanging without a word, or trying that caveman act like you did tonight, and I'm going to do some damage to vital parts of your body. I mean that, mister!" Her eyes and the tone of her voice told him she meant every word. He nodded, but before he could say anything she continued, whispering brokenly, "I've missed you so much."

The pieces of his heart cracked even more and tears ran down his face. "I'm so sorry for putting you through that." He pulled her close and again their tears mingled as he kissed her tenderly. The kisses grew in intensity and Jaci moved away from him again.

"Stay where you are," she said, pointing to the other end of the sofa. "We need to talk this through. Tell me, what made you feel so threatened about us that you ran away like that?"

With shame in his eyes, he answered, "Well, believe it or not, I let Ron, Walt, and a couple more of my buddies get to me. They came over here one night, and well . . . by the time they left, I was questioning my sanity. Before then, I was convinced that what we have is exactly what I want. But when those guys finished with me, I was totally confused."

"Jason," she looked directly into his eyes. "I've heard everything you've said tonight, and I know you believe you meant it. But if you can be influenced by your brother or anyone else to the point where you question your own feelings, then maybe you need to do some real soul-searching before you make any kind of promises or commitments tonight."

He moved over to her again and cupped the side of her face in his large hand. "Baby, what do you think I've been doing? I've been having some serious talks with the Lord and with my pastor. I've never prayed like I've been praying the last few weeks. I know . . . have known all along what I wanted. I just let the devil get me off track."

Jaci looked across the room. "And you're sure you really have it settled? Like I've told you before, I can't be going down another wrong path. I've been praying about us too. I just want the will of God for my life. If that includes you, then so be it. If it doesn't, I'd rather deal with it now. Good, *Godly*, relationships are not easy and we both need to be certain of what we want before committing to anything."

He smiled in appreciation of her ability to articulate his own feelings so well and felt the rightness of their relationship settle in his mind. "Sweetheart, I'm a hundred and fifty percent sure. But I've never been in love before. Yeah, I was married, and in and out of affairs. But I never felt about any of those women the way I feel about you. The very core of my existence changed when you came into my life. Now that's a very big adjustment and yes, it's taken some time and prayer for me to get here. My heart, my spirit, has been here all along. I just had to fight and win the battle in my mind."

"So, where do we go from here?"

He moved closer to her and put his arms around her, hugging her tightly. "Let's talk about it. We have the rest of the night and for as long as it takes. But you know what? I'm hungry! Now that we've talked, my appetite is back with a vengeance. Come on, let's see what we can rustle up to eat."

Jaci stood up, kicked off her shoes, and headed into the kitchen. "Yeah, I'm starved. Some psycho forced me to leave the dance before I had a chance to eat."

He laughed as he followed her into the kitchen, hugging her from behind. "But look how much more enjoyable the company is."

They worked together and fixed bacon, eggs, and toast. While they ate, he told her about the talks he'd been having with his pastor.

Jason

Jason had grown to appreciate Gerald Robinson since Gerald had become the pastor of his church. He had known the guy in high school when they played basketball and ran after women together. After high school, they lost touch and had gone down different paths. Jason hadn't seen or heard from him in years. He was blown over when Gerald had been introduced a couple of years ago as the new pastor. He was progressive and a serious advocate of the movement to get men more committed to the Lord and a Christian lifestyle. He arrived at just the time Jason was searching for a new meaning in life. Since then, under Gerald's mentorship, Jason had gradually become more committed to living the Christian life. He still blew it sometimes, but Gerald made him understand that continuing to try was the important thing.

"You know what my pastor's had me doing? By the way, he's really anxious to meet you. Anyway, he's had me studying Scriptures. Many different ones, but I've spent lots of time in Proverbs. He said after I read and took in the wisdom of those Scriptures, I would know what the Lord would have me do about any situation. I read, write down any verse that I think applies to our situation, and then discuss it with him. I'm surprised at how much I enjoy it. And I've really learned a lot."

"But has it helped you in a practical way?"

He answered with an "are you for real" expression. "You better believe it. I didn't know all of that was in there to help us live. I've always been told to read the Bible, but truthfully, I haven't done so on a consistent basis. But it'll be a priority from now on. You know, I would like to share some of my favorite verses with you. Can I?"

Jaci felt the joy bubble up in her heart. She couldn't think of anything that would have pleased her more. With a big grin on her face she answered, "I would love it!"

"I'll be right back," he told her as he ran up the stairs and came back a few minutes later with a Bible and a notebook in his hands.

They spent the next few hours poring over the Scriptures that Jason said had helped him the most. But he confessed that his very favorites were found in Proverbs 31.

"Sweetheart, when I read those verses, I thought of you. The more I read them, the more I saw you in there. Everything described in those verses, I've observed about you. It blew my mind, especially verse twenty-nine." He started reading the verse and continued reading to the end of the chapter.

Jaci looked uncomfortable. "Jason, those verses are talking about this man's wi—"

"I know what they're talking about, honey." He looked deeply into her eyes. "Do you know what I'm saying to you, sweetheart?"

Jaci looked away from the intensity of his eyes. She wasn't ready to deal with what she saw there. "You know what? I'm tired," she said as she glanced at her watch. "Oh my goodness! It's way past time for me to be getting home."

"Why don't you just bunk out here for the rest of the night? I promise you'll be safe. And I'll even feed you some more bacon and eggs when you wake up," he told her, grinning widely. "Trust me?"

She looked hard at him, wondering if she had lost her mind to even consider it. But she remembered the times when he could have taken advantage of her, and how he always protected her, even from herself, then answered, "Yes, I trust you. Give me one of your shirts to sleep in."

He stood and pulled her up with him. Cupping her face in his hands, he whispered, "I don't know if I'm thinking rationally tonight. I have a beautiful woman that I'm crazy in love with in my house, and I'm promising not to touch her! I know something is wrong with me!" Taking her hand, he led her up the stairs and into his spacious bedroom. He went into the closet and came back with a T-shirt in his hands. "You can change in there," he said, pointing to the bathroom.

When she returned dressed in his shirt that reached almost to her knees, he had put on some pajamas and was lying on the bed. "Okay. What room can I sleep in?" she asked him.

"This one," he answered quickly. "I want to spend this whole night with you. And don't worry, I remember my promise."

She looked at him as if he were crazy. "Well! Mr. Proverbs Man. Where has all that wisdom gone? Out the window? Hiding under the bed?"

"Honey, I know what I'm suggesting might not be the wisest thing, but I just don't want us to be apart tonight. We've come so far, gotten so much resolved. I'm just not ready for it to end."

She went into deep thought at what he said. She too felt the fragile bonding that she was reluctant to break. But suddenly a Scripture came to her mind. "Jason, the first thing we have to decide is who we're going to serve in our relationship. We both know we're not the strongest when it comes to resisting the temptation of giving in to our feelings. You've been so good at making sure we don't cross any lines and I appreciate it. I know you think you're strong tonight, but I just recalled a Scripture from Ephesians. It simply says: 'Don't give place to the devil.' My grampa used to put it this way: 'Give the devil an inch, he'll take a mile; let him ride, he'll soon be driving; give him a crack, he'll make a door.' Do you get what I'm saying? One seemingly innocent decision can lead us down a path we didn't intend to follow. And we want our relationship to honor God in every way, right?"

Jason surveyed her, the light of understanding in his eyes. "You're right sweetheart. I just got carried away with the joy of having you here. So what do you want to do?"

"We've talked to each other and talked about the Lord, read His Word, and agreed with it. But the one thing we haven't done tonight is talk to the Lord. Can we just talk to Him together and seek His wisdom and direction in our relationship? And then we're going to bed—in separate rooms."

"Thank you, sweetheart, that's a great idea. It's He who will keep us on the right path."

They talked to the Lord together. Each picking up from where the other left off in presenting their petitions to Him. They prayed until they were almost asleep. Then Jason took her to another bedroom.

Mercies

Jaci

Jaci awoke early the next morning after sleeping soundly. It took her a minute to orient herself, then memories of last night returned. "Lord, thank You for Your mercy, because You were surely with me last night," she said quietly. She slowly slipped out of bed to go into the bathroom, then dressed in her now-rumpled dress.

She knocked on Jason's door before sticking her head in and calling to him softly. He stirred, then raised his head, looking at her with sleepy eyes. "Baby, what are you doing up this early? It's barely daylight. Go back to bed."

"No, I need to get home, I have some things I need to do today." She gasped. "I just remembered, I don't have my car. How am I going to get home?"

He gazed at her for a long minute. "I think you're running away from the progress we made last night. Is that it? If it is, it won't work. We're not going back." When she didn't respond, he gave a long sigh. "Okay. If you insist on leaving at this ungodly hour, you'll have to drive yourself. Take your pick, the Jag or the Navigator?"

"Neither one, really. But I guess the smaller one is the lesser of two evils. Why can't you drive me? How are you going to get your car?"

He got out of bed and handed her the keys to the Jaguar. "I'm going back to bed. Then I have some errands to run. I was hoping to take you with me. But you're not cooperating. Anyway, Patrick is supposed to come by later today. I'll get him to drive me over to get the car."

"And what was I supposed to wear when we ran these errands? I'm not exactly dressed to hang out, you know."

"Oh, we would come up with something. Sure you won't change your mind?"

"No, I don't think so." She knew she needed to do some serious thinking about the big change in their relationship.

When Jaci walked toward the door, J.P. went to the closet and slipped on a robe, then followed her down the hallway to the stairs. She found her purse, shoes, and coat in the family room and waited while he disarmed the alarm system and unlocked the door leading into the garage. He showed her which button on the keyless entrance pad to push to gain entry to the car. "It's pretty powerful. So go easy until you get familiar with it," he cautioned.

"You don't have to tell me that!" She was totally intimidated by the car.

By the time she drove across town in the early morning light, relieved there was not a lot of traffic on the streets, she was enjoying the car. She turned down her street and was surprised to see a car parked in her driveway. As she got closer, she recognized it as Gloria's. Her mouth dropped open in amazement when she realized the possible implications. Gloria had come to her house last night, parked her car, and Bill had picked them both up. Could this mean? . . . Had she been so immersed in her own problems that something had developed between her coworkers without her noticing?

"We . . . lll!" she said to herself. "This is a surprising development. Goodness gracious! Uh! Uh! Uh!"

Then she reminded herself not to jump to any conclusions.

She drove the Jag into the double garage and parked it next to her Jeep. Thankfully, she had thought to tuck the garage opener into her purse along with her keys before leaving last night. Seldom did she use any entrance to her house other than through the garage. She went through the process of unlocking the door to enter the kitchen, going straight to the answering machine to check her messages. To her relief, all was well. She had grown so accustomed to expecting bad news that it was almost a letdown to hear routine messages.

After she showered and slipped into comfortable clothes, Jaci realized she was too mentally and emotionally hyped to relax, so she decided to go grocery shopping and cook dinner for Randi and her family. She knew they hadn't enjoyed a good home-cooked meal in a while. Deep inside, she knew she was just seeking a distraction to avoid thinking about last night. She wasn't ready to deal with all the ramifications just yet. Had Jason almost proposed to her, or had she imagined it?

She decided on the popular African American menu that never failed to delight: baked chicken, greens, macaroni and cheese, candied yams, and cornbread. And she knew Randi would be looking for cheesecake. Since she seldom cooked large meals anymore, usually settling for TV dinners or a salad with a piece of meat grilled on the George Foreman grill, she needed to buy almost everything.

Later, as she stood at the sink washing and re-washing the greens, she berated herself. Of all the grand ideas she had ever had, this was one of the worst. She continued harassing herself throughout the meal preparations, regretting her earlier call disclosing her plans to an excited Randi. She could have caught up on some much needed sleep, or cleaned the house, gone shopping, weeded her flowerbeds. Anything but this. A pizza would have sufficed!

Her doorbell rang just as the food, almost ready, began to produce enticing aromas. She swung open the door to greet Gloria and Bill.

"Hi!" Gloria said. "Bill drove me home last night, so we came by to get my car. We just took a chance and rang the doorbell. Whatcha' doing?"

"Cooking a meal for my daughter and her family," Jaci explained, stepping back. "Ya'll come on in." They stepped through the door, sniffing the air.

"Whoo!" Bill yelled. "Something smells really good. What are you cooking? Do I smell some greens?"

"Yep. Along with some other good stuff. They haven't had a good meal in a while."

"Huh! They better get in line behind me. I ain't going nowhere till I eat. How soon will it be ready?"

"Me neither," Gloria said, kicking off her shoes. "You need some help? I make pretty good cornbread. Just show me where everything is."

Jaci, realizing she had company for dinner whether she wanted it or not, smiled. As she and Gloria left the room, she said, "Why don't you see if there's a game on, Bill? There's bound to be something at this time of the day on a Saturday." Bill picked up the remote and started flipping until he found a game that suited him, then got into it so heartily that he seemed to have forgotten all about the food.

As they bustled around the kitchen, it occurred to Jaci that this was the first time either of her coworkers had visited her home for any length of time. They had come by for a few minutes to drop things off or, in last night's case, to pick her up, but beyond that, there had been no hanging out together. In spite of that, they made themselves right at home.

When Gloria pulled the cornbread out of the oven Jaci noticed that the chicken was beginning to fall off the bones, so she removed it too. Bill saw this and jumped up and shouted, "Grub time is on! Where can I wash my hands?"

After Jaci dished up brimming platefuls, they sat at the small kitchen table and ate like they hadn't seen food in days. Conversation intermittently flowed between mouthfuls, but conspicuously missing was any mention of the happenings of the previous night.

They all groaned when the doorbell rang. Jaci looked at the clock hanging above the table. "It's not time for my daughter and her family to get here. Maybe it's Jason."

When she opened the door, Jason and Patrick stood there, both smiling broadly. "Hey, guys! Come on in."

Jason gave her a quick hug and pressed his lips to hers in a brief kiss, before leading the way into the family room, where he had a view into the kitchen. When he saw her coworkers sitting at the table, he continued walking toward them, asking how they were doing and introducing them to Patrick, who had followed him. Seeing the food on their plates, he turned to Jaci with an accusing look. "You didn't tell me you were going to cook all this food. Is it for us? Looks like one of my favorite meals, especially the greens."

"No, I just decided on the spur of the moment to cook a good meal for Randi and her family. Gloria and Bill just happened to drop by and wouldn't leave until I fed them."

"Well, you're not getting rid of us either. Where are the plates?"

"Pat, are you hungry? Do you want to eat?" Jaci asked Patrick, who was still standing in the middle of the room.

"You gotta be kiddin'! You couldn't melt me and pour me outta here! Hey, did you make cheesecake? You know I love your cheesecake," Patrick said, scrambling in the cabinets for a plate.

"Wait a minute! You guys go wash your hands! You know

better. The bathroom is down the hall to your left. The food will still be here. And yes, as a matter of fact I did bake a cheesecake. It's a favorite of my daughter too."

"Aw, man!" Patrick said, almost running down the hall.

Gloria and Bill continued eating, but had questioning looks on their faces. Apparently, something significant had occurred between J.P. and Jaci last night.

Jaci called Randi and told them to come on over while there was still food left. Good thing Jaci didn't know how to cook in small quantities.

Later, after everyone had eaten their fill and left, Jaci and Jason snuggled together on the sofa. "I just realized why I'm so beat!" Jaci said. "I didn't get much sleep last night."

"Uh! Wonder why?" Jason asked with a chuckle, which quickly faded as he turned serious. "Sweetheart, have you given any thought to what we talked about last night?"

He had done all the praying and thinking he could do. His mother was right. He knew his own mind. There was no way he was going to let Jaci get away from him. He would never find a woman more suited to him than she was. All he had to do was convince her that they had something worth keeping. He spent the morning shopping for an engagement ring. Now his only hope was that Jaci would accept his proposal. He felt like a nervous teenager on his first date.

"Not really, why?"

"Because last night changed everything. I meant it when I said that I love you and I hope you did too."

"Yes, I do, but . . . I think we should move very slowly and carefully from this point on. Just to make sure these feelings are real and not just about, you know . . . physical attraction." She hesitated nervously, not knowing how to continue. "We both know there's a real . . . uh . . . a really powerful chemistry between us. To be honest," she looked at him directly, "I admit that I'm human, with all the feelings and desires that go along with being human, but I'm a Christian and I can't give in to them. I made that mistake once, I won't do it again. I . . . we have to exercise self-control, no matter how powerful the attraction. Otherwise, we can't expect God to bless what we have."

Jason nodded in understanding. "Well, I don't disagree with that and I'll try to be patient with your need to move slowly. But I'm sure about what I feel. I love you and as far as I'm concerned, what we have is permanent." He reached into his pocket, pulled out a small velvet box, and opened it to reveal a very large pear-shaped diamond ring. "Jaci, I love you very much. Will you do me the honor of becoming my wife? And as soon as possible, please?"

"Oh my God, Jason! What? I . . . I wasn't expecting this. I don't know what to say."

"You say, 'yes.' And if you had gone with me to run my errands today, you would have had the privilege of picking out your engagement ring. Do you like this one? If not, we can exchange it."

Jaci was still sitting with her mouth open. "It's beautiful, honey. I couldn't have made a more perfect choice."

"Well, are you going to give me an answer or keep me in suspense?"

"Yes, I'll marry you. But . . ." She hesitated, and her eyes filled with tears. "You'll have to bear with me because I need plenty of time. As you well know, I have some trust issues and I don't want to rush into anything that will ultimately make both of us miserable. In fact, I suggest we consider going through premarital counseling. We may find out we're totally incompatible. And I want to make you happy, not sorry you married me."

"I don't think that's going to happen, but I agree, the counseling is a good idea," said Jason. "But Jaci, understand this:

We can't wait too long, okay? I'm ready right now. If it was up to me, we would get married today."

"Jason! See, there you go, didn't we just agree to . . ."

"Okay, okay!" He held up his hands in surrender. "I'll back off for now, as long as we agree not to wait too long. We're not getting any younger and I want all the time I can get with you."

Feeling uncertain about how she should respond, Jaci scrambled for something else to talk about. "Is Wynola a friend of yours?"

His look let her know he was aware of what she was doing, before answering. "More of an acquaintance. I've known her for years." He didn't mention how the woman had always flirted with him. "Why do you ask?"

"Well I saw her sitting at your table last night and I was just wondering."

"She and Linda seem to know each other. That's why she was sitting there."

"She and Linda? Ooookay! That explains why I've been having such a hard time with Wynola lately."

"What kind of hard time?"

Jaci relayed her ongoing problems with Wynola that had caused an uncomfortable working environment.

"What! And you don't know what's gotten into her?" Suddenly, he snapped his fingers. "I wasn't paying much attention last night since my mind was on other things, but as I think about it, they were very chummy. I need to find out what the relationship is between them. Don't worry about it, though, I know how to get her off your back. In any case, you won't have to deal with it much longer. As soon as we're married, you're out of there."

"Wait a minute! Who said anything about me quitting my job? That's something we'll have to talk about."

"Well, I don't want to talk about it now. I just want to enjoy this time with you. But we'll see." He had every intention of winning that particular argument. When the phone rang a few minutes later, they were so involved with each other that it caused them both to jump.

Maxie

axie impatiently waited as the telephone rang on the other end. He hoped Jacetta was home since it was the weekend, but he was prepared to hang up if the answering machine came on. He refused to leave any more messages. He was almost surprised when she answered.

"Jacetta? This is Maxie. What's happening?" There was a long pause on the other end before she answered.

"Maxie, let me give you my daughter's number. That way you won't ever have to call here again." She rattled off the number to him. "She knows you'll probably be calling."

"How're you doing?" Maxie asked. "You can't talk to a brother for a few minutes?"

"No I can't, I'm busy," she said before hanging up the phone.

Maxie wasn't at all thrilled by her action and refused to accept it. He quickly redialed the number.

Again, he heard her intriguing voice say "Hello?" with a question in it. "Jacetta, Maxie again. You know, for the sake of our daughter, I was hoping things could at least be amiable between us. This continued hostility on your part is not helping anybody. Did George call and talk to you?"

Jaci took a deep breath before speaking, then decided she just couldn't let it pass. "First of all, don't insult me by saying things like 'our daughter.' You and I both know those words are not a true depiction. Secondly, what you're calling hostility is really indifference. The hostility went out the window a long time ago. As a matter of fact, it happened on one of those days when I had to take on two more jobs just to make sure my daughter would have food, clothes, and a decent roof over her head. Let me be more specific. It was the day I stopped hoping and gave up on you somehow catching a little decency and maturity and realizing your obligation to a little baby girl you were partly responsible for bringing into this world. Don't try to lay a guilt trip on me, mister. Because as far as I'm concerned, any guilt to be claimed is all yours. Thirdly, yes I did speak to my uncle. And since you're too dense to know it, I've already given you much more than you deserve, and I meant it when I said there's no need for you to call here again, Maxie. Like I said, I'm busy and I would appreciate it if you would adhere to my wishes."

Maxie was quiet for a moment before continuing. "I don't know what that is if it's not hostility. That just let's me know that we need to talk and clear the air between us. I was thinking that I could come down there one weekend so we could get together and . . ." He was still talking when he heard the dial tone in his ear. She had hung up again.

He slowly replaced the phone, fighting back what he recognized as anger. He'd heard a man's voice in the background telling her to hang up. He was tempted to call back again, but figured it wouldn't be wise. His determination stiffened. She was crazy if she thought he was going to go quietly away.

Jaci

*A*round two in the morning, long after Jason left, Jaci's phone rang, dragging her out of a deep sleep. Her heart beat wildly as she picked it up, filled with dread and bracing herself for bad news. She knew a call at this time of night couldn't be good. "Hello?" she answered in a sleepy, questioning voice.

A woman's menacing voice came across the line. "Heifer, you must be real stupid! Or don't you understand plain English?" Cold chills ran up Jaci's spine as the woman continued. "Looks like I'll have to do something else to let you know I'm not playing with you." The woman paused for a second as if she expected a response, and when she didn't get one she continued. "If you don't leave J.P. alone, I'll see to it that you'll be very sorry."

Jaci was still sitting up in bed holding the receiver long after the woman hung up. She knew when she finally laid the receiver back in the phone cradle that she wouldn't get any more sleep. Who in the world could that have been? She searched her sleep-fogged mind for possible suspects. Maybe it was a wrong number, she thought, grasping for any explanation that would make sense. But no, the woman had mentioned J.P. She was definitely the target. She shivered, realizing this potentially dangerous person had threatened her.

After church the next day, she had lunch with Sister Sadie's family, then checked on Randi and the baby, and finally went home and waited to hear from Jason. He called around four, and she told him about Linda's threat at his office and the harassing call she had received.

"Why haven't you told me about this before? Doggone it! Jaci, when are you going to realize you don't have to handle everything by yourself?"

"Well, to be honest, when Linda said those things, I thought maybe she was just angry because you had just yelled at her for making me wait so long. And I was trying to give her the benefit of the doubt. I didn't want to get her into trouble if it was just a passing thing. But after last night . . . well . . . I don't know. I can't be certain it was Linda, but I can't think of anybody else it could be. What about you? Do you have some woman with a fatal attraction for you? If so, let me know so I can cut you loose right now."

"No, I don't know anybody with a fatal attraction for me," he said in aggravation. "And no, you're not cutting me loose. It's not hard for me to believe it's Linda. I know for a fact that she's had a little thing for me, but I didn't think she was crazy enough to do something like this. She's outta there!"

"No," Jaci objected. "Don't do that. Not until we know for sure it's her. She could be innocent. And I'd hate to be the cause of her losing her job if she is."

"We'll see. In any case, I want to know if you get any more of those threats. Okay?"

J.P.

Thanksgiving Dinner

The Gilmore Family Thanksgiving dinner rotated from house to house each year, and now it was J.P.'s turn to host. It wasn't a big deal because he had everything catered, with the exception of his mother's and aunts' stuffing and sweet potato and pecan pies.

Jaci reluctantly accepted his invitation to join his family for dinner. She hated the thought of meeting all of his family at one time, and she hated social affairs anyway, especially with people she didn't know.

"Okay," she told him unenthusiastically. "I'll come, but I have to leave early."

"Why don't you invite Randi and her family? That way, we'll all be together and you won't have to leave."

"No, they always go to John's parents for most of the day, then come to visit me for a while."

"And where do you usually go?"

"Sometimes I go to church, then spend the day by myself relaxing. And sometimes I hit several places where I've been invited. It just depends on how I feel."

"That's over," he said, not liking the idea of her spending the holiday alone.

Jaci arrived on Thanksgiving Day with a beautiful floral arrangement for J.P.'s table. "You told me not to bring any food, but I wanted to bring something," she explained.

"You didn't have to bring anything but yourself," he said hugging her tightly, pleased at her thoughtfulness. He knew the women in his family would be impressed.

Lots of people were already there. Several women bustled around in the kitchen, and, of course, the men and a few women sat in front of the big screen television watching a game.

Jason led her around the house, introducing her to everyone.

"Well, it's about time!" a heavyset, nice-looking woman emphatically stated when they stepped into the kitchen. "I'm Cecelia Gilmore, this guy's mother. He's been in big trouble for not bringing you to meet me. I'm very happy to finally meet the woman who has made my son so happy." She inspected Jaci appraisingly from head to toe, summing up everything about her in that comprehensive look. "We'll have a talk sometime today. After all I've heard about you, it's time I found out a few things myself."

"Don't look so scared," her husband, Big Pat, said, coming over to hug her. "Her bark is worse than her bite."

"And yours is not?" Jaci asked, remembering his proposal on J.P.'s behalf. They both laughed.

Jaci was still carrying the flowers. She handed them to Cecelia and asked, "May I help with anything? I'm not really a good kitchen hand, but I'd like to help if there's anything you need me to do."

"Don't believe that, Mom!" J.P. said laughingly. "This woman can cook. Just ask Patrick. And you know what a picky eater he is."

Cecelia accepted the flowers with a big smile. "These are beautiful. Thank you so much. I'll just go put them on the table right now. And yes, you can help us get the food set out so everyone can serve themselves."

Jaci

Jaci went to work helping Cecelia, glad to have something to do.

More people arrived, including a man with a cynical look on his face, whom Jason introduced as his brother, Ron. He, too, examined her in an assessing way, and Jaci could tell just by his eyes that he might try to start trouble with her.

They finally organized the food and got everyone seated at a table. Most of the older people sat around the large dining room table. The young adults staked out the kitchen area, and portable tables were set up in the family room for the children and those unwilling to leave the game on television.

They all ate heartily, and most of the massive amounts of food disappeared.

After the meal, Jaci wandered into the beautiful living room, which was decorated in white with gold and black accents. She stood admiring the black art in the form of framed paintings and sculptures, as well as the impressive white grand piano, sitting in a place of prominence, when she heard someone walk up behind her.

"What do you think? You like the decor in here?" Cecelia asked, looking at one of the pieces of art.

"Yes, I do. Although it's rather cold and sterile," Jaci answered.

"Well, I don't like it. It's too stark, not enough color, no plants or anything to make it homey. But what do I know? That professional decorator J.P. hired said it was perfect."

"If you saw my house, you would know that I agree with you about the color. I like vibrant colors too. But I do like the clean uncluttered look in here. Probably, what you don't like is that it looks more like a showroom than a living room."

"Hmmm! You're right. It does look more like a showroom than a room to be lived in. What say we sit down and put it to some use?" As both took a seat across from each other on the matching white sofas, she continued. "Why don't you tell me a little about yourself?"

Jaci felt like she was on trial. "Okay. Let's see. I grew up in a small community known as Riverwood, Arkansas. I come from a very large family. After I graduated from college, I moved to Dallas, and later, here. I have a daughter whom I raised by myself, and two grandchildren. I work for the city in the Housing Compliance Department—been there over twenty years. For the last few months, I've had the opportunity to work part-time for Jason, doing some quality control work, and I love it. I'm a member of the Grace Community Church, where I sing in the choir and every once in a while get to teach a Sunday school class. I've been there almost as long as I've lived in Houston. And . . . let's see . . . I think that about covers everything."

"How long have you lived here in Houston?"

"Over twenty-two years."

"And what made you decide to move here? Did you have family already here?"

"No, I didn't. I moved here to take a job. But when it didn't work out, I ended up working for the city. I hadn't planned to be there long—just until I could find something better. But shortly after I started, the bottom fell out of the economy, and jobs became scarce, so I was glad to have it. After I had been there long enough to have a little seniority and get vested, it made sense to stick it out."

"Mom! Are you in here interrogating Jaci?" J.P., followed by his dad, came into the room. His uncle Stanley didn't lose any time following them. Then came Uncle Stan's wife, Aunt Lucille.

"Oh Lord!" Jaci thought. "Now I'm really in for it."

J.P. sat on the armrest of the sofa where Jaci was sitting, facing his parents. His aunt and uncle sat beside Jaci. Jaci felt Jason's arm slide around her, pulling her close to him. She knew he was trying to show his support, but actually, all he did was make her feel more uncomfortable.

"Oh, so this is where everyone ran off to!" Patrick and one of the cousins came into the room with cameras. Patrick carried a video camera, and the cousin a digital camera. "Hold still and smile everybody," the cousin said. "Just act natural everybody and keep talking," Patrick added.

When the cousin (Jaci couldn't remember his name) pointed the camera toward her and Jason, Patrick yelled, "Wait!" He hurriedly put the video camera down and ran to sit on the floor between Jaci and Jason, throwing his arms over their laps. Jason tightened his arm around her shoulders and leaned in even closer to her for the picture. "Will you move?" she said tersely after the picture was snapped.

"Nope!" he answered calmly.

She looked around the room again and her eyes landed on the piano. "Who plays? Or is that just a showpiece?"

"Oh no," his mother said. "J.P. plays, and plays well—both the piano and the organ. So does Patrick if you can ever get him to sit down and play."

Jaci looked up at J.P. with surprise. "Well, I've found out something new about you today. I didn't know you were a musician. I'm impressed."

"I keep trying to tell you I have all kinds of talents. Just keep hanging around, you'll see."

Before she could respond to his bragging, his mother asked, "What about you, Jaci? Do you play?"

"Well, I like to try. But I don't know if I could be called a musician. I love piano and organ music. Jason, you'll have to play something for me sometime."

"We'll have to get ya'll teamed up one of these days," Aunt Lucille said. "Maybe at our next Family and Friends Day program at church."

"Um. I don't know about that," Jaci replied, shaking her head. "I don't know if I'm that good." She looked at her watch. "Oh my, I'll have to be leaving shortly so I can spend some time with my family. I'll be happy to help get the kitchen in order before I leave though."

Cecelia jumped up. "A girl after my own heart. Come on; let's get to it. I'll be ready for my nap pretty soon."

They made quick work of putting leftovers in storage containers and cleaning up the kitchen. They were almost finished when Jason's brother and a guy introduced as Walt strolled into the kitchen.

Uh! Oh! Jaci thought to herself. *These guys are out for blood.*

"Soooo! Jaci. Is that your name? Jaci?" Ron asked mockingly.

"Actually, my name is Jacetta. Jacetta Pauline Winters. It just got shortened over the years to Jaci. Anything else you want to know about my name?"

"So you're a J.P. too? Isn't that special," Ron said sarcastically.

"Yeah, man," Walt agreed. "I'd say that was real special."

"Well, yes, I hadn't thought about it, but I guess I am a J.P. What's your point, Ronnie Man?"

He squirmed. He didn't like being called Ronnie. "Just trying to get to know you. Soooo, what kind of, uh . . . for lack of a better word, 'whupping' you done put on my brother that's got him all bent out of joint?"

"Ron!" at least three people yelled out.

"Now you're being rude, Ronald, and you know better than that," his mother said huffily, hands on her ample hips. "You're not too old to get *your* butt whipped. Just remember that."

"Ron, you're way out of line," J.P. told his brother angrily. "You can't act no better than that, maybe you better leave."

"No!" Jaci stepped in quickly. "Let me and Ronnie Man finish our conversation." She looked at a troubled J.P. "Trust me, I got it, baby."

She walked over to Ron, smiling. "Go for it, big boy! You too, Walt."

Walt, realizing they may have caught a tiger by the tail, backed up a little, hands in the air.

"Like I said before I was so rudely interrupted," Ron rolled his eyes around the room. "What you done put on my brother that's got his mind all messed up?"

"Love, Ron," Jaci answered. "Simple, old-fashioned love. Do you know what that is?"

"Lady, I can write a book on what I know about love. Can you?"

"No, I can't. But I don't have to. The only book I need is already written. And there's more in there than I'll ever be able to use."

"Is that right? Well what part of that book have you used on my brother?"

"Oh, I'm going to tell you. You may want to write it down for future reference. Just so we don't have to go over this again."

"Naw, that's all right." Ron looked a little nervous. The conversation wasn't going as planned. He'd intended to embarrass her, intimidate her, and make her feel uncomfortable. However, she was standing up to him in a way he hadn't expected.

"Well, listen real closely. I know it sounds strange, but I love using this portion of the book on people." The kitchen had filled with people watching the intense exchange. J.P. relaxed against a kitchen counter with a smile on his face as he watched Jaci holding her own with Ron.

Jaci continued. "This book is called the Holy Bible. Ever heard of that book, guys? Anyway, in that book, in First Corinthians chapter thirteen, you'll find the love potion I've been using on Jason."

A loud laugh went up from those familiar with the verses Jaci was about to quote.

Ron looked most uncomfortable. But before he could say anything, Jaci began to quote the verses in a quiet but forceful voice. "This love is very patient and kind, never jealous or envious, never boastful or proud, never selfish or rude to others, never demands its own way, is never irritable, doesn't hold grudges, hardly ever notices when others do it wrong, is never glad about injustice, but rejoices when right wins. It's loyal no matter what the cost, always looks for the best and always defends. This love, Ron and Walt, never, ever ends.

"Now. What part of my love potion do you all object to?" When they didn't answer right away, she snapped her fingers in their faces and said, "I rest my case." She headed straight for Jason, who embraced her, while everyone else who had crowded into the kitchen began to clap and laugh.

Ron and Walt stood there speechless for a few seconds. Then a big grin spread over Ron's face and he hollered out, "I'm in love!" and followed Jaci across the room, reaching for her with outstretched arms.

"Not with this lady!" J.P. said, laughing as he pushed Ron away.

Cecelia and Big Pat crossed the room to where the couple stood. Cecelia folded Jaci in a big hug and said to Jason, "You hit the jackpot with this one, son. You better not let her get away!"

"I'm trying, Mom," Jason replied as he grabbed Jaci's hand and pointed to the diamond ring on her finger. "If you can say or do anything to make this woman hurry up and marry me, you'd make me a happy man. I've gotten down on my knees and begged, stood on my head and pleaded, walked, chewed gum, rubbed my stomach and patted my head at the same time, and promised her anything I think she might want. And she just won't cooperate."

Everyone cracked up as J.P. attempted to act out everything he described. "Will you stop!" Jaci yelled, embarrassed and all of a sudden hot and flushed.

"Jaci," Cecelia said to her. "I want to welcome you to the family. And I want you to know that I didn't raise my sons to be playboys. Those old crazy women out there ruined them. I hope you won't keep this one waiting too long, since he's trying to straighten up." She hugged her again.

"You know, Ron," Big Pat said to his other son. "If you're smart, you'll be trying to find the field where this one came from and get you one just like her."

"You're wasting your breath on that one, honey. He's hopeless," Cecelia told her husband.

When everything had calmed down, Jaci retrieved her purse. "It's getting late and I should've already been across town." She headed toward the door.

"Wait, babe, I'll walk you out," J.P. said, following her.

"I like the way you handled Ron and Walt," he chuckled when they were alone. "You won't have to worry about them again. Now I'll have to watch and keep them from trying to steal you away from me. You're special, honey. You know that? My mother loves you. And that's no small thing. Now, when are we going to set a date?" He backed her up against her truck, trapping her. "I don't like your having to leave me like this. I'm tired of having to snatch time with you. Tired of having to restrain myself with you. It's never enough."

Jaci went on the defensive, knowing she was wrong. "Oh. So what are you trying to say? That if we don't get married soon, you'll have to go out and find somebody else to fill your needs?"

Jason backed up in surprise. "Now how did you reach that conclusion? You know that's not what I meant. You're just trying to start something because you don't want to deal with the issue. It's not going to work, Jaci. And to answer your question, no, I don't plan to go out and find somebody else. You're the only one I want. Sweetheart, can't we talk about this without getting into a fight?"

Jaci pulled him back to her. "I'm sorry. And you're right, I'm not ready to deal with the issue. But we did agree to move slowly. Can't you be a little more patient?"

Jason sighed. "My patience is wearing pretty thin. I talked to my pastor last week about starting our counseling. He said we could start whenever we're ready. I'm ready, sweetheart."

"Did we agree that your pastor would do the counseling?" Jaci inquired. "I don't remember."

"Well, if I remember correctly, the consensus was that since you'll be joining my church, my pastor should be the one to do the counseling. Am I correct?"

"Yeah, I guess so," she answered slowly.

"So when?" he pushed.

"Jason! Now is not the time for this conversation. I need to get across town. I'll call you later."

"Maybe I can come over after I get everybody out of here. Is that okay?" He kissed her softly. "I need to spend some time with you, sweetheart. Alone."

"I'll call you when I get home," she responded, hugging him close. "I really need to go. I'm expected to show up at Sister Sadie's before going to Randi's."

"Doggone it! There's no telling what time you'll get home," he anguished, groaning into her neck. "Well, whatever time you get there, call me, okay?" He gave her a long kiss before opening the truck door and then closing it when she slid behind the wheel. "Be careful, honey."

"Okay, I will. Talk to you later."

Jaci headed out of the cul-de-sac. Jason stood watching until she was out of sight, then walked slowly back into the house.

Across the street and down a ways, hidden from view behind tinted car windows, watchful eyes had taken in everything. As Jaci drove past the car, malevolent emotions, so strong she should have felt them, were sent in her direction.

Linda

Linda's hatred of Jaci intensified, incited by the knowledge that she had lost J.P. to the woman. She knew that drastic steps would have to be taken to get Jaci out of the picture. She had called and warned her off, but evidently Jaci had not gotten the message. She wished she had found a way to really get her point across before J.P. came into the office and joyfully announced that his single days were almost over—that Jaci had agreed to marry him. Linda was so disillusioned that another man was about to get away, she had to take the rest of the day off.

It angered Linda that Jaci was where she should be . . . wearing J.P.'s engagement ring, having Thanksgiving dinner with his family, receiving his kisses. She refused to give up, though! It was time Jaci got the message once and for all. Linda meant to have J.P. by any means necessary.

Jaci

A few days later, Jaci pulled the mail out of her mailbox and noticed a folded piece of paper among the usual correspondence. What she read caused her to gasp and her heart to start beating double time. Written across the page in large typewritten text were the words,

"I know where you live, and your family too. If you value your and your family's lives, you'll stay away from J.P."

She called Jason, who immediately drove to her home, then notified the police. An officer soon arrived, made a report, and said the department would investigate. Unless they could prove Linda was the one who wrote the threatening note, however, there was really nothing they could do.

The next day, Wynola's secretary called to inform Jaci that Wynola wanted to see her. Filled with dread, Jaci prayed silently as she slowly walked to Wynola's office, knowing it would be nothing good. *Lord, please let Your strength sustain me. Thank You for being a present help in the time of trouble.*

A smug, triumphant expression covered Wynola's face when Jaci entered the office.

"Jaci, I've received another serious complaint against you. This time, you've really given me no choice but to take disciplinary actions. And I'm sure Mr. Shannon is behind me on this, so there's no need to go running to him."

"What are you talking about? And I've never run to Mr. Shannon about anything."

"Read this." Wynola threw a sheet of paper across the desk.

As Jaci began reading the typewritten letter, her mouth fell open and she felt herself grow cold.

I am appealing to the management of the Housing Compliance Department for help. I am at my wit's end trying to save my family. I have pleaded with Ms. Jaci Winters several times to leave my husband alone, but though he's told her he wants to end their affair, she ruthlessly pursues him, demanding that he continue it. She has no consideration for his wife and three children. I am outraged that the department would continue to spend taxpayers' money employing a person with such low morals as this woman has demonstrated in her refusal to stop trying to break up my family. I hope I can depend on you to assist me in this matter. Otherwise, I will be forced to seek help from the mayor and the citizens of Houston. I am sure this would prove to be embarrassing and detrimental to your department.

Thank you, Ms. Jean White

Jaci fought to remain calm. "Wynola, this is a bunch of crap. I'm not dating a married man, and this is the first time

I've ever heard of a Jean White. Who is this man I'm supposed to be having an affair with anyway?"

"Don't try to play dumb with me, Ms. Winters," Wynola
responded in an overly professional tone. "No woman would
write this kind of letter unless she were desperate. This has to
be her last hope, bless her heart. And, of course, you can't
grasp this, but being a married woman, I can certainly em-
pathize with her. I have no choice but to issue you a first-step
disciplinary letter. Of course you know, any additional infrac-
tions or complaints will result in suspension without pay,
until we can remove you from the payroll."

"Just like that! Without an investigation or anything, you're
ready to take my job. You're taking the word of someone
you've never heard of over someone you've known for years?
I find this very interesting. Well I want you to know, Wynola,
that I'm not fighting this battle by myself. I've . . ."

Wynola interrupted. "I don't care who you think you have
behind you, Jaci. They won't be able to help you with this.
You should have thought about this before you got involved
with somebody else's husband and brought this kind of slander into this department."

Jaci stood up to go. "You misunderstood. I wasn't talking
about earthly help. With this kind of evil threatening me, I
need more than that. No, I was talking about help from my
Heavenly Father. You see, I've already turned you and this entire situation over to Him. I need a copy of this." She started
to turn with the letter in her hand.

"You ain't turning me over to no doggone body!" Wynola
stood up so roughly that the back of her chair hit the wall
with a bang. "And give me that letter. I'll get you a copy of it
later," she said, reaching for the letter.

"Oh but I have turned you over," Jaci replied calmly. "And
I don't mind making the copy. I'll be right back." She left the
office quickly, praying as she went.

Lord, have mercy! She prayed. *Mercy, Lord! I need Your mercy! Deliver me from this snare of the devil. Mercy, Lord!*

For the next several nights, her phone rang every hour with threatening words from the woman. Jaci had to resort to turning the ringers off every night. Each morning her answering machine was full of vile threats from the same sinister voice. "Get away from J.P. or you'll be sorry! I'm not playing with you, heifer, I'll kill you and your family." Jaci also received the same kind of threatening calls at work.

Jaci endured almost no sleep, concerned about what the woman would do next, and was troubled that the woman had brought the threats to her job. She was sure the bogus letter from "Jean White" was somehow connected to the woman, but she didn't know how to prove it.

Then, Jaci found notes on her truck daily that showed pictures of a woman with a knife in her chest. "You're dead!" the notes read. The same message was scratched into the paint on her truck. She felt like the woman had invaded every area of her life. This woman knew everything about Jaci, even down to the kind of vehicle she drove. *Oh God, have mercy! Help me, Lord*, was her constant prayer.

Bill told her not to worry—that he was working on it. But Jaci didn't hold out much hope. What could Bill do anyway?

Bill was doing a lot! He made sure a copy of the letter got into the hands of Ed Shannon, with a warning that if Ed didn't move quickly, he would go to the mayor himself. It was time for Jaci to get some help in this situation before Wynola succeeded in her efforts to fire Jaci.

After the third sleepless night, Jaci couldn't face work the following day. Jason had been out of town several days and had returned late last night. Although they talked, she had been reluctant to bother him with such stupidity while he was out of town. But she was tired and weary from lack of sleep and knew she had to let him know what was going on. She waited until 7 a.m. to call, hoping he would already be awake. Strangely, she didn't get an answer and wondered where he could be this early in the morning. Thinking maybe he was in the shower, she left a message and waited for him to call her back. Thirty minutes later, he had still not called. She used her cell phone strictly for emergencies and tried not to call others on theirs unless absolutely necessary. She decided this was one of those times and dialed his cell phone.

"What's up, sweetheart? This is a pleasant surprise. Is anything wrong?" Jason asked when he answered a few minutes later.

She was so relieved to hear his voice she was almost in tears. "Jason? Where are you? I really need to talk to you."

"I'm at the office, honey. Remember? This is moving day." She hadn't remembered, but realized that was one reason why he had been so busy lately. Jason had purchased the thirty-story building where his office was located. In addition to moving his own offices to another floor, he was also moving the real estate business and his brother Ron's architectural firm into the building. He decided to keep the current tenants who wanted to renew their leases with him and would begin leasing the remaining vacant space to new tenants the first of the year. Jason wanted the family businesses settled in before he advertised any available space.

"No, I didn't remember," Jaci said softly. "Jason, I have to talk to you. Right away."

"It'll have to wait, sweetheart. There's no way I'll be able to get away from here today. It's total chaos. I'm trying to get my own office ready, as well as supervise everything else going on. Want to come help me?"

"Not really. But if that's what I have to do to talk to you, I guess I'll have to do that. Where should I come? To your old office or to the one on the top floor?"

"You're going to ditch work and come over here? I feel really honored," he said, a smile in his voice.

"Jason, I'm not going to work today. I stayed home because I need to talk to you. I'm sorry, I forgot all about this being moving day. But sometime today, we have to talk."

Finally noticing her serious tone, Jason stopped his trek from one end of the building to the other and said, "Come to my old office. I'll be in and out of there, so that's where you're likely to catch me."

"Okay. I should be there in an hour or so," Jaci informed him.

"Sweetheart? Is everything okay?"

"I don't want to discuss it over the phone. We'll talk when I get there."

"Okay. See you then."

Jaci quickly showered, threw on some jeans with a comfortable blouse and some sneakers, and headed to Jason's office. It was going to be interesting to see if Linda was there. If she was making those threatening calls all night, and was still able to go to work the next day, then she was one tough sister; Jaci admitted it had taken its toll on her.

Sure enough, when Jaci stepped off the elevator on Jason's floor, the first person she saw was Linda, haughtily giving directions to the movers. When she spotted Jaci, her body stiffened and a deep scowl covered her face.

She'll never see me looking defeated, Jaci decided. "Good morning!" she said cheerfully as she passed through the reception area. "How are you all doing?"

"J.P. is not in his office, and he's very busy. He has no time for you today," Linda told her.

"I know he's busy. That's why I'm here to help him. He told me to go straight to his office."

"Well, you're going to have a long wait. There's no telling

when he'll be back. You might as well leave. You'll just be in the way."

"I don't think so." Jaci looked at her challengingly. "I know how to make myself useful."

She entered Jason's office and saw that he had made little headway in preparing for the move. *Where is his secretary? She wondered, then remembered: The woman is off on maternity leave. And Linda is too busy playing Ms. Important to offer any real help.* Shaking her head and thinking he should have hired a company to pack up his offices as well as move them, she grabbed a box from the stack in the hallway and began carefully packing the items from the top of his desk. Once that was done, she took a marker and wrote JPG–DESKTOP–FRAGILE on the side of the box. She emptied his desk drawers and marked the boxes, then proceeded to the credenza. She was working on the first of several bookshelves when she heard Jason's voice in the hallway.

Finally, she thought. *Maybe I can get this over with.*

But when Jason entered his office, his brother Ron was close behind him. "Wow! Honey look what you've done!" Jason remarked, crossing the room to hug and kiss her. "This is going to move me up on the ready list. You think you can stay long enough to help me get my new office set up? I sure hope so."

"I don't know right now," she said softly. "Jason, why didn't you hire a moving company whose services include packing everything as well as moving it? It would have made this so much easier."

Jason and Ron looked at each other. "I made the mistake of delegating that responsibility to Uncle Stan, who said he had a friend in the business who could do it all. To make a long story short, they showed up with four men, and no instructions to pack anything."

"I tried to tell him, but he wouldn't listen," Ron said as he followed Jason across the room. Jaci was a little uneasy, not knowing what to expect from Ron after their little scene on Thanksgiving Day. But surprisingly, he was cordial and friendly. "Hey, Sis," he said, engulfing her in a bear hug. "When you finish in here, can you come help me get set up?"

"Nope!" J.P. answered for her. "She'll be too busy helping me. Go find your own help."

"I was talking to Jaci!" Ron said pointedly.

"I was answering for Jaci," J.P. replied.

"Just let me have the keys," Ron said, agitatedly. He looked at Jaci, who had resumed her task of packing boxes with books from the bookshelves. "Jaci, you wouldn't know how to pick a lock on a file cabinet would you? Somebody locked it and I lost the key to it years ago."

"Sorry, no. If I had time, I could probably fiddle with it and get it open—I've had to do that before—but I gotta take care of my baby now."

Jason handed him a key ring filled with an assortment of keys. "Please bring my keys back. Don't make me have to come looking for you."

Ron gave him a "get lost" look before strolling slowly out of the office.

"Okay, sweetheart," Jason said when Ron left. "What did you need to talk to me about? Make it quick; they're waiting for me downstairs."

"This isn't something we can discuss quickly. I'll just wait here until you have more time."

As if on cue, his cell phone began ringing. When he looked at it, he sighed. "Gotta go." He gave her a brief kiss and said, "I'll be back as soon as I can, okay?"

"Yeah. Okay."

Jaci worked steadily for another hour, then decided to find a water fountain to quench her thirst. She picked her way around the furniture and boxes cluttering the hallway, and walked toward the reception area, fervently hoping Linda was someplace else. No such luck! Jaci saw her immediately after she turned the corner. She glanced around quickly to see if anyone else was nearby. She didn't relish being alone with this woman. As luck would have it, there seemed to be nobody in the near vicinity. Linda seemed to realize this fact at the same time.

"Well, well," Linda said nastily. "I guess you have a really thick skull. Or are you just plain stupid? Frankly, I don't care which one, because you have pushed me too far. I've warned you and tried to give you every opportunity to leave J.P. alone, but you just won't listen."

"Lord, have mercy," Jaci said. "So it is you calling and making threats against me and my family. I suspected as much, but I asked Jason not to do anything until we knew for sure. I was trying to give you the benefit of the doubt."

"I don't need you to do me any favors. What you need to do is get out of J.P.'s life. What do you think a little nobody like you can do for a man like J.P.? He's just stringing you along, honey—having fun. When he's ready to settle down, he's going to do so with a high-class woman, and I'm sure that's not going to be anyone but me."

Jaci held up her hand and pointed to the ring on her finger. "Now, that's a strange thing for you to be saying since I'm the one with his ring on my finger. Why don't you stop all this childish silliness? A truly high-class woman wouldn't resort to what you're doing. Where's the water fountain? I'm thirsty." She turned to leave.

Linda crossed the room and grabbed Jaci's arm, swinging her around. "Don't you walk away from me! Who do you think you're talking to anyway? I'll take that tasteless ring off your finger and jam it down your throat! And don't think I can't do it!"

"What the heck is going on here?" Ron asked from the doorway where he and some other people had gathered.

Now they show up, Jaci thought as she looked down at Linda's hand on her arm. "I know you better get your hands off of me." She pulled away from her and tried to walk off again.

"What's going on, Jaci?" Ron asked again.

"Ask J.P. who went to L.A. with him last month," Linda taunted, grabbing at Jaci's arm again. She smiled confidently. She was certain Jaci hadn't gone with him because she had called her house several times while J.P. was gone and Jaci had answered each time. And if Jaci was home, there was no way she would know who was in L.A. with J.P.

Jaci pulled away from her. "You're crazy!" she said. "As a matter of fact, I went to L.A. with Jason. My daughter told me somebody kept calling and hanging up. Now I know it was you." Jaci shook her head sadly at this woman's desperation. Randi and her family had stayed at Jaci's house a few days while having some work done on their house. And she and Randi sounded almost identical over the phone.

"You're lying!" Linda screamed. "I went with him on that trip. And we had a ball!"

She'd had enough. Jaci looked at the pitiful woman standing before her. "Listen, I'm not going to argue with you. You need to go get yourself some help." She turned to leave and Linda grabbed her again, this time trying to slap her but missing when Jaci dodged out of the way.

"I told you before, you don't run anything in this office, and you don't tell me what to do," said Linda. "Now get out!"

"And I told you to keep your hands off of me and I'm not going to tell you again," Jaci said quietly. "Ron, this woman has been calling and making threats against me and my family. She's even said she was going to kill us. Now I'm tired of her and her threats. Will you tell her to back off? I don't want to hurt her."

"Ha! You hurt me! Heifer, I'll show you who's going to get hurt!" Linda stood a head above Jaci and outweighed her significantly. She rushed toward Jaci again, hand raised to attack.

Jaci acted on the instincts gained from her cousin Buddy's coaching while growing up in Riverwood: *If it's a man, knee below the waist as hard as you can, one fist in the stomach, other fist in the nose. If it's a woman, elbow in the chest, one fist in the stomach, other fist in the nose.*

Before Linda realized what was happening, Jaci's elbow hit the right spot on her chest. Linda yelped, letting go of her hold on Jaci. Before Linda could recover, Jaci landed a blow to her stomach and another to her face. Linda went down. Jaci lifted her foot, kicking her in the side with all the frustration of her sleepless nights going into the motion. She raised her foot to kick again, but before she could land the blow, Ron grabbed her.

"Jaci! Hold up."

Ron looked down at Linda struggling to get up from the floor. "Did you do that, Linda?" he asked.

Linda wiped at the blood running from her nose. "This woman's not right for J.P.! Look at her! Fighting like a street woman. He needs a woman with some class and culture. I was merely trying to get her to stop making a fool out of herself and leave him alone."

"I know you don't think I'm going to walk away from the man I love, and who loves me, because of some perceived relationship in the mind of a crazy woman," Jaci said. "If so, you are sadly mistaken."

Ron picked up the phone sitting on the corner of the desk and dialed a number, then spoke into the phone. "J.P., get up here to your office quick. This is an emergency."

Just as he was hanging up, J.P. and Herbert came hurrying

around the corner. Someone watching the fight had already called him.

"What's happening?" he asked, looking around the room, then running to Jaci, still in the grasp of Ron. "What's the matter, baby?" The shock of what had just happened hit Jaci, and she started crying and hugging him as if she would never let go. He cupped her chin in his hand, trying to get her to look at him. "What's going on?"

When Jaci didn't answer, he turned to Ron.

"Ron! Will you please tell me what's going on?"

Ron pointed to Linda. "This woman's been calling, tormenting Jaci. Making threats against her and her family. And if I heard correctly, Linda told her she was going to kill her if she didn't stay away from you. She just jumped on Jaci and tried to throw her out of the office, and well, you see whose nose is bleeding. This woman is a screwball," he said, pointing to Linda with distaste.

J.P. looked at Linda and said coldly, "I should have fired you a long time ago. Get off my property before I do something I'll be sorry for. And count yourself lucky that I don't knock you out of one of these windows."

"You can't do that!" Linda yelled at him. "J.P., don't you understand? I'm trying to help you and protect you from this conniving little tramp. You need a woman like me at your side. I can help you advance socially and in other ways. Please, J.P., you'll be sorry if you don't get rid of this heifer. And I'm filing charges against her for attacking me." Linda limped to the desk and grabbed her purse out of the drawer. She pointed toward Jaci. "I'm going to get you for this. Just wait." She started toward the door.

"Wait a minute! We can't just let her walk out of here!" Ron said. "I told you, this woman is screwy. We need to call the cops and get her locked up. You think you telling her to get off this property is going to stop her? Not from what I just heard. She's a nut case. She'll keep coming after Jaci."

"No, she won't!" Herbert spoke up for the first time. "Will you, Linda?" he asked hopefully. "If we let you go, you'll go on about your business and leave Jaci alone, won't you?"

"Maybe I will, and maybe I won't," answered Linda. "It depends on whether J.P. wakes up and gets rid of her."

"Lady, I don't want you!" J.P. almost screamed, looking at Linda with a deep scowl. "If I did, I could have had you long before Jaci ever came into the picture. In fact, I despise you. You're nothing but a gold-digging, status-seeking, lowlife. What would I want with the likes of you. I know a woman of class when I see one, and you're definitely not one."

Linda continued to plead. "I know this woman has your mind all messed up, J.P., so I'll forgive you for that. If you would just think about it, you would see what I'm talking about and give us a chance."

"Oh no, honey. It doesn't work that way!" Jason's mother shouldered her way through the crowd gathered in the area. "My son has chosen the woman he wants, and it's not you. Evidently you're too crazy to get the message, so your butt is going to jail." She picked up the phone and dialed the operator. "I need the police but it's not exactly an emergency. What num—? Okay, thank you. Hello? We have a crazy woman in our office making threats against us. Can you send someone quickly? She's saying she's going to kill somebody." She rattled off the address of the building. "We're on the fourteenth floor. All right, thanks."

"You can send me to jail, but I won't be there long," Linda said smugly. She had been through this before.

"Well, let me tell you something, you crazy witch." Ron walked over to her, pointing a finger in her face. "You better get out of there running. 'Cause we take care of our own. You think we're just going to let you hurt someone in our family?

Now, my brother don't want your crazy tail. Ain't never wanted you! I don't think you're nearly as crazy as you're acting. So, let me say this before the cops get here. You hurt Jaci, we hurt you! Got that? Whatever you do to her, you better get ready; the same thing is coming your way. Now, I suggest you heed this warning, 'cause, lady, I mean every word I'm saying. Don't make me regret stopping Jaci from kicking your behind."

"And if you don't believe him, believe me," Jason said. "I'm not going to be nothing nice if you come near my fiancée again. Your problem is with me, not her. I'm the one who chose her. Not the other way around. You want to come after somebody, come after the right person."

Cecelia looked around and noticed the people crowded around the door, watching. "Okay, people, let's break it up. The show is over and we've got work to do." Everyone left except Ron, Herbert, and Cecelia, who decided to watch Linda until the police arrived. J.P. and Jaci walked slowly down the hallway to his office.

"Jason, I'm so sorry. I never meant for something like this to happen when I came over here today." Jaci cried brokenly.

"I know that. You didn't know that woman was going off the deep end. But I am upset with you. Why didn't you tell me about Linda continuing to harass you like that? I've asked you countless times to share things with me. Why do you continue to try to handle everything by yourself?"

"It wasn't a case of my trying to handle it on my own. You've been out of town and so busy that we've hardly had a chance to talk. But after days and nights of her calls and harassment, I'd had enough and that's why I came on over here today. I knew I had to tell you what was going on."

"You should have done that already, like I asked you to," he told her impatiently. "As crazy as that woman out there is, she could have hurt you at any time, and I wouldn't have even known it had gotten to that point. What is your problem, Jaci? I'm about sick and tired of having this conversation with you!"

Jaci decided she didn't need this on top of everything else. "You're tired? You don't know what tired is." She looked around for her purse, grabbed it, and started out of the office. "I'm not staying around here for any more abuse. I'm out of here!"

J.P.

J.P. let her go. He paced back and forth across his office try-ing to process all that had gone on in the past few minutes. He didn't know whether to be embarrassed, angry, apologetic, or what. He was beyond tired after working day and night, and to have something like this happen was totally unacceptable.

"Man, what the devil is wrong with you?" Ron asked from behind him. J.P. turned and saw that Ron and a rebellious looking Jaci had entered the office without his hearing them.

"Jaci can't leave until the police get here. I'm sure she'll have to give a statement. She needs to stay back here. These women don't need to be in the same room."

"I'm sure there's another office where I can wait," Jaci told Ron. "Your brother has informed me that he's tired of deal-ing with me. And I refuse to stay where I'm not wanted."

"I didn't say that! But I am tired of you trying to handle things by yourself and messing up, when I'm here to help you."

"Excuse me," Jaci told Ron, and gave J.P. a dirty look before leaving the office again.

"Do you know what you're doing, brother?" Ron asked. "You better snap, man. You don't want to lose that lady. And you know, that's something I never thought I'd say."

"Two women fighting over me like two dogs over a bone!" J.P. groaned loudly. "Oh Lord! That might be an ego booster for some men, but it's a total turnoff to me." He groaned again. "And in front of my staff! That really blows it."

"And you're blaming Jaci for that?" Ron asked. "I heard her tell Linda more than once to leave her alone. She even asked me to make Linda back off so she could leave. But before I could do anything, Linda had jumped her."

"And you just stood there and let them go at it." J.P. shook his head disgustedly.

"Naw, man, it wasn't like that. When Linda attacked her, Jaci was all over her. Before I could even move, Jaci had knocked her to the floor." He started laughing. "You don't want to ever make that woman mad. You'll get your tail whipped real quick."

"I, I can't believe she did that!" J.P. stammered.

"What was she supposed to do? Let Linda beat up on her? Would that have made you happy?" Ron walked over and stood in front of him. "I don't believe I'm saying this, but you act a fool and let Jaci get away, it'll be the biggest mistake you ever made. She told Linda that no way was she going to let a crazy woman make her walk away from the man she loves. She's quality, brother, as you well know. And I don't know why you're tripping like this. But . . . that just leaves the field open for me or some other lucky guy." He noticed J.P.'s eyes and mouth tightening, and knew he had hit the mark. J.P. was getting angry.

"I'm going back out there and wait for the police," Ron remarked as he made his escape.

The police finally arrived and took statements from everyone. After ascertaining that Linda had instigated the fight and continued her threats against Jaci even in their presence, they arrested Linda. They told Jaci she would have to file charges against Linda, and advised Jaci to seek a restraining order to restrict Linda to a certain distance.

As soon as the police finished with her, Jaci left the building like it was on fire.

"Where's Jaci going so fast?" Cecelia asked, looking at J.P. strangely.

"Oh, Mom, didn't you know? J.P. is blaming Jaci for everything that happened here today. Told her he was tired of dealing with her. So, Jaci said she wasn't staying anywhere she's not wanted."

"Boy, have you lost your mind?" Cecelia yelled at J.P. "You better go catch that girl. You know doggone well Jaci didn't start this mess. We told you a long time ago what Linda was after. And you didn't do anything about it, so if what happened is anybody's fault, it's yours."

"I'm not blaming Jaci for what happened," J.P. said tiredly. "I'm just upset that she didn't handle things differently." He made an impatient sound. "You know what? I just wish everybody would leave me alone." He turned, hurried down the hallway to his office, and closed the door behind him.

Now that he was alone, Jason walked across his office to the window and got there just in time to see Jaci's Jeep leave the parking lot. He grabbed his head, groaning as though in deep pain. "What have I done?" he asked himself.

He sat down behind the empty desk and looked around the office. Everything was ready to be moved. Everything from the walls, bookshelves, desk, and credenza was carefully labeled with appropriate numbers. There would be no problem placing things where they belonged.

His office was ready . . . made ready by the woman who had told him she hadn't slept the past several days. But in spite of that, she worked hard in here all morning to help him. He knew of no other woman in the world, other than maybe his mother, who would have done this without thought for herself. He started feeling like the jerk he knew he had been with her. *What in the world got into me?* he wondered.

He sat in deep thought, ignoring the knocks on his door and the ringing phones. He needed to face up to some things where Jaci was concerned.

She loved him—almost as much as he loved her. By necessity, she was extremely independent, preferring to handle her own problems and issues. She had told him that from the start. He had to accept the fact that she might never reach the point where she was comfortable with his need to take care of her and protect her. She was also as stubborn as a mule when she believed she was right.

She was caring, loving, loyal, dependable, and all those things she had told Ron and Walt on Thanksgiving Day about love. She was cautious and leery. But once her mind was made up, she was in it all the way.

She'd been honest and up-front about everything from the very beginning.

He wanted to kick himself as he questioned the reasons for his anger with her today. Especially when he came up with only one reason. *Male pride.* What was that Scripture about pride goeth before a fall? Why was he upset with her? For standing up to a crazy woman because she loved him? For failing to tell him the extent of the woman's harassment and trying to handle it by herself? When was she supposed to tell him? He'd been putting her off all week, telling her he didn't have time. Hadn't she taken the day off just so she could come to him and tell him what was going on? Maybe if he had taken the time to talk to her he could have kept this from happening. Was this move so important that he would jeopardize their relationship?

Absolutely not! The whole company could go down the drain as far as that was concerned.

He picked up the phone and dialed her number. He knew she hadn't had time to make it home, but he could leave her a message. He had to get her a decent cell phone. Hers didn't work half the time.

"Jaci, I'm so sorry, baby. Just chalk it up to fatigue and stupidity. Will you call me as soon as you get home?"

Forty-five minutes and eight messages later, he still hadn't heard from her.

His door flew open and his dad, who had been out running errands, stormed into the room, a scowl on his face. "I hear there's been some tail kicking going on around here today, and it ain't over yet. 'Cause if you treated Jaci the way they say you did, I'm getting ready to kick yours. Have you lost your blasted mind?"

"Yeah, Pop. I guess I have. I really don't know what got into me. And I don't need you to kick me, I'm doing that real well myself."

"Well, I guess you did Linda a favor," his dad answered. "She's getting exactly what she wanted—Jaci out of your life." He left the office, slamming the door behind him.

Consuming fear at the thought of life without Jaci filled him and caused tears to fill his eyes. He picked up the phone and dialed her number again. "Sweetheart, please call me! And you may as well know, I'm not giving up."

Jaci

*J*aci erased all the messages and turned the ringers off. "I'm not talking to you anymore today," she said loudly to the last message.

Feeling dirty and stressed out, she ran a hot bath, pouring a generous portion of bath oil into the tub. She lit her favorite scented candles, stripped, and sank into the hot water, where she stayed until the water had cooled and she was about to drift off to sleep. She got out of the tub, slipped into a night-gown, and was asleep almost as soon as her head hit the pil-low. She slept soundly for three hours and was jerked awake by her pager going off. She knew it would continue to beep until she stopped it.

She realized she had slept through several pages and hadn't heard a thing. Evidently, she had taken the edge off her ex-haustion enough for the sound to finally permeate. Of course, they were all from Jason, with the exception of one from Randi. She quickly dialed Randi's number, knowing her daughter would be worried about her if she didn't call her back.

"Hey, honey. What's up?"

"Mama, what's going on with you and Jason? He's called me several times looking for you. He said if I talked to you, to tell you he's really sorry and to please call him. What did he do?"

She briefly ran down the situation to her. "If he calls back, tell him I said to go suck a rotten egg."

"I'm not telling him that!" Randi replied. "You'll have to call him and tell him that yourself. So how long is this woman going to stay in jail?" she asked worriedly.

"I have no idea. I'm just sick and tired of the whole situation. She knows now that I can whip her butt, so she's not going to get too close to me again."

"Well, I think you and Jason need to go down there and file charges on her, like the police said. And get that peace bond against her. It's no telling what that crazy woman may do next."

"Yeah. You're right. But I'm not going to talk to him today. I'm still too angry. Maybe tomorrow. I'm going to get some more sleep now. I'll talk to you later."

Jaci snuggled back into her pillow and went back to sleep, praying Linda was still behind bars.

Randi dialed Jason's number as soon as she finished talking to her mother. "Jason, I talked to my mother. She's tired and trying to get some sleep. She said maybe she'll call you tomorrow."

"Is that all she said?" he asked.

"Nope. But I can't repeat it. She's still pretty mad at you."

"I don't blame her. I acted like a jerk. Do you know if she's going to work tomorrow?"

"The way she sounded, no. But you know Mom. If she wakes up and feels like it, she'll probably go in."

"Okay, Randi. I appreciate your help. And don't worry, I'll get things worked out with your mother."

Jaci slept through the night and awoke early Thursday morning, still tired but feeling better. She decided not to go to work since she was off the next day anyway. She would just treat herself to a minivacation (to heck with Wynola). She called the office and after she ascertained that Gloria and Bill had things under control, Jaci went back to bed and slept another couple of hours.

She finally got up, took a shower, and ate toast before checking the messages on the answering machine. The tape was full of messages from Jason, but there was one from Lena, who had called that morning.

She quickly called her back. She needed the kind of conversation she knew she would get from Lena.

"Hey, girl, it's Jaci. How's it going?"

"Hey! I'm free for lunch. Want to treat me?"

Jaci's spirits lifted. "Sounds good to me. Where you want to go?"

"Olive Garden on South Main. Twelve-thirty."

Jaci hurriedly got ready. This was a welcomed distraction.

She expected Lena to be waiting for her, but when she didn't see her, she sat down by the door to wait. When J.P. walked in, she didn't acknowledge him, just simply turned her head. He walked over and sat down beside her.

"Guess what?" he asked without a greeting. When she didn't answer, he said, "I'm your lunch date. I got Lena to set this up for me."

Jaci stood and walked out the door without a word. He figured she would do that, so he followed her all the way to her truck. "I know I blew it yesterday and I'm so sorry for the way I acted. Will you please forgive me?"

"Sure. I forgive you," she quickly answered to his surprise. But before the relief he felt could set in, she continued. "Now leave me alone and go suck a rotten egg or something."

"Doggone it! I knew that was too easy!" he groaned. "Jaci, we love each other. Remember? We can't let this come between us like this. Will you come to the house with me so we can talk?"

"No."

"I need you, sweetheart. In so many ways I can't name them all. If you don't forgive me, I'll never be complete again. You're my essence, the part of me that makes my life meaningful. Honey, I don't even want to think about living without you. Please come with me."

"Just leave me alone! I'm not going to let you hurt me again,

Jason. I may be stupid, but I'm not a glutton for punishment. I know when to get off the short bus."

"You're not stupid. I'm the one who fills that role. Please talk to me, Jaci. At least give us a chance to work this out."

"Ma'am? Do you know this man? Is he bothering you?" The security guard who had been watching them from across the parking lot walked over to them.

"No, thanks officer. I'm fine." She looked at Jason. "Now see. I asked you to leave me alone. Do you want to get arrested out here on a parking lot?"

"If that's what it takes," he answered. "Jaci . . . We have to talk. . . . Please! You owe me that much."

"I don't owe you anything. But since I'm not interested in becoming a spectacle on this parking lot, let's go." She paused, then added, "But I'm not promising anything." She followed him to his house, parked in the driveway behind his SUV, and walked with him inside. He led the way into the family room. "Do you want anything to eat or drink?"

"No. Let's just get this over with so I can go."

They spent the next hour hashing out their feelings and differing opinions. Jaci knew all along that she loved him too much to let the thing with Linda destroy them. But she was still just angry enough to let him stew a little. She understood Jason's reaction yesterday. He wanted to be her protector and fight her battles for her, while she wanted him to learn that he couldn't take care of every situation for her. Some fights a woman has to fight for herself.

They finally reached a truce, realizing that her need for independence, and his need to protect, made it a temporary one. They both knew this would be an ongoing issue.

"Are you working today?"

"No, I took the day off."

"Will you come back to the office with me? I could really use your help. Your hard work yesterday helped me get relocated a lot quicker. But now, I need your help getting the new office unpacked and set up. Besides that, there's a line of people waiting to kick my butt if I don't bring you back with me."

"I guess so. But I'm not promising how long I'll stay. Have you heard anything from Linda today?"

"No! And I confess I'm concerned about what she might do next. She's crazy. That's another reason I'd like to keep you close to me. If I didn't have so much to do today, we'd go and file charges against her, but hopefully we'll be able to do it tomorrow."

"I'm not afraid of her."

"I know you're not," he said with a sardonic look. "I've heard several versions of how you took her down. But I am scared, and I don't intend for her to get close enough to you to hurt you."

"Here we go again!" Jaci said in exasperation. "I can take care of myself, Jason!"

"Maybe. Come on, ride with me."

Tired of arguing, she almost agreed, but the thought of not having her own transportation so she could leave when she got ready prompted her to say, "No, I'll drive myself."

When he began to argue she retaliated, "Look, you'd better be glad I've agreed to go with you. Don't make me change my mind."

Maxie

It's almost Christmas! Maxie thought peevishly as he headed toward Jacetta's house. Randi made him wait all this time before contacting him. Despite his efforts, he hadn't been able to force a meeting with his daughter until she and her mother were good and ready. He pestered Jacetta, leaving messages that she never responded to, or if she happened to answer when he called, she only said, "I'm out of it, it's between you and Randi," before hanging up. His demands that she at least talk to him and tell him what was going on went unanswered.

The only thing that pleased him was their agreement to meet at Jacetta's house. That was right up his alley. He couldn't have planned it better himself.

Finally, he would have the opportunity not only to meet his daughter and grandchildren, but also to satisfy his curiosity about Jacetta. He really wanted to see the woman who had teased his senses with that husky, sexy voice for months. He pressed down a little harder on the accelerator, anxious to get there.

He found his way to Jacetta's street and noticed there were cars already parked in the driveway and along the street in front of the house. Oh well, he thought. Looks like a real party's going on. He rang the doorbell and waited.

A beautiful, curvaceous woman dressed in navy capri pants with a navy and gold matching top opened the door and motioned him in. Silky, thick, reddish-brown hair hung to her shoulders in loose curls, and skin that had the look and smoothness of honey tempted him to reach out and touch it. *Wow! Who is this?* he thought to himself. He entered the foyer and looked to his immediate left through an archway that led into a spacious formal living room, where several adults were laughing and talking as they ate from plates piled high with food. He followed the woman farther into the house, admiring her shapely legs and still wondering who she was.

They entered a family room occupied by more people. On the opposite wall, sliding patio doors provided a view of the backyard, where he saw a large swimming pool. It was too cold to swim, but the yard was full of activity—people playing a loud game of volleyball and children running around getting in their way. He could hear a baby crying somewhere in the house as he searched faces, trying to pick Jacetta and Randi out of the crowd.

"Randi!" The woman who had let him in stuck her head around the door leading into the hallway and called out in a loud voice, "Maxie's here."

His head snapped around as he looked closely at the woman. Shock registered on his face as he asked, "Jacetta?" He couldn't believe the beautiful woman standing before him was the same woman he remembered only vaguely.

A dramatic change had taken place in her appearance. Gone was the chubbiness, the short Afro hairstyle, the bad complexion. The woman didn't say anything, simply stared back at him from large green eyes set in a heart-shaped face with high cheekbones and a flawless complexion. The bow-shaped, kissable lips tempted him to lean down and taste them. But before that thought could take root, a tall muscular man stood up from the sofa and stepped between him and Jacetta, effectively blocking his view and his haywire temptations.

"I'm J.P. Gilmore. And, yes, this is Jacetta, but she's known as Jaci to all her family and friends now." He slipped a possessive arm around Jaci's slender waist as he spoke. "Randi and the baby will be out in a moment. You want to have a seat or help yourself to some food or refreshments?"

Maxie realized the man was effectively staking his claim. He sat down in the recliner in the corner directly behind him. Noticing all eyes were focused on the interchange among himself, the man, and Jaci, he sought a way to divert the attention from them. "No thanks. I'm fine right now." Ignoring J.P., he spoke to Jaci. "Nice home you have here, Jaci. I'm sure your neighbor across the street told you I came by to see you a while back. How long have you lived here?"

"Ten years," she answered, and made no other effort to continue the conversation.

"Looks like a pretty nice neighborhood. Quiet and peaceful." *Not like my drug-infested, run-down neighborhood,* he thought to himself.

"It is."

He was floundering. The next question in his mind was, do you live here alone? But he thought better of asking it, with the Gilmore guy standing there watching him like a hawk. He was wondering what to say or do next, when a slender younger man stepped up to him, hand extended.

"Hi, I'm John, Randi's husband. Our son Sean is running around outside in the backyard. If you want, I'll take you out and introduce you. Randi's changing the baby, so she might be a while."

That sounded like a good plan to Maxie. He didn't particularly want to go outside, but anywhere was better than this tension-filled room. He stood and followed John through the patio doors.

His son-in-law called to a little boy engaged in some kind of game with a teenage boy and another child. The boy looked when he heard his name and frowned as his daddy told him to come.

He shook his head. "No."

"Sean, come here. You can go back in a minute." John walked across the patio, took the little boy from the teenager who had scooped him up, and walked back over to Maxie.

"Sean, this man is Mommy's daddy. He's your other papa."

The little boy looked at Maxie and shook his head emphatically. "No!"

"Remember, Mommy told you about your other papa."

The little boy looked at Maxie again, then said, "P'ay pease." He pointed to the other children running around the yard, anxious to get back into the game.

"Hey, little fella, come talk to me." Maxie reached out to take the child from John, but Sean cowered, hugging his daddy close. Maxie dropped his arms, a strange feeling of disappointment settling in his heart.

"Nice-looking little fellow," Maxie said to John.

John looked at Maxie with a shrug of his shoulders, turned, and put Sean down. Sean's plump little legs immediately went into action as he ran back to the other children.

"Yeah. Some say he looks just like his mother. Of course, me and my folks all think he looks like me. I guess he just looks like himself."

Maxie sat down in one of the lawn chairs under the covered patio. *Nice*, he thought, looking around the yard. Even without the pool, it was a nice yard.

The patio door opened and a young woman who had to be Randi walked out. She looked so much like Jacetta they could have been sisters. She walked over to him. "Hi, I'm Randi."

Maxie searched her face in an effort to decipher her feelings, but like her mother, Randi had a closed, distant expression.

Giving her his most charming smile, he took her hand in his and held it. "You don't know how much I've looked forward to this. If I'd had my way, we wouldn't be meeting for the first time today. I've tried but . . . Well, you have to ask your mother about that. She's the one who . . ."

"Uh, Uh! Stop right there!" Randi said. Snatching her hand out of his and putting her finger in his face, she calmly continued. "Let's get this understood right now. I don't want to hear any negative remarks about my mother. You see, when I was fifteen, we drove all over Dallas and made numerous phone calls looking for you. And that was just the last time. Every time I asked my mom about you, she tried to find you. My mom never put you down or said anything negative about you to me. But I'm not stupid. I know how we had to struggle and how hard my mother had to work to take care of us. And I know who wasn't there to help. So don't even try that, mister."

As Maxie stood there with his mouth hanging open, Randi continued her barrage. "My mother has asked that we leave her out of any relationship we establish. I promised her I would. I'm letting you know right now, if you want to get to know me and your grandchildren, I don't even want to hear her name coming out of your mouth. I don't need you in my life now, but I've been taught to forgive and to love everyone. That's what I'm trying to do. I hope you comprehend what I'm saying. If you can't handle it, then you'd better leave right now."

His daughter's words rattled him. The self-assured young woman made it clear, he could take a hike off of a short pier as far as she was concerned. And for one of a very few times in his life, Maxie was at a complete loss for an appropriate response. "I wasn't trying to put your mother down. I was just saying . . ."

"Yes, you were!" both Randi and John stated. Several pairs of eyes were riveted on them by now and the young man playing with Sean came to stand next to Randi, looking at him with an angry expression.

"Want me to throw him out, Randi?"

"Nooo! Patrick, just be cool, I'm okay."

Patrick threw him a dirty look, then took a few steps away and stood leaning against one of the patio posts, where he continued to toss threatening looks at Maxie.

"Who is that?" Maxie asked.

"My brother," Randi calmly answered.

Surprise and other questioning expressions ran across Maxie's face. *Brother?* George hadn't mentioned Jacetta having another child! Oh man. This was getting more complicated than he expected. But nobody was throwing him out until he got ready to go, he thought to himself, remembering the beautiful woman inside who was now called Jaci.

"I didn't know Jaci had any other children."

"Patrick is my stepbrother." Randi didn't know why she stopped short of saying, "to be." She and Patrick met each other only months ago, but they quickly formed an easy alliance and friendship with one another, jokingly plotting how they could push their parents over the broom.

"Ohhhh . . ." Maxie responded, still with a puzzled look but not saying anything else.

The door opened again and Gilmore stepped out. "Pat! Come here a minute."

With a look on his face that said he knew he was in trouble, Patrick walked slowly toward his dad and followed the man inside.

"Is that his . . . ?" Maxie began.

"Uh, uh, uh." Randi held her hand up. "Remember. This is about you and me. Anything else is none of your business."

J.P.

*P*at, what do you think you're doing out there? I would have left your butt at home if I had known you were going to come over here and jump into something that's none of your business."

"But, Pop, that dude was . . ."

"No, no. Now we all talked about this before anybody else got here and decided to let Randi deal with her father. Now if you can't do any better, you'd better go ahead and leave."

"Okay, okay!" Patrick answered quickly, not ready to leave.

"I don't know about you, but I'm not gonna let him bad-talk Jaci. And all I was saying was that I would throw his behind out of here."

"I know that, son." J.P. was proud of Patrick for wanting to defend Jaci. It showed how deeply he felt about her. "But Pat, let me look out for Jaci, okay? I'm an old man, but I'm up to it."

"Yeah, okay. But I'ma keep my eye on him. That dude is slick, Pop."

"Another word and you're out of here. And I'm keeping my eye on you."

Jaci

With the help of Jason, her cousin C.J., and Lena, Jaci worked to replenish the quickly disappearing food. As she carried on, she fought tumultuous emotions. Jaci didn't like the idea of Maxie's coming to her house to meet her daughter and grandchildren, but she had been outvoted by Randi and Jason. She would rather have had Maxie go to Randi's house for the meeting, leaving her totally out of it. But both Randi and Jason, after listening to Maxie's persistent messages on her answering machine, felt that a big part of Maxie's insistence on this visit was about Jaci, not about meeting his daughter.

Jaci agreed with them that Maxie probably wanted to satisfy his curiosity about her and reluctantly agreed with their plan. Both Randi and Jason were so protective of her that they didn't want her to go through a scene with Maxie alone. So here they were—in the midst of a face-off with tensions so thick they couldn't be cut with a sharp knife.

Jaci watched from the kitchen window as Randi spoke to Maxie. Although she couldn't hear what Randi said, she could tell by the expression on her face that Maxie had said something to upset her. And when Patrick ran over to them, she knew things were not going well. She motioned to Jason to come to the window. He got there in time to see Patrick giving Maxie a dirty look before walking away.

"Let me get that young man in hand," Jason said before leaving the kitchen to call Patrick inside. It warmed her heart to know that Patrick considered himself a part of her family, so much so that he had run to defend them, conveniently forgetting that Randi was to handle everything. *Oh, man! Maxie must have really said something volatile*, she thought.

"This was a mistake," Jaci remarked to C.J., who was busy taking a large tray of chicken wings out of the oven, and to Lena who was making more iced tea.

"I don't know why I let them talk me into this fiasco. Even if the man had come and tried to have some sort of face-off with me, I would have been all right. Why do they think I'm such a wimp that I couldn't have handled him? Heck, I've got so much pent-up anger toward that guy, I could probably toss him out of here with one hand. I prayed that I would be able to keep my cool with him. I'd convinced myself that I had forgiven him and put everything behind me. But I tell you, I could hardly speak civilly to him when he walked in the door. I don't recall ever being that cold to anyone. This lets me know I've still got lots of praying to do."

"Don't be so hard on yourself," Lena said. "You have a right to those feelings, Jaci. The bottom line is, the man dogged you and abandoned his child. Any way you slice it, it comes down to that. There is no justifiable story he can tell, or action he can take at this point, to dispute that fact."

"But I've still had to accept my own guilt and responsibility in the matter. I have to keep reminding myself of that."

"Girl, we been over this how many times over the years?" C.J. almost yelled. "I'm totally out of patience with you in this. Yes, you made a mistake. Because you were in love with him! You didn't set out to use him, and then disappear, like he did. You know what? I agree with Jason and Randi. I'm glad this is happening with all of us here. If he could have gotten you alone, Maxie would have been pushing all your buttons and had you crying in his arms, asking *him* for forgiveness."

"Woooo!" Lena said, laughing. "Did you see how he was checking you out when he came in? Even before he realized who you were, his eyes were traveling. Why do you think J.P. jumped up and got between you like he did? He was sending a hands-off message to Maxie. Now that jerk knows he has more than you to deal with, and if he's smart, he'll slither on back to where he came from."

J.P.

Most of the guests had finally left. Randi and John were still outside talking to Maxie and watching Sean and Patrick, who had finally settled down and were now sitting at a table eating. Jaci, C.J., and Lena were busy cleaning up and putting the leftovers away. Jason was half-lying on the sofa, flipping channels on the television. The baby, who had been asleep in Jaci's bedroom, started crying, and Jaci left the kitchen to go see about her. She came back with the baby in the crook of one arm, retrieved a bottle from the refrigerator, and put it in a pot of water to warm. While the milk was warming up, she walked back over to Jason and handed him the baby. He took the baby and began talking to her. The baby stopped crying and listened with a wide toothless smile.

"Now, look at that. We already know she's going to love men," Jaci said, laughing.

She got the warmed bottle and headed toward the hallway leading to her bedroom. "Come on, lover boy, follow me. I'm not about to break up that love affair, but you can continue your conversation after I feed her." Jason stood carefully, maintaining a tight hold on the tiny baby. Although she had come a long way, she was still too small for him to feel comfortable holding her. When they got to the bedroom, Jaci took the baby from him and placed the bottle into her eager little mouth. Jason stretched out across the bed with his hands behind his head and watched them, making idle conversation about the happenings of the day. He was relating something John's dad had said when they heard footseps in the hallway. Since the master bedroom was the only room at that end of the hallway, they knew someone was coming to that room. Jaci was laughing, but when the expression on her face changed, Jason looked around to see who had entered the room.

Maxie stood there taking in the scene, an indecipherable look on his face. "Uh, Jaci . . . we need to talk, just you and I, privately. Any idea how long it's going to be before everyone leaves? I just need to know if I should cancel my flight or not."

J.P. saw red. He jumped up from the bed so quickly that Jaci almost lost her hold on the baby. "Man, I suggest you get on to the airport and catch your plane. You don't have anything to discuss privately with Jaci."

"I'm not talking to you. I'm addressing Jaci. Who are you anyway? This is none of your business."

"I'm her fiancé—that makes it my business. And whatever you have to say, you can say to both of us. Now, we've tried to graciously accommodate your repeated requests to see your daughter and grandchildren. But the first thing out of your mouth was to try to lie on this woman. Well, I'll settle that once and for all. You don't have a darn thing to do with Jaci. You got that? Nothing! Your only business here is Randi and her children. If that business is finished, then it's time for you to leave. There's no reason for you to call or return to this house ever again. Am I making myself clear?"

Maxie huffed. "I share a child with this woman and any business between us is none of your concern. So like I said, butt out of this."

"Man, you don't share no child with this woman. All you did was plant a seed. You haven't done anything that even re-motely resembles sharing. And beyond that, Randi is no longer a child. She's a grown woman, with a family of her own. We won't even talk about how you did absolutely noth-ing to get her to this point. Nothing! You ought to be ashamed to even show your sorry face anywhere near here."

"Jason, maybe I sh—"

"No, Jaci, you shouldn't!" Jason interrupted. "Whatever you were about to say is not happening. This guy gon' come strolling into your bedroom like he has a right and start de-manding to talk privately! No way! Man, your talking should have been done twenty-something years ago. That's when Jaci needed to hear from you. Not now."

"Well, you're not her husband yet, and . . ."

Jason's voice grew softer and more menacing. "For all in-tents and purposes I am, and if you know what's good for you, you'll get out of here before I throw you out." Jason made threatening steps toward Maxie.

Maxie held up his hand. "Aw'ight, I'm going—for now. Jaci, I'll call you later because we are going to talk. As for you," he pointed a finger toward Jason, "just remember one thing. I had her first."

Jason moved before the gasp left Jaci's mouth. Maxie was

against the wall with one of Jason's muscular arms across his throat, Jason's other fist was busy punching him. Pictures fell to the floor, and it seemed as if Maxie were going to crash through the wall at any time. It looked like Jason was trying to punish Maxie for all the hurt he had heaped on Jaci.

By the time Jaci laid the baby down and ran to pull Jason off him, Maxie was sliding to the floor, groaning.

"You know what?" Jason yelled down to Maxie. "Maybe you did have her first. But you had a young, inexperienced girl that you took advantage of, mistreated, and threw away. I have the best of her. All that she managed to scrape together after you nearly destroyed her. All that she's worked hard to become—all the wisdom, courage, strength, beauty, and love that makes her who she is now. I have all of that.

"You were foolish enough to throw a good thing away. I'm wise enough and man enough to recognize something precious when I see it. And I ain't throwing it away. If you having her first made it possible for me to have who she is now, then I guess I ought to be thanking you instead of beating the crap out of you. But I'm not going to let you disrespect or insult her. Now get up on out of here, and go somewhere and grow up, old man."

Maxie struggled to his feet and stood there for a few minutes to gain his balance, then started back down the hallway.

Randi, John, C.J., and Lena stood at the other end of the hallway watching him. They didn't say a word as they stood back to let him pass. Jaci's hands covered her mouth as she watched Maxie move slowly through the door to leave. She turned to Jason, who was leaning against the wall rubbing his hands, and walked over to him.

"I love you. I love you so much. You just gave me back so much of what he took away from me." They stood there in a tight embrace, not noticing as Randi quietly entered the room, picked up the baby, and left, closing the door behind her.

Jason finally lifted his head and said, "If I had known that was all I had to do to get a reaction like this from you, I would have found him and whipped his tail a long time ago."

After everyone left, Jaci pulled J.P. down beside her on the couch and snuggled up close to him. "Jason, I have something to say to you. I hope you're ready to hear it."

"What is it, sweetheart?" he asked, looking concerned.

"Well, do you think we can start our counseling soon? It's time for us to get married."

He gave a whoop. "Oh, honey! Yes! I'll talk to the pastor in the morning."

Jaci shook her head unbelievingly. "The way I see it, we'd better hurry up and get married before we have to beat somebody else up."

"I heard that!" he said. "What in the world has gotten into us?" They both laughed until tears ran down their cheeks, then settled down with a calendar to work out a wedding date.

"You know it could take a year to plan a wedding. That's if you do it right."

"We won't be doing it right then. There's no way I'm waiting a year. Can we do it around June or July? That's six months and as far as I'm willing to go sweetheart. Heck, as far as I'm concerned we can go to the courthouse."

"I want to have a church wedding. And weddings, even small ones, are expensive. We know ours won't be small since we both come from large families and are part of large churches. I just finished paying for my daughter's wedding. It's going to take me more than a few months to get ready for another one."

"Is that the only holdup?" He reached into his pocket and pulled a credit card out of his wallet. "Here, use this for whatever you need. I mean it, Jaci. Use it and do whatever it takes to make it happen no later than June or July. Okay, baby?"

"What about the last Saturday in June if we can get it set up with the church and find a place for the reception and everything?"

"Yes! It's settled. And we will get everything set up for then."

Jaci

The first of the year found Jaci thankful she had made it through a relatively quiet holiday season, although she couldn't fully relax with the thought of all she had to do to prepare for her wedding. And of course she was unconsciously waiting for the other shoe to drop with Linda and Wynola. Thankfully, Jasmine was doing fine and getting bigger every day, and Jaci was back to taking assignments from J.P., even though he wouldn't send her out of town anymore unless he went with her. More than once, he had mentioned something about her going full-time once they were married. Jaci refused to entertain the thought. She didn't know if she was ready to give up her current position. It wasn't that she loved the job so much. But it was her security—her independence, or so she had thought until this mess with Wynola and "Jean White" had entered the picture.

Lord, thank You for Your mercies that are new every morning, Jaci prayed daily.

With the arrival of February, she panicked. Her wedding was only four months away and there were countless wedding preparations as well as packing up and storing those things she wouldn't be moving to Jason's house. She procrastinated in beginning the packing process because she dreaded leaving the home she had been so happy in. She rallied those closest to her (Randi, Lena, C.J., and Sister Sadie) to help with wedding preparations, and they were all busily at work. Randi took charge of the guest list, along with Jason's mother; C.J. and Lena worked on the program and reception; and Sister Sadie, an accomplished seamstress, created the wedding dress she and Jaci had designed. Sister Sadie also organized everything with the pastor and church, assuring her role as the wedding coordinator. Jaci constantly checked and rechecked her extensive list. Hiring a wedding planner would have made sense but she didn't want to spend money on something she could do herself.

In one of their countless telephone conversations, Lena confessed, "Girl, I was wondering what was wrong with you. I know the story behind Maxie, and I've been with you through thick and thin over the years. But I just couldn't go with you on pussyfooting around with Jason. You were acting like a crazy woman."

Jaci smiled. "Is that why you set me up for him when we had that fight over the Linda incident? I hadn't fronted you on that had I? Some friend you turned out to be."

Lena laughed. "I had to do that, girl. You're never going to find another Jason. And if you know where one is, kindly point me in his direction. Marry that man, quit that sorry job, and do something you like. Maybe do nothing for a while. God knows you deserve it. Whatever you do, don't blow this, Jaci."

Jaci's eyes filled with tears of thanksgiving. "It was only God's mercy that brought us together, and I praise Him every day for Jason. And Lena, you don't know how thankful I am for your friendship."

Maxie

Maxie gleefully thought about his plan as he and his mother, aunt, and brother traveled to Houston to attend his uncle's funeral Saturday morning. It was perfect timing. He knew Jacetta and Gilmore planned to get married in the near future, so he had to act quickly and carefully. He hated to lose. And the way things stood, he was losing. He wanted Jacetta! And he wasn't above using an old woman who had never seen her grandchild and now her great grandchildren to get to her. His plan would work if Jacetta was at home and his do-right brother kept his mouth shut.

After the funeral, he snuck away from the crowd and dialed Randi's phone number. He almost cursed when he didn't get an answer. But that didn't stop him from pursuing his plan. As they prepared to leave the cemetery, his mother and aunt asked if there was a place where they could change clothes for the long ride back to Dallas. Maxie quickly interrupted before they made any arrangements.

"That's okay, Mama. I have a surprise for you—somebody I want you to meet. You can change at her house. Hopefully, she'll be at home. If not, we'll just have to stop at a service station or McDonald's." He refused to meet his brother's suspicious look.

He drove to Jacetta's neighborhood and proudly pulled into the driveway. "Whose house is this?" his mother asked. "Boy, don't be taking me to some stranger's house. Who lives here, Maxie?"

"I think I know," Joe said. "Is this where Jacetta lives, Maxie? If so, I think we need to leave. One of his old girlfriends live here, Mama. And they didn't part on good terms."

Maxie opened the door and spoke before he climbed out of

the car. "Why don't you tell her the rest of it? Mama, if she's at home, maybe you'll get a chance to meet your granddaughter and great grandchildren. That's the surprise I was telling you about. Come on ya'll, get out."

The others got out of the car, curious about who they were about to meet. Maxie led the way to the door and rang the doorbell, thinking if Jacetta was home, more than likely she wouldn't refuse to let them in when she saw the two old ladies standing there.

The door opened and Jacetta stood there with a baby in her arms and a toddler peeping around her. Her expression was a mixture of surprise and irritation. "Hey, Jaci," Maxie said quickly. "This is my mother and aunt, and remember my brother, Joe? We're in town for a funeral and I wanted them to meet Randi and the kids. I hope you don't mind us dropping in like this. I see the kids are here. What about Randi? Open the door," he ordered arrogantly. When she stood unmoving, looking at him like he had lost his mind, he went a step further. "Mama, this is Jaci. And these little ones are your great grandchildren, Jasmine and Sean."

His mother looked at the children and smiled. She saw the woman's reluctance, but she wanted to get a closer look at the children. "Sho is some pretty chil'ren. I would like to meet them if it's okay with you," she said to Jaci.

Jaci's good heart wouldn't let her refuse. She pushed the storm door open and invited the group into her home. She started to show them into the living room where she usually entertained strangers, but Maxie stopped her. "Let's go into the family room where we can get comfortable." He wanted to let them know he had been there before.

Jaci placed the baby into the portable playpen and then turned to them. "Would you all like something to drink?"

Maxie jumped up from his chair. "Yeah. What do you have?" He strolled into the adjoining kitchen and looked into the refrigerator. "Is this tea in this pitcher, Jaci? Mama, ya'll want some tea or some water? Maybe we need to get something to eat before we hit the road. Got anything to eat, Jaci? And they need to change clothes. Joe, why don't you get their clothes out of the car."

Jaci felt like she was in the twilight zone as she took in the visitors in her family room and the idiot trying to give them the erroneous impression that he had a right to be there. She bit her tongue to keep from saying something rude. She knew she had to get these people out of her house before Jason got there!

"Sorry, I don't have anything. It's okay to change clothes, but I'm afraid I'm expecting company, so I can't offer much more than that." She spoke to the old lady who was Maxie's mother. The same old lady she had spoken to countless times on the phone when she called her house looking for Maxie over the years. The same woman who had rudely told her to stop calling because her son was probably at home with his wife, and had even gone so far as to say, "I'm tired of you little sluts calling here, trying to break up a man's home."

"My daughter, Randi, is out, and won't be back for a while," Jaci told them. "I'm babysitting for her."

"Sho' is some pretty chil'ren," Maxie's mother repeated. "Is that Randi on that picture right there? Sho' would like to see her. Maxie, why am I just meeting these chil'ren? I guess if my brother hadn't died down here, I wouldna never seen them. You ever in Dallas, Jaci?" She looked around the room. "Sho' got a nice home."

Maxie's aunt and his brother Joe nodded their heads in agreement. Joe, who had walked back into the house with several clothes hangers, finally spoke up. "Jacetta, I'm Joe, Maxie's brother. You probably don't remember me, but we met a few times when you and Maxie were dating. It's nice to see you again and to meet my nephew and niece." He tried to lift up Sean but the little boy ran to Jaci with his arms stretched to be picked up. Jaci gathered the baby up and looked at Joe in silence, remembering his vague answers when she had asked him about Maxie's whereabouts years ago. His mother went to the playpen and picked up Jasmine. Jasmine favored her with a big smile. Anyone who freed her from her "prison" was a friend. The old lady hugged the baby to her breast tightly. "Oooh! She is so precious." She looked at Jaci with tears in her eyes. "Ya'll ever come to Dallas?" she asked again. "If you do, please bring these chil'ren to see me."

Jaci shook her head. "Ma'am, I wouldn't feel comfortable doing that. The last time I called your house you told me not to call there again. I've tried to adhere to your wishes since then."

The old lady gasped. "I . . . I didn't." She looked at Maxie as realization dawned. Her son had mistreated this girl, and she had unknowingly done so too. "If I did that I'm sorry. It wasn't nothing against you personally."

"No. I know it wasn't. But if you had given me the chance, I would have explained that your granddaughter was wanting to meet you. As it turns out, she just met Maxie a few months ago for the first time. He's been hiding from us all her life."

Maxie walked into the room with glasses of iced tea for his mother and aunt. "There's no call for that, Jacetta. My mother didn't have anything to do with that. You don't have to be rude."

Jaci looked at him coldly. "Oh I'm not being rude. Believe me, if I'd wanted to be rude, you would have never set foot in my house. I'm just being honest. I hate to be inhospitable, but like I said, I'm expecting someone and . . ." Before she could complete her sentence, Jason walked through the already open door. He stopped in his tracks when he saw Maxie and the others sitting around the room. He gave Jaci a questioning look before walking into the kitchen to retrieve a bottle of water from of the refrigerator.

He walked back into the family room, and before he could say anything, Sean ran to him and grabbed him around the leg, while Jasmine was almost jumping out of the old lady's arms to get to him. He walked across the room, picked her up, and grabbed Sean's hand.

He turned to go back into the kitchen, but before he did, he sent Jaci a dangerous look. "Baby?" His look and that one word conveyed his message: *I don't know what these people are doing here, but you need to get them out of here now.* He took the children with him into the kitchen and sat down at the kitchen table.

Maxie's mother looked at Jaci with hurt in her eyes. "Uh . . . is that your husband? I hope we haven't caused no trouble. I'm happy I got a chance to see the chil'ren though."

"Naw!" Maxie yelled. "That's not her husband. Just some guy who thinks he's going to marry her." He looked at Jason who sat at the table, playing with the children. "What do you mean coming in here taking my grandchildren away from my mother? I've already told you, you can't change the fact that Jacetta and I had something going years ago. You don't have a right to come in here and . . ."

"Maxie! Let's go." Joe stood, gathered the clothes, and looked sternly at Maxie, his mother, and aunt, and beckoned to them. "Jaci, thank you for so kindly letting us in to see the children. I realize you didn't owe us that and we appreciate it. Come on ya'll, let's go."

Maxie's mother turned at the door. "Jaci, please don't hesitate to call me. I'm in the phone book under Mabel Jackson. I promise you won't get the same answer the next time. Thank you for letting me see my great grandchildren." She looked at Maxie. "Come on, son. We've intruded on Jaci enough." She grabbed a reluctant Maxie by the arm and pulled him out the door.

Jaci closed the door behind them and walked into the kitchen. She leaned down and kissed Jason. "Please don't be mad, okay? They just showed up here and I didn't have the heart to say no to the old lady."

Jason shook his head. "That guy doesn't miss a trick."

Maxie left the neighborhood in disappointment. He hoped to bring Jacetta around by bringing his mother into the picture. If he could get a relationship going between Jacetta, his mother, and the children, he could work on her from that angle. The Gilmore guy had once again interrupted his plan.

"Maxie, you're some piece of work!" Joe said from the passenger seat next to him. "I'm ashamed you're my brother sometimes. Why did you take us to that woman's house knowing you had no right to even show your face there? I'm surprised she didn't curse us all out and slam the door in our faces."

"Well, I'm glad he did," his mother said from the backseat. "And why wouldn't he take me to see those chil'ren. I have a right to know my own grandchil'ren."

Joe sighed. "That's beside the point, Mama. Under the circumstances, I think we were wrong to just show up at Jacetta's house like that, considering the way he mistreated her and his child. Now that Randi's grown, he wants to show up acting like Daddy and Grandpa. That stinks."

His mother shook her head sadly. "I know what he did wasn't right, but I sho do want to get to know those chil'ren." The old lady wouldn't give up that hope. "I hate you mistreated that girl, son," she said to Maxie. "You shoulda told me about her and Randi. Maybe I wouldna been rude when she called me. I sho do hate that."

Maxie was silent, knowing there was nothing he could say that would change anything.

Jaci

The next week, as Jaci and Gloria drove from one dilapidated house to another taking pictures in preparation for the next hearing, they talked about the stalking situation.

"Linda is not a rational person," Jaci said. "If she were, she would have moved on and stopped all of this foolishness."

"Not necessarily," Gloria answered. "I mean if you want a man bad enough, it's hard to give up on him as long as you think there's a chance."

"Like I said. A rational person would have seen the handwriting on the wall, and moved on. Obviously, Jason has made his choice. But who is she threatening? Me! Now tell me if that makes any sense. Why do these crazy women always go after the woman? It's the man they should have the beef with. Not the woman."

"Maybe they think that if they get rid of the woman, the way will be opened for them to step in and get the man. And in some cases, the woman is either involved with the man, or has been in the past and is just trying to hold on to him."

Jaci felt her blood run cold. She couldn't help wondering if Gloria knew something she didn't about Jason. She hadn't even considered that Jason might have had a previous relationship with Linda. That would indeed shed a different light on the situation.

"Well, Jason knows how I feel about that. I'm not into sharing. If he wants somebody else, all he has to do is tell me and I'm gone. And I won't be stalking anybody either. Anyway, he had the option to choose Linda before I came along, and the fact that he didn't should tell her something." Jaci realized this conversation with Gloria just added to the doubts already swarming in her mind. She had to change the subject.

"Enough about me. I'm curious about what's going on with you and Bill. Have I missed something?"

"Oooh, girl! I'm just as surprised as you are. Bill hadn't said anything or given any indication that he was interested." Secretly, Gloria believed that Bill really wanted Jaci, but now that she was about to marry someone else, he had settled for her. She would take him any way she could get him. "Then, the night of the dance, something just clicked and it's been getting better ever since."

"Could we be talking serious here?" Jaci asked.

"Yeah, we're definitely talking serious."

"I'm so happy for you guys. You're both good people and I'm glad you're getting together. I hope it works out."

Later that evening, Jaci busily prepared the inspection reports for the hearing scheduled in two days. Gloria called good night at her usual time and left. Jaci was having dinner with Jason, so she tried to give him time to get home before heading to his house.

When she made her way to the garage an hour later, she felt uneasy, as if she were being watched. She looked around, hoping it was her imagination, and was relieved when she didn't see anyone. As she approached her truck, she screamed. The front and rear windows were shattered and all four tires were slashed.

Waves of fear engulfed and immobilized her. She couldn't decide whether to run back to the building—what if the person was still somewhere in the garage—or jump in the truck and lock the doors—Then what? Just be there like a sitting duck? She had always scoffed at women in movies who, in the face of danger, just stood there like idiots until whatever it was got to them. Now here she was, in that very situation, doing the same stupid thing.

The footsteps she heard behind her helped make the decision. She nervously unlocked the truck door and jumped in, locking the door behind her. She finally remembered the cell phone that Jason had given her and insisted she carry in her purse. Just as she was about to punch in Jason's number, someone knocked hard on the side window, almost causing her to jump through the broken windshield. It was Wynola Dickson.

"Jaci? What happened? Are you all right?"

Jaci didn't know who to trust. She rolled the window down slightly and said, "I'm calling someone to help me. I'm okay."

"Who in the world could've done this?" Wynola asked. A suspicion of who it might have been entered her mind and a sickening feeling began forming in the pit of her stomach. *Oh doggone! Linda has gone off the deep end again*, Wynola thought to herself.

"I don't know," Jaci answered. "If I did, they would be on their way to jail." Jaci felt the first pangs of anger join the fear. She managed to call Jason on his cell phone, relieved when she heard him answer.

"Jason? Someone has cut all my tires and broken my front and back windows. And I . . . can you come? I'm in the building garage. Please hurry."

"What! Are you okay?"

"Yes," she answered in a shaky voice.

"Is anyone there with you? Maybe you should go back in the building and wait for me. I'll get there as quickly as I can."

"Wynola's here. But I'm too scared to get out of the truck."

Jason thought about it for a second and realized she was right, they didn't know for sure who had done this. For all they knew Wynola could be involved. "Just stay put and keep the doors locked. I'm calling the police. They may get there ahead of me, but I doubt it. Ask Wynola to go back into the building and find the security guard."

"But you just said you were cal—"

"Jaci, just do it!" He didn't feel comfortable about

Wynola's being close to her. "As soon as I talk to the police, I'll call you back."

She sat huddled in the truck with the phone gripped tightly in her hand. She kept shaking her head in disbelief. In typical Jaci fashion, she started examining herself. *Lord, what in the world have I done to bring something like this into my life?*

As usual, that led her mind to where it needed to be—on the Lord. The phone rang and she answered.

"It's me, sweetheart. Have you seen anyone else in the garage?"

"No."

"Well just stay on the line until I get there. You doing okay?"

"Yes, but hold on, I need to pray." *Father, have mercy. I am in trouble and don't know what to do. I am being attacked because Linda doesn't want me to have Jason. Father, I believe You sent him into my life and I thank You for that blessing. I know the devil wouldn't be fighting it so viciously if it were not Your will for us to be together. Lord, I know that where You guide, You will also provide. You didn't give me this fear I'm feeling. So I thank You for power, love, and soundness in my mind right now. Lord, let Your mercy prevail and give me the victory in this situation. In Jesus' name I ask and thank You. Amen.*

Ten minutes passed before she saw the police car round the corner with Jason right behind it. She climbed out just as the police officer got to her truck and began to walk around it, looking at the slashed tires.

"Any idea who did this ma'am?" he asked Jaci.

"Yes, I do. But I'd hate to name the person and it's not her."

"Why do you think it's this person? Has she made any threats against you?"

"Yes, she has. In fact, there's a restraining order in effect, and lots of reports on file."

Jason listened as Jaci talked to the officer, amazed at how

calm she remained. It was apparent—when this woman prayed, God answered. He gave the officer a brief history of the threats and attacks against Jaci. The officer told her before leaving, "Sounds like you have a mighty determined enemy. I'd be careful if I were you. Looks like it's escalating."

J.P.

After they arrived at Jason's house, Jaci felt despair engulf her. She didn't feel safe at home, on the job, or anywhere. Now she didn't have transportation. What next? Jason held her close as tears of frustration rolled down her face.

"I'm sorry. I shouldn't be letting this get to me like this," she jerkily stated. "But I'm just so tired, so weary of dealing with this. Lord, help me."

Feeling helpless and angry, Jason wondered how he was going to protect her from any further attacks from Linda. It twisted his insides to see her hurting like this.

"Sweetheart, why don't you go upstairs and lie down. Later, we need to go pick up some of your stuff. I think you should stay here for a while."

Jaci shook her head. "No, nobody's running me out of my home."

"It's not a matter of someone running you out of your home. Look at you. You're completely shaken. Even if you did stay at your house, you wouldn't get any quality rest. You're staying here with me."

"I just think it's better . . . That I'll be more comfortable at home."

"Baby, will you let me take care of you?" He ran a finger down her cheek and bent to kiss her lightly. "Please."

Jaci didn't argue with him anymore. How could she? Over the years, she had prayed for someone she could lean on during a season of trouble. Now that she had someone, here she was fighting it. One of her grampa's favorite sayings came to her. *"It's wisdom to know when you're blessed. It's a terrible thing to complain when you ought to be giving thanks."* As usual, her grandpa had been right. She decided she would gratefully let him take care of her—for a few days anyway.

After she went upstairs, Jason called Ron and Walt and asked them to come over. When they arrived, he told them what had happened. "I'm about at my wit's end with Linda. We've done everything we know to keep her away from Jaci, and she's still finding ways to get to her. I don't know what to do. We have her arrested, but she's out again before we can turn around."

Ron was thoughtful for a minute before saying, "Remember I told Linda that whatever she did to Jaci, we would do to her. I think it's time to keep that promise."

Jason shook his head. "Naw, man! That kind of retaliation is not the answer. There has to be another way."

"I'm thinking I don't want to hear this conversation," Walt said. "Ya'll do realize I'm an officer of the criminal justice system. Maybe I'd better go."

"All right, Judge. But just remember, you're going to need help one of these days," Ron told him.

Walt threw his hands up. "Okay, but I'll swear I've never heard any of this before."

"What else can we do, Walt?" Jason asked his friend. "We've filed charges against her, put a peace bond on her, and called the police on every incident. But like I said, she's out of jail in no time and right back to her attacks."

Walt thought for a moment. "Well, I think if you give her

a little time, she'll eventually do something that'll send her up for a while. But in the meantime . . ." he shrugged. "I don't know."

Ron made a sound that indicated his irritation. "And what's Jaci supposed to do in the meantime?" he asked. "Maybe ya'll wanna sit around and wait for Linda to seriously hurt or kill Jaci, but that's not my style. What I'm thinking about might not be your way, but it might send Linda a message that enough is enough. I'll take care of it, and don't worry, it won't be anything physical—just something to keep her so occupied she won't have time to mess with Jaci."

"Okay, renegade. Like I said, I don't want to know," Walt said, shaking his head.

J.P. remained quiet for a minute. Ron's words, *"hurt or kill Jaci,"* kept running through his mind. "Okay Ron, I'm with you. But remember, whatever you do, make sure it's nothing that's going to make this any worse than it is. Did I tell ya'll I found out that Linda and Wynola are sisters?"

"What!" "You got to be kidding!" Ron and Walt responded simultaneously.

"No, it's true. And I'm sure Wynola is the one responsible for that crazy woman working in my office. I guess she figured if she couldn't get any play with me, she would sic her sister on me. Herbert hired her on somebody's recommendation. He doesn't even remember whose it was. I almost fired him when I found out those two are sisters. He didn't even read the application. It's right there in black and white."

Ron laughed. "You think he's going to admit to anything beyond what's already known? I know I wouldn't if I were him. Give him a break, he didn't know the woman was crazy."

"Linda even has Wynola harassing Jaci at work, trying to build a case to fire her. She's accused Jaci of working below par, discourtesy to citizens, and anything else she can come up with to discredit her. The latest thing is a letter she produced from some woman accusing Jaci of having an affair with her husband and breaking up her family. Jaci got a formal disciplinary letter, with the threat of total dismissal if another complaint comes in. What do you bet another complaint is forthcoming?"

"Whew!" Ron whistled through his teeth. "The woman just took the letter at face value, huh? Without giving Jaci the benefit of an investigation?" At J.P.'s nod, he continued. "That stinks. It sounds like she's gon' have to be included in our little retribution package."

"Yep. I got that covered though," J.P. said. "That was a big mistake on Wynola's part. I'm on Ed Shannon like white on rice. So are some other people in the department. And Pop has talked to the mayor about it. You know Pop is crazy about Jaci. Anyway, Ed had no choice in the matter, he had to take action. You know Wynola didn't get that job on her own merit. She's a political appointment. Not by this current administration, but she's managed to hang on over the years from one mayor to the next. Somewhere along the way, she forgot her husband's political clout will only go so far. No politician's going to stick his neck out for her over some mess like this. Her butt is already on the way out the door. So what are you planning?" he asked Ron.

"I'm toying around with something very appropriate for Linda. I can't get into it with the good judge sitting here though."

"Man, one of these days you're going to step into something that's gon' cause you to stink for years. Let that be a warning," Walt told Ron with a chuckle.

"Ain't gonna happen," Ron said confidently. "See, I'm a dude who knows how to cover all my bases. And I'm not afraid to steal a base when I need to. You wimps just done got old and lost all your nerve. If you ever had any."

"Have at it, brother," J.P. said. "I bow to your prowess. I'm certainly not one to look a gift horse in the mouth, and if you can do something to help, I'll be grateful, and I know that woman upstairs will be."

Ron was currently designing a facility for a restaurant owner. This client had a long history with the criminal justice system but had managed to stay just beyond the long arm of the law for the past ten years. Ron remembered one of the man's specialties had been breaking and entering. He had bragged that there wasn't a lock anywhere he couldn't pick.

When Ron returned home that night, he looked up the number and called him. "Hey, Johnson! Have I got a deal for you! But first, let me explain the situation. A crazy woman is stalking and threatening my brother's fiancée and nothing has been able to stop her, not even the police. This sicko needs to get a taste of her own medicine, but I don't want her physically hurt, just some things done, you know, like messing with her doors and windows, something that would scare her so badly she won't have the time or the inclination to think about stalking anyone. You with me so far?"

"Yeah. I'm with you," Johnson answered. "What're you offering?"

"I'm willing to give you a break on your fee if you can hook me up and help me out with this."

"Hey, doesn't sound like much of a challenge and I'm definitely interested in knocking something off your high-priced fees."

"I want you to think about this, man," Ron said. "I don't want you jeopardizing your freedom. Like I said, I just want some minor things done to scare this woman off. I stress that no physical harm is to come to her. I just want her to leave Jaci alone."

"Jaci? I know a Jaci. Good-looking lady who works over there for the city. She helped me get some property demolished and got the city off of my back. Is that the woman you talking about?"

"Yup, that's Jaci. And that other woman is making Jaci's life miserable, man."

"Jaci's a nice lady. I would help her without getting paid, but since you offered . . . and Ron, you know I'm not into rough stuff. I did my thing to make a living, and I'm through with all that now. But for a good cause, and a cut in my fee, I can easily get this done."

Misgivings about what he was asking shot through Ron's mind, and he said to Johnson, "It's very distasteful for me to ask someone to break the law, but like I said, this woman is a loose cannon, and I'm afraid she's going to do some real harm to Jaci if she's not stopped. Don't worry, we'll work out something that'll make it worth your trouble."

"Hey, man, consider it done. All I need is the four-one-one on this stalker."

"You'll have it tomorrow. And Johnson, keep it clean, and be careful, okay?"

"Yeah, man. Piece of cake."

Linda

Three weeks later, a frustrated Linda hung up the phone after still another harassing call to Jaci. She relaxed on her pillow. *I'm getting rusty. There was a time when I could come up with all sorts of stuff for a situation like this. There has to be something else I can be doing to get to that heifer.* The calls, threats, attacks—weren't working. Jaci and J.P. were still planning to get married. She wasn't happy with how slow her sister insisted they move on the "Jean White" thing. But it was almost time for Jean White to write another letter. Wynola had assured her that Jaci's dismissal would be certain after it was pointed out that Jean White was so distraught she was thinking about going to the mayor and to the media. Jaci wouldn't be so desirable to J.P. if that happened!

Her thoughts were abruptly interrupted when something came crashing through her bedroom window. She rolled out of bed to the floor, thinking someone was shooting into the house. When she finally lifted her head and looked around the dimly lit room, she saw a brick lying on the floor. She crawled over to pick it up and crawled out of the room into the hallway. She was afraid to turn the light on in the bedroom. With shaking hands, she removed a piece of paper tied around the brick, opened it, and read *"From a friend."* It was after two in the morning, but she picked up the phone with shaking hands and called her sister.

"Wyn! Someone just threw a brick through my bedroom window. It had a note on it that said 'From a friend.' Do you think that trashy Jaci Winters did it?"

"Linda?" Wynola asked groggily. "Where have you been? I've been trying to call you. Didn't you get my messages?" Wynola became more alert as she talked. "Linda! Did you do something stupid like vandalizing Jaci's truck?"

"So, what if I did! I told you I'm going to get that hussy. She's not getting the message so I had to do something to get her attention."

Wynola's stomach began to roll. After receiving a call from Ed Shannon, her husband had torn into her about her harassment of Jaci Winters, demanding to know if she was really foolish enough to do something like that. Her answer left him shaking his head, and he'd told her she was on her own. Her thoughts had been in turmoil ever since. But she was in too deep to stop at this point.

"Why!" Wynola screamed, as she got up, took the phone, and left the room to keep from waking her husband. "That was just plain foolish. Linda, you need to back off and move on. The man doesn't want you! Even if we do get rid of Jaci, he still won't want you. Leave it alone!"

"Huh! It's not even about that fool J.P. anymore. It's a matter of principle now. I'm going to show that little nobody that I'm a woman of my word. I told her I was going to get her for attacking me, and I'm going to do it."

"Linda . . ." Wynola sighed tiredly. "You're the one who attacked her, remember? She was just defending herself. Look. I can't help you anymore. And you need to forget this. Honey, I think you should consider moving back home. After all, you don't have a job or anything else holding you here."

"I'm looking for another job, and I'm not going anywhere until I deal with Jaci Winters."

Wynola realized her sister was not thinking rationally, and she hung up the phone and quickly dialed another number. "Hey, Sis, I'm sorry to wake you up but we've got a problem! Linda again. She's stalking and attacking people again." Wynola took care not to mention the extent of her own part in Linda's actions. "We need to get her out of town fast before she gets herself in more trouble than we want to deal with. I'm about sick of this girl. We should have never allowed her to come to Houston. She causes problems everywhere she goes. I hate to send her back to Mama and Daddy—Lord knows they're tired of her and too old to have this problem dumped on them. But the people she's messing with this time . . . she could end up in prison."

The next morning Linda entered the garage, happily on her way to a job interview, and discovered all four tires on her car were flat. Terrified, she ran back into the house. The car was in the garage, which was locked, but somehow someone had gotten in and cut all her tires. It chilled her to the bone to think that whoever had been there could have also entered the townhouse. Linda was scared!

Three days later, she removed the extensive barricades she had placed in front of the locked door and came out of her bedroom, then walked down the stairs where she stood in amazement. The exterior doors stood wide open and the curtains were blowing out of the open windows. She screamed and ran back up the stairs to the bedroom and picked up the telephone. Someone had been in her house! Had left all her doors and windows open for anyone or anything to get in. They were getting closer and closer to her. There was no way she could continue living in that house alone.

Hysterical, Linda screamed into the phone, "Wyn! Somebody keeps getting in here. They got in the garage and cut my tires the other night. And just now, I went downstairs and found all the doors and windows open. Somebody's coming in here and evidently they have a key because they're not breaking in, and I haven't heard a thing. I'm scared, Wyn! I can't stay here by myself."

Suddenly it occurred to Linda that it had been days since her last attack on Jaci. She'd been forced to switch from the offensive to the defensive mode. "I'm calling the police on Jaci! I know it's her behind this."

"Hold on, Linda, don't do that!" Wynola yelled. "Jaci hasn't even been in town this week. If you start making unsubstantiated allegations against her, you could be sued. No, honey. I've talked to Mama and Daddy, and we all think the best thing for you to do is move back home. Me and Sister are taking off a few days to help you get packed and moved."

"I told you, I'm not going anywhere. I was thinking I could stay with you for a few days until . . ."

"Yes, you are going!" Wynola said through clenched teeth. "Don't you understand? It's over, Linda. You're going if we have to drag you."

Wynola carried out her promise to move Linda back to
New Orleans. She returned to work the next week relieved
that Linda was out of Houston and with their parents who
promised to get professional counseling for her—again. Now,
she hoped, things could return to normal. But Wynola's relief
was short-lived and was quickly replaced with a feeling of uneasiness when she noticed that everyone avoided her and whispered as she passed them in the corridor. Something was up.
Her heart sank when she found a summons from Ed Shannon
waiting for her.

"Wynola. Come in and have a seat," Ed told her cordially.
After she sat down, he continued. "Wynola, I'm forced to do
something today that doesn't bring me any pleasure. However,
based on your actions recently, I'm in the position where I
have no choice." He handed her a letter with a stack of items
attached to it.

Parts of the letter jumped out . . .

*In light of your poor judgment . . . unjustified harassment of
an employee . . . falsified evidence to substantiate misconduct by an employee . . . maliciously seeking to slander, discredit and wrongfully dismiss an employee, . . . you are
hereby requested to submit your resignation immediately.
Your refusal to voluntarily resign will lead to action by the
department and the mayor's office to formally force your re-
moval through civil service procedures.*

The letter was countersigned by the mayor, indicating his
approval. There was more, but she stopped reading at that
point to look at the attached documents. As she perused the
documents, she tried to form an argument in her mind to defend herself. But when she saw the contents, she knew there
was no use. The papers included statements from two department managers, who described their witnessed unfair treat-

ment of Jaci Winters by Wynola; several letters of support for Jaci Winters from citizens, who demanded the department stop unfair disciplinary actions against Jaci Winters; a copy of the bogus letter from "Jean White"; a copy of the denied leave request from Jaci; a copy of the police arrest records, along with records of reported threats and attacks made on Jaci Winters with Linda Adams as the prime suspect; and a document showing Linda Adams to be the sister of Wynola Dickson.

Wynola stood and almost staggered out of Ed's office without a word. She walked as if shell-shocked down the corridor leading to her office. Her cushy, high-paid position was gone. Twenty-five years down the drain. As she walked unseeingly, she remembered Jaci's declaration that she had turned Wynola over to God. Now, it seemed Jaci and her God had won. Wynola's heart hardened. Maybe she had been too hasty in getting Linda out of town. Perhaps if she had helped Linda more in getting rid of Jaci, she would still have her job. But just wait! She was going to fix Jaci and her precious God too!

Matrimony

Jaci

Family Reunion

*J*aci's family reunion was held in Riverwood the last week-end in April. In spite of everything going on in her life, Jaci decided to attend. Her accumulated vacation time had reached maximum levels and she was at the point of losing some days if she didn't use them. She took two weeks off because in addition to the reunion, she also needed to do some serious work on her wedding and to get her house in order. She decided to lease her house rather than sell it. Not only did she have to pack everything and get ready to move, but she was also having work done to get the house ready for the tenant.

She worked ceaselessly in the house Monday through Wednesday. She then got ready for the drive to Riverwood and the reunion, which would begin that Friday night. The more she thought about it, the more excited she became. Her cousins all planned to attend and Jaci looked forward to spending some time with them.

She and Jason left Houston just after daybreak Friday

morning. Jaci wanted to arrive early enough to visit with her father's mother, Grandmother Winters, who was in a nursing home, as well as other family members.

Six hours later, Jaci fought the urge to pinch herself to see if she was dreaming. Riverwood! She was in Riverwood—with Jason! Though only a few hundred miles in distance, River-wood was a world away from Houston.

How much, Jaci wondered, did her relationship with Jason have to do with her decision to attend the reunion?

So much had occurred since she left Riverwood filled with hopes and dreams. Now, she simply wanted to savor the good memories that engulfed her as they drove from house to house, finally ending up at her brother's. Jaci wandered to the back of the house and sat down on the bed, remembering . . .

It seemed as though from birth, the cousins . . . seven of them . . . were enveloped in a mystical kind of charm that no one outside the group could understand or infiltrate. Maybe it had something to do with them all being born the same year. Maybe it was because they spent more time with Grampa and Grammy than their siblings and had the benefit of more of their wisdom and prayers. Maybe it was because they all looked so much alike that most people outside of the family didn't know which child belonged to what parent.

Seven brothers and sisters had all had babies born during one year, much to the delight of the babies' Winslow grand-parents. Four sisters had given birth to four daughters, and three brothers had fathered three sons. Those babies had, at some point, been breast-fed by each of the mothers. And thus had proceeded their lives, sharing every experience all the way from birth to college.

Jaci smiled as she recalled some of the mischievous things they had done. *Lord, it's a wonder we all survived.* Although they'd had every intention of staying in close contact with one another, it hadn't turned out that way. For years, they'd only managed quick hugs when they saw each other on brief trips to Riverwood, or occasional calls to get updates on their lives.

It had only been over the past several years that the cousins had begun reconnecting and reestablishing their closeness, and in the process, discovered that life had lost its charm after they had gone their separate ways. Jaci had prayed that their difficult seasons would soon be behind them. Again she chuckled as she recalled some of their youthful shenanigans and admitted her gratefulness for experiencing them. She had survived many tough ordeals by drawing on the strength, ingenuity, and creativity developed while growing up with her cousins.

Meanwhile, at another Riverwood home not far from where she was, a conversation about Jaci was taking place. "Is Jace coming? I heard she was, but I won't believe it until I see her."

"Yeah. Somebody told me she was already here. I think I'll call around and find out."

As Jaci sat reminiscing in the bedroom, each of her cousins came to the forefront of her mind. Kevin . . . called Buddy because Grampa had nicknamed him Little Buddy the first time he saw him. Robert . . . dubbed Big Ben after he got into a skirmish after a basketball game with a big player named Big Ben from a rival school. David . . . labeled Dusty after he fell into a large sawmill barrel filled with wood shavings and dust and looked like a human dust mop when he was fished out. Regina . . . shortened to Gina, and probably the one who kept them from getting into more trouble than they did. Anita . . . called Nita by everyone, and the one they had all been protective toward. Catherine Joy . . . mostly called C.J., but was often called Red because of her hair color and a temper that lived up to that name.

While growing up the seven cousins had been villains to some—heroes to others—always into something! They were all musically inclined and played either the piano or guitar, and they were singers as well. Typically, the cousins capitalized on their talent by forming a singing group in high school. And not surprisingly, they had become reasonably popular and in demand.

Anticipation filled her, and Jaci knew she was having one of her "moments." There was no other place on earth she'd rather be than Riverwood. Before the thought was complete, she heard the phone ring, and her brother yelled out that it was for her.

A few minutes later, she grabbed Jason's keys and ran out the door.

"I'll be back! I'm going to see my cousins," she called over her shoulder.

Munroe and Valerie Hilliard's house had been the cousins' hangout when they were in high school. In fact, Munroe had encouraged them to form the singing group. Now, their house was the obvious place for the cousins to meet. Some were already there, and others, like Jaci, were on their way.

Minutes after their greetings, the cousins sized one another up. "You cut your hair off." "Where all that gray hair come from?" "Oh yeah, where *is* your hair?" "You eatin' good these days, I see." "How many brats you got?" "Hey, are you kidding, I got grand brats now!"

They eventually settled down, and more than two hours passed unnoticed as they talked, ate, cried, and talked some more.

Back at her brother's house, Jason's concern grew. Jaci had been gone for hours. "Do you think we should go look for Jaci? She's been gone so long; something must have happened. I'm kind of worried about her."

Her brother and his wife laughed. "Heck naw! You don't know country folks, huh? She's stuck at somebody's house and if we show up, we'll be stuck there too. That's probably why she didn't take you with her."

"How are Randi and her family doing?" Jaci's sister-in-law asked.

"They're doing okay now, but you know, Randi had problems with her pregnancy, then the baby had problems. When they got through that, Randi's father showed up making demands . . . they've had a pretty rough time."

Jaci's brother jumped up from his recliner. "He what! Oh man, I should have beat the crap out of that sucker years ago. He must be stone crazy."

J.P. laughed. "Don't worry, I took care of it. And I'm looking forward to doing it again if he doesn't stay away from Jaci."

"You took care of it? How?"

"I whipped his butt. I think he was convinced that he could show up and pick up where he left off with no problem. He's not suffering under that misconception anymore. Man! It felt good! My hand was sore for days, but I'll do it again if I have to. That guy almost destroyed Jaci."

"Yeah, I know it. And I know now we should have done more to help her, but Jaci kind of went undercover."

"I don't have any say over whether Randi sees him or not," J.P. said. "Jaci left it up to her to make that decision. But Jaci . . . He'd better stay away from her if he values his life."

At the Hilliards' home, Munroe Hilliard sat in his old chair, unashamed by the tears that streamed down his face. Munroe and Valerie still missed the cousins, even after all these years.

"Riverwood just hasn't been the same without ya'll," Valerie said. "We still laugh about all the stuff ya'll used to get into. Remember that time ya'll were trying to smoke Grampa's cigar butts and burned the old outhouse down?" she asked, laughingly. They all cracked up.

"Yeah," Big Ben exclaimed, "we ought to beat Gina's butt right now, she was the one who messed up."

"Just try it, buster," Gina responded. "We were all in that

thing together. I think it was your match that set my dress on fire anyway."

"Oh my God!" Nita said, a look of horror on her face. "Ya'll, it's a wonder Gina didn't burn up that day. It took all of us beating away at that nylon dress to put out that fire. We didn't even notice that the cigar butts we had thrown down had set the outhouse on fire. By then that old wood was going up in smoke."

"Yeah," Buddy said. "And our behinds were smoking for the next week. I haven't wanted to smoke since." They all cracked up again and started recalling some of their other escapades that had kept their small community from ever becoming boring.

While the banter continued, Munroe disappeared into a back room and returned with an electric guitar, which he handed to Dusty to hook up to speakers, then steered Jaci to the old piano in the corner. "Kids, ya'll sing some of the old songs. I been waiting for years to hear ya'll sing together again."

"Oh my goodness!" C.J. said. "I don't know if I even remember those old songs."

Amazingly, the tunes and words came back. It wasn't long before they were all shedding tears, remembering and missing those no longer around who had also loved to hear those songs.

Although it was called the Winslow Family Reunion and it had been planned by Jaci's mother and her siblings, most of the community turned out for many of the festivities. The old school principal and several of the older schoolteachers, now all retired, were present to see and be seen by the many they had taught. The cousins stayed together for the most part, getting to know one another's family and friends.

Saturday's activities got underway early at the old high

school that had been converted into a community center. A lengthy program in which the cousins were coerced into singing was followed by lunch, games, dancing, and visiting.

Jaci

*J*t had been so good to be in Riverwood with her cousins. After the reunion Jaci returned to Houston full of anxiety over all she had to do. By the next Friday, she had packed up most of her things and completed several tasks on her wedding. Her vacation was almost over and she dreaded the thought of returning to work.

Jaci sat on the sofa in the family room to take a breather from her packing and looked out through the patio doors. She took in the large backyard filled with greenery and trees and the soothing blue water of the swimming pool. Curiously, she felt peace and contentment rise up within. It suddenly occurred that maybe she should consider Jason's desire that she quit her job. After all, she did have options now. She felt overcome with gratefulness. *Thank You, Heavenly Father, for Your mercy.*

The time spent in Riverwood with her family was the most time she had spent there since leaving after college. She now realized that somehow the visit had sparked a change in her. Oddly, her thinking seemed clearer, her spirit calmer, and her outlook on life better than she had experienced in a very long time. She saw glimpses of the young, enthusiastic Jaci who had left Riverwood filled with hopes, dreams, and plans. Had that person been hiding in her subconscious all these years? Over-

shadowed by disappointment, and disillusionment, and obscured by one stormy season after the other?

Yes, she decided. It was time to let that enthusiasm for life
resurface. She stopped dreading her return to work and began
to look forward to it, deciding to trust that God in His graciousness would restore all that had been devoured and destroyed by the enemy.

It was springtime. Her favorite season! A season of renewal.
A season for hope and faith to take prominence in her life
again; a season for new beginnings; a season to start believing
that good rather than evil would come her way. A season for a
change!

As if on cue, the telephone rang. She looked at it with displeasure, thinking . . . *It didn't take long for that fantasy to end!*

She slowly picked up the phone, half expecting to hear the
resumption of Linda's threats. As soon as she said a cautious
"hello," she heard a scream, then Gloria saying excitedly,
"Girl, I just had to call you! There's big happenings in the
place! You should be here!"

"Hey, girl!" Jaci said to the excited woman. "What's going
on?"

"Jaci!" Gloria refused to calm her excitement. "Wynola is
gone, girl!"

"What do you mean, gone?" Jaci asked curiously.

"I mean gone, like no longer here! She was given a choice—
resign or be fired. I don't know which one she took, but she
cleaned out her office and walked out without a word to anybody." Gloria paused to get her breath. "And get this! Linda,
that crazy woman that's been stalking you, is Wynola's sister.
That's why Wynola has been doing all those hateful things to
you—to help her. They even created that fictitious letter accusing you of having an affair with a married man to get you
fired. I still can't believe Wynola was that stupid. And guess
what? Linda is gone too. Wynola's husband told Mr. Shannon

that Linda is back in New Orleans and under the care of a psychiatrist."

Jaci was speechless. "Oh God, Gloria. I'm . . . I don't know what to say. I'm not happy to see anyone lose their job, but . . ."

"I am," Gloria said with no compunction. "She deserved it. She didn't have to do what she did. Remember when she denied your leave request when you needed to go see about your grandmother and she told you it was because she felt like it? I wonder how she's feeling right about now?"

Mixed emotions flooded Jaci's mind. She didn't want to rejoice over another's downfall, but she couldn't help but be relieved that the trouble the sisters had caused her was over.

"Gloria. Thanks for calling, girl. I need to go so I can take all of this in. I'll see you Monday, okay? Bye." Jaci hung up the phone in a daze. She couldn't believe what she had just heard. As it began to sink in, she jumped up and praised God for His goodness and mercy. Linda and Wynola had made a choice to do what they did. Now they had to deal with the consequences. She didn't feel guilty glorifying God for delivering her from their hateful actions. She ran around her house like somebody crazy, shouting and thanking the Lord. Then she picked up the phone and called. Jason. "Jason? I just heard that Wynola is gone! Can you believe that?"

"Good," he answered. "I knew it was going to happen, just not when. That's why I didn't say anything." It was definitely a day to get a serious praise on!

A strange atmosphere greeted Jaci when she arrived at work the following Monday. The buzzard mentality was in full force as her coworkers swarmed around her, picking Wynola apart and claiming to have single-handedly defended Jaci. She held her tongue, knowing it wouldn't be long before she was back on their menu. She entered her office and checked the work status. A hearing scheduled in two weeks required some attention, and she needed updates from her staff on their activities while she was out of the office. As she went about her duties, she quietly thanked the Lord for His peace. All she had ever wanted was to do her job in peace.

Just as she was getting focused and organized, the phone on her desk rang. It was Ed Shannon's secretary. "Jaci, Mr. Shannon would like to see you in his office right away."

"Okay. I'm on my way," she answered, while wondering, *Lord, what now?*

Jaci sat in shock as she heard Ed Shannon say in his slow Texas drawl: "I want to offer you the position vacated by Ms. Dickson. I realize you have a lot on your mind right now, with your wedding coming up soon, so I don't expect you to give me your answer right away. Give it some thought and get back to me as soon as you can. I have no doubt you'll do well in the position. In fact, I'll even go so far as to say you've been handling the bulk of the managerial responsibilities in the division anyway. You might as well get paid for it."

Jaci was so stunned it took her a moment to respond. "I have to be honest with you, Mr. Shannon. My fiancé would like for me to quit after we're married. It's not a settled issue, but the possibility is there."

"How do you personally feel about it?" Ed asked, thinking what a gigantic loss it would be to the department if she left.

"Well, I would really like to make twenty-five years. That's almost two more years. But like I said, it's still under discussion."

"Tell J.P. to lighten up!" Ed said laughingly. "What does he want, for you to be a housewife?"

"No, not at all. He wants me to work for him."

"Oh!" Ed looked thoughtful. "I can't say that I blame him for that. He knows you'll be a real asset to him. Well, think about it. Even if you take the position for just a short period of time, it'll be to your advantage."

"I will not only think about it, I'll pray about it, and discuss it with Jason," Jaci said as she stood up to leave. "I really appreciate your considering me for the position, Mr. Shannon. I'll try to give you an answer soon."

"You are more than welcome, Jaci. And I hope things turn out favorably for both of us." He watched her leave, thinking J.P. Gilmore was a lucky man.

Jaci sat down at her desk, her mind in a whirl and all thoughts of work definitely out the window. She dropped her face into her hands, wondering if her life would ever settle back into a comfortable routine. It seemed that one thing after another lined up to keep her in turmoil. *What's up with this, Lord?* she questioned, but stopped herself before going any further. *Lord, I'm sorry for complaining. Thank You for the blessings that are being manifested in my life. I ask for wisdom, guidance, and direction for myself and Jason. Whatever decisions we make, Lord, let them be according to Your plan and purpose.*

She was, without a doubt, in a new season, and life as she had known it was over. She was almost tempted to yearn for the old, comfortable struggles. At least she had known how to handle them. Now she was drowning in the unfamiliar—her quickly approaching marriage already had her in a tailspin of doubt and confusion. Now this job offer added to that. But the changes were good, she reminded herself, and began to pray *Thank You, Lord, for bringing these good things to me. I know it does not have to be so.*

She picked up the phone to call Jason. Might as well let him know what was happening. She knew to expect the very heated discussion her news would set off.

Jaci

Bash at J. P.'s House

Jaci was surprised to find a catering truck parked along the side of the house, tables and chairs already set up around the spacious backyard and pool, and bustling activity underway by the caterer and his staff. A huge barbecue pit emitted mouth-watering aromas, and long tables filled with every conceivable condiment were set up under a large tent. The kitchen was a mass of activity as the caterers prepared the usual side orders of baked beans, potato salad, green salad, macaroni salad, and rolls.

Jaci arrived early, thinking Jason might need help with the preparations. She should have known better. After Jason let her in, and they had settled in the family room where they could observe the activity going on in the backyard, she looked at him with admonishment. "Wow! This is going to be a big event. Had I known that, I probably would have chosen not to come. You know I don't like large social events. Maybe I should leave now before everyone arrives."

"Nope. That's exactly why I didn't tell you. And remember, I had to endure your family reunion last month. Not that I'm complaining."

"Yeah, right! Who had smoke blowing out of his ears when I got back to my brother's house that Friday evening?"

Jason smiled, remembering. He had been upset with her for leaving him alone with people he didn't know for so long. But she had warned him that would happen and tried to talk him out of going with her. So he couldn't complain too much.

"This is something I do every year. It's simpler for me to

have one big event and invite everyone—family, personal friends and acquaintances, employees—and whoever just happens to drop by. It fulfills my obligation to throw a party and gives everyone a chance to network and get to know each other. And of course, this year I want everyone to meet you. By the way, did you invite Randi and her family, and your cousin and Lena?" At her affirmative nod, he continued, "Are they coming?"

"Yes. They said they would be here. Lena's a big if, though. She'd already made plans with her friend. So it depends on whether he agrees to stop by. Thanks for inviting them. That was nice of you."

He looked at her with annoyance written all over his face. "You don't have to thank me! I want your family and friends here."

He grabbed her left hand, pointing to the large diamond ring there. "Sweetheart, I didn't put this ring on your finger without giving it a lot of thought. When are you going to get it through your head that our separate lives are over? We'll be married in a few weeks."

"Oh Lord, Jason, don't remind me." She groaned as though in torment. "I'm praying we're doing the right thing I don't want us to make a mistake with something as serious as marriage. I just can't do that to you."

"Will you stop that! We're both adults and know our minds well enough to know what we want. I'm just thankful God let us find each other before we get too old to care one way or the other."

She punched him playfully in the side and changed the subject. "How long does this usually last?"

"Well, the invitation said six to ten. But you know people. They ain't going nowhere until they think every chicken leg and rib is gone. It'll probably start clearing out around ten. But we'll have some stragglers around until eleven or so. Why?

You have somewhere else to go? If you do, I suggest you cancel those plans right now. You want to freshen up and put your purse up in my bedroom? When you get back, I'll have a nice cold drink ready for you." He caught her arm and gave her lips a quick kiss before he released her and watched her walk away.

Jason

*D*ang! She looked good!

When he opened the door and saw her standing there, he was tempted to put a sign on the door saying the party was canceled, then he could have her all to himself.

He was so in love with the woman he couldn't see straight. It still surprised him, the consummate playboy, having his nose open so wide the proverbial freight train would have no problem getting through. He had always been the one who ran while the woman clung. Now, he found himself clinging to Jaci and reluctant to have her out of his presence. He had it bad!

Two hours later, he looked around in satisfaction. The house and yard were filled with people having a good time. He was thankful the weather had cooperated. It was May and warm enough for those who wanted to, to take a dip in the temperature-controlled pool, but not so scorching hot that it was too uncomfortable to enjoy being outside. Patrick was vigilant in his role as lifeguard and enjoying it immensely. He had also invited some of his friends, and although they only came to eat as much as they could before heading to their own parties, Jason was glad they came so Patrick would have some company.

Jason's parents were holding court with his aunts, uncles, and other older adults in the comfort of the house. Every now and then they came outside and walked around the yard, observing the various activities, but never for long, preferring the cool quiet of the house to the loud music and noise outside. Cardplayers had a Bid Whiz tournament underway on one end of the long-deck. Jaci's cousin C.J. had teamed up with Jason's friend Walt and they were whipping everyone, to the chagrin of long-standing champs, Ron and Herbert. Jaci enjoyed herself as she moved from group to group talking and mingling. Since she loved to dance, she and some of the young crowd designated a corner of the yard as the dance floor and she was trying to learn the latest steps.

Every female, young and old, had a ball spoiling C.J.'s infant nephew, Geordi, who had been left in her care by her brother. The little guy happily went from arm to arm, enjoying all the attention.

"Hey, baby!" Jason walked up behind Jaci as she was taking a breather from dancing. "Having a good time?"

"As a matter of fact, I am! But I'm starting to get a little concerned about Randi. They should have been here by now."

"There they are now. You worry too much," he said as Randi came around the corner of the house with the baby carrier, while John followed with Sean in tow. "Come on, let's introduce them to everyone."

Baby Jasmine didn't stay in her carrier long. One of Jason's aunts rushed to grab her before anyone else could get to her. The baby was a charmer, and gave her famous, toothless grin to everyone who paid any attention.

"Randi, you guys go on over and help yourselves to whatever you want. I'm really glad you made it."

"Thanks, Jason," Randi answered. "Where did Mom go? I've got something to tell her." She looked around until she spotted Jaci, who had walked over to the card table to check out a big commotion going on there.

"Mom," Randi spoke softly after walking over to her. "Just before we left home, Aunt Nita called from Dallas. She sounded upset. She had tried to call both you and Aunt C.J., but called my house when she didn't get an answer. I told her I would have you call her back, but she said no, she would call you. I had to find Jason's number for her because she said she really needs to talk to you all right away. I figured she would have called by now."

Concern fizzled through Jaci. "I don't think so, unless no one heard the phone. Or someone may be talking on it. She didn't say what she wanted? I hope that crazy husband of hers is not up to his old tricks. The Winslows might have to take a trip to Dallas to kick his tail again."

"Oh Lord. You and your outlaw family!" Randi exclaimed before shaking her head and walking off toward the food tables.

Jaci went to the house to use the phone. As she walked in, Jason's mother beckoned her over.

"Jaci, you have a beautiful family! All of ya'll have those gorgeous green eyes and beautiful smiles. Even the babies. Those eyes must be a family trait."

"They are," Jaci confirmed. "Passed down from my maternal grandfather. All seven of his children have them. And all of the grandchildren. Now it's down to the great grandchildren. No one can deny, those are some strong genes."

"They sure are," Jason's father pitched in. "I wonder if you and Junior's babies will have them?" he said with a sly grin, trying to dodge his wife's "hush your mouth" slap across the shoulder.

"I don't think so," Jaci said, trying to hide her embarrassment. "Our baby days are long gone."

"Don't be so sure," his mother said, a hopeful expression on her face. "You don't know what the Lord has in store."

"Well, I'll just be glad when you put the boy out of his misery before he drives us all crazy," Uncle Stanley said. "I ain't never seen him like this before." He looked pointedly at Jaci, suddenly dead serious. "You see that woman over there in the white shorts? Give her half a chance and she'll be on your man like a chicken on a junebug. Eyes been on him ever since she got here."

"Uncle Stanley! Are you trying to make me jealous?" Jaci asked jokingly, although she knew he was telling the truth. She had noticed the woman watching Jason all evening.

"Naw," Uncle Stanley said seriously. "I'm just saying. It's plenty women just like that ole Linda, who would do anything to get off in this big house with him. But he ain't got eyes for nobody but you. That boy loves him some Jaci! You know that, don't you?"

"I know," she said softly. "I love him too. Now I'm getting outta here! It's too hot in here for me!"

Jaci

Jaci found an empty chair on the deck and pretended to watch the volleyball game, forgtting all about the phone. But her mind was busy trying to process the conversation she had just had with Jason's family. Whew! She couldn't believe the pressure she was getting from him *and* his family. She felt as if she'd been in a battle.

Although the wedding was just a few weeks away, she was scared— plain and simple. Scared of hurt and disappointment;

scared her own issues would mess things up; scared Jason would completely take over her life and she would lose herself in him; and although she had seen no signs of it, scared his reputation as a player would prove to be real. She hadn't forgotten the ugly seed of doubt that Gloria had planted in her mind. She kept reminding herself to trust in the Lord, that everything would be all right. She knew that if she allowed herself to dwell on those thoughts, the torment would drive her crazy.

The sun had gone down and the air started to cool down too. Parts of the yard grew shadowy, and someone finally put some oldies music in the CD player. Jason took a break from his hosting duties and came over to where she was sitting. "Why are you over here looking like you've lost your best friend? Come on, sweetheart, dance with me." Other couples had already begun to dance on the grass.

He led her over to a dark corner of the deck. As they danced, he pulled her close, wrapping both arms around her. "You feel so good in my arms," he whispered to her. "I'm ready to throw everybody out of here so we can spend some time together. Or better yet, let's just go on upstairs, lock the door, and forget about them. They'll leave when they're ready."

"Don't even go there, honey," she scolded him. "We're having enough difficulty controlling things in that area already. Anyway, just think about it. What if we did do something like that. Which we won't. But what makes you think your parents and Uncle Stanley wouldn't be up there banging on the door, with a shotgun in their hands, demanding that I make an honest man out of you."

He laughed at the scene she described and she soon joined him. To the amazement of those watching, they stood there with arms locked around each other, laughing uncontrollably.

A young man stuck his head out of the door. "Is there a Jaci out here?" he yelled, looking around.

"Yes. I'm Jaci," she said, untangling herself from Jason and walking toward the house. "What's up?"

"You got a phone call," the youngster answered. "You gon' be long? I'm expecting a call," he added, handing her a cordless phone.

"She may be," Jason answered for her. "You've been on that phone all evening. Man, you better get a cell phone if you have that much business."

Jaci punched the talk button on the phone and spoke into the mouthpiece. "Hello?"

She heard her cousin Nita's voice on the phone. "Jaci?"

"Hold on a minute, Nita." She glanced around, looking for a quiet place to hold a conversation. She figured no such place would be found downstairs, since there were people scattered all over the lower rooms.

"I'm going up to the bedroom. It's my cousin calling from Dallas," she said to Jason, who was still close by.

"Sure, go ahead," he answered.

She quickly ran up the stairs to Jason's bedroom and closed the door behind her. "Okay, Nita, now I can hear you. Girl, how're you doing? What's going on?"

"Jaci, is C.J. there with you? I don't think I can say this more than once."

"She is. Hold on, let me get her."

She came out of the bedroom, leaned over the banister, and yelled down to Jason, "Would you get C.J. please. I need her to come up. Tell her to hurry."

When C.J. bounded up the stairs and entered the room, Jaci handed her the phone from the bedside stand. "It's Nita," she whispered.

"Jaci? C.J.? Are you both there?" Nita asked.

"Yes, we're here," they both answered.

"G . . . G . . . Guys." Nita's voice broke and they could barely hear her as she continued. "Frank is dead."

"What!!!" they yelled.

"He's dead, ya'll. They found him in a hotel room today. Probably been there all night, since he didn't come home last night."

"Oh God. Nita, are you okay?" C.J. recovered enough to ask.

Nita responded slowly. "Yes, I think so. I guess I'm still in shock."

"When do you want us to come?" Jaci asked.

"I need ya'll now! But I guess I can wait until tomorrow. I'm just holding on by a thread, waiting for ya'll to get here so I can crack up. Where's Gina? Can ya'll find her and see if she can get here?"

"Sure, honey," C.J. answered. "I'll track her down."

They were surprised at the family reunion when Gina told them she was thinking about leaving California and moving back to Riverwood. Before she left the reunion, Gina whispered to them that she was definitely going to do it. True to her word, Gina was currently in the process of buying their grandparents' old house. She was doing a lot of traveling between Riverwood and California to close the deal.

"What about Buddy and them? You want them too?" Jaci asked her.

"No. I just need you girls with me right now."

"Nita, you're not there alone are you? Are the kids? . . . anybody, . . . there with you now?" Jaci asked her.

Nita sighed. "The boys are on their way now. I guess they'll be here shortly. Right now, my friend Lynn and a couple of ladies from the church are here. And Frank's family will probably be here before long too. Oh God. I just don't believe this is happening!"

Both Jaci and C.J. were quiet—both thinking *good riddance*—but too caring to say it.

C.J. finally said, "Nita? You know that it'll be tomorrow afternoon before we can get there. We have to get everything situated here before we can leave. But we'll plan on being there for a while, okay?"

Jaci looked over at C.J. gratefully. She had been trying to figure out how to say the same thing gracefully.

"Will you be all right until then?" Jaci asked. "Just go to a room and cry, pray, whatever, until we get there. Don't let anyone pressure you to make any decisions right now. We'll help you with all that. You did say all of Frank's people have been told?"

"Yes. And I'm a little worried about how I'm going to deal with them? What if they blame me?" Nita's voice broke.

"Whoa! Blame you for what? You're not the one found dead in a hotel bed," C.J. said. "But like Jaci said, go in a room—not yours and Frank's—close the door, and refuse to talk to them. Don't try to explain anything, let 'em call the police to find out what happened. And tell them that you're not making any decisions until we get there, got it?"

"Yes," Nita answered quietly.

"Nita," Jaci said softly. "This is all probably a lot easier said than done. But just do your best, honey. You've got that strong Winslow blood flowing through you. And most importantly, God has promised to never leave or forsake you. Draw on His strength and power. He'll see you through."

"Now how do we get to your house from Interstate 45? Do you remember how to get there, Jace? No?" C.J. asked, then said, "We'll call when we hit the city limits, Nita. Don't take no mess off of nobody. Tell them when your cuz's hit the door, we'll be taking names and whipping tail!" They were relieved when they heard Nita laugh.

"Thanks, guys," Nita said in a stronger-sounding voice. "I

can hardly wait till you get here. It's going to get crazy around here, and I don't know what I would do if I didn't know ya'll were on your way."

"Nita. Got a pen handy? Okay, take our cell phone numbers down. If something comes up in the meantime and you need to talk, call us! Anytime between now and when we get there. The phones will ring in the car. Now I want you to remember that and do it. We'll check on you first thing in the morning before we hit the road."

"C.J. has spoken," Jaci said. "Now you better do it! We're going to go now so we can get things rolling. We'll see you tomorrow afternoon, and hopefully Gina will be rolling in about the same time."

They hung up and sat there in silence, not knowing what to say. It wasn't an easy one to call. Their last encounter with Frank had not been pleasant. In fact, they had gone to Dallas and whipped his butt for beating up on Nita. Of course after that, Frank had forbid them to ever set foot in his house again.

"We'll be back if you ever lay a hand on her again, you can count on that," they had yelled back at him on the way out.

Since that time, they kept in touch with Nita by phone, calling when they knew Frank wasn't home and making sure she told them if he hit her again.

"Jace?" C.J. finally whispered. "I don't know what I'm supposed to be feeling right now, but I'm having a hard time feeling sorry Frank is gone. All I feel is relief."

Jaci took a deep breath, thankful C.J. had voiced her thoughts. "Same here, Cij. All I can think is that it could have been Nita. I was worried sick that the sucker would kill her one day. At least we don't have to worry about that anymore."

"What time do you want to leave tomorrow?" C.J. asked. "I'll drive. But I gotta try to figure out what to do with Geordi if his parents don't show up tonight like they promised," she said disgustedly.

C.J.'s brother and his wife left the baby in C.J.'s care for weeks at a time, leaving most people under the impression that he was her baby. "I guess we might as well plan to stay all of next week, since the services probably won't be until next weekend. Tell you what. Just call me in the morning and let me know what time you'll be ready. I don't think you'll be getting out of here anytime soon tonight."

Jaci thought hard. "Why don't we see if Randi will keep Geordi until they show up? If you don't feel comfortable with that, we'll just have to take him with us."

A quick knock was immediately followed by the door slowly opening and Jason peeking in.

"What's going on?" he asked, entering all the way and looking at Jaci.

"Nita, our cousin in Dallas, called to let us know that her husband was found dead today."

"Oh God! Where was he found?"

"In a hotel room," Jaci answered with distaste.

"Oooooh!" Jason looked shocked. "That's not the noble way to go out is it? What happened to him?"

Jaci and C.J. looked at each other. "Oh Lord. We didn't even ask. We were too busy trying to deal with the fact that he's dead," C.J. answered as she walked toward the door. "Thanks for inviting me, Jason. I had a really good time. I'm going to gather up my little guy and go on home. Jace, you got a really nice guy here. Treasure him, girl. And remind him what happens to men who mess with the cousins." She gave a wink as she walked out the door.

"What's she talking about?" Jason asked, looking puzzled. "What do ya'll do to people?"

"Nothing. Just ignore her," Jaci said, following C.J. through the door with Jason right behind her. They walked slowly down the stairs in silence. C.J. immediately gathered a now-sleeping Geordi and his things to leave.

Jaci walked over to Randi and spoke quietly to her.

"Oh my God!" Randi said in a shocked voice.

"C.J. may need a babysitter until her brother and sister-in-law get back. Can you keep Geordi for her?"

"Sure," Randi answered. "Just pack him up and bring him on over. When are ya'll leaving?"

"As early as we possibly can tomorrow. We promised Nita we'd be there as soon as we could."

"Well, I guess we'll go ahead and leave now too," Randi said. "How much longer you staying, Mom?"

"Girl, please! You see that man headed this way?" C.J. pointed to Jason. "He'll have a conniption fit if Jaci tries to leave anytime soon. She'll get home when she gets there.

"Call me in the morning, Jace. Oh! I'll get in touch with Gina," C.J. called over her shoulder as she headed around the side of the house toward her car.

Jaci waved okay to her as she walked back to Jason and gratefully accepted his hug.

"Okay. What time are we leaving tomorrow?" he asked.

Jaci thought for a minute before answering. "Jason, to be honest, it's not a good idea for you to come. We're going to be busy helping Nita with the arrangements and everything, and trying to keep her from falling apart, I don't think . . ."

"I know you don't think I'm going to let you go up there without me? Not with that fool Maxie lurking around!"

Sensing a battle in the offing, Jaci shored up for it. "Honey, Dallas is a big place. There's probably not the remotest possibility of even accidentally running into Maxie. And what do you mean, let me?"

"I meant . . ." Jason said with a stubborn look, "I don't think it's a good idea for you to go alone."

"Well, I won't be alone, my cousins will be there, and furthermore, how do you think I've survived all these years without you? I'm not exactly Winnie foo foo! I'm fully capable of taking care of myself."

"I disagree. That guy has been trying to get to you for months. After that stunt he pulled bringing his mother to your house, I don't put anything past him. I'm going."

"Your concern warms my heart, but no, you're not."

He gave her a hard, determined look, turned away from her, and walked over to his parents. She knew he was telling them what had happened.

His dad immediately stood, went outside, and said in a loud voice, "Okay, people, party's over! We've had a death in the family. Time to break it up and go on home."

Everybody looked surprised, then questioning, as they stood and prepared to leave. It was still early for them. Only a little after nine o'clock.

Jason came back to her, grabbed her hand, and pulled her down the hallway and into his office, only to find his brother there with a woman in what looked to be an intimate conversation. He closed the door and redirected their path upstairs to his bedroom.

As he watched the unfolding scene, Big Pat said to his wife, "I see a fight brewing. Junior probably don't want Jaci to go up to Dallas. I need to talk to that boy. You can't put a harness on a woman. You gotta let her run free. If she's yours, she ain't going nowhere."

Cecelia chuckled. "Well, I don't think Jaci needs any help. She's not going to let him harness her. I can tell she's not going to take any mess off of him. She's just what he needs."

"You're not going with me!" Jaci stated as soon as the bedroom door closed behind them.

"You can't stop me from going. I'll follow you up there whether you like it or not."

"That would be stu . . . uh . . . illogical."

"You started to call me stupid," Jason said accusingly.

"I did not! I said 'that,' not 'you,'" Jaci responded.

"You meant me!"

Jaci looked at him with irritation. "Why are we arguing over whether something is stupid or not? That's not the issue here."

They looked at each other and laughed.

"We're wasting time, aren't we?" Jason asked.

"Yes, we are," Jaci answered. "I'll have to leave real soon so I can get home and pack."

"You're not leaving here anytime soon. And that's one argument I will win tonight."

Jaci smiled and remained silent. She knew to quit when she was ahead.

They walked back down the stairs hand in hand. Jason heard his dad in the kitchen, giving directions to the caterers, while his mom and aunts busily put food in the freezer and cleaned up the kitchen.

Everybody looked around, surprised when they saw them approaching. Big Pat said, "We were trying to shut things down for you. We didn't know what time ya'll might resurface. Ron and Pat are outside helping the caterers load up."

"What he means is, he didn't know 'who' was going to resurface," his mother said. "My bet was on you, Jaci."

"Mine too," his dad admitted. "And looks like we won. You going to Dallas, son?"

"I don't know."

"You going to Dallas, Jaci?"

"Yep."

His parents and the others cracked up and continued laughing as they finished up in the kitchen and said good night.

"Now what in the world was that all about?" Jason asked, looking at Jaci.

"I have no idea," Jaci answered smilingly, but she had her suspicions.

Jason locked the doors and led the way into the family room.

"Oh man!" Ron yelled from outside. "They've locked us out! I wanted to take some food home with me!"

Patrick went to his car, a big smile on his face, and drove off.

"So how are you going?" Jason asked when they got comfortable on the family room sofa. "I know you don't plan to drive. If so, you'll have to take my car. I don't trust yours on the highway."

"I'm riding with C.J."

"Is she taking the baby?"

"No, I don't think so. His parents are supposed to get back tonight. If they don't, Randi will probably keep him. Or C.J. may decide to take him with us. Right now she doesn't know."

"Dang! Ya'll sure got that together quick. So how long do you plan to be there?"

"I don't know, honey, that's hard to say. But I don't foresee any services until the end of next week. And I'm saying that hoping it'll work out that way. This couldn't have happened at a worse time for me, but I have to go. Nita needs us with her right now."

"So where will you be staying?"

"Hon . . . ey! I don't know. At the house with Nita, or at a hotel. None of that can be determined until we get there."

"Be sure to take your cell phone so we can stay in touch, okay?"

"Yes, dear," Jaci said with a smirk. "Anything else?"

"Will you let me know when the arrangements are completed? Maybe I can drive up for the services and we can ride back together."

"Sure. But have you forgotten about the men's conference? That's next week isn't it?"

"Oh man! I think you're right. I'll just have to find someone to cover my sessions for me."

"You can't do that! You're one of the main speakers. And they couldn't have made a better choice for someone to do a session on black entrepreneurship. You're the best, baby."

Jason grinned. "You're just saying that to help you win this argument. I know what that's about. We'll see."

Maxie

Maxie sat in his regular spot—in his old recliner in front of the television. As usual these days, he was unable to get his mind off Jacetta—the mother of his child and the sexiest grandmother he had ever seen. He had been stupid, he sadly acknowledged. When they first met, Jacetta's youth and inexperience had made it easy for him to take advantage of her. He'd made a lifestyle of duping ignorant women, getting what he wanted, and dumping them. He hadn't thought or planned anything beyond that. But even back then Jacetta had plans to do something with her life. She had already graduated from college and had started work toward her master's degree. He wondered if she ever completed it. Perhaps if he'd been as smart as he had thought, he would have envisioned her as she was today. But maybe it wasn't too late, he thought, smiling with delight at the opportunity before him.

Maxie called George every week to keep tabs on Jacetta. He was still angry and humiliated at the way things had happened on both of his visits to her house. He'd lost out on both of those encounters, mostly because of her so-called fiancé. He wasn't a good loser, and one way or the other, he would find a way to come out on top. If nothing else, he would show that Gilmore guy that he would not be pushed out of Jacetta's life until he was ready. Jacetta needed to get that message too.

He'd felt like jumping with joy when George mentioned that Jacetta would probably be coming to town for a funeral. Maxie didn't care what brought her, he was just glad she was coming. He immediately began to make plans. He would get her alone so they could talk, confident that he could talk her around to his way of thinking. He would steer clear of their past . . . that would be the wrong strategy. He needed her to forget that. He would appeal to her as the woman she was now, and would convince her to give them another chance because of their daughter and grandchildren. In truth, establishing a relationship with his daughter and grandchildren had never entered Maxie's mind.

Jaci

They arrived in Dallas midafternoon Sunday. C.J. decided to bring the baby because she hadn't heard from his parents and she didn't want Randi to have to watch him indefinitely. They found Nita's house easily but were disconcerted to find several cars already parked in the driveway and lining the street in front of the house. They were surprised and delighted when Gina came running out to meet them. Thankfully, she was in Arkansas when C.J. tracked her down. Gina's drive from just across the state line in Arkansas was slightly shorter than their drive from Houston.

The cousins excitedly hugged each other, crying and laughing at the same time. Anytime one of them was hurt, the oth-

ers swiftly rallied to their defense. Anyone outside of their circle soon learned that to tackle one cousin was to take on them
all—as Frank's family was about to discover.

When Gina met them outside, she explained what was
going on inside the house. "Guys, get ready! Frank's family is
in there trying to take over. They're running Nita to death fixing food and waiting on them hand and foot, just like they did
when Frank was here. Now that I have some backup, I'm ready
to fight!"

Sure enough, Frank's parents and siblings were ensconced
in the house with much attitude on display, and it was apparent they were staking out the house and its contents, ready to
oust Nita and the children and claim as much as they could for
themselves.

Not long after they arrived, C.J., the most outspoken of the
group, began to set things straight. "We're so glad you're here
for Nita, but she really needs some time alone to deal with her
loss. Would you all mind giving her the needed privacy to get
herself together, take care of her children, and start making
arrangements? I'm sure you all understand."

"We're just as much family as you are!" Frank's brother
spoke with hostility. "And any arrangements to be made will
be made by us. Frank was my brother and this is his house.
We're not going anywhere."

Jaci tried hard to control her anger. These people, who lived
in a small town near Dallas, sat back in full knowledge of what
was going on and allowed Frank to abuse Anita for years and
had not raised a hand to stop him. She couldn't hold her
tongue.

"Sir, I don't mean to be insensitive, but this is not your
brother's house now." She looked at him pointedly. "And
until we learn differently, we'll have to assume that it's Nita's.
Now you know her well enough to understand that you're
welcome here, but right now she's overwhelmed with the sud-

den and unexplained loss of her husband. She needs peace and comfort and shouldn't be expected to play hostess or fight off any conflicts of interest."

Frank's sister, who weighed at least four hundred pounds, stood with hands on her expansive hips. "Like my brother said, we ain't going nowhere. Where ya'll get off coming in here trying to take over anyway? Ya'll wasn't nothing to my brother. He didn't even allow ya'll to step foot in this house!"

C.J. and Gina came to stand beside Jaci, fierce looks on their faces. Nita was sitting with her head down, silently crying.

"Oooh!" Jaci said. "So you know about that, huh? Well, if you know that, you also know why he didn't want us here. And for anyone here who might not know, let me tell you. It was after Frank had beaten this woman so bad he'd almost killed her. We came up here, gave him a taste of his own medicine, and told him he'd better not ever lay a hand on her again. And to answer your question, we're here at Nita's request."

Anita's friend Lynn came to stand beside them. "That's right! And if I had had some help, I woulda been over here whipping his butt long before they got here. It didn't make no kinda sense the way he treated this girl."

Opposing sides took position, with the cousins and Lynn on one side of the room and Frank's family on the other. There was no telling what would have happened at that point if Frank Jr. hadn't spoken.

"Grand Momma," he said, appealing to his grandmother, whom he considered the most reasonable. "I'm sure you understand what my aunts are saying. My mother has a lot facing her right now, and I'm asking ya'll to leave so she can get herself together."

Frank's mother stood up and gathered her purse. "Come on ya'll, let's go." She was ashamed. Ashamed of her son and herself. She had known for years that Frank had abused Anita, but failed to speak up. Maybe if she had intervened and tried to help her son deal with whatever demons were driving him, he might be alive today. She couldn't let her family pick up where Frank had left off in mistreating his wife. She had fought the same battle for years with her own husband, but the Lord had finally answered her prayers when he repented and stopped beating her. She looked around, expecting her family to follow her to the door. When they didn't move, she yelled, "I said, let's go! Frank was Nita's husband. And they're right. This is Nita's and them children's house. They got a right to their privacy right now." She walked determinedly through the door, then called over her shoulder, "Nita, I'll call you later so you can let me know how I can help you with the arrangements." The others reluctantly followed her out.

The cousins promptly went into action. They made lists of everyone they needed to call, and everything they needed to do to make the funeral arrangements, split them up, and went to work. To make room for relatives who would insist on staying at the house, they decided that Gina would stay at the house with Nita, but Jaci and C.J. would get rooms and spend their nights at a nearby hotel.

Jason

It was Monday and Jason was having trouble keeping his mind on work matters. Jaci called to let him know where she was staying and how everything was going. It sounded like things were under control, but he still had concerns about Jaci being in the same city with Maxie, and without him. The men's conference was set to take place from Thursday to Saturday. He was scheduled to do several workshops Thursday and Friday. Jaci didn't know yet when the services would be, but said the family was pushing for Saturday. He hoped it would be Friday so Jaci could come home. But if it was Saturday, he planned to leave Friday evening or early Saturday morning. In the meantime, he was worried about Maxie. Jason didn't trust men like Maxie, who operated like a dog and had a "dog with a bone" mentality. If the dog didn't want the bone, he buried it just to keep another dog from enjoying it, or on the off-chance that he might want to dig it up for himself at a later time. Maxie had been sniffing and digging around Jaci like the dog he was, hoping to get lucky. This made Jason very nervous. His male instincts told him Maxie was as low-down and conniving as ever, and he didn't want him anywhere near Jaci.

Maxie

Maxie hung up the phone, excitedly rubbing his hands together in satisfaction. He had managed to get the information he needed. He knew from George the name of the funeral home handling the arrangements for the late Dr. Frank Stanhope, and it didn't take much effort for him to get the home address of the dead guy from a silly woman who worked at the funeral home. According to George, Jacetta would be at that house with her cousin.

Maxie spent the remainder of the day preparing. He went to the barbershop for a fresh trim and even got his shoes shined and bought a new shirt. He washed and cleaned his car, sure that before the day was over, Jacetta would be in it with him.

Later, he smiled confidently as he found his way to the fashionable neighborhood.

Jaci

As soon as she knew, Jaci called Randi and Jason to let them know Frank's funeral was set for Saturday morning at eleven. Randi wouldn't be able to attend the services, but Jason had already made tentative plans to leave late Friday or early Saturday. Jaci decided she would drive back to Houston with Jason, while C.J. would stay on in Dallas with Nita for a few days.

Surprisingly, their cousins Buddy and Dusty showed up at Nita's house Thursday evening. Big Ben, unable to leave his high school coaching duties, called to express condolences. As the cousins sat around the kitchen table Thursday night, reminiscing and laughing over their antics as children in Riverwood, the doorbell rang. One of Nita's boys came to the kitchen door. "Aunt Jaci, there's some man here to see you." Jaci frowned in annoyance. There was no one she wanted to see badly enough to interrupt her time with her cousins.

"Did he say who he was, baby?" Jaci asked him.

"No. He just asked if you were here and when I told him yes, he asked to see you."

Jaci left the kitchen with a questioning look. When she saw who it was, aggravation and anger consumed her. "Maxie! What in the world are you doing here? You're not welcome, so you need to leave right now."

Maxie salivated as his gaze boldly traveled over the gorgeous woman who stood before him. Her beautiful eyes glinted angrily as the kissable lips tightened in irritation. *It was going to be fun kissing those lips into submission*, he thought. Shoulder-length hair framed her heart-shaped face in loose waves, and the midthigh shorts she wore showed off big shapely legs and voluptuous curves. He wondered again how he had let her get away from him. He was convinced his life would have been different if he'd had sense enough to hold on to her. The woman had everything . . . looks, intelligence, a good job, and a beautiful home. He could be enjoying all of that right now. When she told him she was pregnant, he should have been the one insisting they get married as soon as he could dump his wife and find a preacher. Darnit! He had been foolish.

Maxie pushed past Jaci and arrogantly walked into the sitting room, where he took a seat. "Jacetta, uh, Jaci," he said with a smile. "I went through a lot of trouble to find out where you were staying." He sounded as if he had actually done her a favor. "The least you can do is speak to me. I came over here because I need to talk to you. You've made it impossible for that to happen in Houston, so since you're in my town, I'm making it my business to talk to you. Is your watchdog here?" He chuckled as he looked around nervously.

Jaci looked at him contemptuously. "If you mean my fiancé, no. He's not here right now. But don't think you won't still get your butt tossed out of here. I suggest you leave now, while you still have a chance."

Maxie grinned and looked at her searchingly. "I can't get over what a beautiful and desirable woman the mother of my daughter is. Just how serious are you about marrying that joker? I'm asking because I think you're making a mistake. You should back off and think about it. And I want you to consider giving us another chance. We're older, more mature now. We already have something between us to build on, meaning our daughter and grandchildren. And I think our daughter would love for us to get back together." He turned on his special smile—proven to melt even the hardest woman.

Jaci let out a loud laugh and sat down across from Maxie. "You must be out of your doggone mind! Just what gives you the idea that I would do something that foolish? And you can leave my daughter out of this conversation, so that eliminates your 'something between us to build on.' You effectively removed that possibility when you disappeared after I told you I was expecting your child and begged for your help. As far as I'm concerned, you gave up all rights to my daughter and grandchildren." She looked at him like he was something nasty.

Maxie cringed at her words and the look she leveled on him. Then, he noticed that several people had entered the room and were standing around them. They too looked at him like he was something they would wipe off the bottom of their shoes. A sense of desperation suddenly filled him. He needed to get her away from these people so he could bring her around to his way of thinking. "Jacetta, let's go for a drive, maybe a drink or something, so we can talk privately. And my mother wants me to bring you by to see her."

Jaci looked at him for a long time before she finally spoke. "What gives you the idea that I would go anywhere with you?" she asked coldly. "But you know what, Maxie, I'm glad I have this opportunity to say some things to you. For years I struggled with how I let myself be taken in by you. It took a while, but I finally came up with the answer. It's not a complicated answer and now that I've talked to you and observed you over the last several months, I wonder why it took so long. It's obvious. I had to be either stupid or stone crazy." She laughed and relaxed in her chair.

"Since you showed up again, I've searched for something . . . anything . . . in you, to justify my stupidity or at least explain why I let you make a mess of my life, but all I've seen are signs of you growing physically older. There's nothing to indicate any mental, emotional, or spiritual growth. You're still the same low-life jackass and the most pitiful excuse for a man it's been my displeasure to know."

Jaci continued. "I feel sorry for you, Maxie. You're so pathetic that you actually came over here tonight convinced you had something to say that I'd want to hear. What's wrong? Have you finally discovered, after a lifetime pursuing a good time, that you've gone the wrong way and bypassed the meaningful and valuable things in life? Do you find yourself at a dead end with nowhere else to go?"

Maxie reeled as though Jaci had delivered a physical punch. Her words echoed what had recently been drumming through his mind. He fought the same urge he'd given in to years ago and refused to run as fast as he could. He realized she was still talking.

"A whole lot of people have failed you, Maxie. It's a real shame that no one was able to instill some modicum of decency and wisdom that would have helped you understand that one day, you would be at this point in your life. You could have had the love of at least one good woman, but you didn't have the sense to accept it. The only good thing you've accomplished in this world was planting a seed that resulted in my beautiful daughter."

Maxie felt anger growing at the way she was talking to him. "Now wait a minute! You don't have any right to talk to me like that. When I met you, you were nothing but a dumb little country hic—"

Maxie's words were interrupted when Buddy, a much larger man, grabbed him by the collar of his new expensive shirt and pulled him up from the chair he was sitting in. "I'd be real careful if I were you. I hear you've already gotten one good whipping being disrespectful to this woman, and to tell you the truth, we're all looking for an excuse to give you another one." He pushed Maxie back down in the chair roughly and stepped back, rubbing his hands against his stylish trousers as though to wipe them clean.

"You through with this scum, Cuz?" Buddy asked.

Jaci shook her head. "No. I need to finish what I was saying before we throw him out."

Maxie jumped back up. "I'm leaving. I don't have to stay here and take this crap."

Dusty, wanting to get in on the action, pushed him back down so hard the chair almost tipped over. "My cousin has some more to say to you. Since you presented your ignorant butt over here without being asked, you don't leave until we say you leave. Now sit down!"

Jaci struggled not to laugh at the expression on Maxie's face. "You've been given a second chance by the grace of God. You could have the love of your daughter and grandchildren. But are you grateful? No. Are you doing everything possible to gain their love? No. The only thing important to you is the chase and the conquest of women. I'm just another challenge—one you have to triumph over again. That's all this is about. Whatever I thought I saw in you was never there. But I was in love with that delusion. Did you cherish that love? No. You balled my love up like a used Kleenex and threw it back in my face. Now, you have the audacity to stroll in here uninvited, expecting me to be the same stupid idiot I was then. I don't think so! This time you're the crazy one."

Maxie dropped his head, unable to look at her. "You see, Maxie, I'm abundantly blessed. I have a beautiful daughter and two healthy grandchildren, for which I am grateful, and a wonderful man who loves and appreciates me. The only thing I can offer you now is forgiveness and Jesus Christ. God's been good enough to bring you through some health problems, but are you thankful? No. While you still have time, I encourage you to grow up and find your way to a good church where Jesus is exalted and the Word of God is taught. I forgive you for everything, Maxie, because I have to. But hear this well . . . there's absolutely nothing you can do for me but get out, and don't ever come near me again."

Maxie left the house and walked quickly to his car. Feelings of déjà vu reverberated in his mind. Another encounter with Jacetta had left him reeling with humiliation and other undefined feelings. He got into his car and sat there for a long time, replaying her coldly spoken words in his mind. For some reason he felt like crying. But naw! He shook his head in denial. That wasn't happening. He started the car and drove slowly down the street.

For reasons Maxie didn't quite comprehend, he attended the funeral on Saturday. He needed to see Jacetta again—needed to hold on to the last flicker of hope that she would see him and smile at him with the same loving expression he had seen her give to others. Although the large church was crowded, from his seat in the balcony, he searched until he finally spotted her. However, she was with the Gilmore guy, who had a protective arm around her, and the other two men who were at the house Thursday night. If she saw him, she looked right through him as though he wasn't there. He watched her circumspectly, trying to memorize her beautiful face, before walking slowly to his car. Maybe he would call Randi and his other children. Maybe he could ask his mother about a good church.

Jaci

*T*he following Saturday, Jaci wanted nothing more than to sleep as late as she could before getting started on her long to-do list.

But she reluctantly agreed to meet a coworker for breakfast at the local New Orleans Poboy. The place was popular on any day, but especially on the weekend.

Albert Michaels was a whiner, and some days she could take him, others she couldn't. He was not only a coworker, he also happened to be from Riverwood. Perhaps that explained why she often acquiesced whenever he begged to talk to her about his woman problems.

After they settled into a booth with their food, Albert started right in with, "I don't know what to do Jaci. I love Wanda, but I think I might be too slow for her. She likes the club scene and takes off to Vegas or somewhere to gamble every chance she gets. And you know me, my money's too hard to come by to throw it away like that. And my clubbing days are way behind me."

"Well, like I've told you before, Al, I'm not the one to be giving advice, but have you tried to talk to her? Maybe that's what you need to do, sit her down and have a serious conversation about what she wants out of life. Or better yet, tell her what you want. Do you know what you want? You have to be clear on that. Maybe you all are incompatible."

"I've tried, but . . . you know how hard it is for me to put what I really feel into words. I can't seem to get my point across to her."

The two had their heads bent over large platters of pancakes and bacon. They were unaware that two men who had just come in were now staring at them from across the room.

J.P.

*R*on awakened J.P. with a phone call and badgered him into going to breakfast. He would rather have slept in, but got up, took a quick shower, dressed in some comfortable jeans and a sweat shirt, and waited for Ron in the driveway in front of his house.

"I just want you to know, you're buying . . . waking me up this early on a Saturday morning. And the only reason I'm going is because I can really chow down on some of those big pancakes."

"Hey, man, don't get in here with all that yak. I need to talk to you. I got a little situation going with this girl, and well . . ."

J.P. looked at Ron like he had lost his mind. "What's wrong with you, Ron? What girl are you in trouble with now? Man, when are you going to get it through that thick skull of yours that all you need is one woman—just the right woman. You getting too old for the kind of lifestyle you leading."

"I told you, I don't want to hear all that. I don't need lecturing, I just need you to listen and tell me what to do."

J.P. released a long tortured breath. "I knew it! I should have stayed in bed."

They reached the restaurant and continued the conversation while they stood in line to get their food, and were still talking as they looked around for an empty booth. As usual, the place was packed.

Ron, who had forgotten to get cream for his coffee, went back to the counter. Returning to their table, he noticed the couple in a booth across the room.

"J.P., is that Jaci over there? If that's not her, it's her twin."

J.P.'s head snapped around to look in the direction Ron was pointing. Sure enough it was Jaci, in deep conversation with some man. His face—his whole body—tightened as he dropped his fork and slid out of the booth.

"Now, man, don't go over there and start nothing. You don't know who that dude is, it could be her brother."

"I know it's not her doggone brother," J.P. said as he started across the room.

"Oh darn!" Ron said as he slid into the booth. "Why didn't I keep my mouth shut. I ain't in no mood for fighting this morning."

J.P. leaned over the booth and planted a proprietary kiss on Jaci's surprised mouth, then turned to the guy, extending his hand. "Good morning, J.P. Gilmore, Jaci's fiancé. And you are?"

"Al Michaels," the guy answered slowly. "I'm a coworker of Jaci's. And a homeboy too. I hope you don't mind, I coerced Jaci into having breakfast with me this morning."

"I can see that," J.P. said, looking hard at Jaci. "Come on over when you finish, sweetheart. Ron and I are right across the room over there."

Jaci didn't say a word, just sat there with an amused look on her face.

About twenty minutes later, Jaci stood beside their booth. "Good morning, Ron, how're you doing?" She then turned to J.P. and just looked, waiting for him to speak. When he didn't say anything she asked, "Did you need to say something to me? I'm getting ready to leave."

She looked cool and collected in a red V-neck shell blouse and navy blue midthigh shorts. A pair of shades sat atop her head amidst her beautiful reddish-brown hair.

J.P. stood up quickly and guided her into the booth before slipping in beside her. "I don't have anything to say to you. The question is, do you have anything to say to me?"

"No. I don't. Why?"

"Well, if you walked in here and saw me in an intimate

conversation with a woman, wouldn't you want an explanation?" he asked with agitation.

"No. I would just assume she was a friend or something and leave ya'll alone."

"You're a liar. You would've been over there pouring hot coffee all over the woman."

"Maybe. Let's just hope we'll never find out. It may not be the woman getting the hot coffee."

Ron choked on his coffee and started laughing. "I like your style, Sis. If you ever decide to dump this guy for a real man, give me a call."

"In your dreams. Now butt out," J.P. told him.

"Let me out, honey," Jaci said. "I need to go. I've got lots of things to do today."

"Like what?"

"Going shopping with C.J. for wedding stuff. And I promised to babysit for Randi tonight."

"And where do you plan to fit me in?"

"Oh, come on! We talked about this yesterday, when we spent the *entire* day together. I told you then I was going to be running all day today."

"You didn't tell me you were having breakfast with another man."

"I didn't know it then. Al just called this morning. What is this anyway? The third degree? He is such a big baby," Jaci said to Ron.

J.P. shot an irritated look at her and stood. "Ready, Ron?" Jaci slid out of the booth behind him and they started toward the door, Ron following close behind.

When they got to Jaci's Jeep, J.P. said to Ron, "See you later, man."

Jaci looked at him in surprise. "What are you doing? I told you, I have things to do."

"Is it asking too much for you to drive your fiancé home?"

"Yes. I didn't bring you here."

"Well, you're taking me home. Let's go."

"Jaa . . . son!" she said in exasperation.

"Well, we won't have this problem after we get married. I'll probably be pushing you out the door. Oh no. Wait a minute. Not to go meeting some other man."

Jaci laughed. "You can't have it both ways, babe. And you keep acting this way, we might never get married."

He looked at her with a frown. "Don't even think about it. Come on." He took her keys, opened the passenger door of the truck, and motioned for her to get in. Then he went around and got behind the wheel.

"I'm not going in," Jaci said as they pulled up in front of his house. "I'll be late getting to C.J.'s."

"Call her and tell her you'll be late then. We need to talk."

"Talk about what?"

He walked around the truck and opened her door. "Come on in for a few minutes." Jaci groaned as she reluctantly climbed out of the truck. They entered the house and sat down at the kitchen table. He went to the refrigerator to retrieve two bottles of water.

"Do you realize that in two weeks, you'll be my wife?"

"Yes, I do. I guarantee you, I don't need to be reminded. There's so many things I have to get done between now and then that I can't forget."

"I'm reminding you because frankly, I think you do forget sometimes. My point is, how do you think I felt when I walked into that place this morning and found you sitting there with another man? I'll tell you! I didn't like it one bit. We need to come to some kind of understanding."

Jaci heard a tinge of anger in Jason's voice and knew he was upset. She honestly hadn't thought about her upcoming marriage when she agreed to meet Al. She suddenly realized she had a lot of adjustments to make in her thinking. Everything would have to be considered in a different light. She was about to become somebody's wife. "Jason. I'm sorry, honey. I didn't even think about it in those terms." She spoke softly. "But don't you trust me?"

"Yeah. I trust you. But I think you're too naïve sometimes. I don't know what kind of bull that guy was laying on you, but from the way he was looking at you, I'd say it was all about you . . . and him!"

"Aha! You're jealous! That's what this is all about."

"Doggone right, I'm jealous! I know what I have, sweetheart."

"Jason," she sighed impatiently. "I think the fact that I've lived all these years without even a serious prospect for marriage should tell you something. Think about it. Remember our first serious conversation? What did I tell you then? I don't play games, and contrary to what you think, I can easily tell when someone is trying to run a game on me. There was nothing like that going on with Al. He just likes to talk to me when he's having woman problems. I love you. I wouldn't do anything to hurt you or destroy what we have between us. Trust works both ways, honey. You know how I've had to struggle with the trust issue. Because I know if we don't trust each other, it's over before it even begins, and we may as well call everything off right now."

"We're not calling off anything. But . . . Okay, so I let jealousy kind of cloud my vision. I do trust you, sweetheart. But that's not to say I appreciate seeing you out with another man. I'm never going to like that. And like I said before, you're too naïve. Remember, I told you Maxie was going to try something when you went to Dallas. But you didn't believe me, did you? I know how men think, sweetheart. 'Cause I'm one."

Jaci smiled. "Yeah, you did. But I handled it, just like I said I would. And if you think I'll appreciate seeing you in the company of some other woman, you should think again. But realistically, it's something we're both going to have to deal with. We both work with the public and interact regularly with the opposite sex. I guess we need to set some ground rules and agree on what's acceptable and unacceptable. I'm not going to be nothing nice if you ever step outside the boundaries, I'm telling you that right now. And I know the same applies to you."

Jason grinned as he grabbed her hands, squeezing them. "You better believe it."

Jaci looked down at their entwined fingers, thinking now was as good a time as any to approach her job situation with him. Jason kept putting her off, but she had already kept Ed Shannon waiting too long for her answer. "Jason, while we're having this talk to settle some things, we need to talk about my job. I have to give Ed Shannon an answer on his offer."

"Dang! I was hoping you would decide to turn it down, honey. You know I want you working with me. In fact, I need you. Have you even given that any thought?"

Jaci pulled away from him and drew a deep breath. "Yes, I have. And to be honest, beyond practical considerations, there are some other issues involved in this for me. The primary one being my need for independence. I . . . ." Before she could continue, Jason jumped up and walked across the room to look out of the window, agitatedly running his hand through his hair.

"Here we go again with this blasted independence thing! Don't you realize you're going to be my wife and as such, under my care and protection? I take my responsibility toward you seriously. If you want to work, then like I said, work for me and I'll pay you. And you can do whatever you want to with your money, because I'll take care of your needs and wants. Now any other woman would be standing on her doggone head to have something like this. Why the heck can't you accept it?" His voice escalated several decibels as he spoke.

Jaci's head was lowered and she was almost in tears. "Don't yell at me!" she said quietly. "Surely, we can discuss this calmly and reasonably. We already know we have differing opinions on this issue. If we can't talk without yelling at each other, then I don't know how we're ever going to resolve anything."

"Okay. Okay. You're right. I'm sorry, but when I get emotional, my voice tends to go up. I'm just having difficulty understanding. Sweetheart, don't you trust me to take care of you? To treat you right? I'm not trying to make you so dependent on me that you won't have any freedom. Don't you know that?"

"No, Jason, I don't. Maybe it's because of all my years of struggle with no one to depend on but myself. But what I see is your desire to control. And I can't give you that right now. I don't know if I'll ever be able to. It has nothing to do with my love for you. I guess it's all about my own insecurities. We went over this in our counseling sessions and you said you could handle that. Now what's it going to be? Either you can or you can't."

He grabbed her hand again and began rubbing his thumb over the back of it. "Do I have to? Baby, you're messing with my pride here. As your husband I need to be everything to you."

"You can't be everything to me. If I were younger and not used to taking care of myself, then maybe I would be standing on my head and clicking my heels together. But that's not the case. I promise you, as my husband, you'll be honored as the head of our household and I'll do everything in my power to make you feel like a king. You're the love of my life, and if this wasn't such an important issue for me, I wouldn't fight you on it. But . . . as it stands, I would like to accept that position and work in it at least until I reach twenty-five years of service.

That's not a long time. But I don't want to do so if you don't agree. We need to settle this one way or another."

He gave her an intense look. "I love you, you know that?" At her nod, he continued. "I've made my position clear. You know what I'd prefer, but I'm not unreasonable or selfish. If it's that important to you, I can't ask you not to accept that position. But let me say this, you do so with it clearly understood by you and everybody else that it'll just be for the time it takes you to make twenty-five years, and that the job will not ever come before your husband, and under no circumstances do I want you going into those dangerous buildings anymore. Do you know how many nightmares I've had about that? If you agree with those stipulations, I'll go along with it, unhappily."

"Okay, understood. Now. Is this matter closed? I mean you're not going to be bringing it up every time we get into a fight are you?"

He shook his head slowly. "Naw. I won't do that."

She jumped into his arms and hugged him tightly. "Thanks, baby, you won't be sorry. Now are we straight? I have so much to do. I need to go."

"I don't promise not to be sorry, but yeah, sweetheart, we're straight." He hugged her close and kissed her tenderly. "I'll be so glad when you don't have to leave me."

Jaci

The next two weeks passed in a frenzy of activity, leaving Jaci exhausted to the point of collapsing. She worked almost around the clock tying up loose ends for the wedding, packing and securing storage for the belongings and furniture she wouldn't be taking, and moving things she was taking to Jason's house and getting settled in. She had talked to Ed Shannon and set things up to start her new position after her wedding and honeymoon. But she was trying to get as much as possible squared away so she wouldn't be too swamped when she returned.

On the week of the wedding relatives began to arrive, and she had to deal with those who refused to stay in the hotel rooms she had reserved, preferring instead to stay at her house. She tried to discourage this since she didn't have time to play hostess. But some, like her parents and a few others, insisted, because they wanted to be near her and in the mix of things, believing they would be able to help her. Her cousins Nita and Gina were the exceptions. She welcomed their presence and their help since they understood what needed to be done and went about doing it. Although the plan had been for them to stay with Jaci, with the convening of so many other houseguests, they decided to spend their nights with C.J.

She'd had little quality time with Jason, who was also extremely busy. By the time the rehearsal dinner rolled around, Jaci was almost asleep on her feet. She just wanted everything to be over.

Her wedding day began with overcast skies and the threat of rain. Jaci's heart sank when she saw the clouds. Houston had a reputation for sudden storms, accompanied by torrential rains and widespread flooding. If that happened, she knew people would be unable to attend. She prayed for sunshine as she went through the rituals—getting her hair and nails done, taking care of final details, dealing with the constantly ringing telephone.

By noon, the Lord answered her prayer. The clouds moved on, leaving a blue cloudless sky and moderate temperatures. It was a perfect day for a wedding. But Jaci was petrified!

The air in the small room set aside as the bride's dressing room was nonexistent, and the tormenting doubts and fears had affected her so badly that Jaci's shaky legs refused to support her any longer. The one conclusion she had come to was that she loved Jason. She made it to a chair and was about to sit down when she heard Sister Sadie yelling from across the room. "Don't even think about sitting down. You'll ruin your dress." Jaci sighed heavily and grabbed the back of the chair. "I'm so nervous, I'm about to fall. Is everything ready? Oh Lord, I'm really stressing, Sister Sadie."

"Jaci! Everybody's here and ready. Everyth—" A knock on the door interrupted her, and Sadie hurried across the room to answer it. One of the hostesses stood there smiling. "Jason sent this to Jaci," she said, handing Sadie a long-stem rose and a small envelope. Sadie walked back and handed Jaci the items.

"Here. This is from Jason. Maybe it will help settle you down."

Jaci looked at the rose and the envelope. Fear gripped her again. "What if he's telling me he's changed his mind?" She took a deep strengthening breath. "Oh well, better to find out now than when I'm walking down the aisle." She tore open the envelope and pulled out the folded note. Tears quickly flooded her eyes as she read:

Sweetheart.

We're almost there and I can't wait to meet you at the altar. In just a little while we will become husband and wife. P.S. Don't be nervous. It will all be over in a few hours. I love you.

'J.'

Seeing the tears in Jaci's eyes caused alarm for Sadie. She grabbed one of Jaci's hands. "What's wrong, baby? Is everything all right?" Jaci handed her the note.

"Now ya'll about to get me to crying," Sadie said as she read it and handed it back to Jaci. She turned and walked into the adjoining room, clapping her hands to get attention. "Okay, bridesmaids. Let's get you lined up and ready." She ushered them from the room.

Sadie reentered the room a few minutes later. "Things are going beautifully," she joyfully announced.

"Randi! We need to get you into place." Randi ran to give her mother a quick hug and followed one of the other coordinators out of the room.

"Baby, your moment is almost here." Sadie stood back, looking at her from head to toe. "You look absolutely beautiful, honey. I am so proud of you. Now let me say something to you. I know you're nervous, but remember this is your hour. You can't do anything wrong today. So walk proud, girl. Walk in the strength and power of the Lord!"

"I just pray I'm doing the right thing. I guess I'm just having some last-minute jitters."

"You are, and that's normal. But you know yourself well enough to know you said yes because you can't stand to see Jason in misery." They both laughed and Sadie Brooks drew a relieved breath.

"It's been a long journey to this moment, Sister Sadie," Jaci said softly, thinking reflectively back over her life.

"I know what a long journey it's been, honey." Sadie took Jaci's hands into hers and squeezed them tightly. "But here you are! Jaci, I'm going to talk to you like a mother, 'cause that's what I consider myself. God has sent you a good, handsome, wonderful man. Focus on God's grace and goodness that brought you to this point. And honey, you have to accept this great gift God has given you. Don't question it or try to figure out why He's doing it or why it's taken so long. In order to move beyond the years of trouble and struggle and into this new life, you have to accept His good and perfect gift, and His perfect timing for bringing it to you. Now come on, let's get you into place." She hesitated. "Baby, I just wish you had agreed to let your father or someone escort you. So many wanted to, you know that. They considered it an honor."

"Yes, I know that, Sister Sadie. But right or wrong, I just couldn't. I have to take this walk with the Lord, and you know why."

Sadie did know why and understood it. Jaci had taken so many walks alone and struggled alone for so long, when a little love and support would have made a big difference. Now, wanting to be a part of her victory, several, including her own father, had wanted to escort her down the aisle.

"Baby, just remember, you can't move into the future and hold on to the past at the same time. Leave the past behind you. It's history."

Sadie's words of wisdom hit their mark and somehow strengthened Jaci. "Thank you, Sister Sadie. I needed to hear everything you've said," she said quietly.

Jaci moved slowly down the long corridor to stand at the back of the sanctuary. The church was packed, with people even standing along the walls. "Smile," the photographer whispered from his squatting position in front of her. Her off-the-shoulder ice-blue dress fit her curvaceous figure like a glove. The low-cut dress fell at her knees in the front, showcasing her beautiful legs, while pleats of graduating lengths on the sides and back fell all the way to the floor. The pearls and sequins embroidered into the dress caused small starbursts around her each time she moved. The matching headpiece peaked in the middle of her forehead and crowned cascading curls that fell below her shoulders. Jason's birthday gift, an exquisite set of pearl and diamond earrings and matching rope necklace, glittered against her skin.

Jaci watched as Randi, in her role as Matron of Honor, slowly took the long trek down the aisle, and tears filled her eyes, threatening to run over. On no! I'm not going *there!* she told her emotions. Her eyes fastened on Jason, who looked simply gorgeous in his black-and-gray pin-striped tux. His eyes were glued to her and a big smile lit up his whole face.

As the soloist began singing "Great Is Thy Faithfulness, O God Our Father," she saw that her cousins—C.J., Nita, and Gina—and her best friend, Lena, all bridesmaids, were looking toward the back of the church at her, trembling smiles on their faces. "Ya'll better be praying for me when I'm coming down that aisle," she had admonished them earlier that day, "Otherwise I'll probably trip over my own feet and fall."

"All rise!" the pastor said with arms raised. As the guests stood and strained to get a look at her, some pointing cameras to capture her on film, she began to take small slow steps toward the altar, leaving one season and beginning a new one. This . . . was a journey symbolic of God's faithfulness and love.

It was important to Jaci that each step represent a segment of the journey that had brought her to this point. If not, she feared she might, in her victory, forget the struggle. That would be the ultimate in ungratefulness to God.

Remember! She reminded herself with each step. *Remember all the struggles that brought me to this victory. And never, never forget, lest I become ungrateful. Remember!*

She unlocked the memories that had been relegated to the back of her mind, bidding them to flow freely. Years of agony and aloneness as a single parent; years of rejection by her own family, on the job and even in the church; years of seeing hope after hope crash in disappointment as men insulted and tried

324 / Bonnie Hopkins

to dishonor her; years of wondering if her season would ever change.

She worried that the aisle wasn't long enough to complete her physical and mental journeys, so she slowed her steps even more. She noticed Jason's brother, Ron, handing him a white handkerchief and grasping his arm in a tight grip. *Oh God. If he cries, I'm a goner and I don't look good when I cry.*

She smiled at Jason, trying to send him a message of love. That did it! He pulled away from Ron and walked toward her, his eyes holding hers.

She shook her head, NO! But he kept coming, meeting her when she was only three-quarters of the way down the aisle. He bent to place a tender kiss on her lips before grabbing her hand to walk the remaining steps with her to the altar. She heard someone in the pews sniff loudly and go "Ooooh!"

"Oh Lord!" Jaci mumbled under her breath.

While she battled to control her rampant emotions, she mentally pulled at the thread of memories, commanding the tapestry of her past to unravel, but knowing that remnants would always be a part of her. As she stood at the altar, clutching Jason's hand, she silently thanked God for the memories, moments, mercies, and even manipulations that had brought her to this point, and for the beginning of a new season.

"Brothers and sisters!" Her pastor's voice resonated over the microphone. "We are joyfully gathered here this afternoon to witness and share in the joining of two lives—two paths, as they merge into one. God has done a great and mighty thing in bringing this couple together. And we praise Him for what He will do in and through their life together. Before we go any further, let us pray." The ceremony passed in a blur. Jaci couldn't have told anyone what happened from that point on. She was totally zoned out.

Jason

After what seemed to be an endless round of picture taking, they ran out of the church and through a flurry of bubbles, applause, and comments from the crowd gathered on both sides of the sidewalk. "God bless you!" "Beautiful! Just beautiful!" "Ya'll better show up at the reception!" "No detours!"

They reached the waiting limousine and sank gratefully into the seat. As the driver pulled away from the church, Jaci looked back at the dispersing crowd with disbelief, then said nervously, "I can't believe all those people showed up. The church was packed."

When he didn't respond, she looked up at him questioningly.

Jason was looking down at her with "that look." "Hello, wife," he said softly.

Jaci relaxed into his embrace as she felt their love encompass them. She looked into his eyes and answered in a voice filled with so much emotion it shook, "Hello, husband. I love you."

He kissed her softly, then groaningly deepened the kiss. "I don't want to go to no darn reception. I want to be alone with my wife."

Jaci giggled. "Sorry, honey. You know we have to. I think things went very well. I gotta tell you though, I was tripping really bad until I got your note and this beautiful rose." She still had the rose clutched in her hand along with her bridal bouquet. "Sister Sadie was having a hard time trying to calm me down. I was so afraid something would go wrong. Thank You, Heavenly Father, for causing everything to go well," she said softly.

"Amen to that!" Jason said. "You look so beautiful, honey. I know I wasn't supposed to but I had to come and walk with you. I couldn't help myself."

"You almost made me lose it!" She punched him in the side. "I was already struggling to hold it together when I saw you crying. Then when you did that, the only thing that kept me from boo-hooing right there in the middle of the aisle was the fact that I know I don't look good when I cry. And I didn't want to scare all of our guests out of the church."

"Baby, those people weren't going anywhere. They were as captivated by you as I was."

She threw her arms around him. "Don't you dare get me started." Her voice quivered with tears. "I still have to get through this reception."

The reception had been going on for a couple of hours and Jason was frustrated. He was ready to have his wife all to himself. Jaci had somehow got her second wind and was enjoying herself. She kept expressing amazement that the grand ballroom of the fashionable hotel was packed. They'd noticed that members from both their churches were in abundance. Jason's employees and surprisingly, quite a number of Jaci's coworkers and citizens she had worked with, were mixed in with their large assortment of family and friends.

After greeting people in the long reception line, then barely touching the lavish meal, they laughed at the numerous toasts and savored their first dance as husband and wife. Afterward, they were constantly separated, dancing with others and accepting endless congratulations and well wishes. Jaci moved about the room, laughing and talking to people and thanking them again for attending. If Jason turned around to speak to someone, Jaci once again was drawn away from his side. He soon tired of it and looked around for his brother and Walt.

"Ron. Go tell the limo driver we're about ready to leave.

Walt, find Sister Sadie and tell her we'll be ready to leave in about ten or fifteen minutes or as soon as I can get Jaci out of here. Heck, I don't even know where she is right now. She keeps wandering off."

"There she is." Ron pointed toward the opposite side of the room. "You sure you're ready to leave? Looks like she's having a good time."

"She is having a good time. But I know she's about to collapse from exhaustion, even though she might not look like it," Jason replied. "We're leaving, so go get the limo. We're going to the house to change clothes, and then we're hitting the road. I'm planning to be gone by the time this thing is over. I'm holding you guys responsible for getting the people out of our houses tomorrow. I'll be in touch sometime next week."

More than thirty minutes passed before they were finally in the limousine and on their way home. They rushed into the house and upstairs to the master bedroom. "This bed looks so inviting, I wish I could just fall into it and stay there," Jaci told him, looking longingly at the bed. "Will you unzip me? I think I'll take a quick shower. We have time, don't we?"

"Yeah, I guess so." He walked over to her and unzipped her dress, which immediately fell from her shoulders to the floor. She bent to pick it up, not realizing the impact her scantily attired body was having on his senses. She went to the walk-in closet to hang up the dress, came back a few minutes later wearing nothing but a long robe, and walked into the bathroom. Jason hadn't moved. He still stood in the middle of the floor, fighting a battle he knew was already lost. The sound of running water broke his immobility and he quickly moved into action, shedding his clothes on the way to the bathroom.

Jaci let out a little scream when the door to the glass-enclosed shower stall opened and he stepped in with her. "Now, I know you don't expect me to miss an opportunity for us to take our first shower together, do you?" A second later, her look of surprise turned to one of mischievousness, and she grinningly said, "I don't think this is a good idea. We may never make it to Galveston. Ohhh! Watch it! I don't want to get my hair wet! Get out, Jason!" His lips captured hers, effectively stopped her words, and they were both soon groaning. A few minutes later, the shower door opened and he picked her up and headed to the bed. "Sweetheart, you're so beautiful and I love you so much." He spoke softly to her as he laid her on the bed and began to kiss her in a way that told her their time of restraint was at an end.

A long while later, Jaci, who was fighting to keep from drifting off to sleep, roused herself, pulled out of his arms, and crawled out of the bed. "Jason, if we don't get up we're going to go to sleep and people are going to be coming in from the reception finding us in bed. If we hurry we may still be able to get out of here before they get here." As she spoke, she walked into the large closet, pulled the door partly closed, and started pulling on some freshly starched jeans and a comfortable top.

Jason lay there with his hands behind his head and a lazy smile on his face. "Why did you close the door? I was enjoying the view. And what would be wrong with them finding us in bed?" he asked. "If we want to stay here the rest of the night in our home and in our bed, there's nothing anyone can say about it. We're married, remember?"

Jaci

Jaci made a frustrated sound. "Baby, please, get up!" she yelled at him. "I don't want everybody knowing we detoured from our plan. It's embarrassing."

Totally unconcerned about his nakedness, he stood, walked over to her, and pulled her into his arms. "Sweetheart, you may as well get over being embarrassed. Everybody knows what we'll be doing tonight, and every chance I get from now on. In fact, why don't we lock the door, get back in bed, and forget them. They'll get the message."

Jaci looked at him in agitation. "No. Jason, please hurry and get dressed so we can go. Please!"

"All right, all right! But I don't know why you're carrying on like this." He started putting clothes on just as they heard a car pull into the driveway and doors slam.

"Oh no!" Jaci groaned, looking as though she wanted to hide under the bed.

By the time they made it downstairs, several people, accompanied by Patrick who had let them in, were sitting around the family room with shoes kicked off, making themselves comfortable.

"What are ya'll doing still here? We figured ya'll would be in Galveston by now," one of Jason's cousins blurted out before thinking. "Oh. I guess ya'll must have gotten delayed or something."

Everybody started laughing, while an embarrassed Jaci walked into the kitchen. "Anybody want something to drink?" she asked.

"Yeah." She got several responses. "Hey everybody, why don't we order some pizza and play some cards?" another relative asked.

The suggestion met with enthusiastic approval and the guests ran upstairs to get into comfortable clothes. Jaci picked up the phone to place the order for pizzas, but Jason stopped her before she could dial.

"I know these people are not hungry, not after watching them eat like they were starved just a little while ago. If they want something else, they'll have to order it themselves." He laid the phone down and hugged her tightly. "You just can't help it, can you? You just have to try to take care of everybody's needs. Well this week, the only one you have to worry about is me. And with all these people in here, I'm ready to go so I can have you to myself." He kissed her lightly, then again, deepening the kiss and pulling her closer.

"Man, unhand that woman! What's wrong with you?"

They jumped apart and looked around to see a new group arriving, led by Ron. He was followed by C.J., Anita, Gina, and Lena. Walt and the other groomsmen brought up the rear.

"We're about to get the real party started," Ron announced. "Ya'll may as well stick around at this point, cause I know ya'll ain't been packing all this time. What happened to your hair, Sis? It wasn't looking like that when you left the reception."

Jaci walked over to Ron and hit him in the chest. "If you don't want me to tell these beautiful women all about your dirty, low-down ways, I suggest you shut up. I know you're trying real hard to impress them."

"Ron, man, you better back off!" Walt told him. "The last time this woman told you off in this room, it wasn't nothing nice! Remember?"

Ron laughed. "Oh yeah. I do remember." He held his hands up in surrender. "Sorry, Sis. You know I was just kidding."

Jaci walked into the family room where the others had gathered, sat down, and began to talk about the wedding. As they rehashed everything, the guys came in and put their two cents in. Jason squeezed into the recliner with Jaci. As the conversation continued, he hugged her close and whispered, "You were right. We should have gotten out of here while we had the chance."

"It was a nice wedding, guys," Walt told them. Then he spoiled it and made everybody laugh when he continued, "It almost—not quite—but almost, made me want to think about getting married. That didn't last long though. My sanity re-turned real quick!"

Jason awoke early the next morning to the sound of waves crashing against the seawall. He smiled as he remembered. Yesterday. The wedding. The reception. The impromptu party. Last night. Last night! It had definitely been the best day—and night—of his life.

They arrived at the beautiful beach house in Galveston much later than planned, tired and unbelievably hungry. Jaci slept all the way there. After they unpacked the car, then made sandwiches from the well-stocked refrigerator, they sat on the deck outside the lavishly furnished bedroom to watch the moon's reflection on waters that seemed never ending. Rubbing his thumb over the back of her hand, he said, "Sweetheart, as vast as those waters out there are, I want you to know that my love for you is larger. I know the battles you've had to fight to bring you to this moment. As much as it's in my power, you will never regret becoming my wife. I love you with all my heart, and in honor of this our wedding day and as a pledge to our love and our life together, I have a gift for you."

Jaci gasped. "Oh my God! Jason, I . . . wish you hadn't done that. I don't have anything for you."

"You have yourself to give to me. That's enough," he answered as he went inside and came back a few minutes later with a large envelope. He pulled a large stack of papers out and handed them to Jaci.

It was dark, so there was no way she could read what it was. "What is this?" she asked. When he didn't respond, she stood, went into the bedroom, turned on the lights, and sat down on the bed to read the papers. Before she got very far, she looked up at him in alarm before looking back down at the papers.

"Jason, I don't believe this! You actually remembered!" Her

voice quivered and she knew she wouldn't be able to hold back the tears threatening to overflow. "You bought this . . . for me?"

"Yep, it's yours. Lock, stock, and barrel. The only condition that comes with it is that you will always treat it as our special place. I don't mean you can't invite other people down here to visit. I just mean that this is our place to come whenever we need to get away and spend some uninterrupted time together. I've never forgotten what you said about watching the sunset and the sunrise with your husband, and being in harmony with God, nature, and each other. I want this to be our place to come when we need to get back in harmony with God and each other."

Jaci cried, "Sweetheart, this is the most beautiful thing anyone has ever done for me." Jason told her he'd rented the beach house for the week. She stood and walked over to where he stood by the balcony doors. "You know, I would have been happy to spend our honeymoon right here. We're so tired, I'm afraid we won't reap the full benefits of the cruise." They had reservations for a five-day cruise from Monday through Friday and planned to come back to enjoy the beach house until Sunday night or Monday morning.

Her arms went around his neck and she stood on tiptoe to kiss him tenderly. "God bless you, my husband," she whispered softly, "I love you so much." When she kissed him again, the flames exploded that always sparked to life whenever they touched.

Now, Jason smiled as he basked in the memories. Jaci was God's gift to him. One he planned to cherish. He drew a sigh of relief and contentment. He had found his woman, his wife, his mate. He pulled her closer to him and silently thanked God for her.

Jaci

*H*as it really been nearly six months since her wedding? Jaci shook her head in amazement as she inched along in bumper-to-bumper rush hour traffic. To distract herself, she pondered the changes in her life. They were good changes, *thank God*, but they required adjustments and modifications in her thinking and daily routines. As she considered the changes, she conceded that her adaptation from a solitary lifestyle to a married one had not been smooth. The first fight came during the first month of marriage when Jaci, following old habits, became immersed in a project at work and lost all track of time; she completely forgot her husband, waiting at home. She smiled as she remembered their fight and the resultant makeup. Since then, she made every effort to go home on time.

She sighed in relief as she drove into the garage. The drive home had been torturous. Heavy rain caused the streets to flood in places; therefore, traffic had to move at an even slower pace than usual. Thankfully she didn't have to worry about dinner because she had beef stew simmering in the Crock-Pot. She had prepared it during her trip home at lunch; now it should be about ready. A quick salad and they would be eating dinner in no time. She hoped Jason would be home and was disappointed when he wasn't. It seemed their ever-busy schedules made it difficult for them to spend quality time together. Jaci was still settling into her new position as division manager, and Jason was currently dealing with some legal issues on one of his software patents. He had just returned from D.C. Friday and would have to leave again as soon as he heard from his attorney.

Jaci entered the house and ran up the stairs to the bedroom, deciding a hot shower would be nice. Although she would have liked to stay under the hot, pelting water, she got out, quickly threw on a sweat suit, and went back downstairs to finish dinner. The cold rainy weather made it a perfect night for beef stew. The phone rang and she gave an impatient grunt, hoping it wasn't Jason calling to tell her he would be late. She smiled when she heard the male voice coming across the line.

"Hey, Sis. What's going on?" Ron asked.

"Not a thing. How are things with you?" She listened as Ron told her about his day before finally asking, "Is J.P. around?" She was about to tell him no when she heard the garage door opening. "He's just driving into the garage now. Want to wait? Or can he call you back?"

"No, I'll wait."

Jaci remained amazed at the drastic change in Ron's attitude. In fact, he had gone from one extreme to the other and was almost as protective toward her as Jason was. She had to confront him about his protectiveness a few weeks ago when she and Jason had argued and Ron put his two cents in. Jaci prepared to go shopping one Saturday afternoon, but Jason contended that it was too late, especially since Jaci, Lena, and C.J. refused to leave the mall until it closed. Ron was at their house—where he seemed to be a lot these days—and he joined Jason in the objection.

"Sis, just the other day a woman was abducted in the parking lot of a mall. Ya'll need to go early before the crooks start riding around the parking lot, looking for easy victims. Naw. You don't need to be going to no mall this time of day."

Jaci looked at them in disgust. "How do ya'll think I made it this far without you? By being stupid? I know how to take care of myself. And anyway, we're going to the galleria and will be parked in the underground lot. There are security guards and people constantly going and coming." She looked at Ron with a scowl. "And I don't believe you, Ron. What's gotten into you?"

Ron smiled sheepishly. "I don't know, I guess I must be getting soft in my old age. Beside that, I was getting ready to beg you to fix me one of your special sandwiches. That's what I really came over here for."

"Oooh!" Jaci laughed and wiggled her finger in his face. "I knew there was an ulterior motive in there somewhere. Sorry, buddy, you're out of luck today. I'm outta here." She hugged and kissed a still pouting Jason and headed to the garage.

Jason

Jason entered the house and sniffed appreciatively as the mouthwatering aroma of the stew greeted him. He would never get over the difference his wife made here. He recalled how he had dreaded coming home to an empty house before their marriage, but now could barely wait to get there. Jaci's presence filled the house with warmth and made it feel like a home. He could barely stand to be there without her and was unreasonably upset if he arrived and found the place empty.

He found Jaci in the kitchen with the phone propped between her neck and chin, pulling the makings of a salad out of the refrigerator. Jason walked across the room and planted a brief kiss on her lips before taking the phone she was handing to him.

"Who is it?"

When Jaci mouthed "Ron," he frowned. "Hey man, what's up? I'm just getting home and my wife is just finishing dinner, so I've got to . . . Huh?"

Ron, on the other end, repeated his question. "I said, what are ya'll having?"

"I don't know," Jason answered. "I told you I'm just walking in. But it smells great. Looks like some stew or someth— what? Okay." He hung up the phone. "Baby, I'm going up to change clothes. I'll be back in a minute. Oh, Ron's on his way so you might as well make enough for him."

The back doorbell rang a few minutes later and Jaci went to let Ron in. "Hey, Sis," he said, hugging her. "What's for dinner? Something sure smells good."

"Oh just some beef stew—nothing fancy. And I'm making a salad. I'm debating whether to make some cornbread or make do with some crackers. Want something to drink?"

"Nope. Not right now. And please make some cornbread. We can't be having stew without cornbread," he stated as Jason walked back into the room.

"Oh look, babe," Jason mused. "Our regular dinner guest is here. Man, don't be coming over here telling my wife what to cook." He laughed at the embarrassed grin on Ron's face. "This is about the fourth time you've shown up at mealtime in the last week. I'm beginning to think you ain't got no groceries at home."

Ron gave a dirty look. "I just happen to like my sister-in-law's cooking. Anything wrong with that?"

Jason chuckled. "Naw, man. Ain't nothing wrong with that. I like it too."

All during dinner, although he tried to act carefree, Jason remained preoccupied. He realized he didn't fool Jaci when he noticed her concerned look more than once. After Ron left, she asked him what was bothering him.

"It's this patent thing, honey. I know I haven't done anything wrong, but it's worrying me, distracting me and taking up a lot of time that I should be giving to other things. I hate this."

Jaci scooted closer to him on the sofa and wrapped her arms around him. "It'll be okay. Like you said, you haven't done anything wrong. And the way I see it, this other company is trying to rip you off. I think they're just trying to bluff and harass their way into winning the case. You can't let them beat you down, honey. You've got to stay strong and keep your faith. God's with you. He's not going to let you down."

He smiled and pulled her closer. "I don't know how I survived without you, sweetheart. You always know what to say to make things better. Come on, let's go to bed." After making sure everything was locked up, they headed up the stairs to bed. Once in bed, Jason found his mind going back over the patent lawsuit. He had handled this patent the same way he had others. Why were those bloodsuckers trying to steal this one?

Jaci laid her head on his chest and began talking. It took him a minute to realize she wasn't talking to him, but to the Lord.

"Lord, bless my husband with Your peace. Father, he's Your child, and he loves and honors You in every way he can. Lord, You are faithful, and Your grace is sufficient, and You have promised to be a present help in time of trouble. Lord, Jason is troubled. And I know You know what needs to be done to make him more than a conqueror in this situation. So, Lord, I ask right now for Your mercy, Your deliverance, Your overcoming victory. Father, let Jason experience peace that passes all human understanding, and send forth Your power into this situation that has him so burdened. Father, I thank You right now that no weapon formed against Jason shall prosper, and every tongue raised against him shall be condemned. I ask these blessings upon my husband in the name of our Savior, Jesus Christ. Amen."

Tears ran down the sides of his face, soaking the pillow. His heart felt as though it would burst right out of his chest. "Oh God!" he moaned, as he crushed his wife in his arms. "Thank

You, Father! Thank You for giving me this woman. Lord, if You don't do another thing for me, You've already done more than I deserve. Praise You for Your blessings unto me." His voice broke as he gave way to the emotions that had burdened him the past several weeks.

Jaci

*J*aci surveyed the large office that Wynola Dickson had once occupied. She had never in her wildest imagination even remotely pictured herself in this office or in the position that Wynola had revered so much. Jaci had been so wrapped up doing her job and surviving the day-to-day struggles that she hadn't taken the time to think or strategize about anything beyond that.

Now, as she tried to focus on her plan for reorganizing the division and placing everyone in more efficient positions, she reminded herself to prepare for a fight. She deliberately waited several months to give everyone a chance to adjust to her as manager, but there was always resistance to change. As division manager, she took a more active role than Wynola had in day-to-day operations and had carried the responsibility for both positions until she could make the needed changes and decide who would fill her old position. Several coworkers vied for the position, but she determined to appoint the most qualified person. Unfortunately, that came down to her two most dependable employees—Gloria and Bill—which made the decision even more difficult. Gloria had the administrative side of the job down to an art, but lacked experience in the field, while Bill was the field expert, lacking in the administrative side of things.

She sat agonizing over the decisions she had to make when the phone interrupted her. She smiled when she heard her husband's voice, a voice that still made her shiver.

"Hey sweetheart. What are you doing?"

"Thinking about how my husband's voice still has the power to give me goose bumps," she answered with a smile. "Why?"

"Oooh, sweetheart! You always know what to say to make me happy. Can you get away for lunch? I want to see you, plus I need to talk to you about something."

"You just saw me a few hours ago and will see me again in a few hours," she answered, grinning widely.

"And I have to say no to lunch. I can guess what you have in mind and, uh! uh! you're not getting me involved in your games. I've got too much to do today."

He chuckled. "Lunch at Ruggles. That's all I'm looking for today. I know all you're going to do is grab a sandwich or something and sit there working all day if I don't rescue you. I'll pick you up in twenty minutes, okay?"

Jaci sighed regretfully. "Baby, I can't. Really. I'm swamped with this reorganization and trying to keep routine things going at the same time. Can't it wait until tonight?"

Jason hesitated because he didn't like what he heard. "No, it can't." He drew a deep breath. "Since I can't talk you into lunch, I guess we'll have to talk about it on the phone." Again, he hesitated, which raised Jaci's concern about what he was about to say. "I just heard from the attorney on the patent case." He paused to give her time to digest that information. "And I have to leave tomorrow. The hearing is at ten Friday morning and babe, I want . . . I *need* you to go with me." He waited for her response. He knew she was extremely busy, which was why he had been reluctant to ask. But he needed her with him.

Jaci sat with the phone clutched tightly in her hand and tried to find a way to soften her response. There was no way she could get away now. She had taken more time off during the past year than she had in all the other years combined and had committed herself to making up for that lost time. "Honey . . . I can't. I just told you, I'm totally swamped. You know if I could, I would drop everything and go, but that's not the case right now."

Jason dug in his heels, determined to get his way. "Did you hear me? I said I need you with me. This isn't just a desire, this is a need. Listen to what I'm saying, sweetheart."

Jaci was just as unwavering. "I heard you. But are you hearing me? I'm dealing with too much to take off right now. That's the bottom line."

"Can't or won't? I'm only talking about a day or two." Jason's voice escalated as he continued. "See! This is exactly why I wanted you to leave that job. I knew you were going to be more committed to it than you are to me. I told you up front that I won't take a backseat to that job, Jaci. And I meant that! Now I'm asking you again, will you come with me to D.C.?"

Jaci felt anger rise up within. She knew she had much to learn about the submissive thing. Maybe she was supposed to submit to his request and go with him. But anger took control. How dare he make this an issue! He knew she was struggling to get the division restructured. It wasn't a matter of putting the job first, it was just bad timing.

"I told you, I can't get away right now," Jaci told him sharply. "This is not about whether I'm more committed to the job, it's about timing. You're not being fair about this, Jason. How can you demand I take off from my job at a moment's notice? Well, I'm sorry, I just can't do it." She was about to say something else when she realized she was talking to the dial tone. Jason had hung up.

Not to be outdone, Jaci hurriedly dialed the private line to his office. When he answered, she yelled into the phone. "Why did you hang up on me? I don't believe you did that. That was so childish, Jason."

He didn't answer for a long minute. "I didn't have anything else to say and I didn't want to hear what you were saying. Unless you're calling to say you've changed your mind, I still don't want to he—" Now she had hung up on him. There!

Her desk phone immediately rang again. She knew it had to be him. She couldn't believe they were carrying on like this. As soon as she answered, he said, "Now who's being childish? Huh?" Then hung up before she could answer.

Jaci dropped her head into her hands, glad her office door was closed. How in the world had her life gone to hell in just a matter of minutes? Ten minutes ago, her biggest problem had been the reorganization. Now she was over her head in a marital standoff.

Any further work today was impossible. She stared out the window for the remaining hours of the workday, vacillating between wishing she could go home, *meaning her own house*—which was out of the question since the house had been leased—and being ashamed of herself for even feeling that way.

She was tempted to call Jason back and apologize, but knew he would probably just hang up on her again when he learned she hadn't changed her mind. She turned the volume up on the radio, which was always set on a Christian station. She needed to hear something, anything, from the Lord. Satan was winning this battle so far. How had such a small issue grown so big? How could she justify her refusal when her husband had almost begged her to go with him? She hadn't even asked why! Her only concern had been her job, her responsibilities, her need to do well in this new position.

"Oh Lord, help me," she cried. "I've lost my way, Father. Please lead me in the right direction."

She slowly made her way to her truck when it was time to leave. It wouldn't do to arrive home late and give Jason even more fuel to add to the fire. She shook her head as she approached the truck, another issue that should have been resolved but due to her stubbornness remained a bone of contention. Jason wanted to buy her a new car. He absolutely hated her old unreliable truck. But because it was hers, something she had managed to get on her own, she refused to let go. She drove toward home, and for the first time, hated the thought of going there.

Jason

Jason was already home and packing when Jaci came into the bedroom and kicked off her shoes. She sat down on the side of the bed to watch him place things neatly into his bag. He had nothing to say to her. He was angry and hurt. Why couldn't Jaci understand how much he wanted her with him on this trip? For some reason, he felt vulnerable in this fight, as if all that he stood for was also under attack. His strength seemed small and he couldn't understand the weakness since he had fought more intense battles than this one, and hadn't been affected like this. He needed his wife's strength to help him through this battle.

"Are we going to Bible study tonight?" Jaci asked. Jason looked at her and wondered how she could even think about it. "I'm not. You can do whatever you want." He answered in stilted words.

"Okay. I think I'll go," she told him. "Have you eaten anything? Do you want me to fix you something before I leave?"

He looked at her sharply. "Like I said, you can do whatever you want. You're going to do that anyway."

Dang! Jaci thought. To conclude that this man was pissed off was putting it mildly. She stood, put her shoes back on, and walked out of the room, down the stairs, and out the door. She still had enough anger to propel her actions.

As soon as he heard the garage door open, Jason almost collapsed on the bed. What in the world had gotten into him? His wife was trying to offer him an olive branch and here he was acting like a fool. She might have been getting ready to tell him she had changed her mind. Now that possibility was gone.

If ever he needed to hear a word from the Lord, it was now. He closed the half-filled bag, set it on the floor, grabbed his keys, and followed his wife's path out the door and to the church. He got there just as the pastor began the lesson.

"Brothers and Sisters, tonight we're going to talk about vision," Pastor Robinson said, looking around the room. "I don't mean physical vision and what we see out of our eyes. No, no. I mean our spiritual vision—what we see and understand in our spirit. The question I'm asking tonight is: Have you lost your vision? your sight? your way? your faith? Have you willfully taken your spiritual eyes off the One who is your guide, your source, your deliverer? I contend that many of us have done just that, and are now groping around in the dark wondering which way to go. The Word of God says in Proverbs 29:18 that where there is no vision, people perish. I further contend that many of us are literally perishing. Perishing in our souls, our spiritual walk with the Lord, our marriages, our relationships, our finances, our bodies . . . because we have lost our vision.

Jason had taken a seat in the back as soon as he walked in, not even bothering to seek Jaci out. When he heard the pastor's opening remarks, he started searching the audience intently, finally finding her sitting near her usual place. He quickly made his way to her side.

Jaci

The pastor's words had such an impact on Jaci that tears began streaming down her face before she realized it. Her first impulse was to get out of there before she made a real spectacle of herself. But before she could move, she felt someone slip into the seat beside her and a strong arm pulling her close. She looked up to see Jason, his face also wet, looking down at her.

"I'm so sorry," she whispered to him. "I don't know what got into me."

His arm around her tightened. "Shhhhh! . . . we'll talk about it later."

The pastor continued. "This is not going to be a long lesson tonight. I just want to give you some food for thought and prayer, then I want you to go home and deal with your loss of vision by repenting for choosing your own will over God's. Everyone in here knows how you have gone wrong, and that's between you and the Lord. It's up to you to find your way back to the right path. God loves us enough to let us make the decision. He's not going to force you back into the light."

Jaci didn't have to hear anymore. She had already admitted to the Lord that she had lost her way as a wife. She did exactly what Jason had asked her not to do when he agreed to her staying on her job. She still subconsciously thought unilaterally instead of as a wife. Every serious disagreement between them had been about her job. Did she in fact put her job first? Did she hold so tightly to her job because she was afraid to trust her husband—her marriage? Did she value her marriage enough to put the job in its rightful place? Did she love her husband enough to change?

Oh Lord! Please show me the way that You would have me to take. Then she cringed. *That's a dumb prayer, Lord. I already know what I should do.*

She drove into the garage, got out of the truck, and, without waiting for Jason, who had pulled in right behind her, made her way into the house and up the stairs to the bedroom. She went into the closet and began selecting clothes suitable for the D.C. trip. Jason walked into the room, and, realizing what she was doing, went to her and pulled her tightly into his arms.

"Sweetheart, I'll understand if you can't go. I was wrong to expect you to take off on such short notice. I should have told you last week that I needed you to go with me, rather than springing it on you at the last minute. Maybe if I had, it wouldn't have come to us fighting about it." He led her to the bed where they sat down.

"I don't want our marriage to perish because we mess around and lose sight of God and what He would have us to do. But we also need to stay close and communicate with each other. That's the only way we'll know what we need from each other."

Jaci began to cry. "I know," she agreed tearfully.

Jaci arrived at work at her usual time the next morning. She waited anxiously for her boss Ed Shannon to get in so she could talk to him about taking off the next couple of days. She had packed last night and with the exception of clearing things with Ed, was ready to go. Not going with her husband was no longer a consideration, whatever the outcome. She smiled as she considered the dramatic change in her attitude since yesterday. Her job was still important, but not to the point of jeopardizing her marriage. She silently thanked God for His guidance and prayed for favor and understanding from her boss.

"Jaci, what do you expect me to do? Fire you on the spot?" Ed Shannon asked, noticing Jaci's nervousness as she explained her need for time off. "You have a lot of surplus built up in your time bank, lady. It's understandable that you'll be using it now that you have a demanding husband." He paused. "And you tell J.P. to lighten up a little!" he added, laughing. "Jaci, its not a big deal, and I don't have a problem with it. I know you're going to take care of your job responsibilities, and do them well. And I don't want to upset the boat in any way and make that husband of yours insist on you leaving just yet. I like what you're doing with the division so far. So I'll see you when you get back."

Jaci thanked Ed profusely for his understanding, then held a hurried meeting with her staff to assure that things would go well while she was away. She called to let Jason know she was headed home and wondered why she had made such an issue of going with him. *Ooh Lord! I've got a lot of adjusting to do.*

Jason

*J*ason smiled as Jaci squirmed around in her seat by the window until she found a comfortable position. Her head rested against his arm while her hand sought for and found his. He remembered their first plane ride together and smiled at the differences. That time, Jaci had been careful, even in sleep, to stay as far from him as possible. Now, she couldn't seem to get close enough. He was happy. Now that he had easily won the patent case, he wondered why he had been so worried. Then he caught himself.

"Thank You, Father," he whispered. "All Glory to Your Name for the victory today."

He was surprised when Jaci whispered, "Amen." He thought she had dropped off to sleep. "Sweetheart, you don't know how much I appreciate having you with me today. I know it was a big sacrifice for you to leave your job and come on this trip. I promise I'll make it up to you."

Jaci raised her head and looked into his eyes. "I love you. I know I have some things to learn about being the right kind of wife, but if you'll bear with me, I'll keep trying. By the way, Ed said to tell you to lighten up." She smiled at his obstinate look. "He also said there was no way he was going to upset you because he doesn't want you demanding my departure from the job. He's a nice boss."

Jason snorted with disdain. "He can forget it. I think one of the things we've learned is that your departure is inevitable. That job has to go!" He felt her stiffen. "I'm sorry, honey, but that's the way it is. I don't want to fight every time I need you to go out of town with me. And I don't plan on going too many places without you." Jaci looked up with combat blazing in her emerald eyes. Before she could relay anything, he quickly said, "I guess we'd better pray about it huh?" She laid her head back down on his shoulder, smiling and choosing to say nothing.

Jaci

A week later on Friday evening, Jaci was glad to see the weekend. She hadn't rested up from the trip to D.C. and her extremely heavy workload this past week. She rushed home from work with nothing more on her mind than a relaxing bubble bath and a quiet evening with her husband.

She slipped into the large Jacuzzi tub with a satisfied sigh. She just wanted to sit and let the hot water and fragrant lavender aroma ease the tension from her body.

She let her mind drift and reflect on all the blessings from God. Life was good and there was nowhere else she'd rather be than here in this house with her husband. She chuckled. "Oh yeah! This is definitely a moment! Thank you, Father." The only thing that could have possibly made it any better was her husband's presence in the tub with her. The ringing telephone interrupted her praise-filled reflections. She groaned in irritation. "That was bound to happen," she said, thinking it was probably Jason and rushing to get out of the tub to answer it.

"Hello!" she said hurriedly, hoping she had caught it in time. There was a brief pause before she heard a familiar female voice and felt the bottom fall out of her world.

"Ha! You thought I was gone, didn't you? Well, I've got news for you. I'm not going anywhere, and my sister isn't either until we see you dead. You've taken things from both of us—things that should have been ours. Well, heifer, just know this: You better be looking over your shoulder because we're going to get you. And nothing and nobody's going to stop us this time!"

Jaci dropped the phone and backed away from it as if it were a snake. "Oh God! Oh God! Oh God!" she repeated over and over, her mind filled with horror and fear.

An hour later Jason found her curled into a tight ball on the bed. Her eyes were red and swollen, and she looked as if all the life had been knocked out of her. His heart pounded as he realized that something traumatic had happened to his wife. Why hadn't she called him!

"Baby, what's wrong? What happened? Tell me!" he said, pulling her into his arms.

Jaci hugged him tightly. "Linda . . . called . . . and . . . and said she and Wynola were going . . . to get me. Oh God! Jason, she's back . . . I thought that was all over, but now both of them are after me. I'm scared, Jason." She cried uncontrollably.

Jason

*J*ason was shaken! He too had believed that Linda and her attacks on Jaci were behind them. But it sounded like Linda, and Wynola, were as determined as ever to do harm to Jaci. He lay down beside her and started talking to her softly.

"Sweetheart, I know you're upset and scared. This is another satanic attempt to destroy our joy and peace. But you've got to remember that God is with us. He's brought us this far, and I don't believe He's going to leave us at this point. We'll get through this. And this time, we have to trust Him to end it once and for all. We can't let Satan defeat us. We've got to trust God." He was encouraging himself as he spoke to his wife. He felt like crying too, but his wife needed him to be strong.

"Come on, honey, we've got to pray." He got up and pulled her to her knees beside the bed and started talking to the Lord.

"Gracious Master, You already know why we are seeking You tonight. And Father, we really need a breakthrough in this situation. We thought it was over, but these women are again threatening our lives. Lord, You are God Almighty, all powerful, all knowing, all seeing, all everywhere, and all in control of this world and everything and everyone in this world. Father, we need Your power, Your strength, and deliverance in this situation. Father, we need You to stop the way against those who persecute and seek to destroy us. Father, we need the manifestation of Your promise that no weapon formed against us will prosper in this situation. Father, we need You to fix it so that any ditch these enemies dig for us will end up being for them.

"Father, we admit that we're weary and overwhelmed, but we know that Your strength is made perfect in our weakness. We ask that You will answer us speedily because we have no other help or source to call upon but You. We praise You right now that this trouble will be sent back to the pits of hell, triumphing over Satan and all his army. Father, we thank You and praise You for the victory. We ask all of this in the precious name of Jesus our Savior. Amen. Hallelujah! Praise be to God."

Both Jaci and Jason jumped up and embraced each other tightly. They both felt relief in their spirits as faith took over where fear and defeat had been.

"Oh sweetheart, thank you! And thank God for you," Jaci hugged him close. "I believe that God has heard our prayer and that the victory is already on the way." In her spirit she spoke to the Lord. *Thank you, Father, for leading my husband to remind me that this battle is Yours. I stand still and wait to see the salvation of the Lord. Thank You, Father.*

"Baby, we know that God is with us, but we still have to do some things for ourselves," Jason said. "We have to be watchful because this adversary is out there waiting to attack. And we have to garner help in both the spirit and earthly realms. We'll report this to the police, ask all our family, friends, and coworkers to pray with us and help us. And we'll get this situation on the church's twenty-four-hour prayer chain. This thing is going to end. Soon!"

Jaci

*T*hree weeks later, although the phone calls and threats continued, Jaci's faith remained strong. They alerted the police, and their family and friends had formed a strong support system around them. Jaci went nowhere alone. Her coworkers made sure she wasn't in the office or leaving the building alone. Someone even accompanied her to the grocery store. The consistent prayers of the church encased her and enabled her to endure the situation with peace. Jaci's constant prayer was, *Thank you, Heavenly Father, that by Your power, we have the victory over Satan in this situation. I send forth praise and glory to Your name right now.*

Saturday afternoon, Jaci was upstairs in the game room watching a movie, when she heard a loud commotion coming from downstairs. She got up to investigate. Usually when Jason and his friends were together they got loud, but this was ridiculous.

As she descended the last step, she heard Walt saying, "I told you! Didn't I tell you that one day you would step in something that would make you stink? I knew it had to happen. But this! I never woulda dreamed it would be something like this!"

He fell back in the recliner and laughed uncontrollably.

Jason, T.C., and Charlie sat on the floor laughing their heads off, while Ron slumped somberly in his chair, watching them. He finally said, "I don't see what the heck is so darn funny! I've got a real problem here! That dude won't leave me alone."

His words caused another round of loud laughter. Jaci walked into the room with a puzzled look. "What in the world is going on?"

The men tried unsuccessfully to collect themselves when they realized she was in the room. Jason got up, straightened his face, and walked over to her. "Sorry, sweetheart. Did we disturb you? I know we're pretty loud. We'll try to keep it down."

Jaci looked around the room, which was littered with soda cans and plates that held the crumbs of chips, chicken salad sandwiches, and the chocolate cake Jason had asked Jaci to make that morning. Something worth knowing was going on, but it was apparent they would not be sharing it with her. The men looked anywhere but at her. She turned slowly and went back up stairs, where she flopped down on the sofa and re-wound the movie.

As soon as the men determined she was gone, loud laughter erupted again. Jaci knew this had to be a doosie! And she couldn't wait until the others left so she could worm it out of Jason. Her mind kept mulling over Ron's words, *"That dude won't leave me alone."* What in the world was he talking about? Jaci wanted to know!

As soon as everyone left, Jaci flew down the stairs. "Okay! Tell me what's going on. This must be good the way you guys were carrying on."

Ignoring her request, Jason said, "Baby, will you help me clean up? We really made a mess in here. And there's not a crumb of food left. Those guys ate up everything."

She stood there with her arms crossed and looked at him in

exasperation. "I'll help you clean up if you'll tell me what's going on," she told him.

He shook his head. "Sorry, I can't. Ron asked me not to. You wouldn't want me to break my promise, would you?" Mischief danced in his eyes.

"Yes! I want to know. Tell me!"

"Can't do it, babe. Come on, let's get this place cleaned up."

Jaci began to tidy up. She knew if she kept after him, he would eventually tell her. They worked together to get the family room and kitchen in order, then went upstairs.

"You're not getting any rest until you tell me what's going on with Ron. So you might as well come clean."

Jason laughed, "Okay, okay! But you better not let on to Ron that I told you." He began, but before he got very far, she interrupted him.

"What!" Jaci's jaw dropped almost to the floor. "Some dude is in love with Ron? How in the world did Ron get mixed up with this person?"

Jason laid across the bed on his back, laughing. "Baby, some of these female impersonators, or whatever they call themselves, can fix up to look like beautiful women, and . . . well . . . they can fool the best of men." He chuckled some more. "That's what happened. Ron met this beautiful woman, went home with her, and discovered at a crucial point that he and the 'lady' had the same equipment. He punched the guy out and left, but the guy has other ideas. He's in love and refuses to give up on Ron. But Ron is about to have a conniption fit."

Jaci's hands went to cover her mouth. "Some dude is in love with Ron!" Her giggle started out slowly, then evolved into uncontrollable laughter. She and Jason rolled on the bed and laughed until they cried.

When they sobered, Jason said, "We need to be in prayer for Ron. Not just about this, but about his relationship with the Lord. Have you noticed how much time he's spending here? And how he's in church almost every Sunday now? I think the Lord is working in Ron's heart and circumstances to draw him into the kingdom. Something about our life—our home—is attractive to him. And you know what else? Ron was asking about your cousins, wanting to know if all of them are married."

Jaci smiled. "Hallelujah! But, baby, you need to start witnessing to him more, telling him what the Lord has done for you, letting him see the peace and contentment God has given you, even in the midst of all we're going through right now."

"Right. I have been talking to him a little, but you know how he is. He won't let me say much before he goes off."

"Well, this might be the right season. Let's pray hard that the Lord will touch his heart and make him receptive."

The next time Ron came by their house, Jaci left the room after a while, leaving the brothers alone. Jason took the cue, and started right in.

"Ron, I've been there, so I see signs that you're getting tired of your lifestyle. You're hanging around me and my wife more and more. That tells me you see something in us that's attractive to you. And you been in church the last several Sundays without anybody having to harass you about going. That's great, man! Take it from me, you won't find true life in the streets and running from woman to woman. You'll find that only in Jesus, and in loving and being loved by a good woman. Jesus will take you just as you are. But a good woman doesn't want anything to do with a street hound. Jaci wouldn't have given me the time of day if I hadn't already turned my life around before I met her."

Oddly, Ron sat quietly and listened before he looked up from staring into his coffee cup. He knew a change was occurring in him, but didn't know how or why. It certainly wasn't something he had sought.

"I never thought I'd say this, brother, but I'm jealous of you and the life you have with Jaci. I love coming over here just to be around ya'll. Yeah. I'm kind of wishing for the same thing. But I don't know, man, I might be a hopeless case."

Jason laughed. "Nope! With God, all things are possible. Just think. If He changed me, He can change anybody. All you have to do is go to Him with a sincere heart. He'll do the rest. Trust me, I know. Just continue on the road you're now on. You'll see. By the way, why don't you come to the Men of Power meeting with me next Saturday? There'll be lots of men there at the same place you are. I think you'll enjoy it. And God will even work out this little problem you've got." He chuckled as he dodged the pillow Ron threw at him.

Linda

Linda and Wynola had given up on finding Jaci alone somewhere so they could attack her. They had lurked around the office building and garage and followed her for several days, looking for a chance at her.

"There's always somebody around her," Linda complained to Wynola. "I even have Leo watching for a chance. I'm anxious to see a knife sticking out of her chest. I'm not going to rest until that witch is dead."

"Yeah. I'm with you on that," Wynola agreed. "That heifer caused me to lose a job I had been on for twenty-five years. And nearly cost me my marriage. She got this coming. I think we've come up with a pretty good plan, though. By the time Leo gets through with J.P., he'll be so mad, he'll kill her for us. He's got her up on some kind of pedestal. But when he hears all that Leo is going to put in his ears, he'll hurry up and get to that house. And when he finds Jaci there with Bob, she's coming down real fast. But we'll be there watching, so that if J.P. doesn't do it, we'll kill her ourselves. We'll just make it look like he did it. I hate to do this to Bob. He was pretty good between the sheets, but he should have never started sniffing around Jaci. That was his big mistake."

Linda picked up the phone and called the man she had already partially paid to help them. "Hey, Leo, this is Linda. We're all set. You make your call at ten in the morning. Just follow the script we gave you. Yeah. And Leo? Make it good, okay? I want to send that sucker into shock and have him running to his precious wife with murder in his eyes. Me and my sister are taking care of everything else. After you make the call, come on over to the address I gave you." She gave a slightly out-of-control laugh. "You might even get a bonus if things turn out the way they're supposed to."

Jaci

Jaci hung up the phone with a puzzled frown. Jason had never communicated with her through his staff. She called his office and when his voice mail came on, immediately hung up and dialed his cell phone. She made a disgruntled sound when she heard his voice mail instructing her to leave a message.

"Baby, why is somebody from your office calling me to make an appointment for us to meet? Are you too busy to call your wife? And why do you want me to look at a house? Please call me as soon as you can. Oh yeah! Where are you?"

When Linda stalked Jaci before she and Jason got married,

Jason bought her a cell phone and asked her to keep it in her purse and on at all times. Now that Linda had shown up again, he reminded her repeatedly. Jaci had a habit of simply forgetting to turn it on.

They usually talked more than once during the day. If nothing more than a quick "I love you" or "God loves you" was spoken, they both felt the need to communicate. They also agreed to let each other know where they were going if they had to leave the office. This habit had started after a major argument erupted when Jaci had been out of pocket one day.

Jaci's staff had a tradition of celebrating birthdays by going out to lunch. The day of the argument, they left the office before eleven to beat the lunch crowd. Jaci's cell phone was on the charger, and she forgot it when she left for lunch. Apparently, Jason called the minute she left the office. When he didn't reach her, he called the cell number and of course got the voice mail on that too.

He then called the main office number and talked to the receptionist, who had no idea where Jaci was. Jason panicked, and by the time Jaci returned from lunch two hours later, he was in her office pacing nervously with smoke steaming from his ears. Someone finally told him she had gone to lunch with her staff, but the minute she stepped into her office, he tore into her, pointing to the phone lying on the credenza. Jaci felt like a jerk for putting him through that and had since made it a point to be more careful.

Now, he was the one out of pocket and sending strange messages through his staff. She looked at her watch. It was too late to cancel lunch with C.J., who was probably already on her way to pick up Jaci. Everyone knew her routine of going to lunch early on Tuesdays so she could get back for staff meeting at one thirty.

Oh well, she quickly decided, they would swing by the address where Jason was and leave from there to go to lunch. Her desk phone rang, and, thinking it was Jason returning her call, she hurriedly picked it up.

"Hey, girl, you ready? I'm almost there." C.J.'s voice came over the line. Jaci, trying not to sound disappointed, said, "Sure, I'll head down and meet you in front of the building. But I need to make a little detour. Is that all right? Do you have time?"

"Sure, I have time. See you in a few."

Jaci stuck the piece of paper with the scribbled address into her purse and walked to Bill's office. "Hey, Bill, I'm sorry to bother you, but I'm leaving for lunch. You have time to walk down with me?"

"Absolutely. And you're not bothering me," Bill answered, standing immediately to accompany her.

"Well, I must admit, I do feel like that. But I don't have a choice right now. Hopefully, this thing with Linda and Wynola will soon be over, but they're still calling regularly, telling me what they're going to do to me."

She stepped outside just as C.J. arrived. They drove to the address, thankful it wasn't too far out of the way. It turned out to be a patio home in a nice neighborhood. She thought it was strange that a car with the department logo was already parked in the driveway and was disappointed to see no sign of Jason.

Jaci sighed. "I wonder where Jason is?" She pulled the cell phone out of her purse and called Jason again. His voice mail clicked on immediately. "Jason! I'm here at this house. Where the heck are you?" She ended the call and sighed again frustratedly. "Doggone it! I hate this. He's the one wanting to meet and he's late. Well, the woman from his office said the door would be open because there are people working in the house. But if I wasn't so curious, I'd leave. Come on, let's go on in."

The two women entered the house after a tentative knock. Jaci gasped in surprise when Bob Johnson from her office met them at the door. "Now what are you doing here, Bob?" A sliver of unease shot through Jaci. Something was off about this whole thing, she realized. If Jason got here and found her here with Bob, he was sure to be upset. They'd had words about Bob more than once.

Bob also looked surprised for a minute, then started smiling delightedly at the two women. "Well, I could ask you the same thing, but I'm not complaining. Who is this vision of beauty with you?"

Jason

Jason ignored the ringing telephones and numerous knocks on his office door. He couldn't recall a time in his life when he had been more angry and upset. Ever since he received that call this morning, he had been in an uncommunicative mode. The man's words kept reverberating through his mind.

"Just consider this a friendly heads-up, brother. I hate to see you getting played like you are. You can find your wife and her lover at this address at eleven thirty today if you play it smart. She thinks her game is still cool, so I wouldn't do anything to tip her off. Her and this guy have been together, ripping people off for years. And they're planning to take you for everything you got, man. They've done it to his wife, who happens to be my sister, and no telling how many others. I just don't want to see them do it to somebody else. You don't have to take my word for it, just show up there and I guarantee, you'll see more than enough to know I'm telling the truth. And I wouldn't go over there unarmed, man. This dude is known for packing a gun. You need to be careful."

The address the man rattled off was burned into Jason's brain. He was so angry all logical thought left him. He knew exactly who the dude was. It had to be Bob Johnson. Jason wanted to punch him out every time he saw them together.

Had the man been telling the truth? Was he running some kind of scam? Jason knew a man in his position couldn't be too careful. But if it was the truth, how could Jaci do this to him? Just the idea of his wife with another man sent him into a red haze of anger that blocked all rational, reasonable thought. The haze filtered into his mind and produced dangerous impulses. He reached into his desk and pulled out a gun, pointing it toward imagined images on the wall across the room. He realized at that moment that he was capable of murder. The thought chilled him to the bone but refused to leave his mind. When they talked this morning, Jaci told him she had a lunch date with her cousin and would then be going into a meeting. "Just leave a message if you call because my cell will be muted."

"Yeah, right!" he said sarcastically. "That's really convenient."

Deep down he didn't believe Jaci was capable of cheating on him. But he remembered the way she had danced with the guy and recalled how he had walked unannounced into her office one day before they were married and found them sitting close together in deep conversation. The guy simply smiled arrogantly and walked out when Jason had threatened him.

Jason knew he needed to let somebody know what was going on. In a city like Houston, you didn't run around like a lone ranger. Too many bizarre things went on every day. He thought about calling his best friend Walt, but knew he was probably in court. His dad was out of the question. Most everyone that he felt comfortable calling for help was out of pocket at this time of day.

His brother came to mind. But he hated to involve Ron in this when he was trying so hard to win him to the Lord. However, Ron was the only one who might possibly be available to go with him, so he picked up the phone and dialed Ron's extension.

"Yeah, what's up?" Ron answered the phone in a rushed tone. "I'm on my way out to a site, so talk fast."

"Ron, I need you to go somewhere with me. Can you come up here now?" Jason spoke in a shaky voice.

"Naw, man! I just told you, I'm getting ready to leave. What's up?"

"I can't discuss it on the phone, but there's a serious situation going on involving Jaci. I need your help."

Ron's heart kicked into overdrive. Right away, his mind went to Linda's threats against Jaci. "I'll be there in a minute."

When Ron walked into his office, Jason was holding the gun in his hand, checking to see if it was loaded. "What's going on, man?" Ron asked, looking concerned. "What are you doing with that thing?"

"I might need it," Jason answered. "I got a call this morning from some dude telling me that if I go to a certain address, I'll find my wife there with her lover. I'm getting ready to go over there, and I want you to go with me. I know the dude. I've seen them together on more than one occasion. In fact, I've told him to stay away from my wife. Needless to say, I'm ready to do some damage to both of them if what I was told is true."

"What! J.P., did you call Jaci?" Ron asked, shaking his head in disbelief. "You know Jaci wouldn't do something like this. That woman loves you! Think, man! Somebody's running a game on you."

Jason pushed the gun into his belt. "When I talked to Jaci earlier this morning she conveniently told me she would be unavailable to take any calls. Besides, I'm so angry, I don't know if I want to talk to her."

"I don't believe you, J.P.! What has Jaci ever done to make you distrust her like this? You're wrong brother. Your anger is clouding your mind. You need to get a grip."

"I hope you're right. But if you had heard that guy telling me what a fool I've been behind this woman, you would understand why my head is so messed up." They left the office in a heated argument.

When they pulled up in front of the patio home and saw the car identified as one from Jaci's department, J.P. cursed and Ron felt sweat pop out on his forehead. There was another car parked in the driveway but it wasn't Jaci's. *Must be the guy's personal car,* Jason thought.

They got out of the SUV and walked slowly toward the house. "Now, brother, I want you to keep your cool until you find out what the deal is. Okay?" Ron talked softly and urgently to Jason.

But Jason was in his own zone. Refusing to think about what he would do if his wife was in that house with another man.

They walked across the small porch, pushed the door open without knocking, and walked into the house.

Jaci

*J*aci stood in the middle of the room with Bob, while C.J. walked around the room, checking out the decor.

When the door was roughly pushed open, and Jason and Ron walked in, she drew a breath of relief that quickly turned to dread. Relief that Jason had finally arrived. Dread over his reaction to finding Bob there.

"It's about time!" Jaci said nervously. "I was beginning to think you were going to stand me up. What's the deal? Why did you ask me to meet you here?"

Jason's face was totally blank, but his eyes held a violent

anger that Jaci hadn't seen before. Her uneasiness increased as Jason walked up to her and looked into her eyes a long time before speaking.

"What are you doing here? With him?"

C.J. walked toward the group standing in the middle of the room. "Hey, Jason. Hey, Ron. How are you? Ya'll getting ready to buy this house? It's pretty nice. I've been looking around while we were waiting on you guys to . . ." Her voice trailed off when she felt tension fill the room.

Jaci knew something was desperately wrong. She looked into her husband's closed face, trying to decipher what she saw. "Is your cell phone working? Why didn't you call me back? And since when did we start communicating through your staff?"

Ron grabbed her arm. "What did you just say, Jaci? Who on J.P.'s staff called you?"

Jaci looked from Jason to Ron, confused. "I don't know what her name was." She tried to remember if the woman had even given her name, or just said, "I'm calling from your husband's office."

Jaci's eyes returned to Jason. "She said she was calling from your office and that you wanted me to meet you here. Baby, I called you. Didn't you get my messages?"

"No. I didn't," Jason answered coldly, his eyes now on Bob. "What's your story? Why are you here?" His furious expression caused waves of fear to run through Bob, who had faced enough angry husbands to know he needed to answer carefully.

"I got a call from Wynola Dickson this morning, asking me to come by here and do a structural inspection on this house. She's thinking about buying it and wanted to make sure everything is okay. She was supposed to meet me, but when I got here, there was a note on the door telling me to go on in, that she was running late. I had just gotten here when Jaci and this lady walked in a few minutes later."

C.J. looked into the faces of the people gathered in the room and sensed danger. Something was terribly wrong. Jaci and Jason were immobilized—Jason with anger and Jaci with confusion, while Bob's face was filled with fear.

"Wait a minute, guys!" C.J. said. "Let's get to the bottom of this before it goes any further."

"You got that right," Ron said. "I knew something didn't sound right when J.P. asked me to come over here with him. Some dude called him this morning and told him that Jaci and this dude would be here together and . . . well . . . a lot of other stuff. He got all bent out of joint and came over here gunning for . . ." He pointed toward Bob.

Bob's knees shook so bad, they almost gave way under him. Cold chills hit at the same time he felt perspiration rolling down his arms.

C.J. looked around the group again. "Don't ya'll see? Somebody set all of you up. Each of you got a call to come to this house at a certain time today. Now if things had gone as planned, Jaci and Bob would have been here alone when Jason got here, after he'd been told they would be here doing the hanky-panky. Whoo! That's some treacherous mess. I'm just glad I was here and that Ron came along with Jason. Otherwise, something bad could've happened." She looked at Jaci, who was still staring at her husband. "Jace? You okay? I think we should get out of here now. Whoever did this could call the police and accuse us of breaking in here."

Just then, a tall, thin man with a cap on his head appeared at the door. "Ya'll need to get outta here! Them women crazy!" He took off at a run around the corner of the house.

Jaci stood as though in shock, while Jason, who's mind had started clearing, looked at his wife with mixed emotions.

"Jaci! Come on, let's go!" C.J. said, urging her toward the

door. "Are you still up to lunch? If so, we need to hurry. Don't you have a meeting this afternoon? We'll probably have to settle for some fast food at this point. But we need to get out of here fast!"

Jaci moved slowly and answered as if she had to force the words. "No, Cij. I don't think so. Just drop me back off at the office." At C.J.'s urgent pull, she broke out of her daze and walked around Jason toward the door, refusing to look at him as she passed.

Jason caught her arm. "Baby, we need to talk. Let me drive you back. C.J. can drop Ron off."

Jaci pulled away from him. "Not right now." Her eyes were a turbulent gray. "I . . . uh . . . I need to come to grips with the fact that my husband knows so little about me that he thought I would cheat on him."

"Let's go, Jace! Something's not right here. We need to go now!" C.J. said again, pulling her through the door. C.J. knew her cousin well enough to know she was very close to tears. But they didn't have time to stand around right now.

"I'm out of here!" Bob said. He started toward the door, then turned around and spoke to Jason. "Look, man. I apologize if it seems like I've been coming on to your wife. I guess I have, but I come on to all women. Jaci knows me and has ignored me for years. If I ever had a chance with her, it disappeared when you came on the scene. You have a good woman here. I hope you know that."

Bob wished Wynola was somewhere close so he could kick her from one end of town to the other, and shivered when he thought about what could have happened. That lady had some retribution coming. She had callously set a trap for all of them that held the potential for somebody getting hurt. Most likely him! Yeah. She had something coming. He just had to figure out what it would be. He and Wynola Dickson had a history that her husband probably didn't know anything about. Until now.

Ron grabbed Jason's arm. "Man, you heard that dude. We need to get out of here. Quick!" They all walked swiftly from the house and started toward their cars just as two women jumped out of a car parked across the street and ran toward them.

Linda and Wynola, both with wild looks on their faces, yelled, "Ya'll ain't going nowhere!" Linda dug in a large bag she was carrying.

J.P. pulled out the gun and pointed it at them. "I will blow ya'll away," he said in a cold, hard voice. "You better turn around and get back in that car!" The women stopped, but didn't turn around. He pointed the gun and fired into the ground near where they stood. "I said get back in the car. I'm so mad right now, I'll empty this gun into you, reload, and do it again."

Linda and Wynola turned and ran back to the car, fearful expressions now dominating their faces.

Jaci and C.J. hurried to their car and got in. C.J. didn't lose any time starting the car and driving away. "I can't believe what just happened!" C.J. said. "Those women are crazy!"

Jaci's shaky voice filled the car after they had gone a few blocks. "He thought I was cheating on him." Tears ran down her face. "My husband actually thought I was screwing around with another man. How could he even think that I would do something like that? It scares me to think what might have happened if you and Ron hadn't been there. He had a gun! He was ready to do something stupid. Oh God! Cij, what am I going to do? I don't know when or if I'll ever be able to talk to him."

"Well, I'm glad he had it," C.J. said. "There's no telling what those women had in that bag. And I don't think they would have hesitated to use it. I feel like we just left the O.K.

Corral. My knees are still shaking. As far as Jason is concerned, just take some time to think about it. You don't know what he'd been told."

Jason

As soon as they got in the truck, Ron said, "Brother, I don't have to tell you. You just blew it with your wife. Jaci is pissed! And I don't blame her. I told you from the beginning that Jaci wouldn't do something like that. If you had been thinking clearly, you would have figured out that Linda and them had something to do with this. As a matter of fact, I should have thought of it myself." After a moment he said, "To be honest, I probably would have reacted the same way if it had been my wife."

Jason's angry haze had cleared and he was busy thinking. He pulled out his cell phone and called the detective working on Linda's stalking case. He explained what had just happened, including having to fire at the women to get them to back off. "Yeah. I'll come down right now and file a report. I need to get to my wife, but I want this on record in case something else happens. But I think those women are so scared that they probably won't try anything else right now."

After he hung up, Jason hit the steering wheel with his fist. "Darn it!"

Ron looked at him and asked, "What are you going to do about Jaci? She's pretty torn up over this."

"I don't know, Ron. Hopefully she'll be ready to talk by the time she gets home tonight. Now will you just shut up!"

Ron held his hands up. "Hey! Don't take your frustrations out on me. I'm just trying to help your pitiful butt."

J.P. took a deep breath. "Yeah. You're right. I'm sorry."

Linda

Linda and Wynola drove down the street, pulled over and sat in silence for a minute. Then Linda hit the dashboard hard. "I don't believe this! We just missed another chance to take that little heifer out. It's no telling when we'll get another chance. I could kill that chicken-livered Leo! I thought we had the right man for this. I can't believe he ran in there and warned them."

The trio had sat behind tinted windows in a car across the street and watched as their plan unfolded. Their glee faltered when they saw Ron and C.J. arrive with J.P. and Jaci. It was supposed to be just Jaci and Bob in the house. The plan went downhill from there. When they tried to get Leo to storm into the house and shoot everyone there, he jumped from the car. "I ain't shooting all them people! Ya'll can't pay me enough to shoot all them people!" He then ran to the house and yelled something through the door. That's when Linda and Wynola decided to take matters into their own hands and do it themselves. They didn't expect J.P. to pull his gun and shoot at them.

They sat there another hour before deciding it was safe to drive to Wynola's house.

Jaci

Jaci went directly to her car after C.J. dropped her off. She pulled her cell phone from her purse and called Gloria.

"Hey, Gloria, this is Jaci. I ate something that didn't agree with me, so I'm going home. Will you lock my office and cover the staff meeting for me, please?"

Fortunately, Jaci sounded as sick as she felt; although her sickness was more emotional than physical, it was real.

She drove away from the building with no idea where she was going. She was in no condition to go back to work and was not ready to talk to Jason. She didn't even consider that Linda and Wynola could still be around looking to hurt her. After driving aimlessly for half an hour, she finally thought of a place to go. She drove to her house, praying that Jason wouldn't be there, and hurriedly packed a bag. Then she headed toward the Gulf Freeway and Galveston Island. The beach house was the perfect place to get away for a while.

She called C.J., Randi, and Sister Sadie to tell them where she would be and asked them to tell Jason she was okay, but needed some time alone. For the next few days, she did nothing but walk on the beach and pray.

Jason

Jason knew he had blown it. His parents barely spoke to him, and Patrick wanted to take a swing at him. Ironically, Ron was the only one who stood by him. When he got home and discovered Jaci had left, he called around trying to find her. The only thing her family and friends told him was that she was okay and needed some time to think. He could understand why she felt that way. He spent the next days at home, waiting for Jaci and praying.

He called Wynola's husband to tell him what had happened. Josh Dickson seemed to be coming apart at the seams. He told J.P. that Bob Johnson had already informed him about his affair with his wife, and about the latest stunt his wife had pulled. The police had also called looking for his wife and sister-in-law.

"I don't need this, man!" Josh screamed into the phone. "I got enough problems of my own. I feel like killing them no-good women myself."

J.P. hurriedly said good-bye. He almost regretted calling the man, but Josh needed to know what his wife had done. Little did he know that Josh would carry out his angrily spoken words.

Linda

When Linda and Wynola walked into Wynola's palatial home almost two hours after the incident, they expected it to be empty. They jumped in surprise when Josh walked out of his study to greet them. "Josh! What are you doing home?" Wynola asked nervously.

"Well, ladies. You all have done it this time, and I am thoroughly sick of you. I came home after being indicted for embezzlement, losing my job, and having all my assets frozen, and now I find some mess like this going on." He looked at a shocked Wynola and continued his barrage, "I'm in all this trouble trying to keep you in this!" He waved his arm to indicate the large house. "And what do I have to show for it but two crazy women off terrorizing folk for no reason. I just didn't need that today!" He let out a string of curse words, calling them every vile name he could think of. "All these years of torment, trying to live with you and get along with your snooty family. All for nothing! Well, I called your parents and told them everything and what I was going to do. They're too old to be trying to take care of ya'll and it's time for me and everybody else to get some relief from ya'll screwing around and causing misery everywhere you go. Ya'll straight out the pits of hell, and I'm sending you back. I decided that I don't have any reason to go on living, and that while I'm at it, I might as well rid the world of ya'll." He pulled a gun from behind him and started shooting. When he was sure both women were dead, he reloaded the gun and put it to his own head. By the time the police arrived after the alert from Louisiana by Wynola and Linda's parents, all three were dead.

Jaci

Jaci drove her truck into the garage and pushed the remote, letting the door down. "Jason's home. Oh Lord, am I ready for this?"

By the time she started into the house, the door flew open and Jason stood there. He looked haggard. He hadn't shaved in days and his clothes were rumpled, as though he had slept in them. His eyes pleaded for understanding.

Jaci walked past him into the house and dropped her carry-all bag on the floor. She turned to him and said, "I had to come back. I love you."

Before the words were out of her mouth, Jason grabbed her in a tight embrace. "Oh honey. You don't know the agony I've been through wondering if I would ever hear those words from you again. Please forgive me for losing my mind like that. I was consumed with such jealousy that I couldn't even think straight. Sweetheart, I was ready to commit murder and go to jail. I know I had no reason to go off like that. I just wasn't thinking clearly. I'll go to counseling or do whatever you say, but please, don't leave me again." He hugged her close once more.

Jaci pulled away from him and sat down. "All this time, I thought I was the one with trust issues. Little did I know! Jason, what about our love for each other? Our commitment? Our promise to communicate with each other? If we had just talked that day we might have realized something wasn't right. But you wouldn't even answer my calls. Yes, I think we need to get some more specialized counseling. Otherwise, if something like this happens again, I don't know if we'll survive it. We need to strengthen that weak place in our marriage so Satan won't be able to get in again. I love you and I believe that God has joined us together and no man has the right to put us asunder. Not you, me, or Linda and Wynola."

Jason looked at her searchingly. "Baby, where have you been? Haven't you heard the news? The same day all that happened, Wynola's husband was indicted for embezzlement. He was definitely going to jail for a long time. He'd been stealing for years, trying to keep Wynola happy. Anyway, when he learned what Wynola and Linda had done, it was all too much for him. He shot them and then killed himself."

Jaci gasped. "Oh God!" She sat in stunned silence for a while, before saying, "I don't know how I should respond. I didn't wish them dead, even after what they did. But I can't feel any sorrow for them right now. They tried to kill me and almost destroyed our marriage. I think they would have kept trying until they succeeded."

Jason hugged her close. "Baby, they would have kept trying. It had become an obsession with them. They had to blame someone for their failures in life, and you happened to be the most convenient target. You didn't cause their deaths, they did that themselves. If they had been rational women and made different choices about how they lived life, things might have turned out differently for them."

Jaci

Two months later, Patrick, sick with a bad case of the flu, called Jaci at work. "Mom, I'm sick," he told her, sounding like he was at the point of death. "Can I come home for a few days? This crud really has me. I'm almost too weak to go to the bathroom."

Jaci didn't hesitate before answering. "Honey, you don't have to ask to come home. Why hadn't you called us and let us know you were sick? Can you get somebody to drop you off or do you want me or your dad to come get you?"

Patrick, in the middle of a long bout of coughing, took a while to answer. "I guess so," he finally said.

"You guess so, what?" Jaci asked, not understanding him.

"Yeah. I guess you better come get me," he answered weakly.

Jaci called Jason immediately to see if he could pick up Patrick. She had to go to the grocery store and pick up a few

items, and then home to get things ready. Jason had an important meeting and was unable to get away. So, Jaci made a
rushed trip to the grocery store, then home, before driving
over to the campus to pick up Patrick. The boy was really sick!
He crawled onto the backseat of her truck and fell asleep on
the way home. Thankfully, Jason made it home by the time
they arrived and was able to help her get Patrick in the house,
and into bed.

When they were back downstairs, Jaci told him, "Baby, I'm
worried. That child is very sick. Maybe we should try to get
him in to see a doctor. This thing could turn into pneu-
monia."

"Let's give it a day or two. Maybe if we can get some good
food into him, he'll start improving."

Jaci looked doubtful. "Okay. Let's hope so." She went into
the kitchen and started a big pot of chicken soup.

Patrick was scarcely over the flu when Jason came down
with it. If Jaci thought Patrick had been a bad patient, Jason
quickly proved her wrong. Nothing satisfied him! If she
brought him juice, he wanted tea. If she brought soup, he
wanted bacon and eggs. If she fixed both, he wanted nothing.
If he wasn't too hot, he was too cold. The bed was too lumpy
or the pillows too soft. He drove her crazy!

After a full week with Patrick, and the third day with Jason,
Jaci had had enough and decided to return to work, assuring
Jason that his mother would look in on him. He objected. He
didn't want his mother, he wanted her. She hadn't left Patrick,
so why was she leaving him?

Jaci almost ran out of the house. She was ready to slap the
living daylights out of him!

It was inevitable that Jaci would be the next to succumb to
the virus. Jason, along with Patrick, tirelessly catered to her,
putting up with her whining and bad temper. Strong woman

that she was, she insisted on being back on her feet and at work after a few days.

But a month later, she was still feeling tired and lethargic. She assumed it was the results of not getting completely over the flu before getting back to work. She determinedly went about her business, vowing to rest more.

A couple of weeks later, as Jaci led a song in the church choir in Sunday morning service, she became suddenly so hot she could barely stand it, and her stomach felt like it was full of fluttering butterflies. She barely made it through the song before darkness consumed her, and she felt herself falling. She was lying on a couch in the lounge when she came to. A crowd of people gathered around her, Jason sat beside her looking frightened, and a woman whom Jaci knew was a nurse checked her pulse.

"She's coming around," Jaci heard the nurse say. "I think she just fainted. She probably started back into her routine too soon and never really got over that flu. Make sure she gets some rest, but just to be on the safe side, you might need to go ahead and get her in to see the doctor."

Over Jaci's objections, Jason managed to harass her doctor into seeing her the next day. Jaci endured the usual battery of tests and was sent to the doctor's office. Jason was already sitting in the office when she got there. "I hope you're happy," she grumbled. "This has just been a waste of time."

Before he could answer, the doctor entered and took a seat behind the desk. She opened the file, read a while, and finally looked up, smiling. "Well, what color do you guys like? Pink or blue?" They both stared at her blankly, not understanding the question. The doctor laughed, thinking, *I can see I'm going to have some fun with these two.* "I said, what color do you like? You get two choices: pink or blue."

When they still didn't get it, she broke down and explained. "Jaci, Jason, you're pregnant."

Jaci knew she was in the middle of a nightmare and tried to shake herself awake but couldn't get any part of her body to move. She was opening her mouth to scream when she heard Jason's loud "What!"

She managed to turn her head to look at him and discovered a shocked expression on his face. Tears filled her eyes and she prayed, "Lord, please let this be a dream, and let me wake up now!" She looked back to the doctor who was smiling.

"Jaci, honey, it's no dream. You're going to have a baby in about seven and a half months. Now, I'll be keeping a close eye on you, but you're healthy and I don't see a problem with you having a healthy baby."

"Nooo!" Jaci wailed. "This can't be! It just can't. I'm on the pill. I'm too old. I'm a grandmother!" She began to cry so brokenly that the doctor jumped up and came around the desk.

She rubbed Jaci's back in a comforting manner, while she questioned her. "Jaci, now I want you to think about this. Have you missed any of your pills in the last six weeks?"

"No. I'm really careful about not missing a dose. I take them at the same time every day, just so I won't forget. I'm sure I haven't . . ." She stopped, thinking hard, trying to remember.

"Well, something went wrong, because you're definitely pregnant. What about when you were sick with the flu? Are you sure you took your pills then?"

Jason snapped out of his shock enough to answer. "To be honest, she was so sick a couple of days that she probably didn't remember to take them. But would missing two or three make a difference?"

The doctor looked shocked. "Absolutely! Jaci, you should know that. At any rate, you are going to have a baby. Now, I'm going to give you some prescriptions that I want you to start taking immediately. This is very important, understand?" When it looked like she wasn't getting through to Jaci, she turned to Jason.

"J.P., do you understand what I'm saying? She needs to take these pills every day."

He nodded, then asked, "What is it she'll be taking?"

"I'm putting her on a prenatal vitamin and some iron tablets for now. Like I said I'll be monitoring her closely, and there's a possibility that she might have to take something else, but we'll cross that bridge when we get to it."

Jaci, still crying, found the strength to ask, "What about birth defects? I've always heard that older women have a higher percentage of babies born with defects. I can't . . . handle that . . . I'm sorry, I just can't."

Jason grabbed her hand. "Honey, we have to trust the Lord in this. And we will handle whatever happens."

Jaci cried more brokenly. The doctor rubbed her back and tried to calm her down. "Jaci, I can't make any promises. It is true that some older women have babies with defects. But many older women have strong, healthy babies. We'll do everything we can to make sure your baby has every chance to be born healthy. The rest, like your husband said, is up to God."

Jaci struggled to gain control. She took a deep breath and stood up. "Thank you, doctor, I really appreciate your patience. I don't usually fall apart like this. I'm really sorry." She walked toward the door.

"That's okay, honey. I understand what a shock this has been. Now be sure to make an appointment for next month. In fact, you can go ahead and get on the book for the next eight months."

"Okay," Jaci responded numbly, then ambled through the door.

Jason

As soon as they were in the car Jason turned to Jaci and began speaking to her urgently. "Baby, I am not Maxie. I'm not going to leave you and my child. In fact, you would have to melt me and pour me out of your life now. I want you to know that I am honored to have a child with you. I'll always take care of you, no matter what. I don't want you to worry about anything, okay? Your only concern right now is to have a healthy baby."

Jaci threw her arms around him. "I know this already. Thank you for saying it though."

"Well, why are you so unhappy about it? Don't you want to have my child?" He was actually rather hurt at that thought.

She let her fingers travel over his face in a gentle caress. "Don't ever think that. It's just that I'm not a young woman, and I thought childbearing was behind me. I was looking forward to spending the years ahead with you without the hassles of parenting. It's not that I don't want the child, it's just that the timing is off. Even five years ago, it would have been more . . . acceptable. But not now! I just don't know if I'm up for this right now." Tears filled her eyes and spilled over.

"What choice do we have at this point?" Jason asked softly.

"We don't have a choice at this point. That's why I'm so upset. I did what I knew to do to keep it from happening, but it happened anyway. Oh God, Jason! What if it's . . . not normal? That's the next big concern."

"That's out of our hands, honey. We're going to have to trust God that the baby will be healthy in every way. And we have to believe that this is God's will for us. Otherwise it wouldn't have happened."

They drove home, where Jaci went into the family room and

fell onto the sofa. She kicked off her shoes and curled up in a knot.

"I'm going to get your prescriptions filled and get something to eat. What do you want?"

"I'm not hungry."

"Hungry or not, you've got to eat something. Now, what do you want? Or do you want me to just bring you anything?"

"Yes. Anything," she mumbled softly.

"Honey?" Jason sat down beside her on the sofa. "That job definitely has to go. You know that don't you?"

Jaci groaned. "Jason . . . ! Not now. Let's talk about this later. Please."

"I want to give our child every possible chance. That won't happen with you under constant pressure from that job."

"Can we talk about this later? I just need to get beyond the shock now."

"Yeah, sweetheart. I'm sorry. We'll talk about it later."

Jaci

Three months was as far as Jason would agree to let her work. But she had enough sick and vacation time built up to get her to the twenty-five-year mark.

As word of her pregnancy spread, so did excitement among their family and friends. The most cherished call came from their pastor. After speaking with Jason for a long time, he asked that she get on an extension. With just a few words, the pastor quieted her worries and built her faith.

"Jaci, I want you to remember something. The child you're carrying is a gift from God. However it got here, it came from

God. If I understand correctly, that sperm and egg overcame tremendous odds to get together. Just knowing that makes it even more of a blessing. Now remember that, and start looking forward to this great gift, okay?"

Jaci cried as she hung up the phone. "Jason, I'm so ashamed. I've been selfish, thinking only of myself. Can we pray?"

They slid to their knees and Jaci began praying. "Father, I give You praise and glory for the great gift of life that You have placed within me. I ask for Your hand of protection to be upon that life right now. Bless that life with grace, mercy, and goodness and deliver that life into this world as a whole and well and healthy human in every way. Father, we thank You right now for the victory. You've done it before, now, Lord, we trust You to do it again. And Father, work in us and do whatever You need to do to help us be the kind of parents You would have us to be. We pray for Your wisdom and for Your guidance every step of the way in helping this child to grow up to bring glory to Your Name. In Jesus' name. Amen."

Epilogue

Two Years Later...

aci had been in a reflective mood all day. She tried to shake it as she rushed around the kitchen, preparing for tonight's dinner party.

Her son, Jarrod, was impeding her progress. The toddler held on to her leg and screamed at the top of his lungs. His twin sister, Jarea, sat in the middle of the floor happily beating the bottom of a pot with a wooden spoon.

"Where is your daddy?" Jaci asked in frustration. "He should have been here thirty minutes ago." She picked up the phone to call him, but before she could dial, the phone rang. She answered on the first ring, thinking it was Jason.

"Jaci, baby?" her mother-in-law inquired.

"Oh. Hi, Mom. How are you?"

"I'm fine," Cecelia answered. "How are my beautiful grandchildren? I can hear one of them is unhappy about something. I bet it's Jarrod. Jarea never carries on like that."

"Yep. You're right. He's a little upset that I can't play right now."

"Well, I'm just making sure you don't want us to keep them tonight. It's been a while since they spent the night with us."

"Thanks, Mom, but my cousins are bringing their kids, so mine might as well be here. We're hoping they'll all go to sleep early. By the way, where is that son of yours? Is he still at the office?"

"No, he's on his way home. But he did say he had to make

a stop. Well, call me if you want me to take the kids tomorrow night so you can get some rest. Okay? Bye now."

Jaci hung up the phone. "That grandma is in need of a grandchild fix. I might as well pack their bag."

Her reflective mood returned as she thought of all that had happened over the past three years. "Thank You, Jesus!" she yelled out. A startled Jarrod stopped crying and looked up at his mother for a second, before resuming.

Since her marriage, her cousins had followed suit and gotten married. To everyone's shock, Jason's playboy brother Ron married Jaci's cousin Anita. C.J. and the chief of police caused a stir when they decided to get married. And after a twenty-year separation that had been viciously orchestrated by someone else, Gina reconnected with her son's father, who was now a minister. It was weird how they had all ended up with babies in one way or another.

The door opened and Jason carried in a beautiful floral arrangement. She sighed in relief as he walked over and kissed her. "Hey, sweetheart! Flowers for a beautiful lady," he said, kissing her again.

"Thank you, honey." She blinked back tears. "They're beautiful. Honey would you please get your son off of my leg. I have just two hours to get everything ready."

"I told you to use a caterer," Jason admonished. "I don't know when you're going to learn to make things easy on yourself."

"I know and I should have listened," Jaci groaned.

Jason picked up Jarrod and held him above his head, talking to him all the while. "Man, why are you carrying on like this? You're not doing a good job of taking care of Mommy. We gotta talk about this." He started into the family room, stooping to pick up Jarea on the way. "Hey, little sweetheart. We have to work on your brother, don't we?" Her smile caused all sorts of meltdowns in Jason's heart.

Later that night, after the meal, and after the last die-hard child closed his eyes in sleep, the men gathered in the family room while the women took over the living room.

Jaci told her cousins about what she had been reflecting on all day. "Ya'll, I've been thinking today about all that's happened over the past three years. Who would have thought we would all be married, with babies now?

"We are definitely in a new season. And I don't know what this new season holds, but I'm so thankful that the cold, harsh winter we were in so long is finally over. Remember how excited we were about all of our grandiose plans twenty-five years ago? Then suddenly, we were all in the midst of a cold, stormy season that seemed to go on forever. If it hadn't been for God's keeping power, I think we would have been totally destroyed."

"I agree," Gina said. "We were all almost destroyed during that season. We lost husbands and children, were beaten and abused, abandoned, stalked, and nearly killed. Lord! I know the Word of God said we would have tribulations, but that was ridiculous!"

"Amen to that," Anita added quietly. "But God is good! He has given us another season. Godly husbands, exciting vocations, and another opportunity to raise Godly children."

"Jaci, I thank God for you and Jason," C.J. declared. "I don't think the rest of us would have had the courage or faith to try again if we hadn't had you as a testimony of what God can do. I know I wouldn't have been marrying nobody else," she added laughing. "God is awesome!"

"Yes, He is!" Jaci agreed. "I am so thankful that God brought us through those difficult times. But ya'll know what? I've discovered that in every season, there are blessings wearing different faces: enough joys to keep us thankful and enough troubles to keep us praying. The important thing to remember is that whatever the season, trusting in God's faithfulness is the only way through it. If we didn't experience the scorching heat of summer, and the harsh cold of winter, we wouldn't appreciate the refreshing spring and autumn seasons. The reality of life is, we have to go through every season, and only God controls how long they last. Thankfully, He gives us the strength to endure."

"Amen!" her cousins shouted.

Their husbands heard them praising the Lord and quietly entered the room. Personal testimonies of God's goodness flew from person to person. They had all been through difficult seasons and were grateful for God's delivering power. It wasn't long before they were in the midst of praise and worship—the most rewarding season of all.

"And let us not get weary in well doing, for in due season, we shall reap if we faint not." Galatians 6:9

About the Author

BONNIE HOPKINS is a retired management and community relations consultant who resides in Houston, Texas. She is a graduate of Arkansas A.M.&N. College, Pine Bluff, Arkansas (which has since become the University of Arkansas at Pine Bluff).

In addition to writing, her time is spent with family, volunteer work, reading, and travel.